Second Law

SECOND LAW

Peter Lawrence Kessler

The Book Guild Ltd.
Sussex, England

**For Kate and Jana,
The deliverers of
inspiration**

This book is a work of fiction. The leading characters and situations are imaginary. Whereas descriptions of several persons in the 'supporting cast' have been drawn from individuals no longer living, they are complimentary tributes and in no way disparaging. The same applies to the named officials of high rank.

———————————

The Book Guild Ltd.
Temple House
25 High Street
Lewes, Sussex.

First Published 1990
© Peter Lawrence Kessler 1990
Set in Baskerville
Typesetting by Cable Graphics, Eastbourne,
Sussex (0323) 644660
Printed in Great Britain by
Antony Rowe Ltd.,
Chippenham, Wiltshire.

British Library Cataloguing in Publication Data
Kessler, Peter Lawrence
 Second Law.
 I. Title
 823' .914 [F]
ISBN 0 86332 513 0

CONTENTS

PROLOGUE

505.98.65

The war was over.

Its final confrontation had been a bloody climax to a conflict whose fortunes had swung from side to side before settling in favour of the opposition. Almost until the last, the Earth-centred Service Navy had played the part of the underdog. Out-manoeuvered and out-gunned in all respects, only patience and planning had brought about this unexpected victory. The Service itself had suffered relatively mild losses in the battle which, all in all, had been a triumph of strategic planning and execution on its part. The end to hostilities had come almost sixty years after the war's bloody beginnings, when the forces of the intensely tribal Larr had exploded into space protected by the Allied Planetary Grouping in a mad frenzy of killing.

The one person who had become unintentionally responsible for that final victory was newly assigned Captain Christopher Nilsen Rickard. He was seated in the command chair, feeling nervously exhilarated at his new position. This was his first command, his first ship. She was the SNS *Emputin,* commission number GCC 1905, a command of which to be proud. She was a member of the brand new Eagle-class of cruiser, the Service fleet's secret weapon in the final stages of the war, one of the most powerful vessels currently in operation. Rickard still felt noticeably uncomfortable in the centre seat with so many people obeying *his* orders. It was one very strange and unaccustomed sensation.

But it was something that he would enjoy getting used to.

'Captain, the sensors indicate an unbroken line of vessels approaching the fleet with full shields raised,' a woman's voice said. Commander Ichikawa Kiyami, the ship's extremely pretty science officer, straightened up from multi-display banks of electronic scanning equipment and swung around in her chair to face Rickard. A head of soft, black hair framed her delicate features. Her wide eyes were pale blue, a result of Eurasian blood in her maternal ancestors. She was slender and finely proportioned. And she was dedicated to her profession. It was clear from what she said that the hostilities had not yet ceased.

'Command ship *Searcher* sends fleet-wide message. We are to intercept incoming enemy ships, sir,' communications officer Lieutenant Kathrynn Watts immediately adjoined.

Rickard felt the usual wrenching of his insides. He had grown to expect the sensation but it remained uncomfortable. It was the thought of one more fight, of yet another battle. He was rapidly becoming used to the ever-present horrors of war. The continual carnage and mutual slaughter. But he realised that the momentary sensation of panic at the start of each fresh encounter would never leave him. Instead, he strove to control and direct the released adrenalin, concentrating upon channelling it to aid him in the task ahead. His hand darted to a button on the arm console of his chair and he spoke in what he prayed was a steady voice.

'This is a red alert. Battle stations. All hands to battle stations. This is not a drill.' He disconnected and snapped more orders across the bridge. 'Raise the shields and inform Engineering we will be needing full power. Accelerate to subspeed and plot an intercept course for the nearest target.'

The bridge lights dimmed to a deep shade of red. Console lights glittered more brightly, more easily read now that the darkness around them excluded any distraction. A surge of energy briefly hummed through the ship. It accelerated forwards alongside dozens of other Service vessels towards the closing enemy fleet - a fleet which eagerly sought retaliation against its once subdued enemy. Extra personnel entered the bridge to take up emergency auxiliary stations dotted between the major consoles and on the low platform behind Rickard.

'Tactical display on approaching craft,' he requested.

The relayed picture of deep space was relegated from the main viewer to the two secondary ones either side of it as a computer imaging display of the surrounding ships and asteriods came on screen. Continually changing figures marked out the narrowing distance between the opposing fleets.

'Arm torpedoes and all power banks. Ready needle beamers,' Rickard snapped out. He was feeling calmer, surer of himself now that they were under way. The main viewer switched back to its standard display.

'Course plotted, sir,' the navigator, Lieutenant James Boyd, said. 'Heading for vessel bearing two-nine-one by two-zero-nine.'

'Initiate. Helmsman, accelerate to full subspeed...now!'

'I know the moves, Cap,' Helmsman Lieutenant Mori Bentowski muttered quickly. He was a rather brash, self-assured man of no more than Rickard's own age and he responded like lightning. Sliding the speed controls forward to a point barely below that of actual hyperdrive levels he sent *Emputin* darting out to meet its chosen combatant, slowing barely in time after the sudden spurt of power to avoid overshooting. It was an old trick that every half-decent helmsman could pull, even one of Bentowski's temperament.

The Larr vessel fired first - before *Emputin* had come to a complete halt. A long, raking needle-beam of destructive energy hit *Emputin's* protective shields. The ship rocked and shook under the impact.

'Fire two torpedoes,' Rickard heard himself call out over the hubbub of readouts, computer warnings and blaring alarms. A pang of doubt caressed the outer fringes of his mind as to the resilience of the ship. *His* ship.

His worry was unfounded. Lieutenant-Commander Thom Howarth, the chief weapons officer, thumbed the firing button. Two sparkling bolts of light exited the ship's forward firing bay to smash with satisfying force at

9

the enemy.

Ichikawa Kiyami was busy scanning at her science bank for weaknesses in the other ship's shielding. She discovered the perfect target. 'Captain, I have found indications that this ship has suffered a power loss in its port shielding. The shield will not hold for much longer.'

'That's what I needed,' Rickard enthused - then wished he hadn't. There was something to be said about the experience of war being a great leveller of enthusiasm. It was not wise to get too carried away with the emotional headiness of a battle. 'Mister Howarth, concentrate laser banks one to four on the enemy's port side,' he said, forcing himself to be calm. Outwardly, at least.

Bolts of deadly light immediately shot out to strike where they were needed, causing havoc. The attack was followed by a short explosion which tore ragged sheets of metal plating from the Larr's hull.

'Fire again.'

More beams lashed violently to strike in the same place. Larger chunks of metal were torn out as more explosions followed the first, effectively crippling the ship.

Kiyami looked up again. 'Their shields have failed completely.'

'Cease firing,' Rickard said and turned to the comm officer. 'Lieutenant Watts, send to the enemy ship: surrender your vessel. Prepare to be boarded.'

'Yes, sir,' Watts' willowy figure swung around and she moved her delicate hands rapidly over the controls, speaking into a voice-activated pick-up mike. 'Commander, enemy ship, This is SNS *Emputin,* You are asked to surrender your vessel and stand by to be boarded. I repeat: surrender and stand by for boarding.'

The other ship's answer was to fire again at *Emputin.* The shields held but the ship rocked amid a display of opposing energies as if it were an ocean-going vessel in a particularly heavy storm.

'Damn!' Rickard exclaimed. He'd wished they would give in gracefully. He hated to be forced into destroying them. It was another needless waste but if that was how they wanted it... 'Fire a torpedo at the bridge,' he decided.

Howarth thumbed a control and a single bolt was

released to strike and destroy. The bridge of the enemy vessel was gutted in an oppressive display of destruction and, opened to space, debris and stiff, bloated, corpses were sucked out by the irresistable force of explosive decompression.

Rickard began: 'Repeat the message-'

The Larr ship was unexpectedly destroyed in a flowering blossom of released energy that spread rapidly outwards, causing *Emputin* to rock in an extremely unsteady fashion. Several banks of controls began to spark spectacularly as circuits overloaded and cutouts failed under the severe pressure, Watts hastily scaled down the brightness of the viewers as the brilliant white light threatened to blind them all. Backups switched on, taking over from damaged instrumentation. The few small electrical fires that burned dimly on smoke blackened consoles were hurridly extinguished and the thin pall of smoke wafting upwards was eagerly sucked away by the air filters.

Rickard was the first to recover from the shock. 'They self-destructed. They knew they were beaten so they self-destructed!'

'Dumb sonofabitch,' Bentowski growled, rubbing his dazzled eyes.

'The commanding officer must have been a Larr native,' Kiyami observed with typical informativeness. 'No hired mercenary would have done that. They would instead have surrendered and thrown themselves at the mercy of the Service, or else tried to escape.'

'True,' Rickard admitted, closing the incident from his mind. He was, despite all, in the middle of a battlefield. 'Damage reports, Lieutenant Watts?'

'Nothing serious, sir. Minor damage only.'

'Excellent.' Thank God for that, he added to himself. He hadn't thought it would be this easy. 'Mister Boyd, tactical, if you please.'

The standard picture of space was once more replaced by an over-all computer view of the field of battle. Rickard could see by the constantly updating readings that the Service was steadily winning the exchange of fire but weren't there slightly fewer Service ships now than

11

there had been before? As Rickard pondered on it, a blue shape on the tactical, which represented a Service vessel, began to flicker.

It was obviously in trouble.

The vessel in question was the SNS *Red Star,* the single cruiser to be crewed entirely from members of the disbanded and distinguished Cymma Major resistance army. Its captain, Rhos, the ex-resistance leader, noted that the officer at the weapons console had been killed by the last on-board explosion. The explosion had also knocked out most of the vital circuits including mains power. The ship was now channelling all auxiliary power through to the rapidly failing shields in the extremely faint hope that another Service cruiser could get to them in time to effect a rescue.

Red Star was a light cruiser that had mistakenly picked a heavy battleship as its target. Now most of the bridge lay in ruins and a great deal of the crew were dead. The situation looked hopeless.

The bridge was a mess, an unrepairable shambles. Smashed consoles, burning wiring and crushed, burnt and battered bodies littered its once spotless deck. A thick, dirty cloud of acrid smoke hovered over everything like a thundery grey cloud waiting to descend and cover all from sight, perhaps mercifully hiding the appalling damage. The main viewer screen had shattered, showering long, jagged shards of perspex everywhere and probably adding to the high death toll. Of the two secondary screens there was no sign. Most of the interior wall at that end of the bridge had been blown away, revealing the stark, fire-scarred plainness of the centre plating, great bolts of sealed metal holding it together. The single bridge door repeatedly attempted to seal itself. The mutilated corpse of a crew member prevented it from doing so. The continual whining of the door's straining mechanism created an extra distraction amid the tortuous jumble of noise.

'Best reverse speed,' Rhos called through the din of wildly sparking circuitry to his helmsman - the sole surviving bridge officer apart from himself. The helmsman wearily nodded in acknowledgement and bent over what remained of his instruments.

The time between Rhos giving the order and his receiving the reply was only very short but it seemed to him like an eternity. The answer came nonetheless, and Rhos had fully expected its content. 'I am sorry, sir,' the helmsman said. 'We have no energy to the drive. We are stranded here.'

Rhos felt his hopes collapse. The fight had been dashed from him. His career in space had been so brief and now it seemed to be over. And all he could do was pray to gods he knew did not exist. Could not exist, to allow such tragedy.

The enemy battleship closed in a leisurely fashion on the doomed cruiser. It fired a volley of needle shots and the ship trembled and shuddered to its core, as if it knew its fate. The helmsman's console exploded in his face. Both console and face were ravaged by extreme heat and the body was hurled backwards over the rear of the seat. It crumpled limply onto the navigation bank in the centre of the bridge. A following tremor sent the corpse rolling off.

Dust and smoke. A tearing of metal. The end was coming fast. And then a sudden hush, singular in its intensity.

Rhos shook his head, as if to clear it of engulfing cobwebs, and activated the ship-wide intercom. 'This is Captain Rhos. All surviving crew members are to proceed to the life-pods.' Thinking distantly to himself, he wondered if anyone was left alive to hear him. 'All crew members are to abandon ship. Repeat: abandon shi-' .

He was sharply cut off as the bridge exploded. The expanding fireball burnt away his skin to reveal the boiling muscle and bone beneath. The flash of heat melted the deck beneath him. He died quickly but violently.

Red Star briefly became a miniature sun as it

vapourised, before rapidly dying and dissipating into the cold, dark reaches of airless vacuum.

The flashing blue shape on the tactical display on *Emputin's* bridge faded, leaving only an afterimage burned onto Rickard's retina. One by one the remaining red shapes, the Larr ships, also faded out or were connected onto more of the blues - meaning that they had been successfully captured and boarded.

'It seems we got them all - but only just,' Rickard observed.

Kiyami nodded, 'We have suffered some losses. The second flank is down almost fifty per cent.' She indicated to the appropriate section of the display. 'It was a costly victory, Captain.'

Rickard agreed completely. But he had found that it was always the way with war. 'Return viewer to normal,' he said. 'Cancel red alert. Resume all normal stations.' The emergency personnel secured their equipment panels and departed the bridge. The automatic bridge doors on both sides of the raised platform behind Rickard hissed shut.

'Lieutenant Watts, send a full report of the Larr vessel's self-destruction. Advise that the fleet be warned of this, especially when about to board.' They probably already know, he thought, but it's usually better to be safe than sorry, as the old saying went.

'All systems now secured from battle conditions, Captain,' Thom Howarth, the black security and weapons chief, reported.

Rickard acknowledged him and turned to Watts, who was seeking his attention. 'Captain.' Her tone was hushed.

'Yes, Lieutenant. What is it?'

'Searcher Command says...to inform you that Captain Rhos's ship was destroyed by superior enemy fire. There were no survivors.'

Rickard felt a cold hand of ice clutch at his heart.

14

Rhos...dead? It had been his idea that Rhos accompany Intelligence operative Joseph Brians from Cymma Major to Earth. Brians and himself had helped free Rhos's people from the control of the Larr mercenaries based there. In a way he was reponsible for Rhos.

'Thank you, Lieutenant,' he answered Watts quietly.

He should never have allowed Rhos to go, Rickard realised furiously. He struggled to conceal his intense sense of loss from the bridge crew. If only he hadn't landed on Cymma Major - not that he'd had much choice - Rhos might still be alive. And what a stupid idea on the part of the Service, to turn over a cruiser to a group of people who had only been in space for, what, less than a month? And to let them take part in a fight as dangerous as this was sure to be - not that the strong-willed, overconfident and bold Rhos would have been deterred. Dammit! he mentally cursed. There was absolutely no point in his blaming himself. Rhos would have joined the battle whether he wanted him to or not. It was *not* his fault.

Rickard knew he was trying to make himself feel angry at Rhos to block his own feelings of remorse. Fortunately for his own peace of mind it was working. He would still feel the pain of Rhos's sudden death but not to the cost of his work, or his duty. He couldn't afford to mourn his personal losses now. There was work to do. He shut off his feelings with an ease that was uncharacteristic with him.

'Captain,' Watts' voice broke through the subdued quiet. '*Searcher* has given the go-ahead for the fleet to disperse to home sectors.'

'Oh, yes. Fine,' Rickard said absently. Then he gathered himself and put his mind to work: 'Make ready for hyperdrive. Plot a course for Earth.'

'Aye, sir,' Boyd answered. 'Course now entered. Destination Earth. Sector one of quadrant one.'

'And not a moment too soon,' Bentowski muttered irrepressibly from the helm station.

On the main viewer Rickard could see the remaining ships of the fleet darting off, one by one, some hauling their still locked-on captives. They began disappearing as they reached the space-eating speeds of hyperdrive. One ship, coming up from *Emputin's* rear at near hyperdrive velocity, appeared blue in colouring on the viewer screen switched in that direction. The ship shot past and accelerated into hyperdrive. Rickard noted its colour shifting to red as it sped away in a clear example of the Doppler Effect.

'Hyperdrive engage,' he ordered. 'Go to hyperspeed five.'

'Hyperdrive activated at speed five.'

Space leapt forward on the viewer and the stars ahead blurred and seemed to merge as the ship entered a distance-devouring faster-than-light speed.

Rickard made all the standard checks necessary in his capacity as captain before settling back in his seat. His mind wandered back, recounting the events that had brought him to this place. The sudden transgression from the rank of lieutenant and a position as an auxiliary power controller. A short but eventful posting into the branch of the Service known as Intelligence. Capture by mercenaries and a near-miraculous escape from an enemy base, taking with him important information to aid the failing Planetary Grouping. An Intelligence posting that delivered him to Cymma Major after an almost fatal brush with a Larr warship. On from there to a Larr mercenary base in the guise of a freshly deceased mercenary. A later posting within the enemy organisation to the command headquarters and enough damage caused to render the base shieldless by the time the Service fleet had arrived. He had joined the fleet to receive his reward: a command of his own. His first. Now he was captain of one of the front-line ships of the Allied Grouping.

Rickard roused himself from his reverie and realised he had a little spare time to kill. He decided to take a walk and inspect a little of *his* ship.

'Lieutenant Watts,' he said as he rose, 'If I am needed I'll be below.'

'Yes, Captain,' Watts nodded.

Rickard left the bridge. The doors snapped shut behind him.

Thom Howarth paused a moment before leaning over to talk in a quiet, almost conspiratorial tone to Kiyami who turned to face him. 'Well, Commander? What do you think of the new captain?' he asked.

'I think he is a very fine and reliable officer, which is a definite improvement on the last one we had.' Kiyami was acting protectively towards Rickard.

'You do?' Howarth was unsure if he should be surprised or not. It was unusual for the commander to make up her mind on such matters so quickly, and he had known her professionally for a number of years. However, he had not witnessed an apology she had made to Rickard earlier for doubting in his command ability. She was not in the habit of ignoring her mistakes. This had been no different. 'Are you sure?' Howarth asked.

'Yes, I am,' she said. 'If he seems a little unused to his position, you must remember that he has not long held it-'

'The best part of an hour.'

'- And I think he will become more practised with time. We should aid him to the limit of our abilities. Also, I do not think we should be talking about him in this manner.' She looked Howarth straight in the eye. 'He will be all right.'

Howarth was not so certain. 'We'll see, Commander. We'll see.'

1

505.98.65-06

The lift deposited Rickard outside the entrance to Engineering.

The whole area before him was designated as an Authorised Personnel Only section of the ship. It was a place he had never before visited. Certainly in his old position as a power output controller on SNS *Constitution* he had not been permitted to do so.

The solid double protection doors, marked boldly with the section title, hissed ponderously open as he neared them. Revealed beyond was a bright, busy interior, full of hustle and bustle. Rickard stepped in and observed. This was the very heart of the ship's drive system, the barely understood, almost magical device that pushed it into hyperdrive and kept it there in faster-than-light motion. This immediate portion of Engineering was a fairly wide and extensively elongated area of metal plating, mazeworked piping and clusters of bewildering instrumentation. Dominating the scene was a five metres wide, almost transparent, plastic-like piece of tubing which fed the fuel mixture into the drive system. Strange swirling patterns could be glimpsed flitting along in the direction of the generators. The dull thudding of continuous pumping filled the passage-like compartment. Operating consoles were dotted about. A myriad lights, readouts and monitors gave out displays on a massive variety of subjects. From the mixture level between the neutronic fuel and its reactant gasses, to the intensity of the overhead illumination, everything was carefuly watched.

Personnel buzzed through like angry flies, never settling in one place for more than a few moments before darting off to tend to some other console, feeder pipe or any one of a dozen other operations. Readings had to be continuously checked and double-checked. Monitors had themselves to be monitored. If the fuel reactant level became too high there could be trouble. Never mind that such possibility was out of the question. Even though there were a number of separate alarms that would be triggered, automatics working in conjunction with the ship's mainline computer, failures had been known. If the warnings failed the ship ran the risk of being blown apart. Alternatively, if the levels fell too low no fuel at all would reach the drive, resulting in a dead halt to all motion. Every function had by necessity to be watched, and then watched again.

The uniforms of the engineering staff differed from the standard in colour. The black front and rear sections were the same but instead of the grey that ran down the sides to the legs and on the underside of the arms these were white. Not an overlarge number of the uniforms were of the normal one-piece tunic designs, either, but were instead of a rubbery, thickly moulded material which protected the wearer from the radiation levels in the drive's intermix chambers. Breather lines filled the shape of the protective coverings even more. They were a necessary nuisance while on duty. But many a life had been saved by them after a pipe had come away or a line had broken, filling the air with highly toxic and fatal gasses.

A panel close to the entrance doors suddenly began to spark and hiss as overload systems and cutouts failed. A nearby technician hurried over to it, not noticing Rickard's unmoving form as he dashed by. He was totally engrosed in his duties and worried what a shortening panel might do to the rest of the system. He was fast to shut off the damaged circuits with an expert movement of his hands across the console which, by now, had charred and blackened in places in much the same way as those on the bridge had done earlier.

A second engineer, his protective suit unfastened halfway, joined the technician, they both bent over to closely examine the damage to the unit.

19

'What do you think?' the technician asked of his colleague.

'It'll hold until we get back, it's going to need a bloody good overhaul though, even if it is brand new.'

'It's not the only one.'

'Don't I know it.' The engineer, named Stringer, according to his suit name tag, spoke in a soft but clipped English accent. 'Which circuits went down this time?'

The technician flicked a digital display on before answering. 'There were quite a few. Lines AD3 to AE9 are down for sure but I will need some time to check the rest.'

'Okay. You'd better get on with it.' Commander Stringer - Rickard recognised him as the chief engineer - straightened up to see Rickard's careful observation of him. He was painfully thin, almost skeletal, wiry man with a generous proportion of fine but listless-looking mousy hair framing his Anglic features. His face was high-boned and his features were sharp. He instantly recognised his new commanding officer and gave him a welcoming smile as he strode towards him, taking his hand and shaking it vigorously.

'Glad to meet you, Captain. Sorry about the mess but we've had a good deal of trouble down here since that last explosion outside.'

Rickard was thoroughly taken by his open, friendly manner. There were no doubts in his mind as to Rickard's command capabilities. He returned the warm reception thankfully. 'I apologise for the trouble. The Larr we hunted self-destructed when we caught it. There's no real damage done, is there?'

'Any damage to my engines is real, Captain. Nevertheless, nothing so far is irreparable, so long as we go straight to Earth and suffer no detours, that is.'

'Don't worry, I think that can be arranged. I need a rest as much as the ship.'

'I'm pleased we have that sorted out. Is there anything I can do for you or are you simply making yourself known to the peasants?'

'Basically, yes. I had some spare time so I thought I'd take a look around, seeing as I plan to be here for a while.'

'Your command is a permanent posting?'

'It was when I last saw Admiral Peterson. He made it sound as though it were permanent so who am I to argue?'

'No. Peterson's usually pretty reliable, so I am told.'

'Good. I'm looking forward to some real work. Some exploration out in the third and fourth quadrants, they're the places to be.'

'Well, as long as you take good care of my engines I'll be satisfied.'

'I promise, Rickard grinned wryly. 'I'll be seeing you later.'

'Right, look forward to it.'

Pleased with his first foray outside the bridge, Rickard departed Engineering and made for the lift. Although nothing more than polite introductory chit-chat had passed between himself and Commander Stringer, he felt he had made a reasonably good impression on one of his most important officers. Not bad for a rookie captain, anyway.

The lift doors opened and he entered, this time heading for the sick bay, ten levels above, The elevator network diagram on the interior wall of the lift showed Rickard exactly where he was in the complex maze of shafts. He watched as the flashing blip that signified his lift transported him in the direction of the bridge. Then it branched off at a sharp angle to speed horizontally until it reached the required exit, then the doors snapped open.

Sickbay was a small place, especially in comparison with the seemingly endless spread of engineering. It looked as though it would barely be able to hold more than a few patients, let alone any sizeable amount of the two hundred strong crew. The bay was divided into two areas. The first was filled chock-a-block with as many beds as was possible to cram into such a confined space. No more than eighteen, and all bunched up close together. Each bed had a diagnostic readout panel attached to it and one or two were fitted with straps - secure fastenings for unconscious or uncontrollable patients, no doubt.

The second bay was even smaller and more compact than the first, containing fewer beds and more specialised equipment; prognosis analysis compterminals and a portable drugs synthesizer unit in which, Rickard knew, any known drug could be constructed in a matter of moments. In the far corner a partition fitted from floor to ceiling cordoned off the tiny office built within. Although the office had no door it did provide some seclusion from the rest of the sick bay.

A nurse, the head nurse Rickard judged by her insignia, was finishing tidying and straightening one of the beds when Rickard entered the bay. She turned at the sound of the doors clicking shut and stared at him for a few seconds in non-recognition. Then she realized who was standing before her. 'Oh Erm...it's Captain Rickard, isn't it?'

Rickard nodded in affirmation. 'Ah. If it's the doctor you want to see he's in his office, through there,' she said, directing him to the second bay.

'Thanks.' Rickard walked through to see the doctor crouched low over his desk, completing some paperwork. He was considerably older than Rickard had expected - he had to be at least forty - but his sparse head of hair was still dark with only a light scattering of grey and his face was smooth and unlined. As Rickard neared him he glanced up - and his act went into unstoppable motion.

'Hello. Captain Rickard, I presume,' he uttered almost melodramatically, rising from his seat. 'So very glad to make your acquaintance. I am Philip Beck, your friendly neighbourhood ship's surgeon. As you may have cause to notice, I'm constantly on the prowl looking out for new victims - sorry, patients for me to work on. You'll be seeing a lot of me, don't you worry, especially as I'm the man to make sure you are always in a fit state to command. As far as I know, and people are always telling me, I'm pretty good at my job so you needn't have any fears at all about coming to see me at any time you feel you should. I'll always be there, although my mother always said I should be on the stage. By the way, you look a little worn out.' Surgeon Lieutenant-Commander Philip Beck finally stopped for breath.

'I have been rather busy lately,' Rickard eventually managed to get in.

'Yes, I heard, News travels fast on the ship's freechat line, although bad news moves much faster I have always thought.'

'Pardon me,' Rickard put forward hesitantly. 'But do you always go into verbal overdrive when you first meet someone?'

'I'm sorry?' he frowned, then caught on. 'Oh my speedy conversation, you mean? Yes, I like to get the formalities out of the way as soon as possible so we can progress onto more important things a bit faster. I get a variety of comments on my vocal ability but the nicest thing I am called is 'quaint'. I think it's rather cute, myself.'

'I'm inclined to agree, if only to squeeze a word in edgeways,' Rickard chuckled.

'You should have butted in. Listen, if I ever go on like this again, just tell me to shut up otherwise I'll be prattling on 'till the cows come home and snow falls in the tropics.'

'I'll try to remember that.'

'Good, good, My hearty congratulations.'

'On what?'

'On achieving a great deal to end the war and being rewarded for it by being placed in charge of this motley crew of miscreants.' Beck's obviously natural good humour shone through.

'All I had was the good fortune to be in the right place at the right time, it was nothing.' Rickard insisted. He had been doing so for some time now. He'd lost count of the times he had been congratulated.

'All right. If you do insist,' Beck grinned. 'By the way, you've met my charge nurse have you not?'

'We haven't been introduced.'

'No? Right, then,' he said as he leant out of the cramped little office to call, 'Ginny...here a moment.' The charge nurse entered carrying a small tray in her hands which she placed on top of the drugs synthesizer.

'Charge Nurse Virginia Hicks. This is Captain Christopher Rickard. Captain Rickard-'

'Philip please,' Hicks interrupted. She was always astonished at the boundless realms of Beck's theatrical tendencies.

He, for his part was undaunted. 'Captain, this is

Virginia, or Ginny, as I call her. She's the real boss around here, however much I like to pretend otherwise. Most of the time I just get under her feet.'

'Much to my constant annoyance,' Hicks cut in. 'Pleased to meet you, sir.'

Rickard returned the greeting, still bemused by Beck's unusual manner. Also he found he was unable to restrain his eyes from wandering over the contents of the second bay and wondering at the purpose of some of the newer equipment.

Beck caught his eye, 'Would you like a guided tour around my sick bay?' he asked with an eyebrow comically raised. Before Rickard could answer, Beck went to the head of one of the nearby beds. 'Now let's see. Where shall I start? Aha, this,' he said in a mock serious tone, 'is a bed. We sometimes put patients in them.'

'Only sometimes?' Hicks asked, casting her eyes heavenwards as Rickard turned to her, totally unprepared for the extent of Beck's sardonic sense of humour.

Beck threw her a frown. 'Haven't you any work to do?'

Hicks retorted in the same manner, well practiced in coping with Beck. She still found it hard if not impossible, to repress a smile. 'I have plenty of work to do, so if you will leave those tidied beds alone, I'll get on with it.'

'Sorry.' Beck patted down the crumpled top sheet. Hicks collected her tray and took it into the office. 'As you can see,' Beck added, 'we're all one big happy family here.'

'I did notice. Still, I suppose a medic who cracks jokes all over the place is better than one with a grim look and an urge to cut you open.'

'Too right.'

On the bridge, Watts was making a routine circuit check of her instruments when she perceived an insistent bleeping emanating from the opposite side of the control centre, from Thom Howarth's security console. She watched as Howarth stared at the display before swinging around to face her.

'Kathrynn, reach the Captain for me please.'

'That sounds like trouble,' she said as she activated the ships intercom. 'Bridge to Captain,' she spoke into the pickup. 'Come in please.'

A diode lit up to indicate that an intercom unit had come on line. The conversation now went out on the established link between the two units, rather than on general broadcast.

'Rickard here, what is it?'

Howarth joined Watts at her console to deliver his message. 'Howarth here, someone's been tampering with life support. It could be urgent.'

Rickard was at once thoroughly business-like, 'Meet me there at once. Rickard out.'

Howarth stared down at Watts, making the mistake of perceiving Rickard's sharp manner as a display of personal dislike towards him. 'Yessah,' he commented sourly.

☆ ☆ ☆

Oblivious to Howarth's opinion of him, Rickard switched off the sick bay intercom unit and started for the door.

'Mind if I tag along?' Beck amiably enquired.

'Not at all.' Rickard noticed for the first time that Beck's blue and black medic's uniform seemed to be a size too large for him, although he did not seem to mind. Consigning the fact to a growing list of the personal peculiarities of his crew he hurried out of the door.

The life support chamber was several decks below sick bay and Beck was noticeably out of breath when he and Rickard reached it. Howarth was already waiting outside the closed door when they arrived.

'Have you gone in yet?' Rickard asked without preamble, still trying to establish an air of authority.

'No,' Howarth replied shortly, he felt miffed at the way

25

he had been 'summoned' and was in no mood for polite conversation. 'I was waiting for you.'

'Okay,' Rickard affirmed. He seemed to fail to notice the security chief's reticent attitude towards him. 'What exactly is wrong?'

'Someone attempted to disable the support system by force. That's when the alarms on my console signalled.'

'Right, open it up.'

Howarth decided he would be wiser not to open his mouth at present or he might say something he'd regret later. If only Rickard had not called him down in such an offhand manner.

Keeping his expression neutral he placed himself to one side of the door and waited for Beck and the new captain to similarly position themselves before keying the door mechanism. The low-ceilinged chamber beyond was instantly revealed to Rickard and he ducked his head around the corner of the doorway, ensuring that it was safe to enter. All he could see as he quickly scanned the room was the unconscious form of a technician slumped against the far wall, blood welling and dribbling from a deep gash in his forehead.

'It's clear,' Howarth noted of the room and entered, Rickard and Beck close behind. Beck spotted the injured crewman and hurried over to him, producing a sedative-filled hyperdermic as if from thin air.

Rickard and Howarth observed the handiwork that had been carried out on the damaged equipment. Below the main control bank cover plating had been carelessly ripped away, revealing clusters of wiring and printed circuitry. Wire had been yanked out in solid bunches from the unit. They had been left looking wildly twisted and tangled.

'It looks like the saboteur was trying to *pull* the wires apart,' Howarth commented. 'You can see where they've been stretched. I doubt if any real damage has been done but it wouldn't hurt to get a tech down here to check on it.'

Rickard suddenly felt like telling Howarth that he knew at least enough of his job to be able to handle that himself. He managed to stifle the urge and simply nodded in

26

agreement, adding: 'We were very lucky. Get a team in to clear up this mess.'

Stepping over to the intercom, Howarth punched dismissively at the activation button, acting not as if the job was unnecessary but that he should not be the one to do it. It was ridiculous, he thought, that he should have to act like this simply because the new Captain did not want to get along. 'Howarth to bridge,' he snapped into the pickup. 'Send a tech team to life-support.' He cut the link before Watts could reply.

Rickard turned away, directing himself at Beck. 'I'd badly like to find out who did this, I hope that it wasn't one of my crew.'

The intercom crackling into life promptly interrupted him. 'Watts to Captain Rickard.'

Rickard complied, Howarth stiffly making space for him as he passed. 'What is it, Lieutenant?' he asked Watts.

'Captain, Hanger Bay Chief Bulloch reports a launch has left the ship without clearance.'

'In hyperdrive! That's impossible.'

Howarth snorted derisively. 'It doesn't look like it.'

Rickard sharply rounded on him. Speedily interceding before anything more could be said between the pair, Beck tried to defuse the situation. 'The matter of its impossibility is slightly academic now. If I have my facts correct, the remote will have to take over soon or we'll lose the launch.'

There was a definite pause before Howarth backed off, not liking to retreat but not really wanting to confront Rickard. He knew that he should have kept his mouth shut. His temper always managed to get the better of him.

Rickard hesitated a moment longer before deciding not to pursue the matter. In his view Howarth's personal opinions were his own affair, as long as he kept them to himself. He made for the door, calling back as he left. 'Have two security Marines meet me on the hanger bay deck.'

Beck gave Howarth a hard look. 'That was not very nice of you,' he said reprovingly.

'I know. I didn't mean it the way it sounded.'

'Okay, but just take it easy next time.'

27

'Like I said not so long ago, we'll see.' He left before Beck could reply.

In a sparsely furnished area of the ship that lay adjacent to the security cells, or 'brig', two young crew members attired in the red and black uniform of the security Marine section of the Service were seated at a low table playing a round of cards. Security was only a semi-Marine department, its members undertaking the same training as the real corp but adjoining the Navy rather than the ground forces. Their mode of dress reflected this. They each wore over their one-piece uniforms a solid-looking plastimetal derived armour which covered and protected their chests and vital areas. Two red coloured helmets of the same tough material were lying close by. All in all they would appear a pretty formidable sight to any aggressors.

The first security Marine, Senior Midshipman Kirsten Stuart, was an Ergaeli by birth. Her parents had emigrated from the front-line colony to the relative safety of Earth when she was sixteen, though she retained much of the unique Scots-derived brogue of her native world. She was of fairly slight build, her height reaching only around one hundred and sixty centimetres. Dedicated training had hardened her and she could take full care of herself in a combat situation - as she had often proved. Her shoulder length hair was jet black. Its thick, uncurled locks serving to contrast the pale whiteness of her smooth, rounded pixie-like face, although her fiery temperament was anything but pixie-like. Her small but well-proportioned figure scarcely showed any of the hidden strength she possessed.

The other midshipman, Peter Bernerds, was English. The light browness of the hair, closely cropped, failed to hide the faint trace of a scarline running across his temple, a scar which spoke volumes on the man's troubled nature. In many ways he and Stuart were alike. Their facial attributes made them seem almost like brother and sister and Stuart's sense of the macabre matched Bernerds' own in its gruesomeness. In fact, most of the duo's colleagues sometimes found their caustic sense of humour far too biting. But whereas Stuart restrained herself from morbidity, Bernerds continually sank into an uncaring state of introvert moroseness which seemed to border on the extreme. This was an attitude Stuart was sure would get him killed one day.

Bernerds had joined the Service Navy after the violent deaths of his parents in the war. It had been in one of their unceasing raids on Service-held planets. Of course he'd joined up hoping for a taste of revenge but, much to his extreme disappointment, he had seen very little in the way of first-hand combat. Stuart had noticed that there was a distinctly reserved, taciturn quality to his personality. He also possessed a streak of sadistic ruthlessness, and he often showed a distinct lack of self-preservation, as if he no longer cared about his life. It was plain that he at least held an obvious disrespect for it. Stuart thought herself to be Bernerds' close friend - one of his only friends in fact - and she often found she had to keep a careful eye on his actions, troublesome as they were.

'That's another fifty you owe me,' Bernerds muttered. He placed his winning hand of cards on the table.

Stuart belatedly realised she would never get the hang of the game. She threw down her cards and lit up a cigarette, immediately blowing out a well-formed chain of smoke rings. 'Any more and I'll be paying you back for the rest of my life,' she wryly commented.

'Maybe we should call it a day as far as the cards are concerned.'

'You won't find me saying no.'

Bernerds piled the cards in the centre of the table and returned to his usual introspective mood, drifting into silence. Stuart inhaled deeply on the cigarette. Its tip glowed brightly.

'What're you gonna do now the fighting's ended?' she asked, breaking the deepening quietness. She knew he had thought long on seceding from the Service.

'What do you mean, what am I going to do?'

'Are you staying or ...?'

'Oh I don't know,' Bernerds sighed heavily. He had mulled the situation over and over in his head, ever since notice of the retaliatory strike action had filtered through, and with no firm resolution. He had to admit he did not have a clue what he really wanted to do with his life. 'We've got that new captain. Maybe I'll wait and see what he turns out like before I hand in my resignation,' he told her. 'I might join that new boundary force they're talking about setting up. It's going to monitor the Larr and hold them to their territory boundaries, not that there's much left of that, what with the withdrawal and all.'

'Yeah, I saw the vid-tape. The Council have cut their holdings to bits. We now have a whole series of new planets to clear and settle. It'll keep the landscapers busy anyhow.'

'I've been thinking-'

'So that's what the noise was.'

'Ha, ha,' he dead-panned. 'I was thinking that if I did leave the Service and got turned down by the boundary force I might try my hand as a colonist.'

'You! A bloody colonist?' Stuart chuckled. 'Give it a rest.'

'There's a lot of money in owning a chunk of a low population world,' Bernerds protested. 'I could get lucky and strike it rich.'

'Huh!' Stuart snorted. 'You might just manage to dig out a living,' she advised before the ship's intercom came on line.

'Security to hanger bay. Code Five,' Watts snapped out on the channel.

'Christ!' Bernerds exclaimed, jumping up animatedly. 'Here we go. Just when I was getting comfortable.'

Stuart smiled inwardly. She knew Bernerds looked forward to any distraction from the usual monotony as much as she did. She stubbed out her cigarette in the steel-rimmed ashtray.

The pair grabbed for their helmets simultaneously, both careful to lock the clip at the back of the neck to ensure that the helmet could not be knocked off in combat. Stuart scrambled to her feet and reached for a security locker, opening it with her pass key. She removed two hand pistols complete with holsters and belts, one of which she threw to Bernerds. Pistol belts in place, they raced for a lift to take them to the hanger deck, leaving the section deserted behind them. Stuart's cigarette lay forgotten in the ashtray. A thin wisp of smoke drifted up from it to be caught and sucked away by the air conditioners.

Rickard and Howarth arrived outside the main hanger bay at a run. The thick bay doors were sealed firmly closed, a wall-sited indicator light showing that the bay was open to space. Rickard quickly discovered another of his new officers, Hanger Bay Chief Lieutenant-Commander Rem Bulloch, in flight control. The office was a spacious operations area filled along one wall with multiple banks of instrumentation. Over that was a wide, one metre deep, completely transparent perspex window with a direct view of the hanger bay beyond. Bulloch, a short, well-built individual, was standing over a console situated in the far corner. He glanced back when Rickard and Howarth, followed by a panting, red-faced Beck, entered.

'Captain,' Bulloch immediately reported to his new superior, 'I'm sorry, I didn't see who it was. I didn't have the chance. The lunatic pushed straight past me while I was servicing a launch on the pad.'

'You've no idea who it was?' Rickard pressed.

'Absolutely none, sir, I didn't have time. Whoever it was closed up the launch and initiated take-off before I could think of looking.'

'Can you guide the launch back?'

'Certainly can. Everything is set now. I'm ready to switch control over to us.'

'Fine. Go ahead.'

Bulloch pulled on a set of relays and sent out an untenable pulse of electronic energy to grant himself piloting control over the stolen launch. As he manoeuvred the remote flight joystick on the console the craft, which was still visible through the open outer doors, veered around and began heading back to *Emputin*. The launch's small engines suddenly flared into life as its unknown occupant tried in vain to escape, momentarily overpowering the computer link. The craft began to buck and pitch as Bulloch struggled to regain control, finally succeeding while the engines tried once more in a futile attempt to push the launch away from the yawning gap of the bay which eagerly waited to entrap it. It was slowly but inexorably hauled back into the hanger bay. The engines deactivated as Bulloch closed down the flight systems.

'Close outer doors,' he ordered an aide as the launch was rested in the bay.

The aide pressed a button on the nearby main bank and the great twin space doors heaved themselves shut with a rumbling grind of machinery that could be felt through the very framework of the office. Pumps were activated and air began filtering into the vacuum of the bay. The internal heating was applied, without which hands would be burnt by the still icy coldness of the launch and all metalwork that had been exposed to the airless chill while the doors had been open.

Bernerds and Stuart chose that moment to arrive, halting beside the inner doors as Rickard exited the office.

'Open the interior doors, Mister Bulloch,' Rickard said as he acknowledged the middies' presence.

The enlarged group entered the hanger bay through still moving interior doors. The chilled atmosphere was felt immediately, largely damped down by labouring heaters though it was. The hanger bay was not meant to be opened so soon after receiving a launch and, conversely, the exterior spaceward door was not usually kept open for such a length of time as it had been, allowing an even greater degree of heat dissipation than was usual.

The party came to a halt at the tightly sealed entrance of the launch.

'Open her up, Mister Howarth,' Rickard ordered but

before the security chief could move the hatch swiftly hissed open of its own accord and a madman leapt out.

The crazed attacker made his instant jump aimed for Rickard. He tried too late to dodge and was caught by an outstretched arm and slammed to the frosty deck. The attacker's wide eyes were glazed and his mouth opened and closed convulsively, as if he were chewing on an invisible lump of gristly meat, spittle dribbling over the edge of his lips. He grasped Rickard's left hand and pinned it to the deck. As Rickard's unprotected skin touched the still icy surface he let out a yell of pain. The intensely burning cold seemed to bite at him, eating into his bare flesh.

Stuart and Bernerds were quick to recover from their initial shock and they reached for the would-be saboteur. Stuart caught his sleeve and pulled strongly at it, causing the man to lose what little balance he had over Rickard and to be hauled to one side, Bernerds took hold of his other arm and twisted it cruelly behind his back.

Beck closed in and jabbed the ever-present hypo into a boldly prominent vein in the man's neck. The effect was instantaneous and dramatic. The captured aggressor shuddered violently for a moment before becoming limp as he drifted swiftly into unconsciousness. Bernerds dumped him unceremoniously to the floor, regardless of its temperature.

Howarth helped Rickard up, mentally noting one mark against the captain in his reckoning of him. Rickard held his burning hand as he tried to ignore the throbbing, tingling pain. He had seen the sudden reaction that Beck's shot had given the attacker and was inquisitive.

'What was it you used?'

Beck grinned. 'Just ordinary sedatives, although I think I pumped a little too much into him,' He bent down to examine the saboteur's pupil dilation. 'He'll wake up fine in around twelve hours. It's your hand I'm worried about. How does it feel?'

'Like Hell,' Rickard emphasised. He nodded at the unconscious form. 'Who is he?'

Howarth spoke up, any trace of belligerence towards Rickard, meant or not, absent from his tone. 'I know him.

He was a laser bank technician. Crewman Piers Nyman, Laser Operator Second Class.'

'Well either he was insane to begin with or he was a Larr agent who was caught at work and for some reason he flipped.'

'I've heard about something like this before,' Beck frowned thoughtfully. 'There was an entry in a medical paper. An item about an enemy agent who was also caught in the act of sabotage. Before he could be stopped he took a drug that biologically affected certain areas of his brain, turning him insane. Presumably it was to prevent the Intelligence people questioning him.'

'That sounds about right. It would explain what happened to this one. But why attack me?'

'After reading the medical paper I have a theory on that. If an agent does get captured after taking the drug then it's possible they've been 'programmed' or conditioned to attack the nearest and most senior Service officer, in this case you. He would have known exactly who you were seeing as he obviously served on this ship.'

'God! How many more of them are there? We could be defending ourselves from attacks like this for years to come.'

'I hope not. That would make life difficult,' Beck noticed Rickard wince at the pain in his hand. 'Come on, Captain, I want to take a good look at that hand in sickbay.'

'Yes, all right. Mister Howarth, please see that the prisoner is safely secured in the brig. He'll probably be shipped off to a rehabilitation centre after we reach Earth.'

'In that case,' said Beck, 'he'll go to the centre on Tau Ceti Gamma. That's got just the right level of treatment for a case like his. He'll probably be a normal, everyday honest convict in a couple of years. Meanwhile, it's down to sickbay with you.'

Rickard allowed himself to be led off by Beck while Howarth supervised Stuart and Bernerds in the transferring of the prisoner.

☆ ☆ ☆

Rickard's damaged hand had been generously treated with an analgesic spray. It would also help with the recovery of damaged skin and the tissue beneath it. Then the hand had been lightly bandaged by Virginia Hicks to prevent further damage while it was healing, Hicks rounded off by applying a piece of tape to the bandage to seal it in place.

'There, I've finished,' she said. 'You'll have to watch how you treat that hand for a couple of days, it'll still be pretty tender for a while. I'll remove the bandage in a day or two if we're still on board, if not take it to your Local and get him to do it, okay?'

'Fine. Thanks.'

'And make sure you don't go playing with any escaped lunatics again,' Beck added from the safety of his office.

'It's all right, Doc. By my standards it's business as usual.'

Watts broke in on the conversation via the intercom. 'Captain Rickard to the bridge, please. We are making final approach on Sol System.'

Rickard thumbed the transmit button. 'I'm coming up, Lieutenant. See you later, Doc.'

'I'll be waiting, and kindly do not address me as "Doc", *Mister* Rickard.'

☆ ☆ ☆

All was ready for the drop from hyperdrive. Rickard took the conn from Kiyami who returned to her own post. 'Subspeed course plotted and locked in, sir,' the navigator reported.

'Slow to subspeed point seven,' Rickard said.

The brightly glimmering stars took up their normal positions in the dark sky as *Emputin* slowed and came out hyperdrive a short distance beyond the orbital path of gaseous Saturn, the planet's ever-changing swirls of

35

beautifully colourful patterns contrasting with the stark, seemingly motionless vividness of its multitudinous collection of rings, although the relative closeness of *Emputin* barely revealed them to the observers in their full glory.

'All systems secured from hyperdrive. Proceeding on subspeed point seven,' Bentowski said. 'And will I be glad to get home.'

Emputin continued on towards Earth, drifting purposely into the plane of the ecliptic, still travelling a speed of which the early explorers of space could only dream. Rickard watched on the main viewer as Saturn slid past. She took with her a cluster of moons only one of which, Titan, possessed any human life. Jupiter came next, its lurid markings barely changed in so many hundreds of years. A faint, simple ring was visible, clinging close to the gas giant's extended atmosphere. Rickard wondered mildly how much of human history it had bothered to witness, from the first tentative and dangerous steps away from the inner planets to a full blown war waged across an entire quadrant of the galaxy. *Emputin* passed within kilometres of the large moon, Callisto, its crater-pitted surface casting elongated shadows from the pale, distant light of the Sun.

Not far from it was the loose assemblage of tumbling rocks and mining pods that made up the asteroid belt. As it crossed over, the impressive bulk of the cruiser blacked the light out from the multitude of freighters grouped there while they paid their regular visits to deliver supplies to the miners and to collect their products for as little payment as they could wrangle.

Reddened Mars was quickly passed, her twin satellites, Phobos and Deimos, rotating around their primary at a rapid speed. Earth gradually came into sight, the single-person sailing craft cresting the solar winds at a safe distance from its blue-tinged atmosphere. The passenger docking station was revealed, now brimming with customers. The news of the war's termination had sped back through the Grouping at a tremendous speed so that the travel routes were suddenly filled chock-a-block with all types of merchant and private vessels. The once empty vacuum was now transformed. The grand old passenger liner, the SS *Empress,* had been pulled out of retirement and was presently attached to the docking station, her newly repaired bright and colourful hull reflecting the Sun's rays in the cold ambience of space.

The Service Navy spaceport came into view over the Earth's rim, its dazzlingly illuminating beacon lights flashing in regular patterns as it followed its geo-stationary orbit around the planet situated directly over the European continent. The spaceport was roughly two kilometres in length from top to bottom and was designed so that a thick rod-like stem joined onto a mushroom-shaped dome at one end and a tenuous-looking filigree framework at the other. The hollow dome possessed enormous space doors positioned at regular intervals, one to each quarter section to allow the entrance of Service cruisers. Inside, the building and repair work of any great magnitude was carried out in completely safe, airtight surroundings. *Emputin,* not requiring such rigorous attention, would merely be docked onto one of the exterior umbilicals which projected from the rounded dry-dock hull.

'Slow to subspeed point oh one,'

'Point oh one, aye, Sir.'

'Lieutenant Watts, please advise Docking Control that we are ready for them.'

'Yes, sir.'

'This is Docking Control, *Emputin.* You are cleared to dock. Prepare to transfer control to us.'

'All systems are ready and waiting.'

'Release control now.'

Bentowski did so and relaxed in his seat, enjoying the rare experience of having someone else do the piloting for a change. 'It's all yours, pal,' he said.

The spaceport came closer and one of the projections from the upper dry-dock dome was moved out to meet them. Rickard noted that a lone figure in a life-suit was carrying out some piece of minor maintenance on the dock's hull.

The computer which was controlling *Emputin's* flight

briefly ignited the tiny positioning and manoeuvering jets along its bow, giving it the same velocity as the spaceport. It slowed perceptibly. Then the searching umbilical eagerly locked on to one of the main starboard air locks with a reverberating clang of metal on metal and the ship became still.

Lights flashed off on the nav and helm consoles as the computer shut down the flight systems. A voice carried over the comm unit.

'You are fully secure, *Emputin*. Docking completed.'

2

505.98.67

Rickard took one of *Emputin's* own launches planetside rather than wait for transport to be arranged from the spaceport. His coxswain was a young junior officer who seemed extremely capable in the handling of the small vehicle. The launch winged its way down into the thick atmosphere passing through heavily piled layers of persistent cloud which hung low over southern Britain. The sprawling metropolis of London came into sight, revealing its intimate details a little at a time as the ground closed in.

The coxswain directed his craft towards the Service Command structure which dominated the shorter, more compact buildings surrounding it. The building was often compared with an iceberg in its design - a larger proportion of it was hidden under the ground's crowded surface. What little that showed stood out boldly. The pale blueness of its outer walls was in direct contrast to the darker, utilitarian offices and shops that came up to the open, grassy chunk of land which separated the two totally different styles of architecture.

Service Command. Headquarters of the entire Service Navy, controlling the fleet through countless lesser bases on a multitudinous number of planets. Here, the countless arrays of deskbound admiralty staff whiled away the hours plotting new schemes and ideas to keep the lower ranks continuously busy. It sounded like them, anyway. Well, most of them. It was in one of the thousands of offices below ground that Rickard had received his promotion to captain. And where he had first met the admiral's daughter, Karen Trestrail.

Rickard had to admit he was looking forward to seeing

39

her again. In fact, she was his one real connection with his home world. Both his parents were long dead and he possessed no close relations. None to speak of. No, Earth was a lovely place to visit but Rickard could not see himself staying for any extensive length of time. Especially now that he had his own ship to look after. Travel was in his blood. He longed to be out there, amongst the stars, however damned corny it sounded. He almost felt homesick for space if he were planetside for too long.

The coxswain flicked some controls and the launch touched down noiselessly and without a single jar. 'There you are, sir Service Command.'

'Thank you,' Rickard said, and climbed out.

The launch had landed on one of the rooftop grids. Others were visible to Rickard on the lower towers of the Command structure. Higher towers stretched reflectively above, reaching for the sky.

Rickard made for the elevator shaft. It was placed for safety's sake well away from the pad near the edge of the high-railinged roof. The lift arrived after only a short wait and Rickard entered it - to find Vicky Benet standing beside him.

'Hi! I heard you were coming so I decided I'd meet you,' she smiled as the doors closed and the lift began its vertical descent.

'It's good to see you again,' Rickard said, and he meant it. Vicky was an ex-Larr captive he'd helped escape when his intelligence mission had taken him away from the mercenary base of Alpherate II. He had provided her with a means of returning to Earth and she had accepted, only too glad to be away from the enemy camp.

Now she seemed to bubble with renewed spirit. 'I'm doing great,' she said. 'I've even managed to get a pretty decent job,' she enthused in much the same way as Rickard had on *Emputin's* bridge a few hours before. He guessed it was all a matter of where you felt most comfortable.

'What as? Rubbish disposal technician?'

'A dustman? No, don't be daft. I am now personal office aide to a full admiral. I have my living quarters as well. It's in a block only a few minutes away.' Their eyes met for a split second before Rickard looked away.

He wondered if that was meant as an invitation or if his imagination was simply playing up. After all, they had been fairly close for a while. Now, as far as he could see, Vicky had landed on her feet and seemed positively effervescent, and he supposed she had good reason to be. A whole new life was opening up for her, one that did not include mercenaries and their degrading ways. Now she had a job which paid very well and an apartment in one of the newest luxury block complexes. No wonder she looked excited.

'Who is it you're working for?' Rickard asked out of interest.

'Admiral Lamia Melato. A woman admiral, no less.'

'You have a point there. It's not so often a woman reaches such a high position even these days, with supposed sexual equality - and she's fairly young. As far as I know, Admiral Melato is barely forty. It makes me feel less guilty about my sudden rise in rank.'

'Oh, come on. You shouldn't feel guilty. You earned your promotion fair and square.'

'Maybe. Well, I suppose so. I'm certainly glad you've reached so far in one step. It did take me *slightly* longer.'

'Oh, yes-'

Vicky broke off as the lift doors opened. They stepped into a hallway which opened out a short way ahead onto a compact recreational area bordered by perspex surrounds. Off-duty personnel sat about, chatting and involving themselves in entertaining and educational amusements. The potted plants positioned along the hallway made the bright, spacious locality seem more friendly.

'Yes,' Vicky continued in a lower voice. 'I've heard about your new ship. Well done.'

'Thanks,' he grinned self-consciously. His face reddened fractionally at the warmth of her manner. He was about to add more when the wall-speakers along the hallway suddenly burst into life.

'Captain Rickard to Debriefing, please.' The message echoed along the corridors.

41

'It seems as if I'm going to spend the rest of my life being paged. Sorry, but I must go.'

'Okay. Thanks anyway for helping me out. Perhaps you'll come and pay me a visit sometime?'

'I'd love to.' He had been right the first time.

'You'd better mean that.' Vicky tiptoed up and delivered him a peck on the cheek before hurrying off.

Rickard watched as she disappeared, then started off in the opposite direction, enmeshed in his thoughts. She was a lovely lady, he mused. And his own question about her had been answered, albeit unknowingly on her part. He really did hope he could get time to visit her later but where would that leave Karen? Last time they had met matters were left pretty open ended. After meeting Karen Trestrail at his promotion in her father's office - the office of the sharp-tempered Vice-Admiral Trestrail - he had been able to visit her only once before being whisked away by Intelligence. He wondered if he were still welcome. It was high time he found out. Making a decision, he resolved to go and see her as soon as the debriefing was over and done with.

Rickard's trail of thought was sharply interrupted as he rounded a corner and almost collided with Prime Minister Cadir, premier of the nation on Cymma Major which Rickard had aided. Rhos's homeland. With Cadir was an escort Rickard had not seen before. He was a thick-set, thick-featured man with very little in the way of good looks.

'God,' Rickard muttered sourly, not at all pleased to see the Prime Minister. 'This seems to be my day for bumping into people.'

'Captain Rickard!' Cadir cried, 'I heard your name being called but I did not expect to meet you again.'

Rickard thought exactly the same thing, though for different reasons. 'I'm sorry I can't stop to chat, I have a previous appointment. Perhaps we can talk later.' He tried to excuse himself. He did not exactly dislike Cadir but in his book a politician was a politician and Cadir was a prime example of how false and insincere Rickard thought them to be.

'Were it but possible, my friend.' Cadir mimed an

expression of sorrow, 'I am returning directly to Cymma. I have this moment signed the documents initiating my people into your Allied Grouping of Planets so I must return to inform the citizens and prepare them for more visits from off-worlders.'

'Oh, another time, then,' Rickard said, trying also to sound sorry.

'Yes, I'm afraid it will have to be another time.'

'Right, I'll be off.' Rickard made to go but Cadir forestalled him.

'My dear Captain. Have you heard of the sad loss of our heroic freedom fighter, Rhos?'

'Yes.'

'It was so unfortunate a loss. We will all miss him.' Cadir's face dropped.

'We shall,' Rickard said, thinking how well practised the minister's actions were. What a hypocrite he was.

'Rhos was a good man who was instrumental in the freeing of our planet.'

'Rhos was also a good friend of mine.'

'Yes,' Cadir continued, blatantly ignoring the fact that his audience of one was plainly uninterested in his speech-making. 'I *was* thinking of honouring him at the National gathering on Cymma but any award he receives now will have to be posthumous.'

Enough was enough, decided Rickard. 'I'm sorry but I really have to get a move on,' he said and watching Cadir at his play-acting was a waste of time. 'I must go,' he repeated politely but firmly. 'Please give my commiserations to Rhos's wife for me, won't you?'

'I will, of course, Captain.'

'Thank you.' He left.

Cadir called out to him as he reached the end of the passage. 'Good-bye, Captain, I will look forward to the next time you visit our now free home.'

'Some chance,' Rickard muttered under his breath.

He found Rear-Admiral Peterson waiting for him outside the debriefing room. Peterson welcomed him extra-cordially, a sentiment Rickard returned wholeheartedly. This was the man who had vested him with his new command so it was only natural that he feel a pleasant disposition towards him.

'Welcome back, Captain.' Peterson greeted him. 'How did you find your crew?'

'I'd say they'll do quite well for now, sir.'

'I thought you'd say something like that. Most captains do when they've just been given a new command. You wait a while, then you'll find out what they are really capable of. You should be glad of them in time, believe me. Behind many a captain's success lies a good crew.'

'Why the debriefing, sir? I didn't realise the files were incomplete enough to need my report.'

'You'd be surprised. Oh, they're not really that bad. We simply like to find out as much as possible from each agent, so that we can build up an absolutely complete picture of his or her movements. An open operative such as yourself could pick up any number of interesting items. Anyway, there are some areas of knowledge on which we are very unclear. We have to know how the Larr bases are structured so we can safely send in raiding parties and later, full blown takeover forces. Some of them are still resisting. The Council are ready to pull the plug on us if we indiscriminately wipe out "so many people who could eventually contribute to the general good of society", so we have to be careful. Don't worry about it, son.'

'I see.' Rickard began to appreciate the need for what he was about to undergo.

'All that aside,' Peterson continued, 'you have done a remarkable job. One of which you can be very proud. I believe you have some leave owed to you?'

'A little,' he understated wildly. He was owed something in the region of two to four months' backdated leave, especially after the assignment he had just completed.

'Well it's yours to take as soon as we've finished with you. Enjoy yourself, it may be some time before you have the chance again. You are a cruiser captain now. You can't go swanning off whenever you feel like it. Come on, let's get this debriefing over and done with and then you can be on your way.'

Peterson shepherded him into the dazzlingly lit room beyond and closed the door firmly behind him.

☆ ☆ ☆

Rickard took a hired car from Service Command to Karen Trestrail's home complex in the north of the city. Once there, the building's express lift shot him up five hundred floors in a few seconds. After that he was forced to catch a local back down to floor 466, where he found Karen's apartment. He pressed the buzzer and, with some trepidation, awaited an answer.

The door opened. Karen was clearly overjoyed to see him, as her lively, enthusiastic manner revealed.

'Chris!' she cried, crushing him in a welcoming hug that spoke not so subtly of deeper emotions. 'How are you? Oh, it's great to see you again. It was on the news about the end of the war and the battle near New Norway. They even gave you a mention as being the newest captain in the fleet. I'm so pleased to hear you have your own ship. I know what it must mean to you.'

Rickard, a touch overwhelmed, could only manage a strangled, 'Thanks,' in the face of Karen's gleeful greeting. He glanced meaningfully into the apartment, making something of a show of doing so. 'Shall I make myself comfortable out here,' he said drily.

'Sorry, Chris. Here I am chatting away and forgetting to invite you in,' she apologised. 'It's been a while since I saw you and my mouth just got the better of me.' She led him inside, raising a heel to kick the door shut after her, so loath was she to release her hold on Rickard. 'You didn't meet my flat-mate last time you were here, did you?'

Rickard vividly remembered his last visit and, no, there hadn't been anyone else here at the time.

'Nicola,' Karen called, 'come here a minute.'

'Why?' a voice replied from somewhere beyond the lounge. Rickard suddenly felt uneasy. The voice sounded strangely familiar to him.

'We have a guest,' Karen continued. 'A friend of mine. A very good friend of mine,' she added to Rickard with another of her vivaciously heartwarming smiles.

From the bedroom came Karen's flat-mate. She was

45

dressed stylishly in a flowing, ankle length skirt with white blouse. Her moderately short, pale blond hair was tied back in a fetching pony-tail, held together by an oversized black bow. Karen's flat-mate, a woman hard to forget, was none other than Nicola Woods.

Rickard's mouth virtually dropped in astonishment. In his surprise he gaped. There was no thought of trying to cover the shock of seeing *her* here. How many more 'old acquaintances' could he collide with in one day? The last time he'd seen this lady was on a freight-cum-passenger vessel that had been under attack by the group of mercenaries he'd infiltrated. Then she'd acted extremely coquettish towards him, although whether it was simply because he had been cast in the role of heroic rescuer that she had acted the way she did, he couldn't tell. He certainly didn't expect to see her here, in Karen's flat, of all places.

Karen looked from Rickard's stunned gaze to Nicola's pleased expression of remembrance. 'I imagine you two have met before,' she finally uttered. She inflected a tone of warning to Nicola as she spoke. The warning marked the edge of forbidden territory. She did not want Nicola crossing that boundary.

Nicola ignored it, flashing a grin at Rickard. 'Yes. We certainly have met before. He's the one I told you about. You know, my mysterious rescuer.'

'I know,' Karen said. She knew all right. She knew only too well. She also recalled the manner in which Nicola had spoken of her rescuer, the unknown hero. Unknown no longer it seemed.

Rickard made a desperate grab for his fleeing wits and pulled his mouth closed. He attempted a casual approach, hoping he could make himself appear quite calm and collected. He knew the minute he spoke that what he said sounded utterly lame. 'Hi. Fancy meeting you here of all places.'

'I share the flat with Karen,' Nicola said, batting wide eyes beckoningly at him.

Rickard's insides churned. Please help me! He mentally grovelled to whatever higher power had control over the matter. 'Karen didn't mention she had a flat-mate,' he

46

spluttered.

'Oh, didn't I,' Karen stated in mock surprise. 'It must have slipped my mind. How forgetful of me.'

'Oh Karen,' Nicola said with a smile, 'that memory of yours.'

Rickard tried to recover himself. His wits were finally taking hold and beginning to act almost sensibly. He had little trouble in detecting the sarcasm in her voice and felt he should explain. 'We met while I was working undercover for Intelligence. I was with some mercenaries for a while. I managed to help out a few passengers when their ship came under attack-'

'It's all right, Chris,' Karen cut in. 'I've heard the story.'

Nicola gave a shrug and looked suitably apologetic. Her act was good enough for Rickard to believe. Unused as he was to this type of thing, the double meanings and underlying messages the women were exchanging completely missed him.

Karen grasped Rickard's hand possessively. She wanted to strengthen her claim on him. She was damned if she was going to allow Nicola to get away with sheer piracy. It happened that the hand she held was his injured one. For the first time she noticed the bandage there. Concerned, she made a closer inspection. 'What happened?' she frowned.

'Don't worry, it's nothing. I got it in a small fracas on board my ship. An enemy saboteur-cum-spy attacked me after we'd cornered him. We worked out that it was probably part of the man's programming to go for me. The medics patched up the hand. It's fine now,' he shrugged.

Karen looked up at him. His eyes told that he wanted to be away from the flat, preferably with her. She held his gaze for a moment longer hurriedly averting her eyes. She was feeling emotionally unsteady in Rickard's company and she was finding it hard to hide those emotions, more from Nicola than from Rickard. Her flat-mate was undoubtedly bound to play on any weaknesses she could find. With merciless attention to detail. As far as she was concerned, 'All's fair in love and war' was meant to be taken in deadly seriousness.

Nicola was keeping her attention firmly centred on Rickard, and still she did not miss a single movement from Karen. 'Would you like a drink, Chris?' She offered with open hospitality.

Too open for Karen's liking. She could not fail to observe her over-possessive flat-mate's constant eye contact with *her* visitor. Upon impulse she slid her arm under Rickard's to certify *her* claim on him.

Rickard recognised only a scant amount of this bolder byplay. He instead wondered blithely where he could offer to take Karen. It was plainly apparent to him that they would not have much of an evening together with Nicola in the way. 'Karen, how do you feel about driving out for a meal?' he ventured.

'Yes I'd love to. Where are we going?'

'Umm...How about Paris, on the Champs Elysées? I have a car that'll get us there in under ninety minutes,' he said, remembering an enjoyable restaurant he had visited there...what? A month ago? No more than two. It seemed closer to a year considering how much had happened to him in the interim.

Karen was understandably enthusiastic, seeing this as the perfect opportunity to get her man away from Nicola's clutches. 'Paris, great! I've never been to Paris before.'

'Good.' Rickard relaxed, pleased that he had made the right choice. 'We'd better be off.'

'Come on, then,' Karen hustled.

'Sorry I can't stay and chat, Nicola. See you around some time,' he called over his shoulder as Karen bustled him out, giving Nicola a triumphant wave as she disappeared through the front door.

Nicola looked thoughtfully after them.

They picked up the car in the fourteenth sub-basement parking level of the block. Rickard drove straight out of London until they reached the cross-Continental motorway that led to Dover and the south coast. Cruising an auto-drive at a steady two hundred kilometres per hour they reached the port with considerable ease. Once there, the motorway, with its eight lane ultra-smooth surface, ended. A line of toll booths heralded the nearing of the Eurobridge. The bridge had celebrated its three hundredth anniversary not so long before and was scheduled for retirement as soon as its replacement, a stronger, far more adequate version, was completed. Nonetheless, it looked in remarkably good shape for its not inconsiderable age.

Once on the bridge there followed a ten minute leisurely drive across the nine-and-a-half kilometres long, twin lane road, before it came to one of the two huge, mid-channel concrete islands which carried the road down in a gently winding spiral into a tunnel drilled under the sea bed. After another twenty odd kilometres of motoring alongside a completely subterranean rail tunnel the roadway came up on a second, identical island that led directly onto the last section of the bridge. Colossal spans stretched vastly into the sun-drenched distance of a suddenly blue sky. Heat bounced off the road to distort and convolute the images of vehicles ahead. Giant supports stretched seaward to protected concrete shields that held the fantastic feat of engineering in place.

Once past another row of toll booths, intended for traffic coming in the opposite direction, the bridge road became a motorway again. It led on through the verdant French countryside and townscapes, nearing the outskirts of Paris before it headed off towards Spain.

Rickard took a junction exit that brought him into the centre of the ancient French capital. He parked the car in an underground facility basically the same in design as the multiple levels under Karen's home complex. The couple took an elevator to ground level and emerged directly onto the Champs Elysées, where Rickard steered Karen in the direction of his restaurant.

A narrow road ran along between wide pavements, lined each side by a double row of lushly darkening deciduous trees. They swished and swayed gently in the mild breeze, imbuing Karen with a peaceful, contented frame of mind. She noted with interest the numerous young couples seated at the outside tables of bars and cafés along the way. Then her wandering eyes looked ahead and she saw the framework which covered the

49

famous ruin of the Arc de Triomphe in a fine mesh of dull grey metal struts.

'It's good that they've actually got around to rebuilding it at last,' she indicated to the Arc.

'What?' Rickard started, roused from the mine of his own ever-present thoughts.

Karen sighed in mock sufferance. 'The Arc de Triomphe. It's been in that state ever since an anti-government terrorist attack about three-and-a-half centuries ago.'

'I haven't been paying much attention to local events lately.'

'Well you should. It's important to. A pressure group recently began demanding its rebuilding, even though everyone thinks of it as a ruin - like those old castles spread all over the place. The local government relented last week and the work started. That was on the news, too.'

'Last week I was a few thousand light years away from Earth,' Rickard gently reminded her. 'It seems as though I have some catching up to do.'

'I just think it'll look very nice once it's back together again,' Karen insisted. She caught him staring at her with a bemused smile on his lips. 'What are you looking at?' she demanded with faked petulance.

'I was just thinking how beautiful you look.'

'Yuk! Mushy!'

Rickard simply smiled and pulled her closer to him.

In the maze-like internal structure of Service Command, three staff admirals were meeting in a confined, shadily illuminated room bare of all but essential fittings. A data tape monitor and its playback equipment, placed on a lone desk against the wall farthest from the room's entrance, had been activated. The old-fashioned hinged door was left ajar, awaiting the arrival of the third participant.

Vice-Admiral Robert Trestrail fidgeted restlessly in his seat, impatient for the meeting to begin.

'Tis nae bloody funny anymore, I wish that woman would get a move on,' he growled, his Ergaeli accent emphasised to the full.

'Show some patience,' Rear-Admiral Peterson chided from his own uncomfortable seat near the desk.

Trestrail cursed, 'Patience ma ass. We're called down here tae this.... *cellar* all o' a sudden, wi'out any warning, an' told tae wait fer a top secret meeting. What's top secret about this place, that's what I want tae know?'

Peterson did not like to agree with his bad-tempered colleague but he had to admit Trestrail held a valid point when he voiced his dislike for cloak-and-dagger secrecy - which he did frequently and with generous volume. Peterson himself liked it just as little but he knew it *was* sometimes necessary.

Trestrail's grumbling did not cease when Admiral Lamia Melato entered the room. She was a tall woman. Her height of almost two full metres gave her a dominating appearance. A head of uniquely reddish-blonde coloured hair did nothing to detract from that image. Her face was soft and unwrinkled, a credit to the most modern creams and oils available, and her firm figure filled out the tight contours of her uniform quite elegantly. She was an elegant beauty, fully self-composed, and she was nobody's fool. She and Trestrail were old and well-established enemies.

She closed the door behind her and sat in the vacant chair placed centrally to the other two.

'I'm sorry to be late, gentlemen,' she said, taking a data tape from her pocket and slotting it into the playback system.

'Why all this secrecy?' Trestrail instantly demanded, his hard-headed stubborness refusing to rest the matter without proper explanation.

Melato delivered him a sharp look. 'This tape I am about to play contains information of an important and sensitive nature to the Grouping,' she snapped. 'Service Command is not yet ready to release that information to the general populace. It could, and probably would, arouse fears of another war.'

Trestrail was surprised. 'Tis that serious, eh?' He ceased his complaining, momentarily satisfied. He did not apologise for his outburst - that was not in his nature.

'I'm glad you see now why I had to be so secretive. The Council have already seen the tape and have recommended me to find a captain suitable to take the job of entering and investigating the "hostile zone", as it is presently being termed. Now-' she activated the machine, bringing a computer graphics illustration onto the monitor. 'This is a map of the sectors controlled by us on this side of the zone. Nothing is known about the geography of the zone itself, except that its occupants have presently limited their territory to the edge of this remarkably large asteroid belt which splits sector seventeen of quad three in half. The nearest planet to the Belt is LA921, called Alpheratz, in sector sixteen. This has only recently been liberated from the Larr, so we have only a minor outpost there.' She pointed out the appropriate items on the screen.

'Excuse me for butting in.' Peterson said. 'Where does this tape come from?'

'It was copied from the computer central file of the Larr command base, before its destruction, by ex-Intelligence operative Christopher Rickard.'

'Oh.' Peterson comprehended. Now he knew what Rickard had handed him in the hangar bay of *Searcher* before the fleet had gone in to attack.

Trestrail was noticeably less civil. 'Humph!' *That* rank-climbing amateur,' he said contemptuously.

Melato had read Rickard's file prior to attending this meeting so she knew how he had been promoted suddenly and, to some, unnecessarily from the rank of lieutenant. She sympathized with him, understanding only too well how he must have felt - and how others felt about him. She, too, had gained a surprise promotion, this time *from* the rank of captain, when her ship had come under attack during the war and had been badly damaged by Larr vessels while she was transporting Council officials. She had used an old trick, fooling the enemy into thinking the ship was dead, enticing them to close in for boarding. Waiting until they were close enough before firing every working laser bank at them at almost point-blank range. The officials had been greatly impressed by her actions, not to say relieved, and had consequently ordered her immediate promotion to the rank of full admiral. That had all been some time ago but she too found she had to deal with rude and often malicious remarks from people such as Trestrail - until her work results showed her to be fully competent in her post. She expected that it was much the same for Captain Rickard.

'If you will remember, *Vice*-Admiral,' she said in reply to his comment, putting extreme emphasis on the fact that he was a grade lower than her in rank. 'You once called *me* a rank-climbing amateur. No longer, I think.'

Trestrail blustered, realising he had put his foot in too far and was in danger of having it bitten off. 'Aye, well, mebbe he will prove himsel'...eventually.'

'I'm so glad you agree, Admiral,' Melato smirked victoriously. 'Now, to show you the only visual recording we have in our files. This was taken from a Larr cruiser. At the time it was escaping back into what was then its own space.' She let the tape continue. The picture was of airless vacuum filled by the menacing bulks of three battleships of unfamiliar design. They were closing inexorably on the fleeing Larr ship, firing all the way. The alien ships suddenly filled the entire picture as the camera operator magnified the picture. Unreadable, almost Arabic in appearance, was the writing etched onto the upper bow of each ship. It was hard to see even that, such was the violence of the rocking of the Larr cruiser as the alien battleships continuously scored direct hits. Few shots were forthcoming in the opposite direction. 'Now you will notice their arrival in the Belt,' Melato mentioned redundantly, as the asteroids were already on screen. The large and small, rounded and flattened shapes of asteroids came between hunters and hunted as the Larr ship entered its own territory. The alien ships at once came to a halt. They simply waited until their quarry had moved out of range.

The tape ended to be followed by a momentary silence. It was broken by the grating voice of Trestrail. 'Well! Who d'ye suggest we send intae *that*?'

'I have thought on the subject and have come to the obvious conclusion that the ship we send in must be one of our strongest and most powerful, one of the Eagle-class. I suggest that the ship should be the SNS *Emputin*.'

'What!' Trestrail exclaimed loudly. 'But that's-'

'Captain Rickard's ship, yes,' Melato finished for him. 'What do you say Admiral Peterson?'

'Hmmm,' Peterson sighed affably. 'I can't say that I find any objections to the idea. I mean, judging from the tape I'd say our Eagle-class ships are more than a match for any three of theirs, so there would be no *real* danger. In addition, if these alien people were hostile to the Larr they might show us a more co-operative side to their nature. I'm inclined to say yes to Rickard's appointment as mission leader.'

Melato smiled. She knew where Peterson's loyalties lay, and they were certainly not with Trestrail. 'I'm glad you agree,' she said. She may not have originally wanted Rickard for the job but she was definitely going to use him now, if only to score one over on Trestrail.

'But I dinna agree!' Trestrail blurted vehemently. 'Why, that untrained, inexperienced-'

'*Admiral Trestrail!*' Melato exploded. 'Captain Rickard has shown quite adequately that he can be trusted with the task. You have to look no further than his work record with Intelligence to see that. If you continue these derogatory outbursts I might begin to think you are carrying out some sort of private vendetta against him!'

Trestrail looked for a moment as if he would argue further but thought the better of it and turned away in disgust.

'That's settled, then,' Melato said levelly, 'Captain Rickard it is.'

54

Rickard and Karen stepped out of the lift, the doors gliding silently closed after them.

The couple strolled leisurely down the deserted hallway, the heels of Karen's shoes click-clicking on the bare floor. She fumbled deep in the cavernous pockets of her jacket for her door key. Eventually discovering the plastic card she flourished it with a sigh of relief.

'I thought for a moment I'd be locked out for the night,' she said, envisioning sleeping on the doorstep. It was not a pleasant idea, even in an air-conditioned complex.

'Wouldn't Nicola have let you in?' Rickard enquired, moderately surprised.

'You have got to be joking! Once she's asleep nothing short of a bomb under the bed would disturb her.'

Rickard chuckled at the notion with the air of a man at last finding contentment in his life. Karen had other things on her mind, having long-since noticed the dark rings around Rickard's eyes. She could no longer keep from voicing her concern. 'You look exhausted, Chris. Are you okay?'

'I'm fine. The only thing wrong with me is lack of sleep, that's all. A good eight hours' worth should see me okay.' He brushed the matter aside.

Karen was instantly relieved. Not so much that he would not be able to stay with her for the night but more for the fact that because of Nicola's presence she was unwilling to invite him to stay, especially *because* of Nicola's presence. It was something she had been loath to tell him. He had unknowingly made it easier on her. Social etiquette for a sophisticated age. They reached the door and Karen slotted the key into the lock. The card was accepted and the door sprang open. Karen glanced inside, hesitating awkwardly. 'I can't really ask you in,' she said apologetically. 'You know...Nicola...'

Rickard smiled tiredly, fully understanding her dilemma, 'Karen, it's okay.'

'I'm glad you're taking it so well. I thought you might be offended.'

'Course not. By this time you should know me better than that. Go on, I need some rest anyhow.'

'Och, ye're full o' blather, as my father would say. You, Christopher Nilsen Rickard, are a smooth talker when you want to be.'

'Can I help it?'

'I doubt it. So now let the all-embracing darkness of sleep betide me until sweet morning breaks,' she suddenly recited expansively, much to Rickard's amusement.

He frowned quizzically. 'Was that a quote?'

'I think so. I can't for the life of me remember where it's from.'

'It doesn't matter.'

'No...' Karen stopped and stared at him, suddenly wishing Nicola was nowhere within a hundred miles of them. They kissed, deeply and with great fervour. Rickard was intently aware of the warm intensity of her body as it pressed into his, making them briefly one and he felt he could hold the moment forever but it ended and they eventually broke apart.

Karen held on a second longer, reluctant to let him slip away for however short a time. However, she knew she had to so she whispered him a heartfelt farewell and entered the flat. The door closed softly behind her.

Rickard released a drawn out groan of contentment. Life had never felt so good.

☆ ☆ ☆

The early morning sun rose majestically over the multiple towers of Service Command, casting elongated shadows over the surrounding architecture. The air was crisply clean and sharp and a thin layer of dew covered the grassy banks that surrounded Command, slowly melting in the rising warmth of day.

Vice-Admiral Trestrail's office looked out high over the waking city. Traffic in the streets below was just beginning to build up. The morning 'rush hour' remained virtually unchanged in its constitution, drawing on an exercise more than four hundred years old. And it was still as arduous an experience. A sudden tap at the office door made Trestrail start in his soft, padded chair and he called out sharply, 'Come.'

Rickard walked in, his uniform tight with the stiffness of newly pressed material. 'You wanted to see me, sir?' he asked. He closed the door and approached the wooden desk behind which was seated the one man in the whole of the Service Navy he actively disliked. He knew for a fact that the feeling was entirely mutual. He had been awoken by the insistent buzzing of his vidcom set less than thirty minutes before and had hurried to discover why the vice-admiral wanted to see him of all people.

'Sit yersel' down, Captain,' Trestrail's tone was neutral, neither friendly nor hostile. Directly businesslike in fact. 'Ye ken full well that I did nae agree wi' ye're promotion but there's nae a thing I can do about it so I'll ha' tae live wi' the fact. We'll ha' nae more said on the matter.'

Rickard was not about to argue. He could not deny that he was relieved, although mildly puzzled to say the least, that Karen's father had dropped his vendetta. Not that he was in much of a position to complain. It was hard enough for him to become used to a command position as it was, without a staff admiral opposing him all the way. But why the sudden change around?

Trestrail gave him no time to think further, getting directly to the subject at hand and trying to hide his intense animosity toward Rickard only because he was wary of Admiral Melato. Until he could find a way of removing the upstart from his post legally he would have to play it calmly.

'Now, wi'out further ado I'll get on tae what ye came here fer,' Trestrail started, his act on top form. 'A'm giving you this mission, this assignment, fer ye tae prove yersel'. Dinna muck it up. Orders: take *Emputin* intae the hostile zone in sector seventeen o' quadrant three, which I'm sure ye're well aware of seeing as how it was ye got the information tape in the first place. There, ye will make contact with its inhabitants. determine if they are suitable or no tae join the Grouping an', if no, what do they have in the way o' armaments. Ye're on yer own. It's yer decisions that will count - or yer mistakes. Full details - what there are o' them - will be available to ye via yer ship's computer.

'Ye leave in six hours. Ye'd better get a move on.'

3

Kirsten Stuart led the prisoner escort detail through glazed panelled doors, leaving behind the launch that had delivered them from *Emputin*. The prisoner under escort was Piers Nyman, sedated mildly enough to leave him the use of his legs. He seemed dozy and confused, apparently unaware of his surroundings. A livid red weal marked one side of his face where Bernerds had earlier dumped him on the deck of the chilled docking bay. Behind him marched two security Marines, young faces expressionless under the plastimetal armour helmets. The deep red colouring of their helmets dimly reflected the sparse overhead lighting of the narrow, claustrophobically confined main corridor of the holding centre. Each Marine had a firm hand on Nyman's shoulders, steering his bedrugged form along. Each had their pistols fastened securely in their belt pouches, understandably expecting no trouble.

The group reached the reception desk, a high counter constructed of solid, uncovered metal, as were much of the fixtures and fittings inside the centre. The attendant seated lazily behind the desk looked bored and unattentive, fully disinterested in his work. Lackadaisical attitude revealed to the full, he climbed unenthusiastically to his feet as Stuart called the escort detail to a halt. She produced and handed him a document of transfer to be signed.

The attendant took a sip from the steaming hot drink on his work-top and burped. 'Is this the nut who attacked your captain?' he drawled languidly.

'It is,' Stuart replied crisply. 'He's been sedated but I don't know how long the dosage will last.'

59

'Don't fret on it. He won't need sedation any more. Not once he's shipped out to Tau Ceti, for sure. They'll look after him.' The attendant gave her a wink. She presumed it to mean that he was attempting to be ironic. He followed that up with a single sadistic chuckle.

Stuart stayed silent, not wanting to show her disgust at this foul slur of a person. Honest manic depressives like Bernerds she could take but not the evidently falsity of the attendant. She wanted to be out of the dark, foreboding corridors of the centre and mentally urged the rather unsavoury creature behind the desk to get a move on with the proceedings.

'He's marked dangerous on this,' he waved the transfer paper.

'He is dangerous.'

'Don't look it from here,' he said, shaking his head. He removed a battered ink pen from a desk drawer and scribbled something totally illegible on the form's dotted line before returning it to Stuart.

Stuart gave the form a cursory inspection before stuffing it back into her pocket. 'He's all yours now,' she said, relieved to be rid of the sullen Nyman. She pulled him forward by the front of his clothes and was completely unprepared for the sudden pull from Nyman that sent her staggering against him as he broke into an unexpected rage. Before she could regain her balance Nyman gave her a violent shove and she was smashed against the wall with a force that knocked the breath from her body. She slid to the floor, momentarily stunned.

At the first sign of trouble the attendant jumped for the low ceiling. He grabbed hold of a protective wire mesh and pulled it speedily downwards to lock into the groove on the top of the counter. There he stayed in perfect safety. He was fully content to allow the trained security people to deal with the frenzied prisoner.

Nyman turned from Stuart's crouched form as the two Marines went for their pistols. They were a fraction too slow. With an animal-like bellow Nyman chopped his arms in a surprisingly expert fashion, sending both pistols flying madly away. The first Marine leapt forward, gaining a hold on Nyman which turned out to be very short lived. Yelling incomprehensible profanties, Nyman brought up an elbow and jammed it hard into the man's unprotected throat.

The Marine choked fitfully as he struggled to draw breath. Before his stunned companion had time in which to act, the first Marine had been carelessly lifted into the air by Nyman. In a feat of superhuman, completely insane strength he was thrown bodily to hit the opposite wall with a degree of impact that knocked him into a dazed stupor.

The remaining Marine broke out of his momentary bewilderment and thought to retrieve his fallen weapon. Nyman, spittle frothing forth from the dark cavity that was his wide open mouth, grasped the retreating security Marine by the rear of his armour and yanked him back. He caught the man's throat in a vice-like necklock. The Marine tore wildly at the throttling hold, managing to draw blood from his protagonist's uncovered arms as he gasped for air. Nyman's iron grip forced his head up, allowing the crazed adversary an improved grasp on his bruised throat.

Stuart shook her head to try and clear the misty haze that threatened to engulf her. She looked around and witnessed the trouble in which the second Marine was involved. Brushing back the dishevelled hair that had fallen over her face she pulled herself to her feet using the counter for support. She ignored the pitiful sight of the petrified attendant standing as far back from the counter-like desk as he could manage, not even thinking of sounding the alarm. Gathering all her energy, Stuart launched herself at Nyman in an effort to save the life of the desperately thrashing Marine. Nyman had his back to her and did not sense her approach until it was too late. He began to turn just as Stuart delivered a sharp, hefty kick to his lower spine. He cried out and released his grip on the Marine, tossing him to one side. Nyman spun to face Stuart. There was death in his eyes and explicit menace in his pose as he swung undirected blows at her, all of them missing.

On the spur of the moment Stuart decided she could take a chance and try to calm him. She began speaking to

61

him in low, soft tones, all the while steadily backing away from those large, flailing fists. 'Come on now,' she murmured. 'You don't want to hurt me, do you?'

Nyman seemed to pause hesitantly before again starting forward, fists swinging out with increased violence.

'Hey, calm down will you.'

He paused, suddenly unsure in his madness what to do, confusion written on his contorted face.

'That's better, Nyman. Calm down. Calm down and you'll get a nice rest with no-one to bother you. Don't you want that?'

'For *Chrissake*!' The attendant suddenly exclaimed from behind the wire mesh. 'What the hell are you waiting for? Get him now while he's quiet!'

'Shut it, you cretin!' Stuart yelled back at him but the calm spell had been broken. Nyman lashed out with renewed force and caught Stuart a glancing blow on the side of the chin. She staggered back, barely keeping her feet. Nyman closed in with an evil grin as Stuart backed up against the wall. Desperation lent her a helping hand for she knew she would not survive very long at the mercy of Nyman's incredibly powerful hands. She struck out with her foot, catching him full in the groin. He folded, his rage dulled by the sudden pain. Stuart completed the move while she could by joining both her small hands slicing down to chop the doubled-over Nyman at the nape of his neck. The blow knocked him unconscious and he toppled over, landing spread-eagled on the floor.

Stuart paused for a second, leaning against the wall while she caught her breath. Then she checked the condition of the two fallen Marines. The first was clutching at a deep facial cut, moaning at the insistent, throbbing pain that echoed through his skull. The second was still out for the count, his pulse slow but steady.

Leaving them where they lay, Stuart went over to the desk where the shaken attendant was beginning to comprehend that the trouble was over. The senior midshipman felt sickened by the man's cowardice and showed him no mercy in her ice-cold tone.

'Open this,' she commanded sternly, banging her fist

against the mesh. The attendant emerged from his corner and meekly complied, sending the mesh springing upwards to lock home with a crash. 'I want a medic team here at once for my men and I think you'll need some help in shifting Nyman. I doubt if you have the strength for it.'

The attendant, shamefaced, did as he was told. He activated the vidcom screen set behind the desk. Stuart moved away and started to help the first Marine to his unsteady feet, making sure the cut on his face was not too serious. Then something occurred to her and she swung back on the attendant.

'I think,' she suggested with a grim smile, 'you should make that extremely dangerous on Nyman's form.'

The elevator sped rapidly downwards in the eight hundred storey block, its load a light one, a lone passenger.

Rickard had found that, once the pre-flight checks and the laborious task of stocking *Emputin's* food, fuel and air supplies, as well as a hundred and one other jobs, minor and major, had been put into operation, he had very little to do other than chivvy everyone else along. Instead he decided he had time to pay Karen a flying visit to say good-bye, especially as the remainder of his long overdue leave had been postponed for him until his return. He had brought a launch down solo from *Emputin's* bustling hanger bay and had landed, quite unofficially, on the roof of Karen's towering apartment complex. Using a service lift to get to the top housing floor he'd then switched to an express for the remainder of the trip. It was decidedly easier than setting down at the nearest landing grid and driving all the way.

While the lift continued its descent, Rickard puzzled over Trestrail's sudden change of heart. It was clear the man still did not like him, that much continued to show, but Rickard felt better knowing the admiral would not jump half-way down his throat and throw an uncontrollable fit every time he saw him. That was something for which to be extremely thankful. Life would be a little easier for that. Maybe he had a guardian angel looking over him to ensure he stayed safe. It would certainly help. Even more so with his coming assignment, the hour of embarkation drawing ever nearer. He had hardly realised, when searching through the Larr computer files on Base One, that he would be the person to command the subsequent expedition into the zone. What a break for his career that was. A definite bonus. How much more good luck could a guy get? Things were certainly looking up. First a command, then Karen, and now this. Of course, there was no debating as to which was the best of the three. He'd damn well miss her. This bloody excursion of Trestrail's had better not last too long, he was impatient to get back to her already. But he still wanted to be away from the constraints of Earth. It was too confining for him. He wondered if the ship would be ready in time. His thoughts skipping subjects like an overactive grasshopper Rickard recalled his extra passengers. Was the science team aboard yet? They should be. He'd lose the schedule if they were not. There was so much to work out in such a scant amount of time. How the hell was he supposed to get everything ready in *six* hours? He should have demanded at least twice as long from old Trestrail. The old man couldn't have denied him that, surely.

'Damn. I didn't think the captain's job was such hard work,' he muttered to himself as the lift finally slowed to a halt.

The doors shot open and Rickard emerged into the garden-like plaza of floor 466. Its central square of bushes and shrubs was utterly deserted.

Realisation arrived in a flash and Rickard cried mentally. It was the middle of a working day. Most people would be out earning a living, including Karen. He cursed himself, knowing the fact should have occurred to him. That was one of the drawbacks of working in the Service: he fraternized with such screwed-up hours most of the time that he inevitably forgot ordinary people worked to set times.

'I'll call anyway. It could always be her day off,' he hoped optimistically.

He found the correct door and buzzed. There was no answer. He repeated the operation and waited a minute or so longer before reluctantly coming to the conclusion that nobody was home. He was just moving off when the door opened and a sleepy, ruffled Nicola peered out. She caught sight of his disappearing form and called out to him, immediately wide awake.

'Chris! Hi there.'

Rickard came to a halt and glanced back. He looked apologetic when he saw it was Nicola not Karen who had called. It was probable that he'd woken her, noticing as he did her hair was tangled and unbrushed and she was dressed only in a provocatively thin, well-worn cotton nightdress. He wished he could get away without making a fool of himself. He knew full well what Nicola wanted from him and it was definitely not his mind. Still, there was nothing to do but return. He strolled casually back to the doorway.

'I thought there was no one home,' he offered.

'It's my day off work,' Nicola revealed, 'I was enjoying a lie-in, I only got up to answer the door.'

'At least someone's having it easy. I'm sorry I disturbed you.'

'It's no bother,' she shrugged easily.

'Ah, I take it that Karen is not in?'

'Afraid not, Chris, I think she went to see her father. You might know him. He's in the Navy, too.'

'Oh, I know him all right,' he forced a groan, feeling ill-at-ease talking to Nicola while she continuously eyed him, that ever-intense, persistent wish clear on her face. 'Can I leave a message?'

'Yes, sure you can. Come in,' she invited, opening the front door fully. Her eyes challenged him.

Rickard had meant to relay a verbal message but he reluctantly admitted to himself that there was no escape so he hesitantly passed her, entering the flat. He discovered the flat's normally tidy interior was now disorganised and untidy. There was a scattered mess spread about the floor which seemed to conglomerate into a heaped stack near one corner of the room. Various assorted items, cushions, bundled bed sheets, clothing and music discs, could be picked out amongst heaven knew what else.

Nicola excused the state of the lounge, 'I think Karen started spring-cleaning before she went out,' she said.

'It's okay,' Rickard grinned uncomfortably. He found he could not help but notice the virtual transparency of her nightdress and the way in which it clung to her shapely figure. He turned quickly away and sat on the large, well-padded sofa, pretending to study the cluttered floor.

Nicola's eyes caught his embarrassed avoidance and she was pleased. She hadn't thought it would be this easy. This had been a heavensent opportunity, golden in its perfection. Moving over to a cabinet directly in front of the sofa she reached up to the top shelf to bring down a sheet of notepaper and a pen, deliberately allowing the gauze-like nightdress to ride up and hug her body, fully emphasising the rounded shape of her ample buttocks. Hold the pose for a second and then relax. Display concluded, she deposited the notepaper and pen on the low coffee table that touched at Rickard's bended knees, seeing by his reddened face that her efforts had not been wasted.

He cast a hasty glance at her as he picked up the pen. 'Thanks,' he said. His voice was sounding tight. As he began to write a wave of nervous expectation washed through him and he felt distinctly apprehensive of the imbroglio in which he was enmeshed.

While he scribbled a brief but succint note to Karen, Nicola placed herself beside him on the sofa, purposely letting the flimsy nightdress ride up once more as she slid forward coquettishly to move closer to him. In doing so she revealed a great deal of her deeply tanned thighs, her shaven legs smooth and sensual.

An anxious Rickard could not help but notice Nicola's act, even though he tried furiously to concentrate on writing the letter. Once he had concluded it however, there was no excuse not to look at his flirtatious companion. He knew what it was she was trying to achieve. He remembered the hungry man-hunter glare of desire she had eyed him with. Even though he had been busy trying to rescue her from the distressed ship at the time. Inexperienced with women he might be, but stupid he was not. His mind switched to Karen and he was determined not to permit anything to occur between himself and Nicola. He rose, firmly intent on leaving, but Nicola stood at the same instant, her timing immaculate. The coffee table prevented Rickard from moving fast enough to stop her sliding her bare arms around him.

'I should be going...' he began and Nicola hurriedly silenced him by placing her lips on his. Their mouths closed in a deep kiss, Nicola expelling considerable urgency in the act. Her hands continually moved, caressing his body. His firm resolve shattered into a million tiny pieces and he returned the embrace strongly. His hands pressed onto her, searching, touching, her body warm and alive with excitement. She led him into the bedroom, carefully removing her nightdress to reveal to him the full splendour of her naked body. Rounded, boldly outstanding breasts pressed firmly against him. She led his probing hands to caress her soft, wide hips. His touch raised goose-bumps where he made contact. She raised her chin as he turned his attention to her neck, kissing it lightly and repeatedly.

Rickard's clouded mind had a sudden burst of lucidity and he was shocked. What was happening? he thought suddenly. What was he doing? The answer came clearly and he was abruptly angry at himself for allowing Nicola to break down his defences with such ease. A voice within him cried persistently for him to stop, before this got any further.

He sharply broke away from Nicola, his breath coming to him in short, startled gasps. She for her part, frowned questioningly at him, alarmed by this unexpected event. She thought she had won the battle against Rickard's morality. Now she was apprehensive. A flurry of confused emotions flickered across her face. She comprehended what he was thinking by the confused manner in which he stared. She still felt she had to be certain.

'What's wrong?'

'What you tried to do-' He gulped, his face flushing as he became fully cognizant of her nakedness for the first time. 'What you did was....*insane!* You know full well how I feel about Karen and yet you still make this very convincing play. For God's sake! Don't you have any morals?'

Nicola had her answer and made a feeble attempt at protest as she sank onto the edge of the unmade bed, 'Please, Chris, I...I didn't think.'

'No. You certainly did not think,' Rickard sharply cut in, angry more at himself now for being such an easy catch than at her for wanting to make that catch. 'You should try thinking for a change. It might make a *hell* of a difference! He stormed out of the flat, slamming the front door unnecessarily hard after him.

Nicola lay back on the bed, body trembling with delayed shock of Rickard's justifiable verbal attack, knowing that he had made remarks about her that were closer to the truth than she dared to admit.

'Evacuate hanger bay. Incoming launch. Evacuate hanger bay.' The sharp tones of *Emputin's* computer voice rang out harshly to the accompaniment of wailing klaxons. Personnel hurried to comply, trotting briskly for the scattered exits. Once the bay was cleared, these were then hermetically sealed. The huge space doors were opened by Lieutenant-Commander Bulloch, seated at the console in the adjoining flight control office. A bustling crowd of technicians aided him at the oversized bank of controls. Beck was also present, waiting quietly in the background. He wanted to ensure his newly arrived medical supplies were handled with the care they needed.

He looked away from the solid perspex window to peer over Bulloch's shoulder at the dazzling multicoloured array of readouts on the console. 'Who's this coming in?' he questioned the hanger chief.

'It's the Captain,' Bulloch revealed. 'He popped off planetside to make a visit before we got started.'

Raising a wondering eyebrow, Beck sounded innocent. 'Did he?'

Bulloch disapprovingly shook his head, knowing the surgeon well. 'Don't give me that look. I have absolutely no idea who he visited. You'll have to find that out for yourself.'

Beck grinned shamelessly. There was not much that escaped his ears. He got to hear most gossip of any interest sooner or later. It was for this reason that he was often hailed with the title of chief contributor to the ship's freechat - not that he would ever use or abuse his position as chief medic to further that reputation. In that position he wondered for his own insatiable curiosity rather than for local gossip whom it was Rickard wanted to see with such urgency. There were only two possible reasons in his mind as to why the captain would make such a last minute visit: business or pleasure, and he was pretty sure it was not the former. It couldn't be - there was no reason to leave the ship so near to departure point for something that could be said over a comm-link. So, that left one question; who was she?

It was a woman. It had to be a woman. Well, why not? It was in all the best stories. Anyway, it made better copy. Could there be any truth to the story of Rickard's dating Vice-Admiral Trestrail's daughter? The story was vague but according to Beck's sources the two of them had been seen together. Enjoying his detective like analysis of the probabilities, he wondered strongly on the likelihood of such a pairing. Could it be her? Or was it the ex-Larr prisoner with whom Rickard had returned to the fleet? Everyone knew how close they had seemed. The crunch, when Beck admitted it, was that no-one knew the correct answer as yet, barring Rickard himself. And he could not be asked, not directly at any rate.

Bulloch saw the flow of expressions across the doctor's face as the medic pondered the possibilities. 'I'll never guess what's going through your mind,' he said ironically. 'Tell you what, Phil. I'll bet any money you don't find out who she is before we finish this mystery trip.'

69

Beck realised that his companion had been thinking along similar lines. He came to the modest conclusion that there might be some truth to the saying that great minds thought alike. His eyes glittered defiantly. This was one bet he was determined to win. 'Right. You're on,' he accepted. 'Fifty.'

'Done,' Bulloch stated firmly. 'And you certainly have been!'

The incoming launch cruised gently over the rounded hull of the spaceport. Its pilot was fortunately oblivious to the frivolous smalltalk being exchanged inside his ship. He decelerated the craft, bringing it into the bay to touch down smoothly at its centre. The space doors were duly closed and air was recycled into the vacuum while efficient heating units strained to disperse the frosty chill. Scant minutes later the area began once more to fill with personnel. They quickly recommenced the laborious task of storing away the multitudinous piles of tightly sealed supplies that had been lying secured to the deck while the launch was landing.

Bulloch and Beck entered the bay, the former busying himself in supervising the bustling crewmembers detailed to store the supplies. Beck strode over to the now emergent Rickard. 'Good trip?' he asked innocently.

'Hmm...Oh yes. Marvellous,' Rickard said absently. His mind was still on Nicola. Thinking back, he really *should* have expected something of that nature from her. He ruefully had to admit he felt fairly much the fool now he'd had a chance to recall with a clearer mind. After all, it was not an unpleasant experience to have another woman concentrating her attentions on him. He understood that he was partly at fault himself for fostering Nicola's interest back on the stricken merchant ship. Knowing he should have been less weak-willed he felt he should return later and patch things up with her. He was probably as much to blame as her for what had happened.

Rickard dimly recollected someone talking at him and reluctantly emerged from his introspection.

'Captain Christopher?' Beck was beginning to raise his voice.

70

'Hello?'

'You were miles away, figuratively speaking, of course. I wondered how your hand was doing.'

'It's fine. There's no pain now, I think,' he said illucidly.

'Let me have a look.' Beck took Rickard's injured hand and unravelled the bandage with a doctor's enthusiasm. He made an expert examination of the skin beneath and grunted in a satisfied manner. 'Well, I know you were told to give it a couple of days but it's healing fine, so I don't see any reason not to leave it alone. You, my dear Captain, are a doctor's delight - a fast healer.' He bundled the used bandage into his pocket for later disposal.

'Great.' Rickard caught the deep baritone echoes of Rem Bulloch resounding across the bay. The Chief bellowed exasperated instructions to coax the apparently unconcerned crewmembers involved in unloading and storing, his voice breaking and wavering towards the end of his tirade. 'He's doing a lot of shouting. Surely they can't be that bad.'

'They're not. That's just the Tyrant's way of dealing with them.'

'They don't call him that, do they?'

'Only in fun. It doesn't describe his real personality.'

'I should hope not.'

'Who was it you visited planetside, if you don't mind me asking?' Beck suddenly enquired, seemingly out of the blue.

'Why-' Rickard started but was halted by the timely interruption of the bay's intercom speakers. They blared out a page for him, calling him to the bridge. 'I wonder what they want?' Rickard stared distantly at the speaker.

'Only one way to find out.'

'I'm on my way.' Rickard strode off.

Bulloch witnessed him leave and called across to Beck. 'No luck?'

'Not yet.' Beck said it in a way that promised better results next time.

'Better get your money ready,' Bulloch shouted over. 'You've got no chance, Doc.'

'I wish you would all stop calling me that.'

☆ ☆ ☆

Rickard welcomed the comparative calmness of the bridge after the deafening noise of the bay. He entered the ship's command centre, his outward mask of impassivity concealing his sanguine mood. He eagerly wanted to be away from Earth and all the trouble it seemed to bring him, both professionally and personally. He could barely suppress his impatience to get going. Exploration was a subject dearly close to his heart and that, coupled with the freedom his rank offered him on this type of trip, made him yearn to be on the move. He wanted to be out there, where the action was, not held back alongside all the mouldy relics stuck on Earth. A tangible spirit of adventure flowed within him and he desired to let it free.

It occurred to him that he was staring around like some planet-tied dummy who had never seen a ship's bridge before. He hastily took the deserted conn and made a brief inspectional survey of the bridge stations from the chair's bolstering comfort. The enveloping atmosphere was one of calm expectation, as if nothing out of the ordinary routine was occurring. It was exactly the opposite of the docking bay's frenzied exuberance. Each member of the bridge crew carried out their last-minute pre-flight checks with quiet efficiency.

'Captain, Docking Control allows us clearance to depart,' Watts reported from the comunications bank, saying precisely the words Rickard most wanted to hear.

Bentowski, seated at the helm controls, was moderately nonplussed by the speed with which the prep time had disappeared. 'That was the quickest damned six hours I've ever seen,' he said in amazement.

Howarth gave a low grunt of agreement but said nothing. He still wondered if the Captain had forgotten his earlier show of bad manners. He knew the guy wasn't all that bad, he simply didn't like to admit it yet.

Rickard nodded gladly to Watts. 'Thank you, Lieutenant. Secure all systems for subspeed drive,' Rickard swung round to the main viewer which presently relayed a picture of the majestic bulk of the spaceport as it circled far above the bold curvature of Earth's illuminated sunlit side. He would miss it but he was impatient to see new lands, fresh vistas.

Would the recently arrived platoon of Marines be required to back up security on this excursion? Rickard doubted it. He was feeling too hopeful.

'All systems are secured,' came Bentowski's reply to the preparation order.

'Secure from spaceport.'

'We are secured from spaceport, sir.'

On the main viewer the umbilical joining *Emputin* to the spaceport fell lazily away. *Emputin* was free in space.

'Engage subspeed power, point oh two.'

'Subspeed, point oh two, aye.' The helmsman smoothly slid forward the speed controls and the ship accelerated gently off. The spaceport fell behind.

'Set course for quadrant three, sector seventeen, sub-sector thirty-nine.'

'Aye, sir,' said Boyd from navigation.

'Accelerate to sub-speed point five.'

The ship headed gracefully out into deep space, leaving bustling Earth in its wake. The mission had commenced.

Nothing could hold them back now. They were on their way.

'I'm receiving a Priority One signal from spacedock,' Watts briskly announced. We are to await the arrival of a launch that has already departed from Earth. One passenger to come aboard. It's a...civilian observer sir,' she frowned.

Rickard looked at her in astonishment.

'That's all I need. A civilian to screw up the works and get in everyone's way,' he snapped. Inwardly he cursed. Didn't Service Command trust him? Did he really need a nursemaid? Apparently so, at least according to his so-called superiors. There was nothing for it, though. He had to stop and permit the launch to dock, no matter what degree of reticence he felt. Why did this sort of thing always happen to him? he mused sourly. 'All right, Mister Bentowski. Halt all forward motion.'

'Yes, sir.'

'I'll be awaiting the civilian's arrival on the hanger deck.' Rickard rose from the conn. 'And he'd better have a bloody good explanation for this,' he finished sotto voce.

The launch was inside the bay by the time Rickard turned up and was already being warmed. The captain was met by Bulloch and an ever-present Beck outside the main doors, still hermetically sealed.

'What are you doing down here, Doc?' Rickard asked of the surgeon.

'Oh, I thought I'd come along and see who our new passenger was. After all, I am in charge of the crew's health and fitness. I'll probably have to look after this one, too.'

Rickard gave a grunt of ill-concealed rancour at the mention of the observer. He wondered if this was Trestrail's idea. Little did he realise that he was not far wrong, albeit for marginally differing reasons.

'Perhaps it's more a case of I want to know who it is so I can feed the freechat with some interesting titbits of information,' Bulloch whispered aside to Beck.

Beck delivered him a surreptitious nudge in the ribs.

The inner airlock doors opened and Rickard led the way at a fast pace to the launch's hatch. The hatch had already begun to hiss its way open, revealing a dark, shadowy interior out of which stepped the newly appointed civilian observer. To Rickard's stunned surprise he saw that it was Karen Trestrail.

'What the *hell!*' Rickard croaked, utterly flabbergasted. 'What the hell are you doing here?'

'Surprised?' Karen grinned widely. She stepped off the ramp so the launch's hatch could glide smoothly back into place, tightly sealed. 'I thought you might be. It serves you right for not saying goodbye.'

Wishing he had a better control of his scrambled thoughts in this unbelievable situation, Rickard mumbled a hurt reply. 'I did try, but I only found Nicola at the flat.'

Behind them, Beck gave Bulloch a triumphant grin. They now knew who Rickard had visited on his last minute trip, and perhaps why he'd been so distant afterwards. Who wouldn't be, leaving behind such a beautiful young woman as this.

'Bad luck,' Beck commented, smiling profusely but trying not to gain Rickard's attention. He need not have worried. Rickard's attention was fully occupied elsewhere. 'I hope you've got your cash handy.'

Bulloch gave a low groan. Of all the dumb luck, he mused. 'Listen, I don't have it with me at the moment,' he improvised, 'but trust me. You'll get it when we're paid.'

'When will that be?'

Bulloch shrugged non committally. 'When we get back to Earth, I suppose.'

Beck stared at him sourly, pondering on whether to hit him now or leave it until a more convenient time.

The Chief saw his face and had to smile. 'Don't worry about it, old boy.'

Oblivious to the verbal interplay being enacted behind his back, Rickard was successfully drawing an explanation from Karen, now that he had actually recovered from the very real shock of seeing her here, on *Emputin*.

'What is your excuse?' he asked determinedly.

'It's official, Mister Rickard,' retorted Karen indignantly. Then she decided to mellow her approach, calming her voice. 'My father was going to appoint a Service official to watch over you. He was discussing it with Admiral Melato - if you can call it a discussion - when I went to see him. I put forward the suggestion that I go instead. Of course he wouldn't hear of it but Admiral Melato agreed straight away. I think she saw it as a way of scoring over dad. Anyway, she overruled him and here I am, your official civilian observer. I imagined you'd much rather have me than some old codger who thought he knew best about everything.'

'You walked right into that trap, didn't you. Melato and your father are reputed to be the worst of enemies. I've heard they bicker non-stop. Anyway, pardon me for saying so, but your father's mouth is as large as his brain is small. Any excuse he has to badger me he takes. And I was stupid enough to think he'd given up on me,' Rickard chided himself.

'Be fair, Chris. It isn't his fault I'm here. I know he sometimes deserves what's said about him but this time

75

the blame is mine or Melato's. He was entirely against my coming.'

'But how did you know about all this in the first place?'

'I'm the admiral's daughter. Of course I'm going to find out if I want to.'

'Well, if it wasn't you, he'd make sure someone was pestering me,' assured Rickard. 'I still say it was a damn stupid thing to do, volunteering yourself. Don't you realise how dangerous this trip could be?'

Karen switched her attitude to playfully coy. 'Of course I realise it's dangerous. I didn't think you cared so much.'

'I care,' Rickard sighed. 'That's why I'd rather have left you on Earth.'

'Then why didn't you say good-bye before sailing off into the sunset?'

Rickard paused as he pondered Karen's coquettish flat-mate. 'Have you seen Nicola?' he asked carefully.

'No, I left her a message. She'll understand.'

'Probably.'

She would certainly not be arguing, Rickard thought. In fact, she should be only too glad to see him leave. Perhaps Rickard was relieved the two had not met since his run-in with Nicola. He could not be sure. Their meeting might have created complications he could not deal with. At least with Karen on the ship there was time enough to allow matters to settle. But was it an added complication to have Karen here, on the ship? Damned right it was! How was he supposed to concentrate firmly on his job while simultaneously worrying about her? At the same time he could not help but feel pleased she was joining him. It would do no harm to accept her here, he hoped. He gave a mental shrug of the shoulders. There was not much to worry about. After all, *Emputin* could *"theoretically* handle a significant number of zone ships at one time"*, so the bosses said.

'Okay,' he capitulated. 'Welcome aboard, Miss Trestrail. We'd better keep it formal in front of the crew.'

'I think that comes a touch belated but you're the boss.'

Rickard brought her forward to make introductions. 'Miss Trestrail, this is my chief medical officer, Philip Beck.'

76

'I'm most pleased to make your acquaintance, Miss Trestrail,' suave Beck broadly smiled.

'Call me Karen, please. This is going to be a long voyage and we should get to know one another,' she said, shaking his hand.

'Then I insist equally that you call me Phil.' Beck was smooth, flashing his white, even teeth almost melodramatically.

'Phil,' Karen confirmed. 'Pleased to meet you.'

Rickard groaned monumentally. He fervently hoped that Beck would calm down once they finally got under way. He did not think he could take too much of the surgeon's teeth-and-talk routine.

'We'd better get out of here,' he said as he began steering Karen towards the exit. 'I think the coxswain wants to leave.'

Karen chuckled magnanimously, speaking to Rickard in low tones. 'You're going to have to watch what you say while I'm around, Captain. I have to report to the dreaded vice-admiral when we return.'

'I promise to be completely discreet in your presence,' Rickard swore humbly. 'Now, if you wouldn't mind giving me a couple of minutes of freedom I have a cruiser and her crew to see to.'

'Granted...Captain.'

Rickard adroitly buttonholed a passing female rating. 'If you would show the observer to the guest quarters, Crewwoman?'

'Yes, sir.'

☆ ☆ ☆

Rickard tried concentrating his mind on the matter at hand, putting Karen temporarily out of his thoughts for the sake of duty. It was not easy, to that he could readily attest. Nevertheless...

'Slow to subspeed point one, please, Mister Bentowski,' he instructed.

Space repeated its show of becoming normal on the

viewers as the stars relaxed their coalescence. A heavily populated, thickened mass of asteroids was spread out in a diffused, ragged line that lay directly in *Emputin's* immediate path: the Belt which marked the edge of the hostile zone.

'All systems are secured from hyperdrive,' reported Bentowski, his infamous comic-book humour held in check for the more serious job at hand.

'Mister Boyd,' Rickard was feeling enormously pleased that he was getting somewhere at last. 'Plot a course that'll take us through the thinnest segment of the Belt. Commander,' Rickard directed his attention to Kiyami. 'If you would begin scanning?'

Kiyami bent over her console, standing to gain an improved vantage-point over the startling array of equipment. A small screen over the back of the panel gave constant readouts on the subject of her scan.

Rickard peered back over his shoulder when he heard the opening hiss of the port side bridge doors. Karen and Beck entered and placed themselves unobstrusively against the rail behind Rickard's chair, both permitted in the control section because of their high on-board status. Rickard felt a brief sense of elation at Karen's presence as he caught a whiff of her provocative perfume.

It was not quite the sort of distraction he needed at present. It was a busy time and the male members of the crew had their hands full with the work of the moment without distracting sights such as Karen. But Rickard doubted very much that they minded Karen being here.

He noticed that the subject of his musings was staring in bewilderment at the various multidudes of technology on display around the bridge. It occurred to him that, admiral's daughter or not, she may never before have seen this particular section of a Navy cruiser.

Karen caught Rickard staring amusedly at her. She leant forward and spoke into his ear. 'I didn't think operating one of these ships was so complicated. By the way, where are we?'

'We've just now arrived at the asteroid belt which separates us from unknown space, new territory,' Rickard explained.

'Already! It would have taken three times as long by passenger cruiser.'

'That's because those crates they use on the fun-runs can only manage a top rate of hyperspeed four whereas an Eagle-class can push out hyperspeed ten if it has to. We don't have hoards of heavily insured, overanxious tourists to worry about.'

Karen breathed an understanding, 'Ooh...' as she straightened up.

'Don't worry about it,' Beck said casually. 'I doubt if they know what most of these lights and buttons are for, anyway. They just put them there to make things seem more complicated to the uninitiated.'

Karen equably agreed. She pretended not to notice Rickard's suffering grimace.

While Rickard was otherwise occupied, Howarth, who should have been watching his own instruments, surreptitiously gained Kiyami's attention while she was busy scanning the rock-filled space ahead.

'Hey, Commander,' he hissed. 'Who's the cargo?'

'Show some respect,' she returned mildly.

'Yeah, but who is she? From this angle she looks pretty tasty.'

'Will you stop drooling and get on with your work? You are too late anyway. I have the idea that she is already spoken for.'

'By who?' Howarth demanded indignantly.

Kiyami gave a slight but telling nod in Rickard's direction and looked meaningfully at the surprised security chief.

'Jeez...He doesn't waste much time, does he? Oh well, she ain't *that* good,' he shrugged.

Amused by Howarth's air of faked nonchalance, Kiyami glanced over at Rickard while the latter's attention was absorbed with the newcomer. He certainly seemed happy enough. It was clear that there was more than a purely working relationship between him and Karen Trestrail. It showed in the manner in which he looked at her, the way he talked to her - and she to him, for that matter. The captain was a very lucky man judging by Howarth's values. Kiyami wondered what would have

79

happened to her own career had not her life on Craighferris turned sour. The affair, tempestuous and jagged. She had felt claustrophobically confined, too enclosed in the relationship, and had backed out, consequently throwing herself into her work with a frightening intensity. For a time she had been working towards overload, a breakdown. That had faded and passed when she had been transfered to her present, less demanding post. But the emotional scars were still there, barely hidden under an assumed mask of Japanese inscrutability.

Funnily enough for someone of her rank, she could not function with complete independence. She needed to be able to rely on someone, a person, one person. She needed to have a friend she could talk to, confide in. The inscrutability was only a mask and it occasionally managed to slip and fall away. It helped her a great deal if there was someone she knew who could help her at such times. It did not have to be in a sexual way, just a close companion of equal standing. She could not hide forever the *ai*, the affection she so desperately needed to show. She was beginning to think that Rickard, fresh to this particular aspect of Naval life, could be the person she had been searching for. His personality made him seem right for it.

She vaguely wished she could have known Rickard outside of the job. How then would her career have weathered? Obviously, such ideas were out of the question now. She could not begin to pursue the possibility under the circumstances. That would be unprofessional, she concluded firmly. Neither could she begin a relationship with anyone of lower rank on *Emputin*. That would be equally unprofessional. Instead, she had to control, to repress her emotions. It was possible that she could put more time into such a notion during the post-assignment leave. Until then it was business as usual, work before play. *Shigata ga nai, neh?* The Service could be harsh on one's private life but that was how she had chosen it to be.

Keeping this in mind, Kiyami caught Rickard's attention with the results of her sensor scan. 'Captain, results of my scan show normal trace elements in the asteroids. No precious minerals. Orbit of asteroids added to content leads me to believe that they once formed a complete planet. The planet seems to have exploded or fragmented in the vicinity of one million years ago, consequently forming the Belt in its current state, as opposed to the asteroids of Sol system which never formed a complete planet because of Jupiter's continual gravitational interference.'

'There's nothing overtly unusual or significant here?'

'No.'

'Then there's no reason not to proceed?'

'Once again, no.'

'Good. Continue on course, Mister Bentowski. Yellow alert, I think. Just as a precaution.' The bright glow of standard illumination faded as operational lighting took over. Klaxons sounded and the computer announced the change in status.

'Thanks to our extremely recent but informative briefing,' Beck stated pointedly, 'at least I know now what is so important about passing the Belt, however late in the day the briefing might have been.'

'I was ordered to wait until we were underway,' Rickard said in defence.

Karen grunted softly. 'I'll bet the orders came from Dad.'

'No comment,' Rickard replied.

Emputin began a careful forward cruise, trailing a winding path through the tumbling, twisting, ever-mobile rocks that formed the Belt. Once in a while a larger than average asteroid would appear in the ship's immediate path only to be hit and vapourised in a ball of rapidly dissipating flame. Computer controlled lasers fulfilled the task adequately, programmed to act in precisely that manner in precisely those circumstances.

One craggy sphere of fused rock and silica drifted in from the starboard side, coming too close for the lasers to target in time and stop it. It broke up when it hit the shields, sending smaller chunks scattering away and jolting the vessel uncomfortably in the process. Eventually, space ahead cleared to show the starry void as the Belt was left behind.

81

Emputin was now in the hostile zone.

Kiyami puzzled on a reading that had abruptly appeared on her board as the ship started forward at a higher subspeed velocity.

'There's something out there,' she murmured, almost to herself. Rickard gave her a worried glance. 'I can't quite make it out-'

'Alert. Alert,' the computer suddenly blared, making everybody jump. 'Vessels approaching. Vessels approaching.'

'Three unidentified ships closing fast. Bearing one five oh by one seven five!' Bentowski reported overexcitedly. 'There! On screen now.'

Three tiny blobs materialised at the centre of the main viewer, far too small as yet to be properly identified.

'Approaching vessels are raising shields,' Karen called. 'Arming weapons ready to fire.'

'Red alert! Sound battle stations,' Rickard had to shout to be heard above the computer's amplified electronic din. 'And shut the computer up!'

The warning blasts were silenced, only to be replaced by the increased wail of the klaxons as they indicated the red alert status.

Karen was anxious and disquietened. 'What's happening?' she cried amid the confusion.

Rickard spared her a sympathetic glance, shouting to Howarth at the weapons desk. 'Raise the shields! Arm all laser banks and forward torpedoes for immediate action.' Then he spun in his chair, proffering an urgent explanation. 'We're coming under attack. Three alien vessels from inside the zone. We're now under full battle conditions.'

He just hoped his guardian angel was still on duty.

4

505.98.80

'Magnify viewer picture,' Rickard instructed. The relayed image was abruptly enlargened, and the three unidentified vessels could now be made out with greater clarity. They were travelling in a V-formation with the commanding ship at the apex. Each was rougly two-thirds the size of *Emputin,* smaller and less bulky. The main structural body was rather like that of an oversized atmospheric shuttle, winged tips emerging from the sides like fins from a fish. The bubble-shaped, pod-like bridge section connected to the body via two thick tubular affairs which were segmented by regular, ribbed mounds. A dark opening in the lower portion of the nose signified the presence of a torpedo tube.

Rickard managed to relax a little when he saw how comparatively weak the ships appeared to be. 'We don't seem to be in any immediate danger,' he stated. It was to the immense relief of his passenger who was nervously clutching the rail behind her. 'They don't look strong enough to do us any real harm. Not for a while at any rate.'

'I'm glad to hear it,' a relieved Karen replied. Maybe it hadn't been such a smart idea to hitch this ride.

Rickard turned his attention to Watts. 'Lieutenant, send a signal to the Service post on Alpheratz. Inform them of our position.'

On the viewer, only barely noticed by Rickard, the three ships had split from formation. The leader stayed where it was, effectively blocking *Emputin's* forward progress. The others slid one to either side to cover the Service ship on its flanks. Watts, still trying on the communications, altered the viewers correspondingly.

Doing two jobs at once she focussed the main screen on the leader and each auxiliary on the others.

Retreat as it was now presented was impossible, Rickard knew. It would be utter stupidity to attempt to manoeuvre backwards through an asteroid field and it was apparent that they would not be allowed the room to turn about.

'I can't raise Alpheratz, Captain,' Watts reported with some urgency. 'Alien vessels are blocking all attempts.'

'Send out friendship messages on all channels. Tell them who we are and that our mission here is peaceful,' Rickard commanded.

'I'll have a try,' Watts muttered with a pessimistic air to herself and turned purposefully back to the comm console.

Before she could get any further Howarth suddenly cried out. 'They're preparing to fire!'

The main viewer showed the alien lead ship launch a sparkling ball of energy which raced outwards to strike *Emputin's* shields even as Howarth shouted his warning. The ship rocked under the expectedly ineffective impact.

Kiyami made a vocal note on the enemy weaponry. 'The scanners indicate that their torpedoes are composed of much the same material as our own, although they are of a weaker constitution. Perhaps only half as strong.'

Rickard agreed. 'Their ship design shows they've developed scientifically along much the same lines as us. Which is mildly suspicious to say the least, seeing as we've had no previous contact.'

Watts interrupted with a cursory status report. 'Sir, all decks report no damage. Engineering says we can repel attacks to the strength of the last for at least twenty standard minutes. I have no reply on friendship messages from the alien vessels.'

'Keep trying.'

'Should I get sickbay ready for custom?' Beck asked.

'I don't think that'll be necessary, Doc. We've got the upper hand in this one and I don't intend to let it continue for much longer.'

'That's okay by me. The fewer patients I have in sickbay the happier I feel. Not that I expect you'll get much co-operation from these hostiles-'

84

'Port vessel is about to fire,' Howarth broke in.

'-They'll probably shoot you soon as look at you.'

'Hold tight!' Rickard advised them unnecessarily, grabbing for the arms of his chair by reflex.

The warning was more for Karen than anyone. She tightly grasped the back of Rickard's seat, bewildered by the speed of events.

They watched as the bolt left its firing tube and lashed out directly at them, only to smash harmlessly into the defending shields.

Rickard decided it was time to warn the aliens to discontinue their belligerence. 'Mister Howarth, fire the first tube at vessel bearing one five one.'

'With pleasure.' Howarth jabbed at a button and a brilliantly glowing torpedo could be seen screaming its way out of one of the forward tubes. It splashed efficaciously against the alien ship's visibly straining defences in the manner of a fly meeting a fast-moving car head on. The torpedo's detonation was followed an infinitesimal moment later by a second, more excessive explosion which ripped away the whole port fin and a great deal of the internal structure beneath.

Immediately in reply, the lead ship released two torpedoes at *Emputin* in the one-sided tit-for-tat game. As little damage was done then as had been before, bar the inevitably increased rocking of the deck.

'I think I'm going to be sick,' moaned Karen, releasing the back of Rickard's seat to hug the rail behind her.

'It'll be all right in a moment,' Rickard said quickly. 'One more shot to show them once and for all that we mean business and they should stop. Fire needle beamers at the command ship's main structure. Make sure you leave the bridge intact. I want to be able to talk to them afterwards.'

A tenuous stretch of visible light reached out to caress the target. The vessel's central section disappeared under a vapourising cloud of dissipating wreckage. A gaping, blackened hole remained when the pyrotechnics began to die down, yawning like a jagged rip in the flesh of a healthy body. The ship shuddered dramatically under the forceful impact of the counterblow. Great sparks and miniature explosions danced along its hull for measureless seconds as it drifted uncontrollably away. The other ships stayed ominously silent as the occupants of the command vessel eventually seemed to regain some form of control over their crippled craft. They righted it with painful slowness and brought it limping back to its previous position.

The expectant hush on *Emputin's* bridge ended in a barrage of relieved sighs. They all knew it would do their peaceful mission no good at all if they destroyed one of the ships. As it was they had gone further than they dared with the damage they'd done.

'We couldn't have hurt them much more if we tried.' Bentowski was energetically animated after the concatenation of events. He looked as though he would gladly shoot the first hostile face he saw, were he not the helmsman rather than the weapons officer.

'I'm getting a reply to our friendship messages, from the command ship.' Watts sounded pleased that she had finally gotten through. 'Their commanding officer requests ship-to-ship communication.'

Rickard gave a thankful nod and Beck made unsubtle noises of surprise.

'Put them through, Watts,' Rickard said.

The picture of the alien command ship on main viewer was replaced by that of a swirling grey mist. It rolled past in undulating whorls and dips, forming an impenetrable wall. Rickard glanced at Watts, the question clear on his face.

All Watts could do was shrug helplessly. 'It's them, not us.'

The mist was suddenly cleared. A blindly waving hand cut sharply through the blanketing haze. The smoke of several smouldering or burning consoles on the alien bridge was sucked greedily away by struggling air vents and the fires were snubbed out one by one. The various positions of control, as all on *Emputin's* bridge could now see, were arranged in a circular trench above which was the captain's chair, supplying an overall view of the entire bank of instruments below. Seated at the consoles and in the command chair were the ship's alien crew members.

They were not human, that much was apparent even to Bentowski. Neither were they the tentacled, many-eyed inhuman monstrosities that Bentowski had been expecting. They were humanoid in stature and build, being roughly the same shape and size, although marginally bigger, as the Earth normal. They were graced with the standard complement of eyes, legs and arms and looked altogether less alien than some species inside the Grouping. All wore uniforms made of a brown, leather-like material, with totally militaristic overtones confirmed by arrays of fighting paraphernalia and rounded off by the inevitable pistol and belt.

The captain himself had a bright yellow flash on the left shoulder of his uniform, presumably as an indication to his rank. Only one other of the bridge personnel could be seen to carry a similar flash, although this again was inferior in design.

The facial makeup of the aliens was almost reptilian in nature. The crown of their heads were, for the most part, bald. Thick, dark black hair hung in various styles from the sides. It seemed that their spines had not halted at the base of their heads but had instead continued right over the skull to form a wide, deeply veined crest which carried on to stop above the brow where it descended into the flesh to create the wide, flattened nose. The extra-terrestrials' mouth and ears were human-normal, as were their eyes, especially those of the captain, which sparkled with inquisitive intelligence, although they were a little dulled by the burning smoke.

When he spoke it was with a gruff regality that held what seemed to the listeners like a mixture of Terran Eastern European accents which remained undistilled by the language translation device built into the comm console.

'You will tell me who you are,' he demanded sharply, staring impassively down at Rickard through the viewer.

'I am Captain Christopher Rickard, officer commanding the Service Navy Ship *Emputin* from the Allied Grouping of Planets.'

The alien captain looked warily mystified. The expression on his face was easy to read. It was to him as if

87

a species of animal, once thought extinct, had suddenly reared its head and put in an unexpected appearance. 'What is your purpose in entering our territory uninvited?' he said, quickly covering the surprise he'd shown.

It had not gone unnoticed by Kiyami or Rickard but the latter had other considerations. He felt he should be asking the questions. After all, who was the victor and who the vanquished? He ignored the alien's question and issued one of his own. 'Would you mind identifying yourself?'

The alien gave a gutteral chuckle, understanding this stranger's reluctance to reveal too much information and instead turn the tables on him. 'I am Lord-Commander Matz-Vari Kolbooshi-Nyr - called Matz Nyr by my equals and betters...'

'Is that a name or a fatal disease?' quipped Bentowski from the helm. Fortunately he went unheard by the majority. Rickard cast him a sharp look of warning before returning his attention to the alien commander who had continued talking.

'...I am in charge of this ship of the Mighty Rukan Empire and was engaged in preventing you from entering our space.' He paused to observe Rickard's reactions. Rickard remained still. Kiyami looked on from beyond viewer range, totally fascinated.

Whilst conversing the lord-commander had quietly and expertly noted the superior quality of the technology on *Emputin's* bridge. He continued his monologue, feeling impressed.

'When you were first picked up on our deep space scanners you were thought to be a new design of rebel ship. We are at present having some trouble with malcontent dissidents but they will be cru-...dealt with in due course. We then supposed you to be Larr. We have captured several of their destructive vessels in the past and are pledged to the extermination of all their intruding ships. Since it is apparent that you are neither rebel nor Larr I am at a temporary loss as to what action to pursue.'

'We are on a peaceful mission. I would like to be able to

88

convene some sort of discussion between ourselves and your superiors.'

'Discussions? Yes. That might be possible.'

'Perhaps you could guide us to one of your government centres?'

'Certainly you are in possession of the most powerful vessel I have ever seen.' Matz Nyr thought for a second. 'I must contact my command base for instructions. If you will excuse me?'

Rickard nodded and extinguished the volume on the connection by depressing a button on the arm of his chair. On screen the alien captain turned away.

Beck let out a long sigh. 'Well!' he exclaimed. 'What do you think of that?'

'Some first contact between alien races that turned out to be,' Bentowski derided the official brief.

'Yes. Thank you, Mister,' reproved Rickard irritably. 'I think we can do without the informative comments.' He knew he'd handled the meeting badly and was feeling extra-sensitive to criticism.

'He wasn't exactly over-friendly, was he?' said Karen.

'Nope. He also seemed surprised that we as the Service were still in existence.'

'If all they had to go on was captured Larr information, I'm not surprised.'

'I want to know why he stopped when he talked about the rebels. He realised he'd talked too much when he said the rebels would be cru-. Then he changed it to dealt with. Why?'

Kiyami joined the group around Rickard. 'The word he was going to use was clearly crushed.'

'But why change it so suddenly?' asked Karen.

Beck ventured an answer. 'To hide more militaristic a nature?'

'Battling alien races?'

'Why not? Did you see the inside of their ship? It looked fit for nothing but war.'

'That's probably it,' Rickard agreed.

'So what are we going to do.'

Bentowski's point of view came over a little louder than he'd intended. 'I suggest we get up and go home before we have our asses shot off.'

'Thank you once again for your extremely helpful suggestions, Mister Bentowski,' Rickard said dryly, warning him to shut up. 'I think we should follow Matz Nyr's suggestions instead. If we are asked to go along to his base, and I think we will be, we should accept, with full caution of course.'

'Are you sure that's wise?' Beck queried.

'No I'm not. But it seems to me the only way we'll get anywhere on this mission. At least these people seem friendly after our contretemps. Maybe it was a genuine mistake.'

'Then maybe my grandmother sprouted wings and flew off into the sunset,' Beck retorted scornfully.

'What?'

'We know that not every single Larr ship has been rounded up. Some are still out on the loose, right? Right. So it's possible that they still have spies in the Grouping and found out we were coming here. They could have informed these people that we were on our way and told them to get rid of us.'

'But the captain said they were against the Larr,' Karen protested with uncharacteristic naivity.

'We only have Matz Nyr's say on the matter,' Beck pressed on.

Kiyami did not agree. 'It does not do to be suspicious of every move. I suggest we trust them, at least for now.'

Rickard looked at the worried and questioning faces surrounding him and mulled the situation over. It did not take him long to come to a decision. He knew he had no real choice, anyway. Not with Admiral Trestrail waiting eagerly for him to fail. He decided what to do, momentarily ending all argument. 'We go in if invited.'

Kiyami was immediately concomitant and returned to her post. Beck took a moment longer but accepted the decision nonetheless. Rickard noticed Karen's unease and softly reassured her. 'Don't worry, It'll all work out fine, you'll see.'

Karen did not trust herself to reply. She was thinking once more that maybe she hadn't been so smart coming along after all.

90

On the main viewer the lord-commander was returning to his seat. Rickard was about to restore sound to the connection when Beck interjected with a final observation, 'Have you realised? They show no surprise whatsoever at the translator link.'

'They might have one of their own,' Rickard suggested, unworried. 'Or they might think that we speak their language. It's an easy enough mistake to make. We do it often enough, thinking that everyone speaks English even though we know for a fact that some species find it physically impossible.' He pressed the button and faced Matz Nyr.

'My Master-Commander has decided on a course of action,' Matz Nyr said congenially. 'If you will you are asked to follow me to my home planet, the motherworld of all Rukans and the capital of our Empire.'

'We would be most honoured to accept your proposal,' Rickard stated, making clear that it was simply a proposal and no more. 'What are the co-ordinates?'

'Ho! No need for that!' Matz Nyr laughed throatily. 'You have only to follow our transmission tracers which will be sent out after us.'

There was a brief but definite pause before Rickard acknowledged him. 'Okay,' he said lightly, masking his unease. 'Lead on.'

'Good. Excellent,' Matz Nyr cut the link, still grinning profoundly.

Rickard turned his attention to his navigator. 'Log the planet's co-ordinates and our path to it, Mister Boyd.'

Boyd smiled to himself, liking his captain's style. 'Right, sir.'

Howarth notched up one more mark on his mental list of the man's faults and successes. In his opinion the captain was still not fully worthy of his trust. But there was plenty of time yet.

With the dotted blackness of space once more occupying the viewers the remaining Imperial warships could be seen rejoining their battered leader. All three ships turned about in a circle of one hundred and eighty degrees as tiny manoeuvring jets along their hulls flared into momentary existence. Then their subspeed drives lit up and they coasted serenely away, moving deeper into Empire-controlled space. Boyd made continuous checks on the softly humming navigation console as Bentowski slid forward the helm controls to start the ship off after its escort. Every centimetre of the journey was to be logged in the memory banks of the computer to give a precise location of their destination in relation to the Belt.

'Open the lion's den and in walks Daniel,' Beck grimly stated.

Rickard thought it better to ignore him, turning an ear instead to Kiyami who had made a fresh discovery. 'What is it, Commander?'

'You may have noticed, Captain, that their ships are equipped with subspeed and, as far as I can tell, hyperdrive.'

'What? No, I hadn't noticed.'

'This indicates that, if they have not had a working relationship with the Larr, then they have at least copied the style of propulsion from those ships said to have been captured. We should hope for the latter.'

'Damned right we should!' Bentowski's ever-present chatter for once went unnoticed by his preoccupied colleagues.

Another feather in the cap of mystery, Rickard thought. He took a deep, steadying breath and thumbed a switch on the armrest never before used by him. When he spoke into the pickup he could hear his voice echo from the ship's speakers as the general intercom relayed him to every section of the many compartments and corridors of *Emputin's* busy internal structure. The effect made him feel slightly disconcerted.

'All hands, this is the Captain. After our brief battle encounter with three ships of the hostile zone, differences have been settled to an extent and we have been invited to the capital planet. We are now proceeding further into the zone.' He finished and relaxed, looking up when a hand rested gently on his shoulder. It was Karen. Her drooping, darkly ringed eyes revealed the extent of her tiredness.

'It's been a long day. I need some rest.'

Rickard stood up. 'I'll escort you to your cabin.'

'I hoped you might,' she said, low enough for only him to hear.

'Kiyami,' Rickard motioned to the first officer. 'Take the conn for a while.'

Kiyami saw how Karen was eying the captain but made no indication of the fact as she took the command chair. Much luck to them both, she thought, genuinely happy for Rickard but sad for herself. *Nani-mo.* Certainly nothing, not if it was her *karma* to be thus. *Gomen nasai,* so sorry, but there's nothing you can do about it.

Rickard walked his civilian passenger off the bridge, unobtrusively succeeding in convincing none of the onlookers that he was merely fulfilling his duties in escorting the official observer to her quarters, maintaining a calm degree of professional conduct appropriate to the task. Pleased with his performance he called a lift to take the couple down to the guest quarters. Karen hugged close to him whenever the opportunity presented itself and they were alone. After what Rickard thought to be all too short a time they reached her cabin.

'Can I invite you in?' she asked hopefully.

Rickard really wanted to but he had to defer. 'Not this time, I'm afraid I'm still very busy. There's a lot to be done before we reach their homeworld. You get some sleep. Tomorrow's going to be even longer and more trying than today was. We are going to have to be constantly alert when we get down on their homeworld.'

Karen lowered her face. 'Chris, I'm worried. I know from my father the sort of risks a ship's captain invariably faces.'

'There's no need to worry,' he reassured once more, lifting her head. 'One way or another, we'll make out.'

'I hope so.'

'Get to sleep with you. That's an order.'

'Yes, sah,' she said, mimicking the many crew who had to say it as a matter of course. She glanced inspectorially in both directions of the deserted corridor. In answer to Rickard's inquisitive frown she remarked: 'We don't want the crew seeing their captain making out with an official, do we?' She grinned warmly before kissing him in a startlingly urgent contact. Then she vanished into her cabin, leaving him with the moment and the scent of her body in his nostrils.

Earth: Late afternoon sunlight streamed brokenly though the ample window space. Vice-Admiral Trestrail's Service Command office was lit by shafts of brightness angled by the thickness of the glass. Outside was a city almost wholly oblivious to the new chain of events while it continued to celebrate the ending of the old one. Autumn leaves were gathering in scattered drifts around the bases of closely packed trees. Chill, gusty winds blew them up in madly swirling patterns, giving frustrated greenkeepers an increasingly hard time. Their task was made even more difficult by the almost herculean wind that insisted upon relieving the mostly deciduous trees of a great deal of their browning foliage. Leaves shot from branches like hotly glowing sparks flying out from a burning welder's torch. Overhead, the pale blue sky was heavily masked by fast-moving flecks of stark white cloud. They seemed to scurry for the wan sun, as if deliberately attempting to block off its meagre warmth.

Trestrail was sullenly musing over some paperwork when he was startled by the sudden, and unannounced, slamming open of his office door. His head snapped up. He was fully ready to deliver a prompt torrent of abuse to whomever had dared enter his personal domain without knocking and waiting. Instead, when he saw who was striding menacingly towards his desk, he remained silent. The unscheduled visitor was Admiral Lamia Melato.

Melato sat without any invitation, not that she required or expected one from Trestrail. She left him with more than the faintest suspicion that she was very slightly annoyed. The Ergaeli vice-admiral was determined not to let this other 'rank climber' in his life get the better of him a second time. He delivered her his most daunting stare, lowering his head so his glowering eyes met hers through the bushy blackness of his eyebrows.

94

'An' what is it I may do fer ye, Admiral?'

'It is more a question of what you have already done, Trestrail.' Melato's tone was reading several notches below freezing. She did not pretend that she felt anything other than avid dislike for him. 'I received a copy of a report not more than five minutes ago, redirected to me by someone who thought I would be interested in what it had to say.'

Trestrail feigned ignorance. 'What report would that be?'

'You know full well what I am talking about.'

'A'm sorry-'

'Don't play the damned innocent with me, Trestrail. I know you too well for the disguise to work.'

'All right,' Trestrail came off the defence. 'Shall we get down to basics? How much d'ye know?'

'Enough. You personally authorized the dispatching of flotilla of four ships on a heading into the hostile zone following on Captain Rickard's path. Am I correct?'

'Ye are that.'

'Because you do not trust him. Also correct?'

'Aye, A'll gi'ye that. too.'

'Then I am hereby ordering you to halt them before they reach the Belt. I assume that I am in time to stop you?'

'A'm afraid so,' Trestrail admitted sourly, It's a pity that ye dinnae seem tae know nor comprehend the *full* story.'

Melato was taken aback. Momentarily. Trestrail had delivered his ace-in-the-hole. 'So what is the full story?'

Smiling magnanimously, Trestrail continued. 'It appears that we ha' lost all communication links wi' the *Emputin*. Naturally I waited a sensible period o' time, like, ye know, before giving the order fer a flotilla tae follow an' investigate. It's all fully logged, ye can be sure.'

'I don't doubt it for a second. In doing so, however you have irresponsibly and unnecessarily informed more people of our position in regards to a possible second war, should these hostiles prove to be a threat.'

'Och dinnae fash yersel'. It's only a wee flotilla. An' only the officer in charge, a Commodore Bartlet, knows the whole story. It'll be a simple seek an' locate mission. I want

95

tae know what it is that's happened and why *Emputin* has ceased contact, fer ma lassie's sake if fer nought else.'

'Your daughter! She knew the risks involved. It was her final choice to go or stay.'

'That's no the point.'

'That *is* the point! I will not allow you to jeopardise peace for one person. It does not matter how important they may be to you, Trestrail. In case you had not noticed we have just come out of a full scale war. Do you want to start another one? We are not recovered enough to even think of such a possibility. The Grouping would not survive it but I doubt if that would bother you. To cause a war now would be sheer stupidity on your part.' Melato adopted a tone more befitting a judge about to deliver a death sentence. 'You will transmit an amendment to your last command. You will tell Bartlet to halt on this side of the Belt and await further orders from me. Do you understand?'

'Now look ye here, Ye cannae go about-'

'I said do you understand?'

'Fully.' With tightly suppressed emotion Trestrail realised that the meddling woman had beaten him again. He felt a pang of concern that was unfamiliar to him as he thought of the dire straits his only child might be in. He could only hope she would come through safely, unlike that amateurish, inexperienced fool Rickard. The admiral hoped fervently that whatever ailments struck Rickard down would prove to be terminal.

Melato rose and left without another word. She slammed the door victoriously behind her, distinctly enjoying the harsh resulting *crash*. She wondered if it were efficacious enough to show Trestrail that there was no messing with her.

Halting in the adjoining secretary's office, Melato relaxed, satisfied at the outcome of the confrontation. That would teach him. She experienced absolutely no remorse for a second successful verbal battle against the hard-nosed admiral. That would teach the overbearing, arrogant, supercilious son-of-a-bitch not to meddle in affairs that were above his over-sized head. If she could have copytaped the unplanned meeting she would have done, just to view again the expression of animus on Trestrail's face when he finally discovered that she had once again got the better of him. It would have been well worth watching. It was not every day that one gained the opportunity to see such a stubborn so-and-so taken down a peg or two, and quite deservedly so. This had made her day.

As much as she hated to admit it, though, it was remotely possible that Trestrail, forever staunch and firm in opinion, had a point in his favour in sending out a search-and-locate mission. Notwithstanding how out of line he had been, he may have been right. She, herself, did not put her entire trust in Captain Rickard's abilities, no matter how immovable she had earlier seemed on the subject.

Ignoring how much she argued otherwise, Rickard *was* inexperienced in command. By all normal practice he should have spent some weeks in extra training following his impromptu promotion. True, he had attended the basic captaincy proficiency testing, as did most Service people of his rank. And she agreed fully that he deserved his promotion. Especially since it had been her signature on the promotion documents. But success had carried the young man high on its intoxicating shoulders, cresting him far above normal practices. After all the fuss and congratulation he was still a fallible twenty-five year-old ex-lieutenant who had been safely occupied in power control duties only a short time before. His meteoric rise to fame had blinded everyone to that fact, perhaps dangerously. Rickard was not a fool but he was untried and untested and she might have been wrong in sending him on this particular mission.

It did not do to put all of one's eggs in a single basket because it was always probable that some idiot would come shambling along and sit on the lot, and then where would she be? Lumbered with a lot of scrambled egg, certainly. But amusement aside it could mean trouble. That was why she had ordered Trestrail to keep his flotilla near the Belt to remain 'on call', as it were. Better to play it safe, especially in this profession where an important mistake in such a delicate operation could mean catastrophe. Even more so if word of any of this happened to leak out to the popular Press and so on to the general public. There would be an outcry and heads might roll, hers included. She had to agree, at least in part, to Trestrail's idea. If only for personal safety. A kind of insurance against unforseen accidents.

Melato perceived that she had become too wrapped up in her thoughts and cut them off sharply. She headed for the outer door. Trestrail's bemused secretary sat behind much too large a desk, staring on at the busy to-ing and fro-ing, totally nonplussed. Admiral Peterson got up from a low couch in the corner of the room and trailed after Melato in an almost dog-like fashion. His had clearly not been a ringside seat, a state of events he sorely wished he could have altered. Admiral Trestrail did not have many friends in Command and Peterson would have made a hefty profit on selling tickets for the bout of loquacity.

He hurried to catch up with Melato, trying to match her ground-consuming stride. 'I assume that all went well? No hitches or snags?'

'Wrong. There was a hitch.'

'Oh?' Peterson tried in vain to think what it could be. 'I'm afraid it's escaped me. What was it?'

'The hitch, Mister, was that *Emputin* has ceased communicating. Whichever imbecile intercepted Trestrail's command order failed to inform me of that one minor fact.' She looked pointedly at Peterson. Her rapid pace remained doggedly unchanged.

The fast pace might have been great for Melato but it was making the shorter and physically unfit rear-admiral extremely short of breath. He gasped out his reply. 'How was I to know he'd omitted details? I only caught the file in a random check and imagined you'd be interested. Especially since it was your idea originally to send Rickard. He more than anyone else needs protection from Trestrail's callous attitude. The old axe-grinder may have convinced *him* that hostilities have ceased but no-one else is fooled.' He felt he owed Rickard some favour for throwing him in at the deep end.

'Nevertheless, I would much prefer it if you checked

98

more completely should anything of this nature recur. I stopped Trestrail this time but...'

Melato suddenly came to a dead stop. Peterson carried blindly on for a few paces more before belatedly noticing he was alone. He looked around almost comically for his missing companion.

'What? What's wrong?' he gaped in trepidation. A passing middie seemed overtly amused for some unfathomable reason and Peterson glared at him darkly.

'I wonder...Would Trestrail be so obstinately stupid as to risk his career?' She decided that he would and without a word of explanation to Peterson she crossed to the nearest intercom, punching the transmit button fiercely. 'This is Admiral Melato. Put me through to Command Dispatch.'

'Was it something I said?' Peterson queried inanely.

'Indirectly, yes. I believe I am only beginning to know our friend Trestrail.' The intercom announced the desired connection had been established. Melato spoke into the small, highly sensitive, multi-directional receiver grid. 'Dispatch? Get me Vice-Admiral Trestrail's last received orders, please. I want to know if he sent through a Grade One partial mission cancellation order.'

Peterson finally caught on, the light dawning over his features like a long awaited dawn reluctantly breaking over a distant horizon. 'You think he didn't do it, didn't obey orders?'

'Yes,' Melato nodded pronouncedly, as if addressing a backward child. She was not in the mood to suffer fools gladly.

The reply from Dispatch came back, sounding decidedly negative. 'The order to which you refer has not been delivered, Admiral Melato.'

'Thank you very much. I will be sending the command myself shortly by security connection.' She cut the line.

'I never thought he'd go so far,' murmured Peterson, shaking his head in wonder.

Melato agreed. The anger was building up inside her again. She had dangerously misjudged the man and that could have been very risky.

Very risky indeed.

☆ ☆ ☆

The capital world of the Rukan Empire entered the range of *Emputin's* sensors and scanners. It was a large, reflective globe. A sphere of rock which exuded a yellowish aura. The colouring indicated the intensity of its hot and arid, desert surface. There were few clouds covering its heat-baked blue skies from the harsh radiance of its twin primaries. It nestled comfortably in the binary star system; double suns, one a great blue ball of luminescence, the other a marginally smaller secondary star of bright whiteness, lit up the eternal darkness of space around it, creating a symbiotic halo of diffused light.

'Full approach scan, please,' Rickard asked, pleased after the long voyage not to have Beck and Karen hovering behind him.

While Kiyami was bent over her instruments, Rickard conducted the necessary orbital approach. 'I want an orbit fixed geo-stationarily over their capital city, Mister Boyd. Keep at twenty thousand,' he requested.

'Aye, sir,' Boyd mouthed as he continued stabbing at buttons while coloured function diodes gave ever-changing readings and displays. 'We are entering geo-stationary at range twenty now.'

'Initiate prep procedures. Secure all systems from subspeed and ready a launch for immediate departure.'

'Sir,' Watts said. 'Comm signals out of the zone are still being jammed. I can't raise Alpheratz on any frequency.'

'Okay, Lieutenant. We'll let it ride for now.'

Kiyami concluded her approach scan and looked up with the results.

'Anything I should know?' asked Rickard.

'Nothing out of the ordinary. A standard binary system. The planet is second out from the suns, orbiting at approximately one hundred and twenty-nine million kilometres. None of the other planets are habitable but there is an artificial construction on the fourth planet, probably nothing more than an outpost. The sensors reveal that the planet itself has an axial inclination of only

100

six degrees so there are no seasons as we know them. Absorbed ultra-violet reads only zero point eight leaving us safe from radiation. The average temperature on the planet's surface is thirty-five degrees Celsius-'

Howarth gave a resigned groan and Bentowski felt he had to add his say. 'Darnit! Looks like I get to complete my tan,' he grinned.

'Precisely,' Kiyami confirmed. 'It will be hot. Apart from that, there are seven other major cities in the same region as the capital and there are many more on the other visible continents. It seems to be as overpopulated as Earth, although it doesn't appear as polluted as Earth once was. Perhaps animal transport is used to a greater effect here. The air is pleasantly clean, being made up mainly of oxygen plus the correct amount of secondary gasses to make it breathable for us. We will be hot and will perhaps tire marginally more easily than normal because the planet has a gravity of one point two - only just more than that to which we are used. We will nevertheless survive.'

'As long as the natives let us,' Bentowski croaked to no one in particular.

Rickard favoured him with a sour grimace before acknowledging Kiyami's report. It would not have been nearly so much fun trundling around in a survival suit. They had been lucky so far. In a sudden wave of pessimism he wondered how long it would last. His imaginary guardian angel had to go off duty sometime.

'We are now in requested fixed orbit, sir. All systems read green.' Boyd finished his duties.

'Okay. Lieutenant Watts, detail hot weather uniforms and LTUs for everyone who goes planetside. Ask Mister Bulloch to prepared the cutter, a launch is going to be too small.' He readied himself to leave.

As Watts completed that duty her console bleeped for more attention. She activated the personal speaker to discover the cause. 'Sir, Matz Nyr is signalling.'

Rickard paused on his way to the exit door and shrugged. 'Put him on.'

The image on the main viewer faded to be replaced by the large-as-life picture of Matz Nyr.

'Here we must part company, Captain Rickard,' he growled genially. 'I must return to my patrol duties while you are respectfully requested to attend the Emperor. You only have to follow the ground tracers to reach the correct location. One of the Emperor's aides will await you at the landing grid.'

'Fine. I'll be sending down a single craft with a hand-picked crew. We will be armed of course.'

'Of course. We fully expect caution after the greeting I first offered you. But you will find no need for weapons. Our people will welcome you with open arms. You will come to think of my home as your own home from home.'

'I'm sure I will,' Rickard returned diplomatically. 'Goodbye.'

'Goodbye, Captain. It has been a pleasure,' he smiled and cut the connection. The viewer switched back to showing the planet's highly lurid colour scheme as it turned slowly on its axis.

'Mister Howarth, I'd like you to join the landing party. Kit up and meet me in the hanger bay with a couple of security marines.'

'Right...sir,' he decided to add, grateful to be in on the first trip downside.

'Bentowski, you'll be joining him.'

The helmsman was stunned. He even lacked words for a reply. It was not that he was overwhelmed at being chosen to go, exactly the opposite, in fact. He liked life too much to take part in what he imagined would turn out to be a suicide tour. His silence was obvious as Howarth led him off the bridge, making the most of his unenthusiastic mood. 'Come on, Bentowski, old pal. You'll love it. Nothing but clear sun and blue skies. Think of that fantastic tan you wanted to get. Cheer up. Why be such a misery?'

'Go boil your head,' was all Rickard heard in retort before the doors closed on them.

'Kiyami, I would like you to remain in command up here,' he continued, making way for her. 'It's better that one of us stays behind.' She reluctantly accepted and took the conn. Rickard could understand how she felt. She was the chief science officer so naturally she wanted to be

102

among the first to examine a new planet. But he could not risk having the two top officers of the ship on the surface of this new planet at the same time. Not yet, anyway. 'Monitor our progress and be ready to send down a fully armed party of Marines for us if need be. If that proves impossible or the rescue party fails then you are to get *Emputin* out of here at maximum speed. If even *that* proves impossible - they might call up extra ships to block your passage *if* they turn out to be hostile to us - you know what to do as a last resort.'

'Yes. Self-destruction to prevent them gaining this ship with its more advanced weaponry and information storage banks,' she loosely quoted a passage from the command regulations.

'Right. See you later.' He did not bother to add that he hoped there would be a later. He was also relieved that he would not be taking Karen with him. 'Spare baggage' he did not need. Anyway, he'd only be worrying about her safety all the time if she came along. It was better that she remain on the ship. Not that she'd agree with him. Oh well, he mentally sighed. I'll have to live with that. He turned to leave.

'Good luck, Captain,' Kiyami said with sincerity.

'Thanks.'

5

The smoothness of *Emputin's* blue-grey hull, as yet unscarred by the micrometeorites of space, cracked open in one comparatively small corner. Revealed was the brightly lit interior of the hanger bay, straight rows of tiny landing lights shining out into space. A single craft detached itself from the bay deck and cautiously exited, leaving behind the protection of its mother vessel, and headed down towards the dazzling surface of the planet below. As it descended, entering the atmosphere, a thin layer of pale, almost nonexistent cloud seemed to part and move away before it. The gradually closing surface beckoned the craft on. It seemed eager to accept.

Wide, open desert loomed up before the cumbersome cutter. It smoothly levelled at three hundred metres and shot off in the direction of the capital city. Sun-scorched flatlands and hard-baked sandstone mesas shimmered underneath in the excessive heat distortion. Arid landscapes rolled rapidly by.

Rippling, dusty sand dunes were eventually replaced by numerous rocky outcroppings. These grew and quickly built up into a collection of steep, sloping mountains which were scattered in ever-thickening numbers in the open wilderness. These separated, miniature mountains, their craggy, age-worn faces staring belligerently at the newcomer, began joining together as the cutter sped on until they formed a deeply grooved range through which the craft had to weave and twist.

Huge formations of weather-eroded, sculptured rock piled upon rock were passed. Deep gorges of dark and hidden depths could be faintly glimpsed below. As the cutter took a sharp, narrow turn in the main gorge the hotly glowing suns came once more into view. They sent forth a burst of brilliance that lit all the shadowed nooks and crannies and filled the darkened rock with unexpected illumination.

The cutter appeared to hesitate momentarily, as if in uncertainty, before surging onwards towards its destination.

The mountain range ended more suddenly than it had started. The ground dropped away to form a broad, open valley. It seemed overly-verdant after the emptiness of the previous views of the arid planet. Only the occasional batholithic mound of stone rose from the dirt-covered land ahead, breaking its starkness.

From the air a great amount could be seen of the now visible capital city. Confined, hut-like dwellings were scattered in great profusion around its edges. They bordered on a sun-scalded wasteland with only a few thick patches of friendly green to offset it. The valley was only verdant near the city. The green of chlorophyll bearing plants stayed close to the best-kept soil. Only hardier plantlife ventured forth in the outer reaches.

Some way from the city limits the huts grew more and more numerous. Larger huts and solid structures, proper constructions, took over as the norm for most of the rest, before these too were succeeded at the city's very centre by many lustrous abodes lying in a loosely encircling pattern around a regal, extremely decorous palace. The palace was totally covered by a transparent protection dome. A smaller, much less sophisticated companion palace lay incongruously by its side.

Countless blocks of buildings and low towers, mere phantoms of their Earth-bound cloud-reaching cousins, filled the narrow streets around the twin palaces. They formed a maze of twisting, turning spaces, some of which looked only wide enough to allow a bare minimum of pedestrian traffic. To the city's southern edge was a rather miniscule landing strip made up of only three grids. It still stood out as being very modern and out of place alongside much of the city's older architectural designs. They seemed far more recent and progressive than virtually the whole of the remainder of the dirtied, sun-baked capital put together.

The cutter made for the centremost pad, hovering over it briefly. It almost gave the impression of a hawk hunting some unwary prey, before it settled quickly down in a cloud of retro-gasses and disturbed sand.

As the sand cloud settled a lone figure approached the rested cutter.

The officer had the dress and manner of one of high rank. This was amply reflected by the manner in which he carried himself, shoulders thrown back, chest thrust out, and by the quality of his uniform, which was decidedly more impressive than the standard fare. Apart from the usual leather-like top and trousers, these being black instead of brown, he was adorned with a bright yellow band running from right shoulder to left hip. Gold braid at its top hung down midway over the not inconsiderable chest. A pistol not dissimilar to the Service's regulation issue sat comfortably in a brightly polished holster. Balanced on its opposite side was a lengthy sword housed in a grey on brown sheath. The imperial ambassador awaited the alien visitors with well-concealed impatience.

Inside the spacious cutter Rickard was conducting a hurried last-minute briefing with his team. All wore short-sleeved uniforms and all were armed, some not only with pistols. The security detachment, Bernerds and Stuart, each carried state-of-the-art rifles, complete with telescopic, automatic sights and armour-piercing cartridges. Their thoroughly weighty, menacing style of design hid nothing of their true power. The main part of the team was made up of the ship's various scientific specialists; two ecologists, a biologist and a geologist, all of whom would be conducting their own separate studies on the natives and their planet to be filed for complete study by scientists back home. Howarth was there, and an agitated Bentowski was seated on the edge of his chair wondering how he ever came to be press-ganged into this operation. Also present was Surgeon Beck, complete with full emergency medical kit - for minor accidents only. It would not be much use if his fears of Imperial untrustworthiness were realised.

'I want you all to take it easy when we get out there,'

Rickard was saying. He looked especially at the security people for obedience of his word. At the same time he fiddled with a miniature LTU - Language Translation Unit - fitting it to the collar of his uniform. 'This is an alien race with alien customs, some of which may seem...unusual to us. I want no stupidity from any of you. Opinions are best kept to yourselves if they are not strictly concerned with the business at hand. There are only ten of us to a whole planet of them and I have no illusions about rescue from the ship. If they wanted to, these people could have us hung, drawn and quartered before we could blink.'

This brought a shudder from one of the female scientists. Bentowski inwardly cringed at the picture that entered his mind.

'It's okay, Captain.' Beck hoped that Rickard had not gone over the top with his warning. 'We're all on our best behaviour.'

Rickard caught his eye and saw that he was trying to calm the situation. He was grateful. They were all nervous and rightly so, considering what lay outside. Not just a new planet but a new civilisation, a new culture. One never before encountered by any Grouping-based peoples. It was enough to scare the wits out of anyone if they thought about it overmuch.

At the rear of the group, Stuart was fiddling unceasingly with her LTU, tapping and flicking at it. 'I don't think this thing's working,' she moaned to her companion.

Bernerds snorted derisively. 'You spastic Jock.'

'Well I heard that! Thanks a lot.'

'Don't worry about it.'

'Cut it out you two,' Howarth groaned irately.

'Right Boss.'

'Thank you.'

'Can I go home?' Bentowski asked plaintively.

'Open the hatch,' commanded Rickard.

Hot air blasted into the cutter as the door drew away from the hull, transforming itself into a short stairway. The air was dry and dusty, making it awkward to breath without the occasional cough from a moisture-starved

107

throat.

Rickard was first out. He was followed closely by Beck and the science team. Security, and this included Bentowski for the trip, kept out of the way by standing well to the back. Only the coxswain remained inside the cutter. He had already decided that it was the best piece of luck he'd had in a long time. He did not envy the landing team their risky job.

The young captain walked steadily forwards to halt only a few scant paces away from the ambassador. He stoically waited for the ice to be broken.

The high-ranking officer silently regarded Rickard, evaluating him, estimating his strengths and his weaknesses before speaking. When he did speak it was with an abrasive quality that bespoke of a hidden element, some facet of the ambassador that Rickard was not to be permitted to witness, not intentionally, anyhow.

'In the name of the Emperor I welcome you to this world, Home of the Emperor of the Known Planets and Protector of all His peoples,' he stated with grandiose pomposity. It quickly became apparent to Rickard that this was how he always conversed.

Rickard replied in kind. 'I am the chief commanding officer of the Service Navy Ship *Emputin*. I represent the Supreme Council of the Allied Grouping of Planets and have been granted the full and complete power to act in their name. I am Captain Christopher Rickard.'

'So. I am pleased to make your acquaintance.'

'The pleasure is all mine. I'm very glad to be here.' He was also extremely glad that the stiff and rather formal introductions were over. Now he could enter into a more inquisitive type of converse. 'I must ask, most of your technology here looks brand new. How is it you don't seem surprised about our translator units?'

'We have in our possession a minor collection of the devices, appropriated from captured Larr ships that have entered our Empire, on their destructive escapades. It was thought that everyone from beyond our borders must utilise these devices so I therefore neglected to wear one myself.'

Rickard succeeded in concealing his surprise at the

revelation. He knew now that the Larr had more to answer for in terms of technologiclal aid for these people, intentional or not. Utilising the Larr equipment, whether by direct and friendly contact or via captured vessels, these people had come a long way in what must have been a short time, thus explaining the incongruous meshing of old and new on the planet. There were bound to be more of such surprises to come, discovering what the Rukans had and had not gained from their extraterrestrial contacts. This empire could still be a danger to the Grouping despite the undeveloped nature of their fleet and Rickard was only now beginning to realise the fact.

'I feel I must apologise,' the ambassador continued, 'for the brusque welcome dealt you by that oaf of a commander. You may rest fully assured that he will be justly and rightfully punished.'

Frowning mildly, Rickard realised that was another pointer to the differences in their mutual backgrounds. 'There's really no need for that,' he said in mild protestation. 'We suffered no damage.'

'Nevertheless, by necessity obedience must be maintained. Ah! How rude of me.' The ostentatious ambassador suddenly switched conversational tracks. 'I have failed to introduce myself to you, a situation that can be straight away rectified. I am Master-Aide Kal-Tiin Chikan-Nyr, I am one of the Emperor's highest personal confidants.'

Well, how very nice for you, Rickard thought sourly, not at all in the proper spirit the occasion required. 'Pleased to meet you...Kal Nyr?'

'I am delighted to see that you have grasped at least one of our customs with such speed, Captain. It bodes well for future relationships.'

It came to Rickard in a flash that the aide was simply another damned politician, no different to Cadir in his false mannerisms. He was even worse, in fact, were that at all possible. Twice as pompous. Twice as hypocritical. And three times as loathsome. Still, that aside there was something about that surname. Something that seemed familiar. Or was it his irrational imagination?

'Are you by any chance related to Matz Nyr, the

commander who led us in?' he enquired.

Kal Nyr gave a grunt of evident dissatisfaction, effectively covering any deeper emotions he might otherwise have unwittingly revealed. 'I am indeed related by blood to that miserable excuse for a soldier. He is a first cousin. His attitude towards many of the customs and duties of Rukan Imperialism leave much to be desired. Now, if the formalities of introduction are over,' much to Rickard's annoyance, the aide swiftly changed the subject again, 'we will depart for the Imperial Palace, where my Emperor awaits.'

'By all means,' Rickard remained outwardly acquiescent. By the ambassador's description of his cousin, Rickard imagined Matz Nyr to be far more lenient and humane in his conduct than this pretentious individual. At least, that was the impression gained so far.

Kal Nyr led the landing party to a transport vehicle parked a little way beyond the grid. The vehicle was recognisable to the Service people as being a fairly modern design of float-mover, an advanced form of hovercraft developed in the Grouping for city haulage and general transport usage. Another transfer of knowledge from one empire to another. Rickard wondered actively what else this particular empire had learned from his old enemy.

Without waiting for his guests to board, Kal Nyr took the first of the six rows of double seats on the floater, a stern-faced trooper joining him. Rickard noted the aide's lack of manners and sat himself next to Beck in the second row while Howarth and Bentowski took the seat behind. Once the remainder of the landing team had filled the other spaces Kal Nyr gave an unceremonious wave of the hand indicating that the driver, positioned at the rear of the vehicle on a raised platform, could start off. The floater jerked roughly forward, a wake of disturbed sand settling behind it.

As the party neared the first of the outlying huts of the city Rickard came to notice the timid glances directed at the visitors from the visibly downtrodden populace. Wherever Kal Nyr looked, however, there were only hurridly bowed heads, as if the emaciated waifs of the outer dwellings feared for their lives in his presence. Curtains of rough hide fluttered stiffly in crudely chiselled window frames and cracked and warped wood doors creaked open the merest fraction to allow the occupants a more uninterrupted view of the aliens now travelling through the city limits.

Rickard carefully observed the crude style of architecture. How the buildings seemed to be formed of dried mud with jagged gaps forming windows and doorways. This particular area held the overall appearance of a slum. A place to slot the poorer, unrefined section of the populace. Further into the city the style of construction gradually changed, as did the people. The buildings were now made of more solid materials, something resembling brick in its texture and shaping. The houses were outwardly tidier, cleaner. They were fitted with properly shaped doors and there was glass in the windows instead of hide. The people appeared richer, better clothed and fed. They were less cowardly and timid in nature and stood straighter and more firmly. They still bowed their heads to the imperious Kal Nyr but not to such depth. They looked as if they were bowing more as a politeness than a necessity.

Deeper into the bustling capital, the floater came onto a main road. It was wider, superior in surface quality and had a much improved class of citizen milling along its bordering walkpaths. The road pointed directly to the city centre in an unwaveringly direct line. At its end could be seen the Imperial Palace, looming over the surrounding architecture in the near distance.

The journey continued on with the floater cruising along at a bare minimum of speed. Kal Nyr obviously wanted his guests to gain the best possible visual impression of the city's people and places.

It was very considerate of him, Rickard mused thoughtfully. He knew already that there was more to Kal Nyr than met the eye. His suspicions were justifiably aroused.

To the left of the moving floater there was passed a tall, heavily decorated structure which stood decidedly out of keeping with the normal design of building. It was shaped

111

roughly like a rectangular block with a great arched roof sitting over the top. Two main support pillars were inset into the stone at each of the front corners and greatly ornate patterns had been worked skillfully into them and onto the fanciful cornices above the doors. The double doors were of wood with enormous metal handles planted deep into the lower panels on each side, under carved designs. The arched and over-decorated roofing stretched upwards to crown the rather baroque assemblage.

The church - it could not possibly be mistaken for anything else - was the grandest piece of workmanship yet seen by the landing party and it pointed to a hidden wealth not shared by the majority. Still, this community did not appear to be overtly unhappy. Quite the opposite if all the present activity was to be believed. There was a healthy bustling movement from the packed streets that seemed continuous and without reason. Multitudes of native citizens with arms or containers full of strange and unusual foodstuffs and goods hurried in one direction. Others, their own containers empty, threaded their paths through the crowds in the opposing direction.

Not many spared the time nor the effort now to bow to Kal Nyr and yet he seemed untroubled by this. The floater had to slow even more as great surges of people began blocking the roadway, wide as it was. The blockage became steadily worse until it abruptly ceased with the greater part of the crowd flocking down a left-hand sideturn to a noise- and dust-filled, thoroughly overpacked market-place. Immense numbers of stalls lined the side street market with countless forms of consumer goods of all descriptions. Many of the stall-holders bellowed their advertisement pitches in direct competition with their neighbours and this, mingled with the babble of the thronging crowds, created a veritable cacophony, a deafening roar of sound and vision.

'I wouldn't mind paying that a visit if we do stay,' Beck commented, finding he had to speak rather loudly to be heard.

'It looks very interesting,' was all Rickard said in reply

before sinking back to his silent appraisal of the visible aspects of the native way of life. The whole city had the feel of something suddenly and very recently introduced to high technology, an introduction that by many seemed to have gone unrecognised.

Presently, the palace was reached.

Rickard cast his eyes over its structure. His naval training was used in helping him to note its strengths and weaknesses as a defendable position. He realised that it was incredibly intimidating and domineering as it towered over the comparatively miniscule floater. These people might not have much outwardly visible in the way of new technology, but they certainly knew what was what in magnificent architecture. The whole, magnificent, residence shone with inbuilt grandeur.

The Imperial Palace was an eloquent mixture of both old and new architecture. A symmetrical masterpiece combining both indigenous splendour and imported practicality. The palace itself had been built around and totally covered over by a geodesic-like dome, completely transparent, that protected the interior absolutely. It was framed internally by a filigree of tough supports and struts. They created an intricate gridwork that endowed the whole thing with a kind of polished lustre. The dome looked like a sheet of misted glass with the sun's full rays beaming harshly down upon it.

The palace was contained in an expanse of well spaced, lush green gardens, most of which stretched out towards the rear and to the right. Bushy, amply watered shrubs and trees, looking strangely out of place against the sandy dirt surface of the rest of the city's mostly unconcreted roads and walkpaths, obstructed Rickard's view of the lower sections of the palace but he was afforded a clear view of the upper floors. The palace itself was of an elongated, blocky shape with an unglimpsed depth to its main body, a sense of yet to be seen hugeness pervaded. Regularly spaced pillars protruded along the front face. Large, immaculately gleaming windows set in exquisitely crafted frames filled the stretching-spaces between and were offset above and below by ornately worked patterning which had been cut into the stone-made wall.

The palace exuded a firm impression of immense wealth and aristocratic standing. And a surrounding aura of deadly and ostentatiously covered menace.

The high-ridged stone wall which enclosed the Imperial Palace, its dome and its gardens, was separated at the entrance by weighty, spiked iron gates set into a short run of equally impregnable iron railings either side of it. Armed guards patrolling vigilantly inside and outside the gate reacted immediately to the party's arrival by unquestioningly swinging open the double gate to allow the floater entrance to the courtyard from the paved square leading up to it.

The floater jerkily drew to a halt parallel to the outer palace doors. The sealed doors were set firmly into the dome's mildly reflective exterior. Kal Nyr climbed hurriedly off, spinning on his heels to face the Service party.

'This is the palace of His Imperial Majesty, the Emperor. If you will follow me I shall lead you to the presence of the Emperor himself,' he stated pompously as the landing party began disembarking, stepping stiffly off the floater. Before Rickard could reply, Kal Nyr had started off.

'Oh, goody. We're gonna see the Emperor,' Bentowski said with heavy sarcasm.

'And it's about time, too,' Beck muttered.

Howarth replied with an understanding grimace. The guided tour had indeed been overlong and almost tedious. The novelty of seeing new planets and their inhabitants had long ago worn off for many of them. There were plenty of worlds inside the Grouping that bore a very similar resemblance to this so it was really quite unoriginal.

Halting once more before the gigantic outer portal, Kal Nyr snapped his fingers at the palace guards and they hurried to open the cumbersome doors, their muscled forms aided in the arduous task by unperfected pistoning machinery. Kal Nyr wordlessly set off through the now half-opened entrance and Rickard motioned his team to follow.

They entered to find themselves in a spacious,

elaborately decorated hallway. It was topped with rounded arches that were distanced out along the high ceiling and walls, and covered at regular intervals with minutely designed hanging tapestries. Leading off the hallway, as the *Emputin* people discovered when trailing their guide, was a whole wealth of corridors, each interlinking with at least three or four others along its length to form what must be an extraordinarily convoluted, twisting, coiled maze of almost identical passages and halls. The landing party soon became totally disorientated by the distorted and complex path they threaded. They would have become utterly lost had it not been for Kal Nyr's silent lead.

The corridors themselves bespoke of that hidden wealth and prosperity which was noticeably less hidden now that Rickard came to realise the fact. Magnificent arches holding artistic masterpieces between their rounded stone pillars were passed. There were countless valuable items to be witnessed, untarnished vases, invaluable portraits, and general *objets d'art*. Profuse alcoves in many corridors were almost littered with them, like uncut gems in a newly discovered diamond mine.

Howarth, keeping to the rear, looked tersely at an accompanying Bentowski. 'Maybe this is his idea of another guided tour.'

With uncharacteristic wordlessness, Bentowski simply agreed with a concomitant nod of the head.

After what seemed an endless march along the coiled route trailed by Kal Nyr, the helmsman spotted a glittering ornament adorning the nearby wall and he thought he must have seen it once already.

'Hey,' he hissed at Howarth. 'Haven't we passed this route before?' He frowned, trying to recall the journey.

'Don't worry about it,' Howarth told him, pointing ahead. 'Anyway, I'm sure I haven't seen this bit. I think we've arrived.'

At the head of the small procession, Kal Nyr came to a timely halt as the party entered a spacious ante-chamber. They stood in front of what were presumably the throne room doors. The ambassador raised a hand for expected silence, as if he were leading a group of belligerent school

115

children on an educational excursion.

'You will now be entering into the illustrious and highly distinguished presence of the most reverend Emperor of all the planets of our territories,' he uttered reverberatingly and with a notable coldness to his tone. His spined head-crest shifted forward ever so slightly in an expression of extreme warning - or so Rickard imagined - but he kept his thoughts entirely to himself. He had not seen one single guard since walking into the palace and he doubted that a ruler such as this one appeared to be would dismiss all his guards without good reason. Remaining wary of danger, even though all so far had seemed open and above board, Rickard led his team after Kal Nyr as the aide pushed open one of the twin mahogany doors. Its deeply recessed panelling made it closely resemble a similarly elaborate Georgian style.

The throne room was a rounded, circular chamber with an impressive diameter. Its high-domed ceiling was shrouded in darkness, well away from the illumination below. Stretching away omnidirectionally, the chamber at its lowest level was ringed by solid concrete pillars that reached upwards to support and frame a shadowed second level balcony along which could be glimpsed the indistinct forms of well-armed troopers, glaring at the newcomers suspiciously. Leading inwards from the doors in a direct line to the throne itself was a strip of soft, extremely deep, velvety yellow carpet into which feet sank deeply, as if the carpet were reluctant to let them go.

Rickard followed hesitantly after Kal Nyr who immediately set off towards the opposite end of the chamber and the remainder of the landing party stretched out in a struggling, wavery line, making only a gesticulative effort to keep up while their attention was being held on documenting and recording as much information on their surroundings as possible.

On the wall spaces between the overlarge pillars hung vari-coloured tapestries. Sewn in a multitude of rich and glorious hues, there was gold and silver threaded through the exquisite patterns and dramatic illustrations to complete a sparkling amalgamation of artwork which showed a descriptive history of the planet. Judging by the varieties of red shades utilised in the displays, much of the history had been bloody and destructive.

Not to be put off by this show of undisguised magnificence Rickard turned his attention ahead to his immediate destination. Little noticed, at either side of the narrow carpet, were placed, low hexagonal ornamented tables. Around them well-dressed nobles and over-dressed, and very extravagant but obviously prosperous, merchants sat on woven straw matting. Their legs were crossed under them. They sipped silently at enigmatically coloured beverages, their beady eyes never for a moment left the visitors. Blank faced guards, one positioned at the base of every alternate pillar, stared with cold animosity.

At the end of the stretch of yellow carpet was the personage at the moment of most importance to Rickard and the expedition. Framing this individual on either side were two standards, each crested by the vulgar, minutely sculptured form of some native bird of prey. Each was resplendent in a mirroring gold casing, their polished surfaces casting bright, well-definable reflections from the incongruous and ineffectual electrical overhead lighting. Between the standards there was a raised platform, a dais of stone atop which bare, uncarpeted surface was the throne of the Emperor.

The throne was bedecked in more of the inevitable gold casing, this of better finished quality than that on the standards. Intricate shapes and designs were imbedded into it to create multipatterned vagaries of indistinct nature. Pictures without real form which were impossible to describe. Gemstones of many colours and shades had been set into the throne to complete a self-perpetuated image of absolute power and control. An image of which the Emperor seemed so pleased.

Rickard's attention came finally to that haughtily imperious example of supreme political control sat squarely in the centre of the oversized throne. His arms were stretched out on the ornate rests, awaiting the visitors' arrival with a smug air of indifferent patience. From the point of view of his guests the Emperor was a moderately built individual, compared to others of his

117

race, and he appeared to bear no distinguishing marks over his greyish-brown physiognomy. The uniform of the standard Imperial trooper in which he was dressed was just as splendidly adorned as his aide's, if not more so because of the quality of various additions. Apart from the spotless yellow band running down across his chest and the over-expansive gold braiding hanging at the right shoulder he wore an unscratched, totally unmarked skull cap which fitted his head to perfection, it being moulded exactly to the contours of his crest. It completed, in Rickard's mind, the picture of an over-bearing, perhaps tyrannical ruler.

As the last of the Service stragglers trailed to a halt at the foot of the dais, Kal Nyr nimbly sprung up the two steps to stand at one of the forward corners. He quickly but respectfully lowered his upper torso with a delicate, well-practised ease in a deep bow before dropping to kneel before his lord and master.

'Your Supreme Highness,' he toadied with shameless obsequiousness. 'The emissaries from beyond the frontier barrier. Here at your most notable bidding.' The Emperor watched motionlessly as Kal Nyr raised himself to his feet and adopted a subservient position to the side of the throne. Then he spoke.

'It comes to Our attention that you have fired upon and severely damaged one of Our warships,' he glowered reprovingly.

Rickard was taken aback by the Emperor's blunt directness and evident pomposity visible to a degree that shattered Kal Nayr's best efforts. Valiantly he gathered himself and plunged in with a suitably direct reply, calculated to either make or break any future discussion plans. 'Your warships fired first and they were unprovoked. I was simply defending my ship and crew as anyone would naturally expect in the face of such an attack. As now is not the time nor the place to begin an opening, of which my superiors hope will be a long and fruitful co-operative alliance, with a difference of opinion. I suggest we defer the matter until a more suitable opportunity arises. Or do you think otherwise?'

The Emperor eyed him carefully, aware of a deeper

level to Rickard's character, a stubborn toughness that would be uncovered if pushed far enough. His deliberately calculating mind searched for and found a suitable strategy, a temporary stopgap designed to prevent the occurrence of a confrontation for a time in order that he bend the Serviceman to his own will. Sliding into the role with the well-practised ease of a professional at the art of behavioural deception, he suddenly mellowed conciliatorily, discernibly softening his approach.

'I do not deny the right of self-defence and I admit the point in your favour. Let no more be said on the matter. Now, it is an unexpected honour to welcome your arrival here. Tell me, I was under the distinct impression that your civilisation, the Allied Grouping and its military arm, the Service Navy, were under immediate threat of extinction. How is it you are able to make such a journey in such adverse conditions?'

Rickard betrayed, and indeed felt, no surprise at the Emperor's informed usage of information relative to the Service. He had already accepted that these people would hold many pieces of the overall picture from their occasional contact with the Larr. He did wonder why Matz Nyr knew nothing of the Grouping but it was probable, considering the nature of the native power structure, that virtually all knowledge was dealt with on a need-to-know basis. Matz Nyr may not have been required to know about the Service, especially as it was justifiably being regarded as a lost cause.

'The conditions are no longer adverse, as I hope to reveal more fully. This can be done during the discussions I would like to hold with you concerning the possibility of setting the basis for peaceful negotiations and trading connections. There is much more besides that to be discussed but those are my main objectives-'

'Objectives that can all be dealt with in due and proper course. In the meantime We would be honoured to offer you and your crew the hospitality of Our Empire and insist most strongly that you stay, in a suitable accommodation which will be provided, until such time as the discussions you request can be undertaken. Kal Nyr will lead you to your accommodation, I am sure you would welcome some rest.'

'I would prefer to talk beforehand over one or two matters that I'm sure will be of great interest to you. There is a great deal to be covered.'

'Of course,' the Emperor replied condescendingly, much as Kal Nyr had done before him. 'There will be ample time in the future. Now is the time to rest after your long and no doubt tiring journey, Kal Nyr...'

Rickard was becoming increasingly frustrated and determinedly refused to be fobbed off quite so easily. 'I would still like to ask,' he persisted forcefully, 'how you and your people came to hold so much of the technology of the Larr and the Grouping when all the contact you claim to have had is with a few scant captured patrol ships? And why do you insist on jamming our signals out of the Belt?'

The air froze, and along with it, every Rukan in the chamber, trooper, noble and merchant alike. The Emperor stared incredulously down at Rickard, utterly astonished at being addressed in such a direct and demanding manner.

There was an expectant pause which seemed to stretch on without end, lasting forever.

The unsurprisingly agitated Service people nervously fingered their holstered weapons. Trepidation was clear on all their faces. Wary troopers loosened their stances in readiness for whatever might happen. The electric atmosphere in the throne room visibly crackled with life as the long seconds wore on. The Emperor was to be treated with respect, even reverence. It was not right in the minds of his subjects that he accept such rudeness from an alien.

Rickard did not break direct eye contact as the Emperor seemingly tried to stare him out. He was irately nonplussed by the monarch's exasperating attitude but unwilling to be intimidated, no matter what the cost. To relent now would be to invite later harrassment from the Emperor's solidly unbreakable personality. He would undoubtedly take any advantage offered and Rickard was not about to allow him this one.

The strong visage of distaste which had enveloped the Emperor's reptilian features vanished unexpectedly and he abruptly relaxed his posture. It appeared he had forgiven Rickard his outburst and had deigned to supply an answer to his question. The positive-charged atmosphere lessened considerably as the troopers around the room eased their action-ready postures. A dangerously inimicable situation had been surmounted, barely.

'Your enemy, the Larr, made frequent expeditions into what We consider to be Our territory and continually caused much mayhem before they were stopped. Once their ship design had been copied successfully the territories of the Empire were extended a hundredfold and innumerable patrols were posted at the boundaries to capture or destroy the vessels of all further incursions. A modest amount of secondary technology, pistols, translators and the like, was also acquired. The main benefits came from the reading of computer memory banks containing files on their and your bases. My people may not be so very advanced by your standards but they are not stupid, Captain. It is that simple. As for the jamming, that will soon cease.'

'Thank you for confiding in me.' Rickard decided he had to be satisfied with the quite plausible answer, although he did not much care for the manner in which it was delivered. Nevertheless, it did explain every item of high technological value they had seen so far even down to the Emperor's unreadiness for *Emputin's* relative invulnerability. If they had captured a Larr ship and read its data banks it was doubtful they would contain anything on the brand new Eagle class ships, a last-minute solution to a previously overwhelming opponent. This was probably as near to the truth as Rickard was likely to get.

'Enough of this for the time.' the Enperor suggested laconically. 'Tempers are becoming frayed and a disagreement would cause both of us to regret the action. Kal Nyr will show you to your city-located residency. You are quite free to invite the rest of your crew to enjoy our hospitality and to wander around the city to your heart's content. You will remain unmolested and free of worry. I shall give audience in due course. Until then, Captain.'

There was no choice but to go along with his assertive invitation. Rickard was a stranger in a foreign land and he had already tried his luck in pushing for his objectives. He had to keep on the Emperor's good side. The people of this world would have no compunction in butchering him and his party at the proverbial drop of their Enperor's hat - of that he was in no doubt. So he reluctantly let himself be led away by Kal Nyr to the secondary palace, the residency which lay beyond the protective palace dome and bordered the Imperial gardens.

This was to be their temporary home.

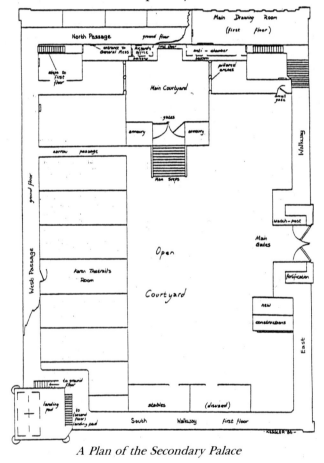

A Plan of the Secondary Palace

6

The residency was minute in scale in comparison with the Emperor's over-lavish abode.

In fact, it was even smaller than that. There was barely room enough to accommodate any sizeable number of Service personnel. Rickard had found he had to organise some kind of rota system to give all his crew equal visiting time on the planet. It had not turned out quite the holiday most had expected but there was a bonus in the singular lack of visible troopers in the vicinity. Nevertheless, it had been ordered that all planetside parties be fully armed. Most carried standard-issue pistols as a precaution, security and Marine teams teams were armed with pulse-firing rifles, their lengthier barrels and generally heavy appearance serving to underline their impressive performance capabilities. Service people ventured out into the city on sightseeing trips or informative gathering missions in large groups to begin with. Then, as no hostile intent was proclaimed by their hosts, the groups dwindled down to twos and threes. In the process, voluminous amounts of computerised literature were built up on the various studying teams' results. More and more was becoming known about the native civilisation all the time, much to Rickard's pleasure. The Rukans were losing their status as an unknown threat.

The residency itself was an entirely different version of its much larger cousin. It was more an open, crumbling brick and mortar assemblage, than a modernised, dome-protected palace. A three metres high stone wall circled and enclosed the entire inner structure. The stones of this shoddy perimeter wall were unevenly placed and, in many places, were actually crumbling away in their decrepitude. Dark, profuse lichen sprouted at its dusty base. Assorted mosses of some local desert varieties crawled steathily upwards over protruding and aging structural decay, groping towards the life-endowing light of the suns.

The dilapidated wall was interrupted in one location by once, but no longer, impressively hefty, slowly rotting, wooden gates. Reaching almost to the height of the wall, the upright beams of the gates were tight-packed together, revealing no spaces in between, lack of solidity notwithstanding. These cumbersome double gates were left open during the long daylight hours as a friendship sign to the natives, none of whom ventured close. At night they were heaved closed and a wooden beam, thick as a man's waist but decidedly less firm, was slid into the eroded metal brackets fixed weakly onto the gates, sealing it as surely as could be managed under the circumstances. A few Marines remained out after that, patrolling the walkways that stretched around three sides of the residency.

Leading off the western passage of the ancient construction, emerging out from underneath the overhanging walkway, were the majority of the living quarters. Smallish rooms were shared by several crew at a time, an effort to allow down as many of them as was possible in one go. At the southern end of the western wall, situated above the walkway, and accessed by a flight of stone steps that were in a better condition that most of the entire remainder of the residency, was something out of fitting with its surroundings. The landing grid was a relatively new attachment to that corner, and it had room - barely - for one launch at a time. Its modern, high-tech style indicated that the residency had undergone some slight modernisation in the not too distant past. It was built so that it leant over the south-west corner, and it was supported by a triad of smoothly plain metal pillars.

To the north were the interior courtyards. They could not even be considered as courtyards in the real sense. Just one rectangular patch of openness in an otherwise overbuilt area. They were separated from the main courtyard by several arches and smaller doors. Above and to the back of these, running to the very edge of the north wall, were the two main drawing rooms. One reached over to the east side, the other towards the west, taking up that entire upper storey section. The easternmost drawing room had been commandeered as the officers' mess; the other, in slightly more unimpressive condition, remained for use as the general mess.

Apart from these few internal constructions there was very little to be seen inside the stone battlements. A low-ceilinged hut on the southern edge had once been a stable for whatever form of haulage animal the planet possessed and was now derelict and abandoned. Two almost new apartment rooms had been put up in the space between the stables and the main gate but these were of such a very shoddy complexion that they were left untouched by the visitors.

At that moment, the main drawing room was playing host to a top level meeting which involved most of *Emputin's* principal officers.

The participants of the meeting were seated on worn, fading lounge sofas placed against the elaborately painted but faded walls. The decorations were rounded off by browning, hanging vines, sprouting from circular pots that reached down from the high ceiling. A thick pile carpet stretched the length of the considerable room and items of wooden furniture, darkly polished but scratched tables and chairs, filled the far end. Tall, unopenable plate-glass windows along two of the walls allowed a fair amount of light to filter in, but the twin suns arched their way across the opposite side of the sky so the plushly furnished room was never directly lit, a mercy for which the Service people were eternally thankful. The luxury, however aged, with which the room was adorned helped create stifling temperatures towards midday, the time in which the room was most ardently avoided. This would not have been helped by the heated brilliance of the sun shining in at full blast.

The officers' meeting, a deliberation upon the complete trustworthiness of their hosts, had lasted for some time and was only now drawing to a conclusion with Rickard ending his own voiced opinions.

'...And although I've not managed to see the Emperor since our first meeting I still think we can trust them, at least for the present,' he finished.

'Are you completely confident on that score?' Beck queried, remaining openly doubtful about Imperial motives. 'Our communications are still being jammed. Alpheratz remains unreachable. You didn't come out of the first meeting with the Emperor too well, and getting a rematch out of Kal Nyr is like trying to punch your way out of a plastic bag using your eyelids, you have to be downright persistent and it's still virtually impossible. I apologise for the comical analogy but it happens to be correct.' There were agreeing murmurs from around the room. 'There have been instances, things. I'm not sure what. Some people are becoming a little worried. These Rukans are outwardly very friendly and pleasant but there's something they are hiding, some...inimicable resentment. I'm afraid I can't quite adequately describe it but it is there, barely hidden under the surface. I think most of us have seen it.'

'I understand how you feel but think of my position in all this. I have to establish an air of co-operation between the two races. I have to ignore vague suspicions and popular beliefs for the success of the mission. We have to trust them. It's all I can suggest for the time being. We have to trust them and hope in time they'll trust us so we can work together. We can't allow irrationalities to carry us away from that task.'

'So how much freedom will you give our people down here?'

'As much as they are allowed by the Emperor. We've encountered no real hardship yet, have we?'

'I suppose not,' Beck conceded reluctantly. 'You know I'm against the small parties venturing out at the moment. I'd rather see groups of ten or more at least. Nevertheless, I realise that your point is valid. There has been nothing concrete to indicate that the Rukan people in general have been anything but friendly once the mistake at the Belt had been rectified.'

Rickard saw that the usually jovial surgeon had relented his stand. He was the last to hold to his views as,

126

one by one, Rickard had broken down the arguments against the free mixing of the two races. 'I was ordered to make contact, socially as well as militarily, and make contact I have. The trick is in continuing that contact. It's going to be extremely hard if large, possibly menacing groups went out. That's why I'm all in favour of smaller parties. Please don't hold it against me, Doc.'

'How could I? I can see the basis of your argument and that's enough. Subject closed in my book.'

Rickard did not bother to voice his own worries about the situation. He had been unable to pay the Emperor a return visit in the six slightly longer local days for which they had been there. As Beck had stated, the main barrier, the hurdle over which he had failed to jump, was Kal Nyr who seemed to be continually blocking his way. He could not as yet comprehend why, and that troubled him. If something were being planned against them then he wished he could discover what it was.

He also desperately wished he could confide in someone. But who? Beck? Kiyami? Who would understand the convoluted way in which his mind worked, the problem his worrier-type nature brought him? Better to leave things be for now. God, what he wouldn't do right now for a quiet life.

'Well,' he breathed tentatively. 'I'm glad we have that sorted. I can now call the meeting to a close.'

Scattered sighs of relief broke through the room and the group split into separate gatherings, each conversing on recent experiences and the meeting itself. Rickard joined Beck as the others drifted off. 'I hope you won't hold anything against me?' he enquired amiably.

'Of course not,' Beck grinned. 'You had a fair case to drive at and I see its merits. So, no hard feelings, eh? At least the comestibles here are worth looking forward to.'

'So I've heard. Hey, how would you like to join me on my first look around town since we arrived?'

'Now?'

'Why not?' Rickard shrugged. 'There's no time like the present.'

Karen, who had been sitting at the rear of the assembled group in her capacity as official observer, came

over to Rickard. 'That was a nice speech, Chris. You had
'em in the palm of your hand. I think you're doing a great
job,' she smiled broadly, her indomitability lighting
Rickard's spirit.

'I'll have no cheek from you, just because you're the
Admiral's daughter,' he lightly returned.

'I know you don't really mean that so I'll forgive you
this once. I was thinking. You haven't been out of this
scruffy, run-down hole-in-the-mud for days and I want to
go lookabouts so...?'

'I'm way ahead of you on that one.'

'Then I don't have to continue. Will you come as well,
Phil?' she asked Beck.

He glanced almost casually at Rickard. Two's company,
and so on, he thought. He did not want to play
gooseberry in their obviously intimate company. But he
saw that Rickard did not mind. Seeing it was fine to agree,
he did so. 'Okay. As it's you who asked, yes. I will come.'

'Can we leave now?'

'I don't see why not. Wouldn't you like to be armed, just
as a precaution?'

Karen deferred. 'Why would I need a gun when I've
two big, strong men to protect me. Anyway, there's a
much more sensible reason; I'm no good with weapons.
I'd probably shoot my foot off if I tried to use one.'

'Perhaps you're right,' Rickard nodded.

'Hey. You're not supposed to agree!'

'Come on you two,' interjected Beck. 'Let's move out
before the suns go down.'

Already out in the city was Howarth who had skipped the
officers' meeting. He did not really care one way or the
other what was decided as he doubted he could do much
to influence the decision, especially as the captain
probably disliked him intensely after his previous
behaviour. Besides, he was still not completely certain
about the man. Sure, he had made a couple of good

128

moves, the asteroid belt for one, but that was not entirely enough for Howarth's overcautious nature. He would doubtlessly get used to Rickard in time but it did not do in his book to rush these matters.

Having seen to his duties in arranging the rota of guards in various positions around the residency he had decided it was time he took a closer look at the natives and, along with the unarmoured Stuart and Bernerds whom he had met at the main gates, had commenced to examine the central area of the city.

The threesome arrived at the high doors of the city's church.

'It doesn't look much like any church I've been to,' Bernerds sourly observed.

Howarth gave him an impatient glance. 'I can't see you as the type to visit many churches, wherever they are,' he said. He often found the middie's distant manner unsettling and wondered why Stuart stuck around with him so much. 'All races have their own different ideas of architectural style,' he added. 'This one is just a bit more...unusual.'

'You're not bloody wrong.'

It was not that the building itself was out of character in any general way with any of thousands of others on a wide number of planets spread from boundary to boundary of the Grouping. It was what was suspended above the doors, something that had been erected since the original landing party had passed this way. It was the object in point that endowed the thing its air of unusuality.

On a large, five-pointed star background plate was a figure, attached, by variously placed nails and bindings which on the whole had seemed to have badly damaged the sufferer's flesh, to a solid three-dimensional block. The subject had apparently died in a rather unsavoury position and in great pain, a scene with which anyone of the Grouping would be instantly familiar. What was unusual to the observers about the carving was the fact that the figure was a Rukan, rather than a human, martyr.

'Their religion looks like it shares a common background with one of our own,' Stuart observed.

129

'Except they got some of the finer details wrong.'
Bernerds added.

'Many beliefs hold a similar story,' Howarth pointed out
knowledgeably. 'Over a hundred non-colonist worlds
have been found to have some variant on the same story.'

'Yeah?' Bernerds grumbled. 'Well it still looks
unnatural to me.'

'I don't care what it looks to you, Bernerds.'

'Whatever you say, boss,' the middie cheekily returned.

Howarth ignored him and entered the church, pushing
past the heavy door. A dark, empty void presented itself
behind the threshold, a veil of inner concealment through
which the security chief gingerly stepped.

Stuart grinned at Howarth's inevitable reaction to
Bernerds' intransigence. 'Stick with it, Pete. I think he
likes you.'

Bernerds gave a grunt of long-suffering dissatisfaction
and trailed after his amused companion as she slipped
through the narrow gap between the doors.

The deeply shadowed interior of the church belied its
superficially congenial appearance. Apart from the fact
that it looked at least three times larger on the inside than
it did outside, it was extremely sparsely ornamented,
showing a remarkably unattractive starkness considering
its unquestionable status in the minds of the natives.
Plain, unmarked stone columns reached up towards the
incredibly distant ceiling, to lock into faintly visible
horizontal support beams which disappeared into the
walls. Below, row upon row of long, uncomfortably
hard-surfaced benches filled much of the floor space,
leading almost up to the very edge of the altar. This were
bathed in a diffused halo of light that descended from a
concealed opening in the roof, and it created an inspiring
sense of awe in the watchers. There were no windows,
stained-glass or otherwise, to be seen in the building and
there was no light save that from the altar to illuminate
the interior, a point that seemed slightly strange to Stuart
as she noiselessly edged down one of the side-aisles almost
blind in the near-blackness, leaving the others at the
doorway.

There was a slight scattering of citizenry seated alone or

in small groups around the many pews, their heads bent low in silent prayer. There they remained, peacefully oblivious to the newcomers until Stuart accidentally bumped one of the pews, causing it to wobble unsteadily. Then they turned as one in a single wave of sudden motion, and they stared unwaveringly with malign animosity in her direction, and their eyes held an unspoken menace that suffused, in its sublime extremity, throughout the enclosed, stifling tense environment of the church. It filled the Service people with irrational foreboding.

First of all she assumed that it was merely because they had trespassed in a very private place. But she quickly dismissed that idea and replaced it with a more nagging suspicion. She started backing up, heading for the doors, unease mounting, pacing slowly as if she were retreating from a wild, man-eating animal that had caught her unawares. Fearless as she usually made herself out to be, it took all her willpower not to bolt and run. She was extremely relieved to escape back to the relieving warmth outside, back into the bright sunlight. Bernerds hurriedly preceded her and Howarth followed after, at a noticeably quicker pace than he'd entered the church with.

'Christ!' Stuart breathed, feeling unnaturally shaken. 'Did you feel the atmosphere in there?'

'I couldn't bloody miss it,' Howarth admitted, visibly disquietened. 'Somehow I don't think our freedom of the city included the church. It must be very important to them, considering the way they acted in there.'

'There was that, yeah. But it was more than that, more as if they didn't have to hide their real emotions. They showed what they really felt. There was an open hostility in there...and it scared the shit out of me,' she ineloquently added.

'That's a load of rubbish,' Bernerds rudely cut in. 'They just didn't want us in there, that's all. There's no big flippin' mystery.'

The middie's abrasive manner brought Howarth sharply back to his normal self and that self objected to Bernerds' curt dismissal of his own disconcerted feelings.

131

'It might not have occurred to you, Midshipman,' he said coldly, 'but some people find your lack of objectivity and senselessness bloody repellent at times. I find the greatest pleasure in telling you that you are the thickest piece of garbage I have ever had the misfortune to come across.'

Bernerds gaped in undisguised astonishment.

'You two are going to have to continue without me. I have a bar to visit.' He abruptly headed off at a brisk pace for the public barhouse on the corner opposite, distinctly annoyed at Bernerds, but more surprised at himself for his uncharacteristic usage of Bentowski's very distinct lingo in his own knock-down verbalization.

With an expression of genuine surprise on his face, Bernerds wondered incredulously; 'What did I say?'

'Look, Bernerds. I know you are always saying things in a way that everyone else often takes offensively and I know you don't really mean it, but I have the slightest feeling you put your foot in it again.'

'You'd think people would learn not to be so friggin' touchy!'

'Like everybody keeps saying, don't worry about it.'

Before they could leave the downtrodden residency on their own tour of the city, Rickard and his two companions were called back to the main courtyard by an apologetic Kiyami who had to clear some relatively unimportant minor matter with him. It turned out to be pleasantly easy to deal with but nevertheless required the captain's personal attention. Once done, Rickard took the opportunity to raise a more pressing topic of his own, feeling rather insistent about the subject.

'I'd like you to get hold of Kal Nyr for me,' he asked. 'I haven't been able to see the Emperor since that first time and I don't like the way I keep being put off. See if you can arrange something okay?'

'Yes, I'll try to find where he could be, but that may present a difficult problem.'

'I know. It's like looking for one particular pebble on a very large beach, but I'm sure he's around somewhere. Send out search parties if you have to. Just have him here, please. I should be back pretty soon so have him waiting for me.'

'I will do my best.'

Rickard rejoined Karen and Beck and they continued on, heading for the bustling crowds beyond the narrow reaches of sand-encrusted grounds.

'Are you by chance having any trouble?' Beck raised an eyebrow, ever suspicious of Rukan motives.

'Not at all. At least, nothing I can't handle - once I get my hands on Kal Nyr.'

Karen glanced away from her sightseeing, frowning. 'Shouldn't he be on hand all the time to see to our needs?'

'He should be. Unfortunately he's not, and that doesn't make my job any easier. It also doesn't do my ulcer such good,' he diversified.

'You don't have an ulcer.'

'I will have at this rate. Anyway, you know what I mean. Don't worry, I'll get the little weasel in the end. The hero inevitably comes out on top, so say all the best stories.'

'This isn't a story, this is the real product. Anything could happen. And will you please stop telling me not to worry. I've done nothing but worry since this mission started.'

'Hey. It was your fantastically smart idea to come along, remember.'

'And I wouldn't miss it for the world, whichever one we happen to be on.' She slipped an arm through his and pulled close to him.

Rickard was unsurprised to find that he did not care at present whether any of his crew saw him this way with the official observer. Let them see. Let them even stare, he thought rebelliously. He didn't give a damn! He was only as human as the rest of them, although he did not expect them to agree to that prospect. Why bother to hide what he felt for Karen? Why not do what almost every other crewmember seemed to be thinking about these days?

'There seems to be an awful lot of traffic in this direction,' an unusually non-garrulous Beck observed,

133

opting on a wistful twinge to change the subject. He gestured towards the widely expansive number of cityfolk, all moving monodirectionally, all dressed from head to foot in bright, gaudy yellow, the first sighting the visitors had made of this shade of colour on a world normally hidden under monotonous greys, browns and whites.

'Yes, it is busy. I wonder what for?' Karen stared on inquisitively at the strangely robed natives.

'Perhaps they're going to some sort of pageant?' Beck suggested.

'Why don't we follow them and see for ourselves?'

They both looked to Rickard for acceptance and he shrugged in agreement. 'Why not. One direction is as good as any other, I suppose.'

They set off after the unusually dressed, thickly bustling crowd, quickly merging with the thronging masses. They shortly noticed every one of the yellow-attired natives was chanting some unintelligible line, a ceaselessly chanted phrase that they repeated over and over, under their quickened breaths.

☆ ☆ ☆

Following their chief's departure, Stuart and Bernerds had drifted over to the market place seen earlier when they had first arrived. They had wandered into the very thickest part of the jumbled conglomeration of stalls, trying in vain not to become overwhelmed by the shouting, bawling voices of the stall-holders advertising their wares all of which, according to the extravagant pitches, were far better in their superbly crafted workmanship than anything available elsewhere in the city.

While being jostled and pushed by the crowds, and continually brushing back her dark hair, which she was wearing loose, Stuart attempted to examine as many of the small, closely packed stalls as she could. She found the whole atmosphere of the market exciting and breathlessly exhilarating. It reminded her of home. As a child she played in busy markets very similar to this in content and, although the goods for sale were markedly different, the general feeling remained the same.

Conversely, Bernerds was thoroughly bored by the affair. He was utterly fed up with having to struggle to keep his feet and found the place completely deleterious - literally. He was sorely tempted to grab the next shopper who pushed him, and shove his fist down the native's throat. He sorely wished these pathetically primitive people would invent for themselves the all-in-one shopping precincts that he was used to, instead of cramming everything together in a idiotically narrow side street so a person could not move without knocking his neighbour flying. The one item that continually annoyed him more than any other was the vile concoction of alien odours that drifted over the area. He thought it sickeningly disgusting, such was its intensity. He valiantly tried to keep an air of calm aloofness about him as he waited for Stuart to tire of her exploration.

The senior middie, however, had a more pressing matter on her mind. She continued to worry over the incident in the church. Gazing rather distantly at the faces of passing shoppers, not directly seeing the market any more, she replayed the events in her mind over and over, always trying to work out what really happened, what the silent worshippers really meant by their stares. Not a worrier by nature she nevertheless continued to puzzle over the matter. A far-away expression clouded her petite features for an instant before reality returned and she was back in the market place.

'Come on.' Bernerds suddenly bellowed in her ear, overemphasising the need to raise his voice for the sake of effect. 'Get a move on, Stuart. This boring place is starting to get on my nerves.'

Wincing at the extra-loud noise, she glared at him before turning serious. 'Bernerds, I was thinking about the church. I still ain't sure why they stared at us like that.'

Taking a moment to understand her above the din, he finally worked out what she had said. 'Don't talk rubbish, I told you to forget it. They were just peeved at us.'

'I don't know. It seems strange, that's all. It gets even stranger the more I think about it.'

'So don't think about it.'

'Something's not right about this place. This whole set-up *feels* bad. It feels as if something bad is going to occur. I don't know how or why, it's just this feeling I kept getting. It's like there are black clouds hanging over everyone, a kind darkness that feels like it's threatening all of us. Nothing here feels right but I can't see what's wrong,' she confided with ominous presentment, looking around at the unnoticing expressions of milling shoppers as they clamoured for custom, the talking, crowding, shouting, oppressive, *alien* faces pressing in on her. 'Unless...'

'Shut up, Stuart. For Christ's sake give it a rest, will you? I've never heard you talk such junk. Relax. Try to enjoy yourself.'

Stuart saw how her frightened suspicions must seem to the darkly pragmatic Bernerds so she put them aside, placing them carefully away to be reviewed at a later date. 'You're right, Pete. I should try to relax more,' she admitted sheepishly.

'That's more like the Stuart I know. Now let's get out of this bloody market before I commit murder.' He moved off, leading the way to the central concourse.

A disturbance ahead, a sudden flurry of movement, caught Stuart's eye and she pulled on Bernerds' arm, drawing him to a halt. He threw her a questioning glance and she indicated to what had caught her attention. A trooper came into view over the bobbing heads of the crowd, shouting and cursing at the bemused onlookers to clear the way, pushing and shoving those who did not. One stubborn elderly citizen shook his head at the trooper, emphatically refusing to be waved aside. The short-tempered trooper raised a fist and callously clubbed the offender to the ground, kicking the barely moving form away from the central passage before subservient bystanders quickly scooped him to safety, removing the cause of the trooper's loss of temper so that he could continue on with his task, still shouting for space.

Into the cleared area came a bejewelled palanquin

bedecked in wildly splendiferous colours and trimmings arranged in a very ostentatious, very showy way designed basically to impress the populace. It was being carried by four struggling manservants, one at each corner. Their ridged, reptilian faces were heavily beaded with sweat, deftly confirming to the human watchers that, although they might look something like reptiles, that was something these people were most definitely not. Set upon the palanquin, seated sprawled out on a low-set ornamental chair, was an official clearly of high-ranking to judge by his manner of clothing. The immaculate robing draped over his broad shoulders was a pale, ochrish-yellow, on it in a tidy arrangement were his badges and braiding, revealing him to be one of the very highest in the native hierarchy.

Trying to become one with the rest of the crowd, Stuart and Bernerds stepped back, moving to the cover of a nearby stall. Their bright, red and black uniforms stood out starkly against the drab colours of the shoppers, making them implicitly more noticeable.

As the palanquin drew level with them the official, breaking his impassive dead-ahead stare glared directly down at the normally tough Stuart, his narrowing eyes implying menace of such magnitude that it sent a shiver of fear running along her spine. The eye-contact lasted but a moment and then the official was gone and the crowd surged in to fill the gap left by his passing.

'Must be some party he's going to,' Bernerds commented dully before he became aware of Stuart's staring eyes, looking disproportionately wide on her darkly framed delicate face as she followed the disappearing palanquin. 'What's wrong?'

Stuart took a moment to recover and when she finally did so she could only manage to speak in a low, tightly tremble. 'I'm scared, Bernerds,' she murmured. 'I'm scared for all of us. I hate to admit to it I'm scared shitless.'

'Don't start that again,' groaned Bernerds, although this time he felt a restraint. He could see that *something* had badly shaken his close friend and companion and he wondered what could be the cause of such a rare

137

occurrence.

☆ ☆ ☆

In a close-by part of the city, on the corner of a well-frequented public thoroughfare, there was a compact, plushly decorated bar of obvious high-repute, going by the quality of most of its customers. The bar, its many windows sheltered from the suns by deep red overhanging canopies, possessed a cavernous, dimly lit interior which hid all manner of weird and wonderful patrons. It was a pleasantly surprising and uncanny sophistication in such a normally basic location. Outside in the smoke-free open air, seated on twin wood stools at a low, rounded table, were two of *Emputin's* bridge officers, Howarth and Bentowski, one of the ship's so-called inseparable duos.

The table was too low to be completely comfortable to any sane man but Howarth was not planning on staying long. Bentowski had been there for some time, sampling and tasting the local produce and finding it fully equal in strength to anything back home, if a touch more solidified.

'...So the boss said to me,' Bentowski was relating to Howarth, 'he said, "Ask him to leave, politely". So I said, in my best polite manner, "Okay, assface. Get your slimy butt outta here before I turn it into cream cheese!" You shoulda seen the look on the guy's face. I never saw anyone go as white as that in my life.'

Though his eyes were alcohol-reddened, an almost sober Bentowski was managing to communicate with surprising clarity.

'It was a helluva hoot.'

'It sounds it,' Howarth said.

'Yeah,' Bentowski gazed into his drink and spotted something swimming there. 'Can I ask you a question, Thom?' he asked, fishing out the drowning insect and flicking it at a passer-by.

'I suppose so. As long as it's nothing too personal.'

138

Howarth looked up over his own glass of thick brown semi-liquid.

'Why did you join up?'

'It's too personal. It's also a long story, one you do not want to hear.'

'No. Come on, tell.'

'Nah. Maybe another time, eh?'

'Well,' Bentowski huffishly pondered on it, 'okay. Seeing as you won't provide the entertainment I guess I'll have to improvise. Although why you should want to be *so* stuffy and mean about it, I can't imagine. I mean, it's certainly no big deal.'

'Stop moaning.'

'Well it's gotta be better than a poke in the eye with a sharp stick.'

'I've never had a poke in the eye with a sharp stick.'

'It can be arranged.'

'Don't you ever stop joking around?' Howarth said, sipping at his drink of sludge.

'Not if I can help it. It's a physical defect. I think my mother had my sour-face glands removed at birth.'

'See what I mean? How come I always end up playing straight man to your comedian?'

'You're too straightlaced. Loosen up a little, it's more fun.'

'Don't try that stuff on me, Bentowski. I know you too well to believe you really talk that way.'

'That's cool. I can relate to your opinion,' he smiled annoyingly.

'Oh, good grief.'

'All right. I'll stop,' Bentowski relented good-humouredly.

'Thank God for that. Do you know. I'm even starting to find myself copying you. I come out with just the sort of junk you keep spouting. It's like a bad disease. Once you've been near it you automatically catch it, and I'm infected.'

'There's nothing wrong in that.'

'That's what you think. I only hope I don't start doing it on the bridge, especially not the way you carry on. I'm surprised you get away with it.'

139

'I'm not. The Captain's a good guy. He don't mind.'

'I don't know if I fully agree with that, yet.'

'What? About the Captain?' Bentowski was surprised.

'Yes. You know me well enough by now.'

'I sure do. You're the most suspicious, untrusting sonofabitch I ever met.'

'Exactly. But that's why I'm Head of Security and you're not.'

'Point taken. I wonder if my credit's good for another bottle of slime.' He eyed the darkened interior of the bar, looking for service.

'You mean you're still drinking that stuff?'

'Sure am, pard,' the helmsman replied in his best imitation wild west accent.

'It's no good for you, you know?'

'Oh, crap. 'Course it is.'

'You're mad. How can that...*gunge* be any good at all for your insides?'

'It can't make them any worse than they already are. Of course it's okay.'

'Of course it is not.'

'Yes it is.'

'It is not.'

'Ooh yes it is.'

'It's bloody not, for chrisake!'

'Well, *excuse* me!'

'Y'know, you may not be the brightest, most sensible pillock I've ever known, but you have to be classed as either the bravest or the most stupid.'

'Ah, compliments. You're so kind.'

Following the flocking crowds, Rickard, Karen and Beck were led to a stone-walled amphitheatre.

Though the faded colouring of the stone led Rickard to believe the amphitheatre was very old, its cleanness belied the supposition. Not a scrap of lichen, moss or weed had been allowed to take root along the tended base of the great stepped walls and there was virtually no outward sign of decay - the precise opposite to the condition of the walls of the residency. This much more awesome structure was built of large, smoothly placed, solid stone blocks, free from any unsightly roughness or projections so that they joined as if moulded together, the edges of each separate stone mixing and fusing at the join. The only visible breakage in the vast monotonous expanse of grey was an ominously dark tunnel yawning out from the even surface like a blackly gaping maw. It was into this entrance that the stream of yellow-robed citizens were disappearing.

'Should we go down there?' Karen asked her companion as the threesome drew to a halt to one side of the busy entrance.

'I'm not sure,' Rickard said. He didn't think so. It wouldn't be wise to go on. Their safety among so many natives was not wholly guaranteed. 'What do you think is going on?'

Beck repeated his earlier suggestion. 'It has to be some kind of ceremony, judging by their clothing.'

'We can't cause much harm if we do go in, can we?' argued Karen.

'I suppose not.'

'The Emperor did say we could go anywhere.'

'He did, didn't he?'

'All right,' relented Rickard. Safety or not, he'd lost his vote. 'You win. In we go.'

'What an excellent idea,' Beck said chirpily.

Karen tightened her hold on Rickard's arm as they descended into the hustling crowd, and were caught up in the flow of bodies. The people seemed not to mind the presence of the visitors. In fact, they gleefully welcomed their participation in the event, shouting and laughing with remarkably unrestrained openness. Whatever was happening, it was important to them, that much was clear, and the more who attended the merrier. They moved into the unlit tunnel.

After what felt like an age the snaking twisting tunnel finally ended, emerging into the bowl-shaped circular interior and the breathtaking heat of mid-afternoon.

Rickard came to a halt, glancing upwards. The high suns were only now beginning to lower themselves from the crown of their orbit across the deep blue sky, and the temperature was still shockingly intense. The marginally heavier than normal gravity did nothing to relieve his feeling of discomfort. Heat rippled over stone. The air was dry as dust, catching in his throat. He cast his eyes earthward, taking in the scene before him.

The interior of the amphitheatre belied its outward appearance, from the outside it looked only over-large. On the inside it looked positively gargantuan. Ringed around the comparatively inconspicuous arena-like sandy centre area, a solid stone catafalque placed in the very middle, were tier upon amassed tier of seats, in reality nothing more than worn rows of raised stone, each reaching a little further towards the heavens up to the final ring, perched right back against the exterior wall. There were three other entrances to the stadium, one positioned for each quarter of the seating space, and wave after wave of native citizenry was pouring out of each of them, filling the vastness of the entire amphitheatre. All were talking, laughing, shouting and yelling to each other in a tremendous cacophony that made the ears of the gawping visitors ring. In a privately reserved box halfway up on the opposite side a well-dressed official in the robes of a master aide luxuriated in blank-faced impassiveness upon a richly jewelled palanquin, surrounding servitors attending him.

Rickard wisely decided to move away from the busy entrance and, keeping firm hold on Karen, proceeded to push a laboured pathway through the swaying, ever-mobile crowds to reach a small clearing in the maze of unsettling natives. Beck, huffing and puffing at the undue exertion required for him to reach this point, eventually managed to catch up.

'What in God's name are they so excited about?' he cried breathlessly over the din.

All of a sudden the crowds filled out, taking up any remaining space, and ceased milling about. A huge tense hush began to fall.

'I don't think we'll have to wait any longer to find out,'

Rickard shouted his reply and pointed downwards to the oval shaped arena.

The others followed the direction of his indication, from a previously unseen entrance tunnel, under the front row of seating, came a single figure, black robed with skull crest gleaming magnificently. He stepped over to the centre of the arena and raised his arms high in supplication, calling for peace. A majority of the assembled audience had also spotted the new arrival, so small and distant, and they quietened their neighbours. The lowered babble of conversation slowly abated until there fell an expectant hush. The silence was almost painful after the ear shattering level of sound before, such was its intensity. The noiseless onlookers eagerly awaited the lone figure's words.

Finally he spoke. He raised his voluminous baritone voice to echo resoundingly, making himself heard through the entire amphitheatre. 'Citizens. She has come. The ceremony will proceed!' Those few, bare words conjured an amazing effect upon the audience. They boisterously cheered and waved and whistled their united appreciation before quietening down to a semblance of calmness.

Down below, in the stage-like arena, the figure waved to someone out of sight and a procession slowly emerged into the harsh sunlight. At its head, borne by six powerfully muscled bearers, was a coffin of polished oakwood with a reflective metallic plaque centered on the upper half of its topmost surface. The bearers were adorned in spotless flowing yellow robes which hung to the ground, leaving a faint trail of disturbed sand in their wake. Their big hands were encased in tight fitting yellow gloves. They carried the coffin with unwavering reverence to the centre of the arena and gently positioned it on the catafalque, leaving it thus raised almost to head height.

Next onto the stage came a clustered group of young females carrying in their hands bunches of many leaved pale yellow flowers of a kind indigenous to the planet. These they delicately placed around the edge of the coffin, completing an unbroken borderline with a

143

particular garish grouping edged around the reflective plaque.

The human visitors in the audience looked on in realisation as Beck mouthed the words they had all been thinking. 'It's a funeral.'

Rickard was just about to add further to that but the glares of sudden annoyance from bystanders held him to silence. This was obviously a very important occasion to the city's inhabitants.

A second party of bearers, also dressed in the now expected yellow robes, came into view hauling between them a hefty, rectangular shaped stone block. The block was ponderously lowered from aching shoulders with the aid of the first party of bearers, and the awkward task was completed with comparative ease. The weighty block was stood upright, placed equidistantly between the coffin and the tunnel.

Rickard stared more closely at the shaped chunk of stone. He discovered there were red markings on both its visible sides, or more clearly, hand-prints. The prints of several different right hands were picked out in red dye and were lined in rows of four, with one side of the stone completed. Whatever this ceremony was it had occurred more than once before judging by the amount of prints on the block. It couldn't simply be a straight forward burial or mourning. There had to be more to it than that.

There was.

Next to emerge from the arena entrance in the morbidly executed obsequies was a large procession of chanting mourners. At the head, clearly recognizable in their priestly robes, were two members of whatever religious group the people supported. Walking side by side they swung tubular flasks gently to and fro, all the while emitting thick clouds of vaporous smoke from the open tops which rapidly wafted into the entranced audience as the slight breeze caught it. A portion of the smoke blew in Rickard's direction and he struggled to stifle a choke as the noxious cloud drifted past his face. The effect on the audience nearby was completely contrary. They greedily sniffed in the foul odour as it reached them and were overcome with ecstatic sighs of fulfilment. Karen glanced up at Rickard, her usually healthy tanned features pale. She gave him an expression of disgust at the smell but said nothing to damage the hushed silence that surrounded them.

Close behind the priests, following their trail, was a female of high position, if one could tell such a thing by quality of clothing. Over the inevitable yellow robing she wore a thin but colourful garland of flowers hanging from her neck. She was covered in an array of rich jewellery, great mounds of necklaces were draped under the drooping garland, and copious numbers of bangles and bracelets covered the lower parts of her arms, jangling loudly whenever she moved. Her dark feet were bare, leaving well-defined footprints in the sand behind her.

After her, there were a great many more mourners, presumably family relations of the deceased, all carrying their own small bunches of the yellow, many-petalled flowers in their clasped hands. As the lone woman reached the stone block and drew to a halt besides it, the rest of the cortége gathered around her in a tight semi-circle.

One of the priests produced from the deep folds of his robes a metal rectangular box of shallow depth. He prised open the lid to show to the cortége and the audience the red dye present therein, before lowering it and allowing the woman to press her right hand hard into the dye. She then withdrew her hand and positioned it carefully on the space next in line to be used on the block. After holding it in place for a long moment to complete the marking, she lethargically pulled back. Her hand print was there on the block for all to see. She had joined the ranks of those privileged enough to be bestowed this great honour, and the audience gave a polite cheer to show their gratitude at being allowed to witness the event.

The second priest now came forward and led the woman by the arm until she stood beside the coffin, beside a wooden step placed against the catafalque. She commenced handing over to the priest all of her resplendent jewellery, valuable piece by piece, until all that remained in her possession was the wilting garland.

Even this she had to remove, putting it over the plaque on the coffin and, using the wooden step provided, climbing up after it, sitting herself down at the opposite end. She joined both hands tightly together and began a low penetrating chant which the enrapt audience took up until the entire amphitheatre was filled with the unearthly, strangely undulating sound.

A party of black-robed youngsters suddenly entered the stage below on which this drama was being enacted, carrying in their arms copious bundles of wood, chopped straight and thin. The funeral cortége, in its circular surrounding of the coffin mound, made way for the new arrivals who began piling wood at the base of the catafalque, spreading and stacking it thickly so that no gaps remained. Then one of their number stepped forward to thoroughly douse it in a thick, effluent liquid. The woman on the coffin dully and dutifully continued her ritual chanting. The audience joyfully joined her.

'It's strange,' Beck murmured, 'But for a desert planet with so few trees there seems to be an awful lot of wood around.'

'I don't like the look of the way this is going,' Rickard mumbled to Karen.

A torch bearer approached the wood pile. After one of the priests had mouthed some few ceremonial words, the bearer lowered his torch and set the wood alight. Rickard looked on in mounting horror as the flames reared up, engulfing the coffin with startling rapidity. The woman in the midst of the roaring circle of fire suddenly broke out of her dream-like daze as the fire licked eagerly at her clothes, and had time for one long, endlessly drawn out wavering scream before she succumbed to the smoke, collapsing limply, toppling forward to lie spread-eagled across the coffin. The hungry flames gorged themselves on the remains upon the mound.

'Oh, God!' Karen cried in horror as the audience rose up in a loudly spontaneous cheer of approval. She quickly turned her face from the scene below, grabbing a hard hold on a shaken Rickard.

Beck licked his lips spasmodically, not averting his gaze. 'I don't think it was such a good idea to come in after all,'

146

he uttered hoarsely.

Recovering from his shock, Rickard found his voice. 'Beck, come on. Let's get out of here.'

Leading Karen along he found the way to the exit, pushing roughly past anyone who was unfortunate enough to get in his way. A few angry looks in his direction did nothing to dispel his mood.

Once outside the amphitheatre and its grim display, he slowed his pace to allow Beck to catch up. Easing Karen off his arm he made certain that she was recovered, staring into alluring eyes now darkened by the events. 'Are you okay?' he asked softly.

She managed a slight smile, nodding. 'I've got over the actual shock of seeing someone burned alive in front of my eyes. I feel a bit more emotionally steady now.'

Beck read Rickard's thoughts and tried placating him. 'There was nothing you could do to stop that you know.'

'Wasn't there?' Rickard snapped vehemently.

Beck shook his head firmly. 'No, even if you did manage somehow to get past all the mourners, the priests, the bearers and the troopers and actually disturb the proceedings, your victory would have been very short lived. The crowd would have ripped you apart for spoiling their day. You wouldn't have stood a snowball's chance in hell.'

Sighing heavily Rickard gave in. 'I suppose you're right, as usual,' he admitted.

'Course I am,' Beck grinned.

'But why the hell would they do something so barbaric?'

'Actually, it bears remarkable similarity to an ancient Earth custom known as a *Suttee*.' Beck declared, his historical interest helping him relate the information. 'As far as I know it was common practice in India up to the mid-eighteenth century when the arrival of the British caused its gradual extinction. The locals thought great honour was bestowed upon them if they attended the ceremony where the wife of a dead ruler would accompany her husband to the flames. They felt it would bring them favour with their god, though it seems here to be no more the exercise of the upper classes as a whole rather than simply the prerogative of the ruler and master. It was a long time ago that it all happened on Earth. I can't imagine how these people know of it.'

'Well it seems common enough here.' Rickard wearily tousled his hair, feeling in no mood for a history lesson, informative or not.

'Remember what you said. We are strangers in a foreign land. Alien customs and all that.'

'Can we just forget that it ever happened?' Karen said plaintively. 'I only want to get back to the residency for a while.'

'Yes,' agreed Beck. 'I think that might be wise, after all, it is getting a little late. That ceremony lasted a surprisingly long time.'

'That's fine by me. I'm in the right mood now to deal with the slippery Kal Nyr so the sooner we get back the better.' Rickard declared. The threesome tiredly moved off.

Elsewhere inside the great amphitheatre, sitting alone and quiet amongst the plangent sounds reverberating mournfully about, was Kirsten Stuart. She had watched stoney-faced as the woman had burned in the fire with her husband's body, and had witnessed the abrupt departure of her captain and his companions, their service uniforms and the observer's bright clothing standing boldly out from the sea of yellow.

The fire was dying down now, the charred embers no longer containing anything combustible, and the audience gradually departed, excitedly passing comments on what an excellent service it had been and how well the woman had died. These were a strange people, Stuart mused inwardly. One moment they could be unnaturally hostile, the next full of sweetness and light. She was not too sure if a permanent embassy here, something which would be a necessity if relations were forged between the Empire and the grouping, would be such a good idea. The people were too unreliable in their outlook and were about as emotionally steady as the reeds in the wind.

She could be wrong. They might make perfect neighbours. But she doubted it.

7

505.99.39

Rickard tramped heavily along the west passage of the residency and up the staircase towards his private office.

He had only minutes before returned from the city and its unexpected surprises to be informed that Kal Nyr was at last to be found, awaiting him with growing impatience in his office. Although he did not mention the fact, Rickard continued to worry at the lack of results on the negotiation front. He had important work to carry out but for some reason he was being blocked. Whether the blocking was deliberate or not he had yet to decide. But one thing was now certain in his mind; he would receive satisfaction by the week's end or he would be forced to leave, returning home with a totally negative report. Apart from doing his status and career no good at all, it could well result in a strong Service force being sent in to demand the satisfaction he had failed to receive, one way or another. It was very doubtful that the Service would allow this particular empire a chance to pose a serious threat to their newly acquired peace. So, he had to try the best he could before that happened.

He reached his office door and swung it open, entering.

The office was quite confined, its narrow walls stood barely two and a half metres apart. On the left hand wall, consuming much of its sparse surface space, was an auxiliary door to the general mess. Between that and the near wall was wedged Rickard's desk, papers scattered across its jumbled top, along with a good many other items and general bric-a-brac. Hanging low over the desk by a fraying material covered lead was a dilapidated electric light, its moth-eaten shade literally falling apart.

The remainder of the office was in a similar condition. Its one bonus was that the plainness of the other two walls was broken by ill fitting louvre doors, which led out onto an exterior balcony. From there one could take in an impressive overall view of the palace. The balcony stood over the interior courtyard, facing towards the wide, cracked stone stairs which led out to the sand-covered courtyard beyond.

Facing the louvre doors, hands tightly clasped behind his stiff back, was Kal Nyr, resplendent in his more informal robes of office. He wore a woven blue-grey overall that closely resembled a smock, with yellow tracelines running down its length. He whirled as Rickard entered, quickly assuming the usual air of polite disinterest that Rickard associated with all politicians, although this time the act seemed a little strained.

'I am not used to being detained for such an extensive period of time, Captain,' he snapped sharply. Rickard noticed he was not wasting any effort on social graces. 'My work is not wholly confined to dealing with your problems and I have a great deal to which to attend.'

'I would like to see your Emperor,' Rickard said in a calm tone of voice, although he felt anything but calm inside.

'Out of the question.'

'All right, I'll rephrase. I *want* to see the Emperor,' Rickard demanded evenly.

'I do not imagine that your extremely impromptu request will be at all possible to realise at the current time.'

'Why not?'

'I am afraid the Emperor is, like myself, otherwise indisposed. Perhaps it would be more advisable for you to wait a short while?' Kal Nyr prevaricated, openly reticent in allowing Rickard his own way.

'I think I've waited far too long already. I want to see him now.'

'Captain Rickard-'

'I said now!' Rickard raised his voice.

'It is not possible. That is a fact that I have already stated quite clearly, or so I thought. I was under the impression that I was most impressive in making myself superbly clear to people.' The high crest on his skull edged forward. 'Could I have been incorrect in such a modest assumption?'

'It is possible, according to what I have seen so far,' Rickard replied coldly.

'How often must I repeat myself to you? An audience with His Imperial Highness is not feasible at the current period of time.'

'I don't believe you, Kal Nyr,' Rickard seethed furiously. 'Why is it that you keep blocking me?'

'Am I, the highest of the Emperor's many distinguished aides, to assume that you impugn my very word? Is it true, Captain? Do you call me a liar?'

'I don't give a bloody *damn* what you think I am calling you!' The veins on Rickards temple stood out boldly, such was the ferocity of his exclamation.

Unmoved by his opponent's heated and stormy temperament Kal Nyr quickly deliberated his position, realising that, having started the confrontation off on its present vein, he would have to change tack or he would continue to lose ground. He could not bluff his way through forever. Rickard was being unusually persistent in his demand for an audience. Persistence was not a trait Kal Nyr would have attributed to Rickard, so his present performance came as no little surprise. The imperial aid decided on another tack.

'As you insist on the matter most strongly, and I must add with great impoliteness, I may be able to speak to His Imperial Highness and construct arrangements for the morrow. As you must understand, it is becoming a touch late for extended meetings of the format that you require.'

'I get nothing but excuses from you, Kal Nyr,' Rickard exploded, smashing his fist down on the desktop, causing everthing on it to jump a few centimetres into the air. He knew he was being put off yet again. 'I haven't seen anyone of importance for days now. You have continually stopped me from seeing the Emperor, something I have consistently requested because there is a bloody great deal to be discussed; trade treaties; territory boundaries, your empire's entry into the Grouping and even tourism to

151

name but a few. I am sick and tired of your continued lack of interest and lack of good manners in this affair! I demand an immediate result or I will have to seriously consider pulling out and returning home with a very undiplomatic report. I wouldn't like to guess what my superiors might do after reading what I have to say about you!'

'I shall see what can be done,' Kal Nyr snorted disingenuously, disguising any surprise he felt at Rickard's unprecedented outburst. Not that it made the slightest bit of difference to him. The Emperor's plans would continue to unfold. This remarkably naive captain still did not suspect anything out of the ordinary.

Rickard had achieved little. He knew nothing had changed and as far as he could see nothing would change. His fading hopes of getting anything positive out of this mission were fast turning into a lost cause.

He eased the pressure accordingly, now assured of the final result. Assured of failure.

'I'll give you to the end of the week to fix up something. Then we will be on our way,' he said a hand going to rub the back of his tired neck in a manner that was becoming a habit.

'As I have previously stated, I will do my utmost to secure an audience for you with the Emperor. I can however promise nothing. I cannot predict the Emperor's thoughts. It is impossible to tell if He may have a change of heart once I speak to him,' the intransigent aide commented aloofly. 'I will now depart. I bid you good night, Captain.'

Rickard sighed tiredly. 'Goodnight, Kal Nyr.'

Kal Nyr brushed past him and strode out of the door, hastily banging it shut after him.

Rickard sank down onto his desk-side seat, facing towards the louvre doors. The irregularly spaced wooden slats revealed the orange-redness of the slowly setting suns. Maybe Kal Nyr was telling the truth and the Emperor was otherwise detained by important business, Rickard thought morosely. 'No, I don't believe that, either,' he admitted to himself.

The Emperor's aide was being deliberately dilatory. He

somehow purposely avoided the issue and created unnecessary delays, blockages. Why? Rickard could only feel that whatever was happening, it would bode no good for him and his crew. Yet what could he do without firm evidence to support his suspicions? He would be made a laughing stock if he went back now saying they left because the situation didn't *feel* right. A failed commander on his first outing. The magnificent superhero of the Grouping comes crashing back to the real universe with a bang. No. He had to stay, at least for a while longer. If only to see what did happen. Damn. Why did it have to be him? Why choose him for this bloody mission?

The tangled maelstrom of his thoughts swirled and raced through his mind, building up the anger at his inability to cope with the predicament. Unable to leave because there was no firm reason to; unable to stay because everything was going nowhere fast and the whole place felt wrong. There was no clear way out for him and he was beginning to feel trapped.

'*Damn!*' he exclaimed aloud, once more slamming his clenched fist down on the desk, harder this time. He instantly regretted the action as a pang of sharp pain lanced up his arm and he quickly tried to smoothe his smarting fist. 'Wrong hand,' he groaned. It was the hand he had hurt in the scuffle with Piers Nyman some many millions of years ago. It just was not his lucky day.

Repositioning the scattered contents of the desk top Rickard rose and went to the louvre doors, swinging them open to let the failing sunlight through. He stepped out onto the balcony and stood looking down at the residency buildings, his hands resting on the elaborately carved balustrade. The stone beneath his feet was warm and strangely relaxing. Calmer now, he tried to clear his mind of the jumble of negative thoughts that prevailed, concentrating on nothing, merely observing the view.

The first sun had already lowered itself out of sight below the horizon. Its brighter twin was following close behind, just edging the topmost outcrops of the jagged cliffs beyond the city limits. A blaze of gloriously coloured cloud was streaked out in front of it, stretching away in a tenuous reach far across the sky. The comforting blueness of the heavens was steadily deepening towards the blackness of night, casting elongated shadows that reached out eagerly from their bases, slowly stretching and increasing their length. The planet possessed no moons but the stars glowed extra brightly on this evening, and even now, with a sun still effusing light, one or two of the brightest stars were clearly visible, twinkling everlastingly in their magical glory. It was starting to get chilly, but it was still a beautiful sunset. One of the most magnificent he had ever witnessed.

Bringing his wandering gaze down to more earthly objects, Rickard passively observed as the security Marines on the main gate dug their booted feet into the sandy soil of the courtyard, trying to heave closed the pitted wooden barrier. The passing of their footsteps left darker patches of bare, deeply dried soil that seemed greatly in need of some water. The Marines finally shut the ponderous gates with a resounding rumble, pressing their combined weight against it to stop its solid bulk rebounding unwieldily backwards. The rotting wood bolt, long splinters spiking out from it in its decrepitude, was slung with difficulty into place. It was held in unsteady firmness by two rusting metal brackets, bolted weakly to each half of the dilapidated gate. Rickard gloomily doubted that the crumbling structure would hold for very long against a determined assault - should such an occurrence arise.

The last light of day was fading fast now, increasing the darkness of the residency's interior. The proliferate weed bushes which sprouted forth from the base of the boundary wall, prim and green despite the dryness of the ground, were beginning to close their attractive blue petals, each one curling itself closed in preparation for the night-time drop in temperature. A small rodent, decidedly lacking in fur, skittered nervously across the openness of the dusty courtyard from behind the protective cover of a dense patch of alyssum, sniffing and testing, searching all the time for tiny titbits of discarded food. Every morsel was eagerly taken up to help fill its ever-empty stomach while it made its way so carefully from the disused stables to the warmth of the occupied quarters, hoping, perhaps, to gain rather more considerable nourishment from someone's wastecan, several of which were placed outside the doors.

Rickard smiled to himself. How lucky the little creature was, he mused. No responsibilities to anyone but itself, and maybe a few dependants. No worries except where it would find its next meal. *It* did not have to worry about the health and safety of nearly two hundred other lives currently in its care. All it had to do was survive from day to day, week to week, in its tiny little world.

His eyes searched along the low, brick-built quarters adjoining the west passage in search of the scaly rodent but he failed to rediscover it. The timid creature had disappeared, probably through some unseen hole in the side of a wall. Instead, his gaze was caught by the fifth terraced accommodation out from the far boundary wall - Karen's residence. She would be alone right now. her co-habitees had been transferred back out that day. There were some perks to his rank, after all.

Making a decision, Rickard re-entered his office, heading for a narrow, confined cabinet jammed into the corner between the louvre doors. He slid the top drawer open, its well-oiled runners creating no noise as it slipped out, and reached inside to remove two drinking glasses and an unopened bottle of vintage wine. He had brought it down from his cabin aboard *Emputin* for just such an occasion, and he was glad he'd had the foresight to do so.

Closing his office door tightly behind him, he descended the stairs to the west passage at a brisker pace than he had shown coming the other way not long before. He soon reached Karen's door, its darkened surface hidden in the gloom of the passage, sheltered as it was by the overhead walkway. The sparse scattering of shoddily erected electrical lighting along the passage's length did not do very much at all to relieve that gloominess.

Rickard tapped softly on the door and waited patiently.

Presently, a voice called from the other side of the door. 'Who is it?' Karen asked.

'Me.'

'Me who?' she returned drily.

155

'Chris,' said Rickard, his teeth beginning to chatter in the late evening cold. 'Now open up. It's starting to get chilly out here.'

He heard the bolt being pulled back and the door was opened the slightest fraction. 'I'm not decent,' Karen said around the gap.

'I don't mind if you don't.'

Karen chuckled affably. 'Hold on, Chris. I'll get my dressing-gown.' She pushed the door to, vanishing for a brief moment before reappearing to open the door more fully. Rickard stepped in, keeping the wine bottle and glasses hidden from sight.

The room was fairly confined and narrow but considerably lengthy so that the three wide beds within all possessed their own private section of space. The bare walls had been covered with a fresh coating of plaster (or the local equivalent) not too long ago but it was even now starting to chip and crumble in places. Above Karen's bed, the one nearest the door, there hung a wall-rug which was handsomely decorated in a dazzling array of bright and cheerful colouring. The bed itself was very plain. It consisted only of a covered mattress upon a wheeled base. Over that there was a double layer of clean, sharp red sheeting brought down from the ship which had been pulled back as if Karen had been preparing to retire for the night. A tatty, threadbare carpet covered the floor, its dull brown colour showing thick piles of accumulated dust and grime. It looked decidedly old and dirty but it was still usable. It had been fitted to the room quite badly. Along the rear wall, where the carpet met the separate bathroom compartment, considerable wedges protruded up the lower reaches of the skirting board, their edges frayed and mouldy. On the whole, the room held an atmosphere of the best made of a bad job, an attitude that all the Service people had nurtured as nothing in the secondary palace seemed perfect, or anywhere near.

Rickard noted that the other two beds were untouched, their neatly made sheets smooth and unruffled. 'What's happened to your room-mates?' he asked.

'They've finished their duty-tour down here. They

156

transferred back to the ship earlier today. The replacements arrive tomorrow so you've got me all to yourself for tonight,' Karen said with a coy smile.

'Well at least I can get a bit of peace and quiet here,' Rickard said, leaning forward to kiss Karen eloquently, the contact stirring strong emotions in both of them.

He stepped back and cast an appreciative eye over her, observing with interest the extra long nightshirt she wore that was only partially hidden by her dressing-gown. It was of a pale red shade that shimmered and clung in all the right places, especially revealing the well-defined form of her shapely legs, before the swirling of her white dressing-gown obscured the view as she moved lightly away.

'You look lovely tonight,' Rickard commented.

Karen turned and beamed at him. 'Flatterer.'

'I've taken the liberty of bringing along a little liquid refreshment,' he said, holding the bottle of wine into view and placing it on the high cabinet beside Karen's bed. The two glasses were placed alongside and Rickard eased open the bottle, pouring a decent measure of the warm, pale liquid into each of the cut-glass receptacles.

'So, what brings you knocking at my door at this late hour?' enquired Karen.

'It's not that late.'

'Okay, what brings you knocking at my door at this not-so-late hour?' she rephrased with a mischevious twinkle in her eye.

'I don't really know,' Rickard admitted honestly. 'I guess I needed some company and yours was certainly preferable to anyone else's.'

'Then I'm glad you came.'

'You are?' he asked hesitantly, all his natural reservedness, his inbuilt lack of self-confidence coming to the fore, despite his readiness for the moment.

'Yes,' Karen firmly assured him. 'I'm in equal need of the company. It was getting pretty lonely in here all on my own. I kept thinking back to this afternoon and the burning. I can't get it out of my head.'

'For me it was easy,' Rickard hinted. 'I had other matters to concentrate on.'

'Phil said the cremation ceremony was originally from Earth, so how did it get all the way here?'

'I don't know. Probably it was passed on; from the computer memory bank of a Grouping vessel, attacked by the Larr, and onto this empire in the same way. That's the only way I can think of it happening.'

'It sounds about right, though. Another bequest of the war. The problems that it caused,' she said.

'There are a couple of problems that I've been keeping under my hat. I'm just not sure if they are worth the worry.'

'Oh, Chris,' Karen finally realised why Rickard was looking so down. 'You know what your problem really is?' she said, sitting on the edge of the bed. She patted the space beside her meaningfully, indicating that Rickard should join her. She continued speaking as he complied. 'You worry too much, especially about other people's problems. Now don't misunderstand me, but I think you should think a lot less of them and more of yourself. Once you sort yourself out *then* deal with everyone else.'

'It's not quite like that,' Rickard protested mildly. He explained his earlier feelings to her of being trapped, unable to move either way for fear that it might be the wrong way. 'I don't know what to do,' he admitted mournfully.

Understanding the extent of the predicament for the first time brought home the reality of the situation to Karen. She fully comprehended why Rickard was not able to make a decision. She understood him enough for that. She only wished he would open up a little and let her understand him completely.

'I see what you're up against,' she said consolingly, sipping thoughtfully at her drink. 'But never fear, for help is at hand. Being the daughter of a vice-admiral does have its compensations. Dad does moan quite a bit about inexperienced officers who aren't capable of taking the weight of command - not meaning you, of course,' she hastily added as Rickard looked up. 'I have picked up a few useful hints and tips along the way. What you should do is this; on your next log entry make it clear that you have some concern over the way things are going and give a couple of examples. First thing in the morning begin unobtrusively shipping all our own goods back to the ship, including the occasional group of crew. Only keep a show force down here to make the Emperor think all is well but that can be evacuated quickly if necessary. That way you're covered from both directions; you prevent an outright massacre if they attack but make it clear to Command that you're not chickening out.'

'That's the best suggestion I've heard in a long time.' Rickard grinned, relieved to have shared the problem with her. 'You're a genius.'

'One does try,' she gestured theatrically.

'And I love you for it,' he said, only half in humour.

Karen became still. 'I know you do. I also feel very strongly about you, Chris. I think you know that.'

Disconcerted by her sudden directness, Rickard shied away. In an attempt to lighten the atmosphere he quoted a phrase, the only piece he remembered, from a play read many years ago. '"Let me enfold thee and hold thee to my heart,"' he said, the words coming with overacted emphasis, attempting to bluff his way out of his own embarrassment. Such closeness was new to him, he had not yet learned to relax and enjoy the sensation.

Karen accepted his retreat and returned his quote. 'And you, Chris, should

"Look like the innocent flower,
But be the serpent under't.

'Of course, if you want a little more, there's another passage that can be related directly to your friend and mine, Kal Nyr.

"That is a step
On which I must fall down, or else
o'er leap
For in my way it lies.'

'You've read it too?'

'Afraid so, Chris,' she smiled apologetically. 'Don't take it too hard. I studied for a couple of years at a drama

159

college. It was hard work and that was one of my first plays. I think it was the best performance I ever gave.'

'I didn't know you were a drama student.'

'Aha! There are a lot of things you don't know about me yet, Mister.' She gently squeezed his arm with her free hand.

Rickard perceived the surge of an, until now, restrained emotion flow unhindered through the whole of his being. The closeness they had felt because of the funeral horror had brought them nearer to each other, cutting down some of the barriers between them. They had shared a tremulous experience and were all the closer for it. The intense attraction they had felt towards each other before was strengthened, doubled in its tangibility. There was no longer any need for the restraint. There was no point in it. And yet he still could not relax.

'Don't fight it, Chris.' Karen sensed what he was feeling. God, why was he so inhibited? Was he afraid of committing himself? She brushed her hand over his cheek, the touch helping to brush away his inhibitions. 'Let it happen,' she whispered gently in his ear.

Without thinking further, he eased the glass from her hand and, along with his own glass, deposited it on the bedside cabinet. Then he draped an arm around her shoulders and drew her to him. Karen's lips found his and they joined in a kiss that seemed everlasting. Their movements were deep with urgent affection.

'Mmmm,' Karen groaned with feelings as she finally pulled back, short of breath.

Rickard's eyes flickered to the door. His face carried a slight frown of hesitancy. 'I've hoped for this for a long time, but do you think we should? Here? Someone might come in.'

'Let them,' Karen mumbled, moving nearer. 'I don't give a damn.'

They kissed again, more strongly this time with ever-increasing passionate desire. Rickard knew what must now happen and he welcomed it with an open heart. This was not something to be avoided or shunned as had been his unexpected encounter with Nicola. This was a moment to enjoy to the fullest extent, the long waiting

160

before this time only adding to the raised level of emotion, making it all the more important for the both of them.

Karen continued to kiss Rickard as he slowly removed her dressing-gown, slipping it gently from her shoulders and allowing it to fall to the floor. Unobstructed by the loosely flowing garment, the two sank back onto the soft, ever so warm comfort of the bed, held in each other's tenderly searching, touching embrace.

The time reached midnight and the alarm on Kiyami's bedside cabinet duly sounded, its short, sharply insistent bleeps echoed around the room.

Kiyami instantly became wide awake and silenced the noisome alarm. It was her turn on the duty rota as officer of the watch, a task she could easily have delegated to a lower rank. She did not, though. This was the time-period she liked the most. There were clear advantages in it most notable in the absence of the searing day-time heat and the chances offered for her to study, via specially set up infra-red cameras, the nocturnal wildlife in the locale. Although she was a science officer versed mainly in the realms of modern technology she did like to engage herself in all the major fields of science as a form of study, finding them greatly educational and a necessary distraction from the sometimes tedious area in which she specialised. Boring was not the correct word to use, and she would never think of using it, but variety did add some spice to life. This time of night also provided a kind of internal peace for her which she did her best to cultivate. She occasionally preferred the calm, tranquil pace of the silent hours to the hustle and bustle of day. Silence could be a blessing. Peace was a gift. In the quietness one was free to contemplate the universe, or watch the growth of a stone. Inner peace was the true blessing. It was also the hardest to attain.

She rose stiffly from the bed, limbering up tired

161

muscles before removing her cotton bedsuit and climbing into the short-sleeved, regulation Service uniform. She fastened the uniform all the way to the neck before shrugging into a thick, comfortable Service Warm Coat, the long jacket's colour scheme blending in with that of her uniform. It would keep the night chill at bay most admirably.

She would not be blessed with peace tonight. Though she had not mentioned the fact, Kiyami held her own doubts on the sincerity of their rather ambiguous hosts, now that her initial fascination of them had faded. She had glimpsed fragments of a hidden layer to the personalities of the common populace and what few troopers she had spotted. It was as if they were striving to disguise a set of emotions or beliefs from the visitors, as if they were masking their true feelings towards what they could well think of as invaders in their territory. Also, the singular lack of any type of discussions between the Emperor and his aides and the command officers of *Emputin* disturbed her. There ought to have been some kind of diplomatic motion by now, not this continued ignoring of what were supposed to be honoured guests. Something was up and she decided it was high time she should inform the captain of her fears and the ambivalence she was experiencing, regardless of the apparent lack of concrete evidence.

Leaving her quarters in the north passage, Kiyami headed for the east wall. Taking the wide staircase beyond the overhead covering of the officers' mess two steps at a time, she arrived on the walkway, its uneven surface stretching down to the minor fortifications either side of the main gates. Peering over the chest-high, buttressed wall, she saw nothing of any wildlife nor much activity of any other description. Instead, with the thoughts of an Imperial dislike for the service people hovering boldly at the back of her mind, Kiyami examined the nearby buildings.

Most of them were the normal, low-built abode, flat-roofed and absolutely no trouble in an attack because they provided no overlooking viewpoint. They were useless as gun posts from any conceivable angle against the residency because of their lack of height. The problems, if any, would come from a four-storey tower lying behind the front row of houses. With a high-powered pulse rifle a crack shot could cause havoc and there would be very little chance of returning any effective fire as the rooftop was bordered by a narrowly slitted wall through which a weapon could easily be aimed without much risk to the sniper. That tower would be one of the first places utilised in the event of an outbreak of violence.

Kiyami broke her attention away from the surrounding buildings and leaned over the wall's edge once more, hoping something native and non-humanoid would show itself. Nothing did. Then she heard a muffled scuffing sound from the direction of the gates which alerted her immediately. She continued to stare at the floodlit area in front of the main gates with a rock-steady motionlessness, but whatever had made the noise had been very careful in concealing itself. The fact that she had only momentarily been thinking on possible warfare made her none the calmer.

A sudden call from a security Marine brought Kiyami to the gate fortification at a run. It took her but a moment to cover the short distance and she was soon standing below the raised stonework upon which was constructed the guard post.

'What is it?' she requested. The single Marine at the watchout turned his head to look down, whilst keeping his position on the confined post. He gladly passed on the problem.

'There's a native outside the gates, Commander. He won't show himself to us, says he has to stay in the shadows or he might be seen by the Emperor's people. He keeps saying we're in grave danger, and that he must speak to the Captain right away.'

'I will deal with this.'

Kiyami clambered up the wood ladder, effortlessly reaching the tightly enclosed raised platform where she negotiated her way past the Marine. She peered over the wall at the sharply illuminated circle of sand below, lit by the twin arcs of beam lights, one at each post. Trying to gain an unobstructed look at the mysterious caller, all she could see was a vague, unmoving shadow lurking back against the opposite gate, staying well hidden.

'Who are you?' she called uncomprisingly, not bothering to hush her voice. She wished there was a free infra-red camera to hand.

'Quiet! Please!' the unseen visitor hissed urgently. 'Talk quietly. I do not want to be taken by the Emperor's troopers.'

Lowering her voice only marginally, Kiyami tried again. 'What is it you want?'

'You *must* listen to me. You are in danger here. I have to speak to your master-commander, your captain, directly. Right away, before it is too late.'

'Stand out in the light so that I can see you.' There was silence. 'Only briefly so I know if you are armed.'

'I assure you that I am not.'

'Then you have nothing to hide.'

The silence returned for long seconds before the mysterious visitor, dressed loosely in dark brown desert robes, ventured out of the protection of darkness into the blinding glare of the mounted spotlights. The caller was a touch smaller than the average native and of decidedly narrower build, as if he had fasted for some time and had lost a good deal of weight. He appeared several sizes too small for his engulfing robes which could have concealed any number of weapons or explosives, so Kiyami stuck to the rules and played it safe.

'All right, you can come in,' she relented, still wary of him 'but only of you submit to a full body search.'

'Anything. Please hurry,' he begged.

'Private,' Kiyami said to the lone Marine at ground level, 'open the gates wide enough for only our unexpected guest to enter. Keep on your guard, though. He may not be alone.' She started down the ladder.

As the Marine struggled and strained to remove the security bolt, three of his comrades emerged from the duty hut - a converted section of the ramshackle new construction - to help, alerted by the noise. Combining their efforts the Marines soon had the bolt off the gates and out of the way. The gate was swung open only wide enough to allow the single visitor to slip through. No chances, no risks were being taken. Once inside, the gates were instantly slammed shut again behind the jumpy visitor, the bolt being almost hurled into place.

'Body-search him,' Kiyami ordered loudly, descending a second wooden ladder that reached from the walkway to the ground. The security Marines duly complied, checking and double-checking every fold, every crease of the visitor's voluminous robes.

'He's clean, Commander,' the corporal in charge of the party of Marines reported.

'Take him to the officers' mess. Wait with him in the antechamber until I arrive,' Kiyami waved them away. She followed at a slower pace as the stolid, hard-faced Marines marched off in tight control of their charge. He was certainly not going to escape. Exposing her slim-line wristwatch, Kiyami turned an almost microscopic dial set into its side, activating the two-way speaker implanted within the watch's super-miniaturised components. The calling signal began to cry out for attention.

☆ ☆ ☆

'Damn,' Rickard cursed as he emerged from the warmth of the bed's thick sheets to grab for his comm watch on the bedside cabinet, almost sending the two partially filled wine glasses flying in the process.

'What is it?' a sleepily recumbent Karen asked, moving to sit up beside him, attempting to retain a hold on the obstinately contrary sheets as they became untucked.

'Don't know. It must be important, though, for someone to call at this time of night.' He finally gained possession of the watch, enclosing a fist over it. Pressing the actuator he spoke into the comm unit clearly and precisely. 'Captain Rickard here. What's up?'

Kiyami's interference-free reply came back through the perfect reception. 'Captain, so sorry for disturbing you, but there is a matter to which I presume you would like to attend. We are holding a native in the officers' mess. He arrived spouting garbled warnings of grave danger for us. He specifically requested to see you.'

Instantly Rickard was alert. The guy could be a nut but if he wasn't then this was it. This could be the confirmation of all his fears.

'I'll be be there as fast as I can, Kiyami. Have Beck and Howarth meet me there, would you?'

'Right away, Captain.' Kiyami signed off, closing the connection.

Rickard hurriedly secured the watch on his wrist and rolled over to face Karen, looking suitably apologetic. 'I have to go,' he said.

'Oh, no.'

'It sounds important.'

'I know,' she admitted reluctantly. 'It seems a shame to go now-'

'I have to.' He silenced her protest by kissing her lightly on the tip of her nose. He placed a finger on her closed, moist lips, sensitively trailing it over her chin, down along the softness of her neck and across the smooth, tanned pinkiness of her extremely lovely body, leaving a faint liquid path and a line of raised goosebumps where the wetness met cool air. He moved his wandering hand over her chest, between the firm, raised mounds of her breasts and on, past her taut stomach to the obstructing cover of the sheets, observing and experiencing the luscious shape of her exquisite figure.

'It's been wonderful, Karen,' he said. 'I don't quite know how to say this but...I think I'm beginning-'

'Ssh.' She placed a silencing finger to his lips. 'I know, Chris. I know.' She ran her hand over his chest, thrilling at the touch.

'I really do have to go.'

'It's okay. By the way,' she added, eyes sparkling, 'I'm coming with you.'

A new, more complete and satisfied warmth permeated Rickard's expression. 'You don't have to, you know. You could just as easily stay here.'

'I know. But I could also just as easily tag along and find out what the commander thought was so urgent about her stranger,' she grinned beguilingly.

'Okay. Come on.'

Rickard energetically yanked back the loose covers and jumped briskly out of the bed, collecting his discarded uniform from the floor and dressing with starting rapidity.

'Hey!' Karen exclaimed with indignation as she rose from the bed. She looked in Rickard's romantically enthused, starry-eyed vision, like a stunningly beautiful mythogical nymph rising from the rolling waves, naked and achingly desirable. 'Wait for me,' his sea-nymph said.

'Sorry,' he murmured, totally encaptured by the sight, his attention momentarily far away from the troubling pressures of command. He waited by the door after snapping the final clasp on his jacket and watched Karen dress, a wave of utter contentedness washing over him as he realised how unusally buoyant he felt.

Kiyami was waiting patiently in the antechamber outside the officers' mess. Her breath left silent puffs of visible vapour in the permeating coldness of the night air. The frugally polished tiled floor beneath her feet gleamed dully, its shine faded and coloured by age. It dimly reflected Kiyami's still image. She would gain no peace at all tonight. The visitor meant the end of the facade. Now the actors would reveal their real purposes. Undisguised by false projections. Now some truth might be learnt.

The sound of footsteps on the stairs made her turn. She saw Rickard ascending fast with Karen Trestrail hot on his heels, their joined hands parting as they saw her. How, she wondered had they come together at this time? Karen could not have known anything unless the captain had informed her, but he would not have had the time to spare to travel from his quarters in the north passage down to hers and then all the way back again in the time he'd taken. So that left only one conclusion. Kiyami mentally shrugged. Why not? she thought, there's nothing wrong in it. What did puzzle her was exactly how and why Rickard had been able to gain permission to bring Karen on the trip in the first place. Surely Admiral Trestrail had not allowed it? On the other hand, why did it matter? It was none of her business. Best to keep her mind strictly on work matters.

Trying to discard her confusing mish-mash of thoughts and wonderings Kiyami greeted Rickard making sure not to indicate to him her conclusions about his private life, a thing she considered to be quite personal and not for open converse. 'Good evening, Captain. So sorry to have awoken you but the matter does seem important.'

'I'm glad you let me know. This is something I've been expecting.'

Well at least she would not have to bother him with her own suspicions, seeing as he already held some of his own. *Domo arigato* to the gods. 'Doctor Beck and Mister Howarth have taken our guest into the mess room to discover his purpose in coming here.'

'Right,' Rickard nodded. 'Let's see our mystery caller.'

Kiyami led the way in. Dim lights barely lit the large room with the window blinds drawn closed and the mess looked different, a much more solemn, repressed place than before, in the daytime. Beck and Howarth were seated either side of the visitor and they looked up sharply as Rickard approached. Two Marines stood statue-like against the wall, awaiting orders.

Beck looked tired, Rickard noticed. The surgeon's normally neat hair was ruffled and uncombed and his eyes were bleary and reddened. In contrast Howarth appeared his usual immaculate self, tidy and efficient, wide awake. How the hell he did it Rickard would never know. Despite his own high-spirited and business-like demeanour, even Rickard did not look that good.

Giving up the train of thought in bewilderment and putting his mind forcefully to the task at hand, Rickard seated himself in a plush armchair directly facing the visitor. Karen and Kiyami sat on the long sofa to his right, the science officer leaning forward with interest at what information the visitor could provide.

'Okay,' Rickard began. 'Firstly, who are you? What do you want here? Why are you afraid to be seen by the

Emperor's troops?'

Their visitor looked pleased that he was finally to be allowed to make his delivery. 'My name in Iad-Nur Tvyl-Kitan. You may call me-'

'Yes. We know that bit,' Rickard interrupted. 'Carry on.'

'To answer your last question first. I am a member of what originally was a political movement called the Freedom against Imperial Oppression group. The Emperor's grovelling minions now call us rebels because we fought them and their power, because we threatened their absolute control over the populace. We are more a military force now, since we were forced to go into hiding in fear for our lives. We are dedicated to fighting the Emperor's rule and although there are at present all too few of us, we are making a growing impression on the common people of the Empire.'

That was not the impression Rickard had but he let the point pass.

'I travelled here at great risk to myself to warn you of the dire peril, the terminal trap you are in while you stay. By the way,' he cut off annoyingly, groping in a deep pocket in his robes.

Howarth's pistol was out of its holster and in his hand in the blink of an eye, the two Marines responding similarly, their speed surprising even Rickard. The three pistol barrels pointed unwaveringly at Iad Kitan. 'Take it easy. We're very jumpy,' Howarth threatened.

Rickard waved him back. 'Relax, Mister Howarth. I think our friend's motives are benevolent.' He cast a warning eye at Iad Kitan, stating unequivocably that he'd better be proven correct - or else.

Reluctantly, but unrebelliously, replacing his pistol, Howarth motioned to the Marines to do likewise. Iad Kitan slowly and cautiously removed a slip of paper from his pocket and handed it to Rickard.

'This is the location of our own planetary base on Tibor. We know your logging system from the Larr ships which came here and were captured. You are invited to visit us when you finally feel the need. I ask you with the utmost urgency to leave this place as soon as possible. The

169

Emperor has only the most selfish of motives for letting you stay, it is a certainty he is not interested in any negotiations of friendship. At an educated guess I would imagine that he wants your extremely impressive ship for his own fleet. With a ship as powerful as yours he could order an invasion of your own space and cause untold havoc. The explicit aim of the FIO group is to bring about the downfall of him and his servile lackeys, whatever the cost to ourselves.'

'I'm not sure,' pondered Rickard. 'I don't know if I trust you that much, but there is Kal Nyr.'

'Kal Nyr's stubbornness will block your every effort,' Iad Kitan affirmed strongly. 'You are in danger. The Emperor wants your ship.'

'But why would he do that. It's not rational.'

'He is not a rational person.'

'We came here in peace,' Rickard protested. 'What can capturing my ship achieve apart from war?'

'He does not care. He is blind to the consequences of his actions. Believe me. I know. He only sees what he wants. And that he takes. If he cannot take, he destroys.'

'That's madness.'

'It's also very melodramatic,' Beck added wryly.

'But utterly true,' Iad Kitan affirmed, driving home the point of his argument.

'Excuse me for being so dense,' Beck cleared his throat. 'But I still don't see precisely what our danger is.'

'Why, is it not obvious?' the rebel said in open astonishment. 'He will attack this shoddily built palace and try to wipe out every single one of your people, simply for the capture of his prize.'

'He'll have a bloody hard time trying,' Howarth said.

8

Rickard's concealed withdrawal was in full flow.

After Iad Kitan's not totally unexpected revelation about the deviousness of the Emperor's nature, the rebel activist had been comprehensively grilled for a solid hour as Rickard strove to discover the full details, to withdraw every last scrap of information. The effort was to little avail. Kitan knew a great deal about the Emperor's motives and drives, but exactly the opposite in terms of factual information. All he could promise with any certainty was that an attack would come sooner or later. Probably sooner for, according to him, the Emperor could not resist such a prize as *Emputin* for very long. In fact, it totally surprised him that the Service people had remained unmolested for this long.

All too soon the night had started to fade and Iad Kitan had insisted upon being allowed to leave before the city awoke, first making one last impassioned plea to Rickard to have the common sense to see the danger in which he and his crew were placed, and leave before it really was too late. He reaffirmed that he would be there to meet him if he came to the rebel headquarters on Tibor which was, according to the supplied co-ordinates, even further into Empire controlled space - in exactly the opposite direction to that in which Rickard would rather travel.

Once Kitan had taken his leave there had followed another discussion, far longer than the first, this one becoming more of an argument on whether they could trust the rebel. It became predictably heated, with Beck insisting that they all leave immediately. Kiyami suggested it might be wiser to look before they leaped, and Rickard stuck in the middle of the two opposing opinions, torn between the choices, both of which made equal sense. Eventually he opted for playing safe and making a tactical retreat. He put into action Karen's plan of quietly moving out and the packing of all their goods was initiated soon afterwards. Shortly after the rising of the suns, in an ominous blood-red dawn, the number of service personnel residing in the palace was cut by half. No-one else was allowed down from the ship and regular shuttling flights helped diminish the number of crew at risk, although their could not be an overt number of flights for fear of needlessly alerting their hosts. After all, the rebel had been able to offer no concrete proof that his word was truthful. All that had won them over was his unrelenting insistence that he was right.

Caution and discretion were the watchwords of the day. A fair quota of extra guard duty was handed around with the Marines being placed on alert status, fully armed while they patrolled along the residency walkways. Extra checks were made on any incoming goods or visitors, for the Emperor had suddenly taken to bestowing them with specially delivered gifts of crated sealed boxes containing native foods and products. It was move that seemed strangely out of place considering what was assumed of their motives, and which provoked a growing suspicion of them on the part of the majority of the crew.

Beck was standing on the east walkway, watching the weather, staring out at the rolling waves of thin aeolian desert sands being blown along in a very untypically blustery day. It was the first strong wind he had witnessed since their arrival, and it cast shadowy doubts in his mind of the whole state of affairs. Was this unusual wind a portent, a sign of ill omen? He wondered as he glanced at the cloudscudded pale blue sky overhead. The tenuous, greying wafts of condensed water vapour were being blown swiftly along. They repeatedly blocked the twin disks of luminescence which struggled to warm the fresh but chilled air of early morning. The day had started with a subdued presence to it. A pernicious presence that refused to be shaken off.

'I continuously wonder if that Kitan person was strictly compos-mentis,' he remarked distantly to Rickard who stood beside him, looking down on the residency's main courtyard.

The young captain was observing the hustle and bustle below. His fashionably short hair whipped about untidily in the swirling gusts of wind. 'I hope he was,' Rickard said. 'Otherwise we are definitely in trouble. I think I prefer the frying pan to the open fire. Still, he was correct about Kal Nyr's stubborn streak. Arguing with him is like hitting your head against a brick wall - the wall doesn't feel a thing. And this wall would probably come after you if you tried to make a run for it. The trouble is, too much has happened in too short a time. A person needs to stand back once in a while and take stock. I've barely been able to relax properly all week...well almost all week,' he remembered with a smile.

'I could supply you with a high quality nerve soothant,' Beck offered.

Rickard laughed shortly. 'With all that's going on now the last thing I need is a nerve soothant, high quality or not. I am more likely to need some stimulants to keep me on my feet. This is going to be a long day and I have been up since midnight.'

'If you come by my sickbay when we're back on the ship I can see about giving you some uppers.'

'I don't know,' Rickard said doubtfully, 'I don't like getting on that stuff.'

'It'll be strictly in the best Kamikaze parachutist style.'

'Pardon?'

'No strings attached.'

'Oh, God,' Rickard dutifully groaned at the awful pun.

Enjoying his brief moment of rest amidst the frenetic activity, he focused his attention away from the comic surgeon and studied instead the hurried comings and goings of his crew below the walkway. He saw the diminutive Stuart leave the dark narrow passage, which connected to the west corridor, and head for the gates. He observed with approval of her curvey figure, graceful yet endowed with a hidden strength. Certainly a woman to watch, if only in the working sense. She might one day make good officer material and it could be an idea to keep an eye out for her, ambition and strength visible in her

173

very stride. If such a thing could be indicated simply from first impressions then she could be subsumed as officer material.

Unaware of her appreciative audience, Stuart arrived at the main gates as a floater pulled to a halt outside. Only one half of the gate was open and a Marine on guard duty blocked the confined entrance space. The floater's driver, a mean-looking huge hulk of a trooper, dismounted and casually sauntered over to the Marine who was rather apprehensively obstructing his passage.

Waiting well to one side, Stuart listened in. She stood out of the trooper's range of vision. The trooper snapped at the Marine in a growling, menacing tone, his speech was confined and basic. 'Boxes of food for you in the crates.'

'We can't take any more yet. They're still loading up the last lot,' the Marine said, his face remaining impassive.

'I have orders to deliver the boxes.'

'I'm sorry mate, there's nothing I can do about your orders. I've got orders of my own and they are to not let anything else through these gates without permission.'

The trooper glowered, his rugose features wrinkling in an attitude of blatant disgust. 'You will make an insult if you do not accept the gift.'

'Look...'

'I'll take care of this, Private,' Stuart broke in with precise timing, The Marine flashed her a look of relief as he stepped back.

The trooper jerked a dirt-encrusted thumb at the floater and its mountainously stacked load.

'Do you want our gifts or not?'

Without a word to the trooper, or even acknowledgement of his existence, Stuart brushed past him and jumped up onto the floater's deck, the surface flat and smooth and filled to spilling point with badly stacked crates. She reached into a pocket and produced a thick handled knife. She forced out the blade with her fingers and jammed it into the sealed lid of the nearest crate to hand.

The trooper jerked to life in a sudden realisation of what she was doing. His face darkened grimly. 'You!' he

174

rapped. 'Stop. You cannot do that.'

'Calm down,' Stuart threw him an unconcerned glance. 'I'm only checking the goods. We have to be sure that they are of high enough quality. You surely don't want us accepting any old rubbish, do you?'

The trooper was silent, irritated no end by her disconcerting attitude.

With little effort Stuart managed to prise up the heavy lid and half push it aside, peering ino the crate. All she could see were stacks of a whole load of smaller boxes and packages, one of which, when its top was lifted, could be seen to contain nothing more sinister than a supply of indigenous vegetable.

Partially satisfied, she replaced the crate's top and climbed off the floater, jumping back to the sand swept soil. She walked once more past the trooper, stopping only when she reached the Marine. She drew him to one side.

Speaking in a low voice so they could not be heard, she said 'Let him bring the floater inside but make sure that it's scanned by explosives detectors before it is unloaded.'

'Right,' the Marine nodded.

'After you've done that, return to your post and keep a look out for me when I get back. I'm going to take one very fast trip to the market and I don't want to find I've been locked out of this sand pit when I get back.'

'Sorry, Mister Stuart, you can't,' the beleaguered Marine informed her apologetically. 'I'm not allowed to let anyone out. Captain's orders.'

'I'm going to be back before you can blink. I ain't spending the day kicking dirt and being stuck in this place.'

'I can't do it, I'm sorry, not for anyone. I couldn't even let Mister Howarth out if he came along and ordered me to. Orders are orders and mine came from the Captain. Sorry,' he shrugged helplessly.

Stuart was about to press further, planning on insisting, when she was struck by a thought. Where was Bernerds? She had not seen him all morning when usually he stuck out of the crowd like...well, like a vicar in a brothel. 'Okay, forget it.' She dismissed the subject and was gone, sprinting off towards the south wall.

The Marine breathed a sigh of relief as one piece of trouble disappeared from view. Then when he turned back to the other piece of trouble, the impatient trooper was delivering him contemptuously black looks of open annoyance.

'Come on you,' the Marine prompted with self-pleasing impoliteness. 'Get your bloody floater in here.'

The trooper's quasi-reptilian physiognomy hid the wave of jubilation that washed over him. He was greatly satisfied with the way matters had turned out but little of his satisfaction showed as he clambered into the floater's driving seat. Face set expressionlessly, he started the vehicle jerking steadily forwards. He knew from his briefing that the delivered consignment would be scanned but their explosive detectors would not reveal the nature of this cargo. All was well.

His load would be transferred to a launch and eventually offloaded inside the magnificently strong Service vessel. All directly according to the plans of his superiors. The time was rapidly approaching when things would change. The tables were about to be reversed in the Empire's favour and they would win out in the oppressive face of their adversity.

Peter Bernerds reached the top of the flight of stairs, energetically ascending to the south walkway. He headed over to the ragged boundary wall and gazed about with an assumed air of innocence.

He made sure the walkway was clear before he ducked under a worn stone staircase, the one that led to the cramped landing grid above. The grating whine of a badly maintained floater humming its way into the residency rung loudly in his ears. He crouched warily in the protecting shade beneath the stairs, staring anxiously out, hoping he had not been spotted. His luck was in, there was no-one about to see him.

Glaring searchingly into the dimly lit niche, Bernerds located the thick, reliable reel of steel fibre rope he had secreted there in the dark night-time hours in preparation for this unofficial escapade. It was all very spontaneous, with only bare planning behind it, but he was thoroughly sick of listening to all the various rumours currently in flight around the palace that they were about to be treacherously attacked, rumours that had really begun to blossom and grow after the probably imaginary visit of some rebel leader. Anyway, he did not believe it. He had finally decided to find out for himself the truth of the matter, one way or another. Additionally, seeing as the captain was apparently pulling out, it would not matter overmuch if a single native official went unaccountably missing. As part of the current yellow alert status, he was still on duty but the efforts for departure were causing a bewildered confusion among the lower officers so he was not likely to be missed for the short time that he would be away.

He had found the opportunity to commence this 'mission' of his own. He planned to work his way into the adjacent Imperial Palace and hijack someone of importance, forcing him to reveal all. He may not have worked out the finer details, like how he was to actually get in through the shielding dome but that was not important. He would succeed against all the odds, no matter what. This in itself could not be without some risk but it was a risk that he was prepared to take, his previously noted lack of self-preservation rising to the fore. It was best looked upon as a challenge, a test of his skills, if only for the chance to experience some much sought-after adventure on what he saw as a dull and incredibly uninteresting expedition.

Poor old Stuart would throw a fit if she knew what he was doing, Bernerds smiled to himself. Thank God she did not. He was fed up with this boring dump of a place that had been chucked at them and he did not want Stuart blabbing to Howarth or the captain. That would get him into real trouble. Not that she was likely to do that anyway, he corrected himself. She was usually pretty easy going.

177

'Hiya.' The voice beside his ear nearly made Bernerds jump out of his skin. He spun to see the very subject of his thoughts beaming inquisitively at him.

'Go away,' he said flatly, turning his back on her.

'I've had better welcomes than that before, even from you.' She crouched conspiratorially beside him, trying to peer over his broad shoulders to see what he was hiding. 'What are you up to?'

'Leave it Stuart. This is private.' His voice was calm but the warning was clear.

'I would never have guessed if you hadn't told me. I ain't going 'till you tell me what you're up to. I ain't missing out on the excitement.'

'Will you get lost?'

'No,' Stuart smiled irritatingly.

'Get lost, Stuart!'

'Wise up, will you. You're up to something illegal here, so what is it?'

Bernerds exploded. 'For Christ's sake! Why don't you just sod off! I am so sick and tired of this whole petty outfit, with its putrid little rules, regulations and interfering, nosey flippin' busybodies! I just want to be left alone to live my own life without the ridiculous dictations of some jumped up, toffee-nosed wally in an officer's uniform who thinks he's God incarnate. All I want to do is to get shot of the whole *fucking* system so I can do what I want to do, not what a prat with stripes thinks he can tell me to do! So just get the hell away from me, Stuart. *Leave me alone!'*

Stuart remained quite unmoved by all of this. She had witnessed many of Bernerds' rebellious outbursts before and was used to his abrasive manner. At least he was no longer behaving as if he did not care. That could only be an improvement. 'Yeah,' She said to him after glancing around to make sure that they had not been overheard. 'That's all very good but what are you doing?'

Bernerds released a frustrated growl through clenched teeth, knowing that there was no way he would rid himself of the woman. She would doubtless want to come along.

'I'm going on a visiting trip,' he said in surrender.

'Where to?'

'Don't ask.'

'I am asking. Where to?'

'The Imperial Palace.'

'Really? Can I come?'

'No.'

'Aww, go on.'

'All right,' he hissed with a justifiably inimical air.

'Great, lead on then.'

Bernerds gave her a dirty glare before continuing his task. 'Keep a look out,' he ordered.

Taking extreme care that he should not be seen he unravelled the rope and secured one end to the support pillar on the stairs. He pulled the knot as tight as it would go, not wanting to be left stranded in the Emperor's own gardens, and allowed the rope to drop over the wall's crumbling edge, noting with approval that it hung only a metre short of the ground.

He clambered briskly over the wall and down, checking once more that the walkway remained clear before dropping out of sight, lowering himself with rapid hand-over-hand movements. Reaching the thickly grassed earth below the wall he dashed to the nearby protective cover of a mass of tangled undergrowth that protruded from untended foliage. A high, bricked wall bordered the gardens at some distance to his right, solid and unworn. To the left the gardens stretched out, seemingly endless in their expanse. Glancing back, Bernerds saw Stuart jump from the rope and dash after him, the rope swinging wildly to and fro after her. Each pass the rope made robbed it of some of its momentum until it had slowed to a gentle sway, no longer a direct attention-stealer. Bernerds fervently hoped that it would remain that way.

Marking their position against that of the palace ahead, Bernerds wriggled forward on his front until he reached the cover of a rounded mound of pulverised rock. The mound emerged from the lush green grass like a rotting sore on an otherwise healthy body. Great chunks of it lay scattered in the overlong grass as if it had been used by some trigger-happy individual for target practice.

Carefully avoiding the sharper fragments of rock, Bernerds leaned around the ragged side of the mound and peered ahead, determining the best route to take. There was absolutely no sign of life anywhere. No-one blocked his path, there was an unnatural silence so intense as to be almost deafening.

Shrugging off his unfounded concerns the young middie pulled himself from the ground and crept forward, ever suspicious and wary of his surroundings. As he waved her to follow, Stuart trailed after him, keeping herself as quiet and noiseless as the very gardens themselves. The pair started through the water-rich greenness so unusual to the desert-like environment. Darting from one tangled mass of living cover to the next they made their way ever so surreptitiously through and around the overgrown, unattended foliage which was analogous to an assault course such was its density. It was vastly different to the way it had looked from the residency. Stuart ran parallel to Bernerds, picking her way inexorably toward the Palace which loomed high in front, its reflective, splendidly constructed exterior surface reaching majestically for the sky. They ran on, dodging the thicker, more bothersome patches of dense bush to finally reach a walled outer courtyard connected directly to the rear of the Imperial domain.

'Quick, find a way in,' Bernerds snapped to Stuart as his companion joined him on the bordering pathway.

The wall's stone-forming appeared much newer and greatly more solid than that of the residency's and it afforded no handholds for climbing. Fortunately for them, Stuart came up with something slightly better. 'Bernerds! Over here,' she hissed, keeping her voice low.

She had discovered a short-set wooden door inbuilt at an position equidistant between the two main corners of the courtyard. Its varnished unroughened surface reflected the harsh overhead light of the suns, creating a pool of luminesence on the gravelled path in a torch-like display of brilliance. Bernerds glanced, with some trepidation now that he was in the middle of what he termed as enemy territory, over the shortish door and examined the deserted courtyard beyond. The protective dome's shell effectively prevented him from being observed. The glare of sunlight that bounced off made it impossible for anyone inside the dome to see out. He wished he felt safer. This place was too exposed.

A row of benches lined the far wall of the small courtyard. Towards its centre was elaborately ornamented fountain. The single sculptured figure in its middle spouted an unceasing flow of crystal clear water which sprayed out into the circular collecting pool below. From there it was ceaselessly pumped back through internal piping. It was an impressive demonstration of imperial architectural design and art.

'What's over there, Pete?' the diminutive Stuart asked impatiently, breaking the deathly silence.

Bernerds said nothing - the sudden opening of an internal door startled him into ducking his head before he could speak. A trooper emerged from inside the Palace, checking the way for the following forms of the Emperor's chief aide, Kal Nyr, and his companion, a balding, stocky officer dressed in the military apparel of a master-commander. A second guard, built similarly to the first in that they were both shaped like minor mountains, came out last of all, securing the door behind him. The two troopers placed themselves at either end of the courtyard while the aide invited his companion to be seated on one of the benches. The soldiers' eyes, Bernerds noticed uneasily as he sneaked a look, were constantly in motion, alert for the merest of movements.

There was an insistent tug at his arm and he glanced back. Stuart let go of his sleeve, 'What is going on in there?'

'Shut up will you, I'm trying to find out.'

Feeling extremely vulnerable in the openness of their position, Bernerds and Stuart strained to listen in on the conversation that began between the two officials. The splashing made by the fountain proved to be an unforseen nuisance, drowning out parts of the conversation. To add to that the wind sprang up once more, blowing blotches of dust and sand in their direction and bringing with it an audible quality that allowed them to overhear virtually nothing that was spoken. Praying

181

that they could not be seen by the guarding troopers they strained to listen. What they did manage to hear chilled them to the bone.

'...I am greatly pleased,' Kal Nyr was saying in his usual manner of pomposity, 'that the Emperor in his supreme wisdom has at long last decided to initiate some positive action. It is high time that we made a gesture in opposition to these aggressive interlopers who barged their way uninvited in to the Empire.'

'I firmly agree,' his companion nodded overzealously. 'They should be eradicated utterly, for the sake of the Empire itself. But they are far in advance of us in terms of weaponry. Their ship, impressive as it is, happens to carry the strength and fire power of many of our own. If we attack we may become the defeated party.'

'Nonsense,' Kal Nyr snorted. 'If you conform to the letter of my plan they will not be afforded the opportunity to establish any resistance. The residency is old and in a state of ill-repair. It will crumble altogether in the face of a determined attack. If you follow my dictates, the plan that I have designed and the Emperor has approved, then we cannot fail to be victorious. Within the next season we will have to construct a fleet of a dozen or more ships similar to our awaiting prize.'

'I shall organise the city troop immediately, Master-Aide.' The officer rose to his feet and threw a crisp salute to his superior, then spun stiffly on his heel and marched into the palace.

'Charming,' Bernerds scowled acrimoniously as he risked another peep over the door. 'So much for our "friendly hosts".'

Stuart was looking the other way, watching the distant corner of the courtyard as a small squad of troopers rounded it in loose formation. 'Bernerds.'

'Hold on,' he replied, intent on watching Kal Nyr.

'Bernerds!'

'All right!'

'I think its time to go.'

Bernerds glanced away from the courtyard in time to see the troopers spot them and unsling their weapons, breaking into a run. 'Shit!' he cried. 'Why didn't you warn me?'

He pulled back sharply from the wood door, in doing so inadvertently showing his head to the troopers inside the courtyard. They moved instantaneously into action, the first bellowing a warning to Kal Nyr.

Kal Nyr's head snapped up and his eyes found Bernerds, the latter not having yet had the good sense to flee. 'Kill him!' Kal Nyr commanded with cold finality, waving the troopers forward.

While Bernerds stood stunned into motionlessness, Stuart was already firing precisely aimed shots in rapid bursts, expertly wiping out the trio of troopers in a hail of controlled fire. By that time the first of the troopers from inside the courtyard had arrived at the door to the gardens.

Bernerds snapped out of his daze and forced himself to face the enemy. He acted with the well trained level headedness of a battle hardened veteran as he stood his ground, awaiting what seemed like certain death. He knew they would be callously shot down if they so tried to run now so instead he placed himself to one side of the narrow door, rifle at the ready and held securely at hip level. Stuart stood well aside, watching the far corner with eagle-sharp vision. She knew fully what it was her partner was awaiting.

The oncoming trooper crashed unflinchingly through the wooden door, smashing it from its solid metal hinges as if it were no more than a thick, cardboard facsimile. Before he could regain his balance Bernerds had a line on him. He fired at point blank range, blasting a large, blackly charred hole in the trooper's broad chest. The unfortunate trooper was hurled backwards by the force of the blast to land in a crumpled heap, limbs splayed in awkwardly entangled positions.

'Good shooting, Pete,' Stuart glanced back, delivering him a complimentary grin.

Bernerds looked distastefully at his first kill, his mouth felt dry and acidic as he flicked his tongue across his moistureless lips. He had no time to prepare for the unheralded arrival of the second of Kal Nyr's guards who came darting into view before he could move a muscle.

The trooper took in the scene before him in an instant, not stopping his heavy forward motion as he crashed sprawling into an unmoving Bernerds. Both figures went tumbling to the hard ground, legs and arms flailing. The two of them lost hold of their weapons almost simultaneously.

Kirsten Stuart whirled at the noise, all thoughts of watching out for further danger forgotten as she took in her colleague's predicament.

The trooper was the first to regain his wits and he struggled to prop himself up, gaining the advantage over his opponent, his lengthier arms a distinct benefit to him. His iron-like grip promptly appeared around the stunned Bernerds' throat, pushing down like a vice. The air was squeezed from his body and physically restrained from re-entering. The outermost edges of panic touched his mind and gained a merciless grip as he spluttered for air. The pinkness in his face quickly altered to a nasty shade of deep red.

Stuart looked on helplessly as the two struggled, unable to fire for fear of hitting Bernerds. Instead, she shouted much needed advice to him. 'Nerve points, Pete. Remember our combat training! Go for the soft spots!'

Bernerds rolled around under his opponent, not hearing her.

'Listen to me you thick git!' she bellowed at him. 'Go for the soft spots!'

Dimly latching on to her words he lashed out, hoping optimistically that the trooper had the same nerve centres and soft-spots as a human. A tightly clenched fist slammed with forceful impact into the trooper's neck, causing him to wince at the blow. His grip slackened at the delivery of a second punch and Bernerds at once started sucking in great lungfulls of life-giving air, the unhealthy pallor rapidly fading from his face. He brought up his large fists and swung broadly, catching the trooper with a severe blow to the jaw. The trooper, his mouth at once streaming with blood, toppled back, freeing Bernerds from his hold.

Bernerds scrambled to his feet and completed his offensive with a wide, sweeping kick that smashed into the kneeling trooper's unprotected skull. He was knocked to the ground, totally senseless. Bernerds scrabbled in the long grass for his rifle as Kal Nyr emerged from the courtyard, stepping over the broken remains of the door. His eyes widened in astonishment at the sight that greeted him. The punishment that had been dealt to his troopers while the Service people remained standing was overwhelmingly astounding to his superior attitude. From his haughty supercilious point of view it had to be seen to be believed.

'Come on,' Stuart cried urgently, backing away. 'Let's get out of here.'

When Kal Nyr saw Bernerds glaring malevolently at him with rifle raised in his direction he retreated a few hesitant steps. The overbearing stance vanished as his hands raised themselves in a supplicating attitude of surrender.

'Bernerds,' Stuart continued to urge, 'will you get your arse moving?'

'I ought to blow the stinking bastard away right now,' Bernerds growled with vituperation. 'It'd save everyone a lot of trouble.'

'That's not the answer. We have to get back to warn the Captain. Leave him, he's not worth it.'

Bernerds clenched his rifle tightly in frustration and came to a hurried decision. Wasting no more time on the aide he darted off alongside Stuart in the direction of the residency before reinforcements could arrive and overwhelm them.

Kal Nyr gave a deep sigh of relief at the narrowness of his escape. Then he once more assumed his mask of superiority as the Master-commander ran back into the courtyard. As the officer neared him he turned with imperious viciousness. 'You blithering, brainless incompetent. Are all of your troops as worthless as these? If so then I fear that we are really in for a massacre - of our own people. Get the army mobile, *immediately!*'

The officer mumbled a half-hearted apology and departed before he could be further insulted.

Kal Nyr stared hard-faced after the disappearing middies, cursing under his breath as the extremely fortunate duo vanished into the dense undergrowth of the bush to warn the rest of their comrades. He cursed the stroke of misfortune. The attack would be without its surprise now but the outcome would be the same - total and utter victory for the Imperial army. The enemy would not be allowed time to prepare an adequate defence. The Empire would win. He whirled away to prepare for the coming battle.

Bernerds, on the other hand, was envisioning a different, opposite outcome as he and Stuart ascended the rope, expertly scaling the wall. They reached the temporary safety of the residency in a state of breathless exitement.

'God I never want to go through that again.' Stuart wiped a line of perspiration from her face using the sleeve of her uniform.

'How are we going to get out in time?' Bernerds said, his mind on the immediacy of the problem. 'We have to find the Captain.'

A passing lieutenant stopped in amazment at the sight of the two midshipmen climbing back over the wall and hauling in a line of rope after them. He frowned darkly as his mind grasped where they had been. He walked up and confronted them.

'What do you think you two are up to?' he demanded, imagining that he already knew the answer. 'Midshipman Bernerds and...Senior Midshipman Stuart,' he discerned their names from their uniform tags. Then he addressed Stuart personally. 'You certainly should know better than to act in this way.'

'What can I say?' Stuart started.

'Where's the Captain?' Bernerds snapped insubordinately.

'What the....?' the lieutenant stuttered in amazement. 'Who the hell do you think you are talking to-'

'Where is the Captain?'

'Listen,' the lieutenant protested in outrage. 'You are in trouble. I'm putting you on report.'

'Yeah? And I think you should shove your report vertically. Forget it I'll find the Captain myself,' he sneered intransigently. He made off at a trot leaving the amazed lieutenant speechless.

'Sorry. There's not much I can do when he's in this mood,' Stuart shrugged apologetically before following on after her companion, trying to repress a smile.

☆ ☆ ☆

The heavy interior doors of *Emputin's* main hanger deck rumbled ponderously into the walls, leaving the way clear for unloading crews to pour into the bay. A single, recently arrived launch rested in a shallow pool of moisture created as the heating units had warmed the cold metal of the hull.

A rating began to mop up the small puddles of water from the deck whilst teams started offloading the launch's cargo, all the while keeping up a steady stream of light-hearted persiflage between them. The piles of boxes and crates were removed, one by one, from the launch's cramped storage space and dumped in an ordered heap beyond the bay's interior entrance. Other teams collected them from there, dispersing them to their various sections and storage holds throughout the ship.

Rem Bulloch entered the bay and moved to one side of the doorway, making sure he did not block the path of busy crew as they struggled out with the bulky wooden crates. The job was hard and laborious, especially without the help of the mechanical loaders which were all taken up running the goods from the secondary pile in the passage. The evacuation was making all of them overworked but they had to keep the bay clear, so it meant shoving the crates out by hand.

Bulloch had spent only a short period on the planet's arid surface. He had found the excessive temperature and the higher than normal gravity not to his taste and had departed on the next launch back to the ship's controlled environment. Now he was busy supervising the evacuation from this end, organising the precise but time-consuming rota drawn up to provide a tidy, efficient departure. A departure that had to remain hidden from

187

the Emperor and his minions until the very last minute, until the captain personally decided it was time to say farewell.

Why they couldn't pack and leave like any normal visitors, he did not know. Not having spent much of the last week in a run-down residency at the heart of an alien city, Bulloch failed quite understandably to see matters from Rickard's point of view. As far as he could see, having a screwball native visit the residency at the dead of night was one thing, but actually listening to what he had to say was definitely another. The captain should be warned by someone in a position to do so, such as the commander, or Beck, that Service Command would not take kindly to his actions without some damned firm proof. Such was Bulloch's idea of the situation.

'Chief,' one of the ratings on unloading detail called him from the launch's open hatch.

Bulloch brought his attention back to the bay. He paced slowly over to the waiting crewman, rubbing a hand down his face and over his stubbled chin. He felt tired. The captain's quiet evacuation was hard work for him, what with the sheer number of times the bay had to be cleared for incoming and outgoing craft and the amount of work that had to be crammed in between dockings and launches. It was all getting to be too much.

'What's up, Oaks?' Bulloch asked the rating wearily.

'There are some more crates in the back sir. They aren't ours and somone's marked them Native Foods on the tops. I wondered what we should do with them.'

'You unload them of course.'

'But shouldn't they be checked?'

'Why? Oh...yes I suppose they should. Look, leave them to one side of the pickup area. No, hang on. Shove them into the spares room instead. We can bring the things out later, when it's a little more peaceful. I'll get someone from Science to run a compatibility check on them, and for the captain's peace of mind they can look for unhealthy additives as well.'

'You mean alien pathogens, sir,' Oaks said smugly.

Bulloch sighed. 'No I mean unhealthy additives, now get some work done.'

'Yes, sir.' Crewman Oaks studied him with drooping eyes, tiredness written all over his face, although Bulloch wondered if Oaks did not tend to overexaggerate.

'Well get on with it, you lazy article,' he ordered not unkindly. 'We're all tired and the sooner you get finished the sooner we can get on.'

Oaks continued with his work with a heavy sigh, motioning to a colleague to help him with one of the large crates while Bulloch walked off, leaving the bay.

The food crates were stacked, two layers high, in the rectangular spare parts room off the main corridor outside the bay. The door was left ajar. Oaks, who was in charge of the work detail, made it clear to the pickup teams that the crates were not to be touched. The launch was duly cleared of its cargo and the bay was emptied of personnel as the over-utilised launch prepared to leave once more. The corridor and its cleared pickup point became quiet and deserted. Silence reigned, the calm being disturbed only by the subdued chatter of distant voices as the crew took what relaxation they could between unloading operations.

The humming wine of the air filters was all that could be heard within the darkened interior of the spares room. The noise overlay the usual *throb* of a ship in operation. Sounds from other corridors came over. Distant sounds. All was still.

With a creak of straining wood, the lid of one of the topmost crates rose and was moved to one side as the emerging form of a solidly built trooper pushed it away. Pistol in hand, he abandoned his temporary mode of transport like a slow motion jack-in-a-box, his eyes darting back and forth as he ascertained his position.

Finding to his pleasure that the room was otherwise empty he jumped down from the stacked crate and studied his surroundings. Peering through the open door he immediately recognised the landing bay hatch, the basic layout of this locality very similar to Imperial vessels of the larger classes. If the whole ship followed these same basic lines of constructional style, then this was the perfect hiding place in which to remain until he was required. Although he did not relish the idea of actually going into hiding, staying away from any possible chance of the oh-so important glories of battle, he knew it was necessary for the plan to succeed.

The single trooper furtively checked outside before pushing the door to, satisfied in the knowledge that the plan would succeed - thanks to him, alone against an entire ship full of his enemies.

He knew he could not fail.

'The natives are getting restless,' Rickard commented, looking over the outer wall at the growing crowd of citizens waiting outside the line of sand that marked the residency's boundary. 'Maybe they know something we don't.'

Beck grunted. 'I have a sneaking suspicion that I know what they think we don't, although they might not know that we know,' he said convolutedly. 'Nevertheless, I do know, and that is what matters. They've given themselves away just very slightly. Look there on the roof of the tower, hidden with all the subtlety of a three-legged elephant on heat.'

Rickard looked. What he saw sent an ice cold shiver racing along his spine. A gathering of heavily armed troopers were setting up their equipment between wide iron railings. Long snouted high velocity pulse rifles were pointed at the residency walkways in a distinctly menacing gesture.

'I have the feeling that the evacuation should be speeded up a little, don't you?' Rickard said, finding his voice curiously level and hushed.

'I find myself in utter agreement.'

Bernerds and Stuart chose that moment to arrive at a run from the south walkway, calling out as they neared.

'Sir! Captain!' Bernerds cried, coming to a sharp halt before his commanding officer and the chief surgeon. His face was flushed and his breathing fast. Stuart pulled up to a halt close behind.

Rickard gave Beck a worried glance as he turned to the agitated midshipman. A sense of presentiment overcame him. He was beginning to think that his imaginary guardian angel had taken early retirement. 'What is it?' he asked, feeling he had already guessed the answer.

'We're going to be attacked.'

'By whom?' Beck asked to confirm the situation.

'What...? By the Rukans of course, sir.'

'How do you know?' Rickard said.

'I - we sneaked into the Emperor's private gardens and overheard the ambassador giving some high-ranking officer orders to move in on us.'

'You did what?' Rickard felt he should be taken aback by the middie's brazen, direct nature but he could not find it in him to be so.

Bernerds' face reddened uncharacteristically as he realised how recalcitrantly he had acted. His former attitude of stubborn intransigence towards officers was suddenly muted. 'We...went over the south wall and-'

'Yes, all right,' Rickard cut him off. Intentionally or not, the midshipman had done the right thing, the one thing Rickard himself would have done had he not so much responsibility, most of it new - not that he would have allowed that to stop him even a few short weeks ago. How he had changed in such a short time. *C'est la vie*, as Beck would have put it. 'Did he say when the attack was supposed to start?'

'Not exactly,' Stuart put in over her companion's shoulder. 'But I got the impression they were ready to start off right away.'

Rickard looked at Beck. 'Time to leave?'

'I certainly think so.'

'So do I. Thank you, Midshipmen. Get yourselves down to the armoury and get properly kitted up.'

'Yes sir,' Bernerds and Stuart snapped a hurried salute before scampering off.

'Well, me and my luck. I certainly got the immediate results I asked for,' Rickard smiled grimly.

'What are we going to do about it?'

'Make sure the crew are armed for one thing.' He hailed a nearby petty officer who quickly responded to the summons. He quickly snapped out his commands. 'It's a red alert situation so inform the section leaders. Begin full scale evac procedures. All other emergency procedures are to go into action. Civilians and non-combat personnel are to be lifted out as soon as possible. The civilian observer will probably demand to see me but I haven't the time to spare. I'm making it your job to get her aboard the first outward bound launch. Break out all extra arms and get the security people and Marines into full armour.'

'Yessir.'

'All right, that's all. Get moving.'

'Aye, sir!' the over-eager petty officer bellowed and sprang off at a brisk trot.

With a satirical glint in them, Beck's eyes followed the departing figure, staring after him as if he were wondering at the man's sanity. 'She won't like that, you know,' he said to Rickard.

'Hmm? Oh, Karen. No, she'll probably give me a stern talking-to when we get back to the ship but it doesn't matter. She's out of the danger zone, that's the important thing.'

'I suppose so.'

Rickard stared into the distance, worrying over more immediate matters. What had happened to his long-cherished spirit of adventure? He wondered morosely. Doubtlessly it had been repressed as the mantle of captaincy had settled more firmly upon his shoulders. There was no going back, he realised. No returning to the old days. He was a man with responsibilities. A man who could no longer afford to think only of himself. The spirit of adventure was gone, vanished forever. In its place was the stark understanding that this was how it was to be for the rest of his life, or at least as long as he was a ship's captain. He would have to look after and protect his crew very carefully - his position demanded it - and he knew he would feel each loss, each death, almost as if it were his own private loss. He dreaded the coming battle and the carnage it would bring with it. Reality had painted a picture different from the comfortable but unrealistic one with which he was familiar.

His insides wrenched with the same old discomfort at the thought of what was to come.

9

505.99.44-68

Down in the open courtyard, the vociferant petty officer could be clearly heard, shouting out a highly jargonised version of Rickard's orders to the rest of the crew as they stopped whatever they were doing to listen, some in numbed surprise, others slowly nodding their heads as if this was what they had been expecting. The petty officer's booming voice rumbled across the residency. With professional control over their fears and apprehensions crew began running to the armoury or were assigned defensive positions, hurriedly being set up in various strategic locations.

Lines of redoubts were fast thrown up along the base and top of the wide flight of steps that led to the inner courtyard; rough constructions of sand-filled plastic food sacks were used for the purpose. The plastic sacks were merged with more than the occasional section of crumbling brickwork, taken from the disused stables and the supposedly new shacks, their comparative strength helped to solidify the protective walls. The work proceeded at a vastly accelerated rate, the defences were set up in scant minutes. Crew and officers scurried about, relaying orders and commands, shouting instructions and generally making themselves busy enough so that they did not have to think too directly about the approaching conflict. The Marines took up positions under command of their sergeant. They were tough. The best. And they knew they could win. Some of them even looked forward to testing the strength of the Imperials.

From the landing grid on the south wall, the frenzied hiss of take-off jets heralded the embarkation of a Service launch, as it rose noisily into what was virtually a straight

194

vertical takeoff, rising rapidly into the blue sky to finally merge with and vanish behind fast-moving cloud.

Still on the east wall, overlooking his crew's battle preparations, Rickard's eyes followed the rapidly receding launch as it became obscured from sight. 'At least Karen is safe,' he said with relief. 'But we are going to have to wait a while for the launches to cycle through the bay. Bulloch may be able to throw them all out at once for us but the damn things can only enter the ship one at a time.'

'We'll still be off the planet and safe.' Beck remained by his side, unobtrusively supplying his experience and support.

'Safe? You have got to be joking. They are going to throw everything they have at us. If they can't get the ship for themselves, they sure as hell aren't going to let us out of the Empire alive with the knowledge and information we have on them. They'll blast us before they let that happen. I'm only sorry that we didn't get the time to evacuate everybody before hostilities broke out.'

'It's not that bad, Chris,' Beck said. 'It's not even as if we've been taken completely by surprise. We've been expecting something to happen for a couple of days, so things could be worse. We weren't so much caught with our trousers down, so to speak, more in the act of pulling them back up.'

'Those launches need time to get down here. We might be left waiting too long.'

'Then again, we might not. Concentrate on the Now, not on what might happen.'

Rickard shrugged his shoulders. He understood the concrete validity of the advice. Beck was right, he was still new at this game. 'Okay. I know we have a battle to fight so let's get on and fight it.'

'That's the spirit, Captain. Never say die. Now, how're your troops doing?'

The front line troops, those who would bear the brunt of the combat, had started taking up positions behind the barricades and along the steps. Security Marines made up the bulk of their number, with the professional Marines giving strong backup with their expertise. Howarth could be seen darting backwards and forwards in his comprehensive organisation of the scattered lines of defence. His own raised voice stood out boldly over the tumultuous mass of others, all similarly raised. Marines with an extremely assorted array of weaponry - pistols, rifles, cussion grenade launchers to name but a few - took up places along the walkways, making sure they kept their heads down, wanting to avoid being shot at by the marksmen on the tower.

Rickard reached into his pocket, intending to call the ship, before remembering he had no communicator. A comm watch did not carry the power for the call. He threw Beck a casual glance. 'Doc?' Beck had anticipated him and had already produced his own communicator.

Flicking it on, Rickard directed himself at the pickup. *'Emputin*, this is Rickard. Do you hear me?'

'Captain, Lieutenant Watts here. I've just received a garbled message from an incoming launch. Something about a forthcoming attack on the residency. What is going on down there, sir?'

'No time to chat, Watts. I'm ordering a full alert. We are about to come under full battle conditions and I want a constant supply of launches to ferry people out while the Marines carry out a holding action. Cycle the launches at top speed through the bay and see if Bulloch can get the cutter mobile. We're making a complete evac of the area. Prepare the ship for immediate departure from this system.'

'On what heading, sir?' For Homespace?'

'Hell, no. To Tibor. You have the co-ordinates by now. The Emperor hasn't heard the last of me, not by a bloody long chalk. Rickard out.' He snapped shut the comm unit with a little more force than was necessary and handed it back.

'Where's Kiyami?' Beck asked as he crammed the battered old unit into his trouser pocket.

'Don't know. I'm sure she's around someplace. She'd better be. I don't want to leave anyone behind. The loss of life will be a total waste as it is.'

'This whole affair is a total waste,' Beck muttered with uncharacteristic sourness. 'As my old Latin teacher used

to say, *cui bono?* Who gains from this? Who indeed?'
'This isn't the Doc I know, surely?' Rickard tried to liven him up. 'I thought you were more resilient.'
Beck recovered himself and beamed in his most charming manner. 'Oh, I am. This was only your imagination. I'll be as right as rain - that is, presuming we ever get any in this desert.'
Rickard hoped Beck would be okay. He was feeling insecure enough as it was without having the surgeon give up on him. Relaying commands in the cold, sterile ambience of a ship's bridge was one thing. It was an entirely opposite matter to controlling clusters of crew in an open, physical confrontation where a single word could save lives or cast them away. The prospect scared him openly.
From one of the gate watch-posts, high up on the scanty plank board base supported by a framework of beams and struts, the lookout saw the first troopers double-marching into sight around the corner. 'Here they come!' he shouted down.
Rickard and Beck peered over the wall. The troopers came to a halt in a straight line in front of the firmly sealed gates. The troop-commander stepped forward and tilted his head upwards, unerringly directing himself at Rickard.
'I have been instructed first to call for the peaceful surrender of your arms and personnel. If you will not comply with this request then I have orders to take the residency by means of force. You will accept that we have the means and motivation to do this.'
'We accept you have the motivation, all right. The answer's still no,' Rickard did not bother to disguise his defiance.
The troop commander turned away dismissively. He began directing his troop to attack. 'Why ask for our peaceful surrender?' Rickard puzzled.
'Why not? It would save them the time and trouble of having to come in and wipe us out.'
'Still a bit of a pacifistic request for one of these people to make.'
'Maybe they need us to tell them how to fly the ship.'

197

The troop-commander waved in his men. They formed a semi-circular double row around the gates and began firing short bursts at the rotting wood structure. The gates began to warp and buckle under the high intensity, wide angle halo of fire.

'Come on,' Rickard snapped. 'Get back to the steps. Everyone pull back to the main steps!'

All the Service personnel on the lower half of the east walkway and along the whole southern end of the residency trailed closely after Rickard as he headed across the sandy main courtyard for the more easily defendable northern end. Howarth had lined a group of Marines along the base of the main steps in three rows. They parted to let through the last of the stragglers as they surmounted the redoubt at the base of the steps.

Coming to a halt at the top of the stairs Rickard called Howarth over. 'I want no firing until I give the order, okay?'

'Yeah, okay,' Howarth affirmed, wondering how the captain would handle his first taste of real action.

Kiyami emerged from the inner courtyard to join them. She looked tired, but no more so than everyone else. She saw Rickard and was pleased that there was still strength in his eyes. She knew she had been right to back him against Thom Howarth. He was more and more used to his position. 'Kiyami, how is it going back there?' Rickard said.

'We are as ready as we will ever be for a battle in this place. There are defendable posts all the way along to the grid except for the west passage. We will have trouble there.'

'I'll face that problem when we come to it. You've done your best. Now all we have to do is survive.'

'Easier said than done,' Beck put in unnecessarily.

'That reminds me,' Rickard said to him. 'I want you off on the next launch. There's going to be a lot of flak flying around here and I would like you upstairs to take in the wounded.'

'With all due respect and all that kind of rigmarole and similar rambling statements, balls...sir,' he dissented with eventual succinctness.

'Huh?' an understandably surprised Rickard gaped.

'I said balls, Captain. Hicks can take care of the injured on the ship just as well as myself and I *can* handle myself. I'm not completely decrepid.'

Rickard was taken aback by the surgeon's unswaying firmness to stay. There was certainly no prospect of him giving up. Nevertheless, Beck's life would be at risk here and perhaps he should be ordered back. He should but...but on further thought perhaps not. Beck was a fellow officer and was fully responsible enough to make his own decision on the matter. Rickard relented easily, respecting Beck's wish. 'Suit yourself, Doc, but don't say I didn't warn you.' He raised an inquisitive eyebrow in Kiyami's direction.

She was equally as firm in her choice. 'I am also staying, Captain.'

'Well, I can only say I'm pleased to have such a loyal band of lunatics with me.'

'How come I don't get a choice?' Bentowski protested mildly from behind Howarth.

Rickard duly noted the presence of his unceasingly presumptuous helmsman, and found he had a need for him. 'Mister Bentowski. As it is so clear to me that you would never leave the side of your colleagues at such a dangerous time, I'd like you to lead a small detachment of men up to the east walkway and try to hinder the oncoming troopers at the gates. If that's all right with you?'

'Yes, sir,' Bentowski groaned wearily.

'Make sure you warn them off first. I don't want to be the one accused of firing the first shot.'

'Anything you say, Captain.' He gestured to a group of ten or so Marines to follow him as he straightened up and finally showed some life. He climbed over the redoubts, followed by his temporary command. The group sprinted down the steps and across to the temporary wooden ladder that led to the watch-post, ascending with rapidity.

'Here's where the fun begins,' Beck said as he watched.

Rickard descended to the base of the steps, wanting to get a clearer view of the proceedings. Bentowski lined his Marines along the walkway, all of them remaining in a

199

crouched positions, cradling their weapons. When the line-up was complete, Bentowski tentatively raised his head, searching for the tower. He was pleased to find that the large gun-emplacement was focusing its attention elsewhere. Also, one floor below the roof, he was unsurprised to see Kal Nyr's anticipating features staring out at the residency.

'The ugly S.O.B. is directing the battle! Goddamn! Let's see what he thinks of this.' He popped his head further into view and shouted at the troop-commander with all his renowned diplomacy. 'Hey! Reptile features! Pack up and go home or you're gonna find yourself stuck in some deep brown smelly stuff!'

Not surprisingly the troop-commander's only answer was to aim a shot at him. He was quick to duck. 'Okay, suckers. This is where you get yours.' With a shout Bentowski gave the go-ahead to open fire.

He and the Marines stood and began pouring fire down on the unprotected troopers below. Many of them fell, instantly killed by the scathing blasts. Others scattered to ineffectually return the fire, their open positions not helping them in the least. The Marines picked off Imperial after Imperial in a display that soon bore a marked resemblance to a shooting gallery - until one of the Marines gave a choked cry and fell back limply, sprawling half over the edge of the walkway. Blood gushed from the skull wound.

There was no time to check if the Marine was dead. A second man quickly fell victim to the accurate shooting of the tower marksman as he finally got his range. Bentowski took permanent care of another trooper below before turning his attention to the tower. Shots were beginning to become profuse from that direction. Another Marine collapsed as a shot found its mark, blood streaming from his wide open wound.

Outside the gates a reinforcement troop could be heard double-marching to the aid of their regrouping comrades. 'Duck your heads down,' Bentowski at last ordered, sensibly reluctant to become the next target. 'Cease fire and take some cover!'

His men complied, thankful to be out of the firing line.

Bentowski threw the watching Rickard an exaggerated shrug to show there was no more he could achieve for now.

There was an explosive splintering of shattered wood. The main gates were spectacularly destroyed, tossing great broken chunks of debris into the air. The heavy crossbar came crashing to the ground some feet from its previous position, still hanging on to one of the metal brackets. Thousands of slivers of wood rained down across the courtyard, littering it heavily. Troopers poured in through the gaping ruins.

Rickard dashed back up to the steps and leapt over the makeshift redoubt, ducking down between Kiyami and Beck. Seeing that his usefulness at the watch-post was ended, Bentowski wisely pulled his men back along the walkway, keeping bent low so they did not fall once more into the marksman's extremely accurate sights. The dead were left where they lay.

The Imperial troop now held the southern end of the residency. As they waited for commands, their numbers in the lower segment of the courtyard were all the time swelling with new influxes of troopers. The newcomers warily examined the enemy for strengths and weaknesses. All they could see were firmly entrenched lines of well-armed men. There fell a grim, unnatural stillness as each side sized up the other.

'I want single volley fire only,' Rickard called out the ranks of Service crew. 'On my command.'

'Why don't we open fire now, before they've had time to group?' Howarth sharply questioned him.

'Because I'd still like to imagine we were still civilised enough not to fire without provocation, instead of blazing away at the first movement.'

'They've already provoked us.'

Rickard stayed silent, not trusting himself to construct a comprehensible argument under the present circumstances, and especially with an officer who plainly disliked him.

Behind the row of command officers, over to the left of the barricade, Bernerds was kneeling beside Stuart. They both watched the troopers with apprehension.

Bernerds was feeling bellicose, fidgety with the intensity of his eagerness to fight, his muscles were tightened in attentiveness for what was to happen and his eyes looked agog on the enemy ranks. The fact that he had made his first ever kill that very morning made no impression upon his eagerness. It had been swept aside and forgotten in the ensuing confusion, Stuart was suffused with a sense of *sang-froid*. She felt completely calm and at ease, as eager to fight as Bernerds but with a greater semblance of self-control and certainly not holding what amounted to a death wish.

The troop-commander pushed his way forcefully through to the front of his troop. He observed with pleasure the intensely belligerent vituperation his troopers were displaying to the enemy. Upon seeing the hastily erected Service defences he stoically readied himself for the attack.

Risking coming into the tower marksman's sights, Bentowski was perched near the walkway's edge to observe the waiting troopers whose ranks were coming into formation. He wished he could take an effective potshot at the problematical marksman who had caused him so much trouble. With him cleared out of the way Bentowski and what was left of his Marine detachment could make a more decisive display of force, spraying the troopers with fire from above. As it was, they would have to make do, firing down whilst simultaneously avoiding the marksman's sights.

As if to echo his thoughts the Marine next to him muttered wishfully to one of his blank-faced colleagues. 'It would help if we had a couple of really heavy duty laser canon on our side.'

'Hmph!' his companion snorted unsympathetically. 'You might as well ask for a soddin' fleet of armoured attack vehicles.'

'Or a ticket out of this flea-pit,' the Marine said and raised his head for a quick peek over the wall. A single shot rang out, shattering the silence. The Marine clutched at his shoulder, losing his balance and falling against Bentowski. Scrabbling wildly for a handhold as he lost *his* balance, the helmsman grabbed the stricken Marine and was in turn grabbed by another Marine to prevent them both falling off the walkway.

Bentowski breathed a heartfelt sigh of relief as he clutched at the comfortingly solid base of the walkway. All heads on the ground snapped up at the sound of the shot, Rickard looked on with concern as Bentowski dragged the injured man away from the edge of the walkway. Only half of the detachment now remained.

Witnessing the disturbances and the fact that the Service forces had been distracted the troop-commander knew the moment had come. Taking his pistol in his left hand he drew his sword, hearing with pleasure the singing of metal scraping across the sheath. With a ferocious bellow he gave the order to charge, personally leading his troopers to the attack, sword arm waving them madly on. Roaring wildly, the massed troop surged forward.

'The friggin' reptiles are suicidal!' Bentowski exclaimed at the sight as his wounded man was helped off in the direction of the landing grid.

Rickard was plunged into a state of temporary stupefaction at the sight of so many blood-lusting troopers charging down on him and it took a hefty nudge in the ribs from Beck to bring him round. Shaking his head to clear it he concentrated on the fast advancing enemy. He waited until they were close, until the distance between them had narrowed to barely more than a few metres before giving the tensely awaited order.

'Fire!'

A single explosive volley cut into the charging troop, the style vaguely similar to that used by European armies more than six hundred years before. Their number was cut, trimmed considerably. Over a third of the troop was left lying in the sand.

'Fire!'

Combined rifle and pistol bursts tore through their bodies, almost wiping out the troop. The harsh *chuff* of grenade launchers sounded, heralding the arrival of a series of concurrent explosions as the earth was torn violently from beneath the feet of many of the troopers. Soil was sprayed out in vast, brief fountains. The few survivors kept on coming, their shrapnel wounded but undefeated commander urging them ceaselessly on through the scattered corpses.

'They're not stopping!' Bernerds cried out as Rickard came to the same conclusion.

'Defend yourselves!'

Opposite forces clashed and the conflict became even bloodier.

The few remaining troopers reached the lower redoubt at the steps and bounded over, forcing the Marines there to resort to hand-to-hand combat. The struggle was intense for a few endless seconds. A trooper managed to lift his rifle and fired point blank at a Marine. Another took a blow to the head and collapsed beneath ever-shifting feet. Using his pistol only when necessary, the troop-commander's sharp-bladed sword continually slashed down, slicing at an armour-encased body without stopping until his blade found an open point. He took advantage of the opportunity without mercy and another Marine fell to the ground.

'Give 'em some help!' a voice shouted out.

Rickard waved a secondary group of Marines into the fray, doubling the strength of the defenders. The tide of the conflict abruptly turned and the aggressors were quickly disposed of. The troop-commander vanished under a mass of smashing, bone-crushing rifle butts.

The Marines emerged triumphant as the fighting ceased. The troop had been wiped out. A relieved sigh coursed through the ranks. 'Don't relax yet,' Rickard advised those nearest him. 'There's got to be more they can throw at us.'

As if to confirm his words a single shot rang out from the marksman on the tower, finding another victim. The unfortunate target slumped lifelessly over the redoubt.

'Damn it,' Rickard cursed through clenched teeth. 'Howarth, who's your best shot with a telescopic?'

Howarth pondered momentarily before pointing to the armoured young woman crouched next to Bernerds. She looked on expectantly. 'Midshipman Stuart's the most accurate. I'm sure she'll be good enough.'

Rickard swivelled in her direction, recognising her

from earlier, and nodded at the tower. 'Do you think you could get him from here, Stuart?'

Stuart smiled grimly. 'No problem, sir.'

She pulled Bernerds unceremoniously between her and her target, using him as a gun-rest. Aiming the long barrelled rifle with unmoving steadiness at the tower she fiddled with the sights, altering the settings, procuring the angle and deflection the shot required. Once set up she gave Bernerds a light warning tap on the shoulder to indicate her readiness and he froze. Becoming one with the weapon she slowly squeezed the trigger, pulling it back ever so ponderously. A single pulse jerked the rifle upwards as she fired and all eyes studied the tower.

A head bobbed briefly into sight before falling back once more. That was followed by a hurried scurrying motion as a single figure rose and shifted an unseen object out of the way. The black barrel of the marksman's weapon was drawn back, the position was apparently being abandoned now that it had been compromised.

'Thank God for that,' Rickard did not disguise his relief.

Howarth was in full agreement for once. 'At least we're having some luck.'

With a clattering of booted feet two more Imperial troops marched into the courtyard in precise military formation, raising minor sand clouds in their wake and headed by what Rickard recognised as a lord-commander. They came to a halt in a double block, each five rows deep, all heavily armed. The solid square blocks reached from wall to wall across the entire width of the courtyard.

'Looks like we're about to have fun and games again,' Beck commented sardonically.

'Wait for my command,' Rickard advised as everyone's attention turned to the newcomers. Rifles snapped up sharply and firing clips were actuated.

The lord-commander drew his sword and motioned his troopers forward. They commenced to advance, keeping in formation. The rifles of the front row held level, aimed along the line of resistance. They reached the midway point in the courtyard. 'Volley fire!' Rickard commanded.

His crew poured a single volley of shots into the approaching troops. Many fell but others from the rear ranks stepped forward to take their places.

Continuing to march, the Imperial front line fired a return volley, many finding targets of their own. The lord-commander snapped a command and his troops broke formation, charging ahead with a disconcerting lack of regard for their own lives, firing all the time.

'Fire at will!' yelled Rickard as the troopers closed in. Shots were exchanged in profusion, Imperial troopers and Service Marines alike finding and becoming victims. Many of the fast approaching troopers dropped but the others still came on. Behind them another two troops could be glimpsed filling in through the remnants of the gates, taking up positions similar to the first party.

Rickard drew his own pistol, felling a hostile face. A stray shot whizzed past his head, blowing out chips from the wall behind. Howarth found time between bursts of pistol fire to shout to him. 'We've got no chance out here. It's too open.'

'I'm beginning to realise that for myself!' Rickard called back. He ducked instinctively as another shot came much too close for comfort.

The remainder of the first party of troops ceased their advance on a further command, stopping just short of the lower barricade. They knelt as one, thinning themselves out in a single row, continuing to fire. The second party trotted forward to back them up, lining behind them, creating a wall of troopers firing non-stop.

Rickard saw the Marines behind the first redoubt were becoming hopelessly decimated under a hail of concentrated fire. Only a battered few of them manning the barricades had survived.

'Howarth,' he shouted, pointing down to the Marines below him. 'Get them out of there. They're being massacred. Withdraw them!'

Howarth signalled his understanding and relayed the order with an ear-shattering yell.

The Marines began the retreat. They started returning one by one in mad, frantic bursts of speed, many not completing the short distance. They were completely open while ascending the stairs. The seriousness of their plight was self-evident.

Rickard snapped out, 'Give them some covering fire!'

'You heard the Captain. Cover them!'

'Watch your side. Look out for the left hand!'

'Shoot the bastards, don't play with them!'

From the protection of the barricade Kiyami supplied stalwart support. She calmly and collectedly marked her targets and fired in short, precise bursts, each shot finding its goal and terminating another life. With extreme patience and cool nerves she took care of many of the leading troopers, more than one unwary captain falling prey to her expert markmanship.

Beside her Beck crouched low, tending to a crewwoman's wounded arm and sorely wishing he'd taken Rickard's advice and pulled out earlier. He knew there was a disorder of the mind running in his family. He had to be mad to want to stay here. But he knew his job was more important than thinking only of his own skin, so that was what he concentrated upon, desperately attempting to ignore the flying pulses of gunfire that whizzed and flew around him.

The din rose around them as the battle became more intense. Pulse charges flew across the narrow dividing space between the two unevenly matched sides. For every Service gun there were now two hostile ones. They were becoming heavily outnumbered and the strain on the survivors was beginning to show.

'Now! Make a run for it!'

An extremely youthful, fresh-faced Marine rose from his position in retreat from the lower baricade, climbing out from a bundle of bodies. He fired back as he moved, shooting wildly and erratically into the bunched ranks of troopers, stepping and stumbling his way back up the unprotected steps. His colleagues above tried to cover him with a prodigious amount of fire, yelling encouragement to him.

'Dodge! Side to side.'

'You can make it!'

His sergeant was particularly vociferous. 'Get moving you bloody anorexic shrimp! Before I come down there and kick you up those stairs!'

The Marine ran, turning and sprinting for the second barricade, snaking from side to side. Gunfire splattered the steps around him as he reached the upper redoubt and caught him full in the back, blowing through his heavy armour like dynamite through paper. The corpse rolled and tumbled back down to add to the ever-growing pile of corpses below.

'You poor little bugger,' the sergeant moaned sadly.

The young Marine was the last of the front line group to live long enough to even make an attempt at reaching the comparative safety offered by the barricade above.

More troopers swarmed into the residency, swelling the already full ranks of attackers. It was time to move to the secondary defences in the interior courtyard. 'Retreat,' Rickard barked vociferously, waving his people back amid oppressive enemy fire. 'Retreat! Pull back!'

Beck scrambled to his feet and made for the open doors, a wounded rating clinging desperately to each arm. Kiyami was close behind, barely dodging a scything volley of rifle bursts which bit into the stonework beside her. The Marines held the troopers off, waiting until everyone was safely inside before following.

Catching sight of a crewwoman in distress a burly, thick-set Marine hurried to the rescue. The crewwoman was fighting desperately in a frenzied hand-to-hand encounter with a trooper who'd managed to find a way through the firing lines. He was steadily overpowering her in an uneven trial of strength. The Marine leapt over the splayed corpse of a rating and flew into the fray. The trooper was knocked sideways by the impact of his arrival but quickly recovered and got off a shot, catching the brash Marine in the leg. The trooper was about to finish his opponent when the crewwoman brought up her own weapon and blasted him in the stomach, the impact having virtually the same effect as a canon shot upon a rag-doll, knocking the trooper away to tumble down the steps. The crewwoman began dragging her would-be rescuer to safety. The damage to his ostentatiously manly pride was obviously worse than the damage to his leg.

'Help the wounded!' Rickard shouted as he determinedly aided an injured rating to his feet regardless of the profuse enemy fire, placing one of the half-conscious man's arms over his shoulders. From the corner of his eye he saw Howarth and several unharmed Marines doing likewise, dragging the majority of the wounded through the gates. A sudden hail of gunfire made Rickard stumble and almost fall as he dodged but he caught his balance, briefly steadying himself before struggling on alongside the still firing defenders.

He reached the interior courtyard and passed his load on. Dashing back to the entrance he hurried on the last of the survivors. Jockeying them constantly he kept up an unceasing stream of encouragement, something of which he himself was in need. He helped a limping rating through with his free hand, firing a covering shot over the heads of two Marines who followed. He saw the unintimidated Imperial forces rise and resume their forward advance.

'Move. Come on, get a move on,' he harrassed a few remaining Marines who struggled to help the many injured.

Beck ran back out, shouldering Marines aside as he raced to help more wounded.

'Beck!' Rickard called out after him. 'Phil!' He made no sign of acknowledgement.

Hurrying past with a blinded Marine corporal in tow, Stuart still found the energy to fire a farewell round back the way she had come.

Out in the courtyard the lord-commander, seeing that his quarry was about to disappear into a more easily defended area, yelled an order to his troops. The massed army broke into a run, heading for the stairs. Beck once more made his way to the doors, casualties clinging to each arm. Solid bullets from a trooper's weapon slammed into the wall bare centimetres from him. He gave a yelp and jumped gingerly to one side, almost losing hold of one of his wards.

'Move!' Rickard screamed at the top of his voice, finding he had been joined by Howarth. In unison they shouted at the Marines who at last realised the danger. They reluctantly abandoned the more seriously injured to the mercy of the innumerable enemy. They pounded their way through the gates, some stopping to return the heavy fire. Only one failed to make it. He was blasted to the ground as the nearing troopers closed in.

Rickard found a gap in the retreating men and placed a well-aimed shot in the enemy ranks.

Bernerds made his way at last to safety, pacing slowly backwards. He continued pouring round after explosive round into the closed ranks of troops. Trooper after trooper fell to his deadly accurate line of fire until they finally found his range. Then shots were wildly forthcoming in his direction. He ducked and bolted.

'Get your arse through!' Howarth bellowed frantically, roughly shoving a bloodied rating on his way. He was the last. The troopers reached the top of the steps and were struggling over the half-collapsed barricade as Howarth and Rickard heaved shut the gates, others joining in the effort. The wooden doors were slammed closed.

A hail of pulse fire thudded into the thick wood, jarring it strongly. Rickard helped throw a crossbar into place to seal the entrance. They were momentarily secure.

'We left some men behind,' remarked a breathless Rickard.

Howarth stared at him. 'Nothing you could do about it,' he said.

'We should have helped them all in.'

'We couldn't, you know that as well as I do,' Howarth told him emotionlessly.

Rickard caught his steady gaze and saw that the security chief's sense of loss was as great as his own, only he was sensibly keeping it repressed. Well, at least Howarth had some heart. No, that wasn't fair, he corrected himself. Don't allow personal disagreements to get in the way of clear judgement. In fact, in this instance, Howarth had the right idea.

On the east walkway, Bentowski was still crouched low with the remainder of his Marine detachment. They had been totally forgotten in the confusion of the affray by both sides, even though they had harried the Imperial army as much as they could from their exposed position. They watched helpless as the Service crew on the ground fled into the residency, some using the small gate below the walkway to reach safety. They continued to watch as the abandoned wounded were allowed to live, being hauled roughly away.

'It's time we were gettin' outta here,' Bentowski finally decided.

His Marines nodded in silent agreement and moved after him.

Bentowski caught sight of the petite Stuart in the sheltered interior courtyard, taking a brief rest amongst the exhausted crew by leaning on her rifle. She looked up at the same time and saw him. 'Hey, Bentowski,' she called, irrespective of his superiority in rank. 'Get your backside down here with the rest of us.'

Bentowski smiled madly and gave her a wave, liking the woman's style. Unrealisably wishful fantasies concerning her coursed through his over-imaginative mind as he pulled his men back. The army of troopers did not even have the courtesy to notice them leaving.

Rickard watched through the gates' wide-angle peep holes as the Imperial captains conferred with their lord-commander. With a sharp gesture from the latter they parted, one of them rounding up a group of troopers. The group was double-marched away from the gates towards the disused stables where they proceeded to break down one of the thick, rounded central support beams. As the beam came away the already unsteady structure of the roof gave an ominous rumbling groan of disturbed woodwork. Slates slid off the hole-filled roof and a large cloud of dust billowed out through the wide entrance. Emerging from the dust cloud like a polar expedition yomping through a blizzard marched the group of troopers, the long support beam held between them.

Its intended use was plainly clear and Rickard's eyes widened in alarm.

'Oh Jesus. They're not going to let us rest.' Rickard gestured sharply to Howarth. 'I want Marines at these peep holes firing out to delay and interfere with the troopers as much as possible. They're going to use a battering-ram on us!'

211

With an eloquent expression of disgust at the news Howarth bellowed commands down the short passageway that led to the interior courtyard. A mixed squad of Marines and ratings piled down to the gates at the ready and fully reloaded.

'See those troopers with the log?' the security chief said without humour. 'You're going to hold them off as long as possible without getting yourselves killed, okay?'

An obedient chorus of 'Yes, sir,' greeted his ears and he and Rickard made way for them.

The gates suddenly shook with a thunderous rattle as the makeshift battering-ram impacted forcefully. One of the ratings jumped back in startled astonishment. The more experienced Marines were unruffled. They calmly slotted their rifles through the peep holes and squeezed on the triggers.

Rifle fire lanced out at the Imperial forces, causing more than one to fall. Others ran forward to take their place in ceaseless streams, flowing unstoppably in one direction. One enterprising individual ran up to the gates, dodging shots from inside with startling dexterity. He brought up his own weapon and fired through the gap.

On the other side of the gates a rating gaped in surprise as blood trickled freely over his uniform from an ugly shoulder wound. He stumbled and fell, not feeling the helping hands that pulled him away. One of the more level-headed Marines at the gates carefully anticipated the trooper's next appearance and put in a shot of his own before there could be a repeat performance. The trooper did not return.

Rickard looked on in dismay as the new casualty was carried past him. 'We can't go on like this,' he said, using a sleeve to wipe dusty grime from his forehead. Tiny droplets of sweat were dribbling down his hot, flushed face.

The gates buckled sharply as the ram made contact. The Marines fired and shots were returned, both with little effect.

'It would be better if we pulled back and defended the interior courtyard,' Howarth opined. 'That way they can't charge at us because they'd be bottled up in this passage.

They'd be sitting ducks. It'd make a nice change, too.'

'That's probably the best way to do it. Okay,' he called to the Marines, 'withdraw to the courtyard.'

They retracted their rifles and backed away from the cracked and breaking gates.

'Where the bloody hell are those launches?' Rickard cursed as he cleared the passage. He glanced up at his office as he came into the paved courtyard. He'd forgotten to close the louvre doors. They were still open from the night before. If the launches did not arrive soon they might as well kiss this battle goodbye and hand over their weapons personally.

Howarth began arranging the men behind the makeshift cover so that they were all fairly well hidden or covered by other guns. They blocked the passage, determined to hold this position for as long as necessary. 'We have to stop them getting any further until the launches arrive,' Rickard said as Kiyami joined him. She looked like he felt.

'It will not be easy,' she said tiredly.

'No, but at least we're relatively safe here...' his voice trailed off as something came sharply to mind.

Bentowski made his appearance on the scene having led his surviving Marines along the sheltered north passage. He reported to Howarth.

'What is it?' Kiyami asked Rickard as a look of horror dawned upon his face.

'That alleyway from the west corridor is lying wide open. A whole army could simply walk in and shoot us in the back. Damn, we're lucky they haven't already done it. Mister Howarth,' he caught the security chief's attention.

'Something up?' Howarth asked as he abandoned Betowski.

'Yes, something's up. We've forgotten to block off access to our rear. I'm surprised they haven't already used it. That connecting alley next to the crews' quarters. It's going to lose us this battle unless it's blocked.'

'I'll see to it myself.'

'Good. Use grenade launchers to blow down the bordering walls. Make as much mess as you can. After that, hold the south side until we arrive.'

213

'Okay. Bentowski, finish setting out the crew to defend this area. You, and you two,' he pointed out three Marines, 'come with me.' The demolition team quickly vanished around the corner.

'Hey, but I'm a pacifist,' Bentowski called after them. 'I even have a medical certificate to prove it.' He raised a hand to pick at his ear as he thought about what he should do with the remaining Marines.

The sound of cracking wood reverberated around the enclosed courtyard. Stuart gave a yell. 'The gates are giving up!' Straight away the gates at the passage's end gave with a gut-wrenching crunch of broken and battered wood.

'Hold your positions,' Rickard ordered. 'Prepare to open fire.' He ran over to one of the concrete pillars that supported overhead arches. Drawing his pistol he edged round the pillar and examined the far end of the stubby passage.

Having found his own problem solved - the Marines had quickly found their own niches at the sound of the weakening gates - Bentowski imitated Rickard's example and retired to the cover of a pillar. He took the one behind Rickard.

Several of Beck's patients were lolling semi-consciously; he had to hurriedly pull them out of the firing line while Kiyami closed in for a better angle on the passage. What she saw confirmed her fears. The gates were utterly beyond repair, slivers of cracked wood crumbling away. Troopers began appearing at the ruins, already shooting.

'Open fire,' Rickard commanded, letting off the first shot.

His crew began pouring staccato pulse fire down the narrow accessway, killing many of their enemy in the wide, peppering spray. Effective fire was quickly returned, the troopers utilising the cover of the half-destroyed gates. A trooper was hit in the face and slumped heavily onto the wreckage. Marines sprayed the accessway with grenade fire, blasting bricks and bodies uncaringly in all directions. Dense clouds of fire and smoke wafted up. The rest of the troops pulled back under a strong deluge of shots. Smoke wafted across the passage, obliterating them from sight.

In his usual overexcited manner, Bentowski maintained a steady stream of meaningless psycho-babble, yelling and cursing loudly, as he pumped bursts of deadly fire down the passage. The persistent explosions of gunfire still drowned him out.

'Cease firing,' Rickard sharply cut through the noise. He lowered his pistol.

Bentowski found himself shouting at the silence and hastily shut up, his face burning red as he glanced around in embarrassment. Fortunately for him, everyone else had been too preoccupied with their own private distractions to take any notice of him.

Howarth's holding action appeared to be working.

A sudden burst of rapid gunfire came from the west passage. It was followed almost immediately by a tremendously powerful explosion that rocked the residency to its foundations, showering everyone with prolific clouds of dust. A second explosion sounded loudly and its force could be felt in the tremoring of the ground. Over the roof of the armoury there rose a pillar of dirty black smoke that speedily bubbled into a large cloud, rising almost vertically over the city.

Rickard strained to see if the alleyway had been successfully blocked but he failed to get the angle he needed - the armoury hindered his view. He stared through the unblocked passageway. His enemy seemed as astonished as he could hope for at the sight of what he prayed was a high pile of obstructing rubble. Thick fumes wafted low across the Imperial ranks as the wind tugged and goaded them towards the dusty soil. Behind the multiplying rows of troopers, Rickard glimpsed two retreating Imperials physically dragging a stumbling, dazed hostage in red and black Service uniform between them. The prisoner suddenly pulled his head erect and glanced back over his shoulder. Rickard was stunned to recognise the man.

It was Howarth, dust-covered and dirty, blood gathering at a cut on his forehead.

10

Howarth was dragged roughly out of the residency, his captors caring little of a few extra bruises to his body. They waited patiently as a lone floater hovered up to meet them, its driver not moving from his forward-placed seat, once he'd drawn to a halt.

His spinning head fast clearing, the level-headed Howarth straight away decided on a course of action. He feigned unconciousness, slumping forward limply.

The trooper holding onto him laughed contemptuously. 'So weak!'

His comrade smirked in agreement and moved off to open the rear door of the covered, van-like floater. Howarth saw his opportunity and immediately made his move. Pretending to wilt forward even more, he quickly withdrew a concealed flick-blade from the side of his boot with his free hand. Springing the blade he slammed it into the first trooper, gutting him viciously.

'Now who's so weak?' he remarked casually as he let the body drop.

The second trooper heard the sound of the scuffle and whirled in time to see his former prisoner making off at great speed in the only direction open to him, into the maze of surrounding houses and sidestreets. The trooper unholstered his pistol and fired wildly at Howarth's legs, hoping to maim him. The burst of shots fell scant centimetres wide in a running line fury that seemed to keep pace with the security chief until he veered off around the sheltering corner.

Out of sight of the trooper, Howarth paused momentarily. He glanced back to the residency as the smoke shadowed form of a launch rose purposefully into

216

the air and ascended towards the clouds. Another launch quickly took its place on the grid amid more firing.

'Hope they all get back safely,' he prayed to himself.

He heard the crunching sound of nearing footsteps, from the direction of the floater, and he disappeared into the city like a fading spectre.

☆ ☆ ☆

'Did you see that?' Bentowski muttered out loud after having watched Howarth being hauled out of the residency. 'Goddamn. We're really in deep shit now.'

That did not say much for his opinion of Rickard's worth, but the fledgling captain decided to let it pass. His eyes lowered, flickering over the few scattered bodies of crewmembers lying around the mouth of the passage in various untidy positions of death. The loss of life thoroughly sickened him, the effect of death on people, faces he knew and worked with rather than unknown nonentities, rammed home the point all the harder. Rage simmered inside him, close to boiling point.

'Has anyone ever told you, Mister,' he said, changing his mind on Bentowski, 'that diplomacy and tact are not your strongest traits?'

Bentowski flicked his attention from the passage to Rickard, surprised by the captain's question. 'On frequent occasions, yup, they have, sir. I guess it was Thom..er, Mister Howarth who last mentioned it.'

'Well you won't have to worry about him doing it any more.'

'I was kinda hopin' we'd get to rescue him back from the Rukes...sir. He's a friend of mine.'

'Ah. Sorry,' he said. Why didn't he learn to keep his mouth shut? True, he was adrenalin-pumped and stuck dead-smack in the middle of a battle zone, but that was no reason to pass presumptous judgements on people he was only beginning to know. 'I apologise,' he offered sincerely. 'I didn't realise you and Howarth were anything other than working acquaintances.'

217

'S'okay, Captain. I know you and him haven't really hit it off but give him time, he'll come around. He likes you really, his brain just ain't told the rest of him yet.'

'I'll bear that in mind when we get back.'

'Like I told Howarth before, you're a good guy, Captain.' His eyes took in the courtyard. 'Now all we have to do is wait for the US Cavalry to ride over yonder hill and rescue us.' Rickard chuckled in agreement.

The majority of the defenders were otherwise occupied, resting as much as they could in the short lull between actions. Some tended to their wounds, others made speedy maintenance checks on their weapons. No-one was expecting what happened. The small gate below the east walkway gave way as a roaring mob of troopers burst through it. Simultaneously the lord-commander outside gave an aggravatingly sudden yell of 'Charge!', as the troopers in his command rushed the confused defenders.

Spirits flagging under the unceasing onslaught, the Service crew and their Marine backups nonetheless fought bravely to hold off the massing Imperial troops but it was plain to see they were fighting a lost cause. Almost immediately large numbers of them were set upon by the combining Imperial forces. Some were gunned down coldly and callously. Others were beaten into submission and dragged off behind the fighting. The Marines in the east section scattered under the extreme pressure of too numerous an enemy. Many of them were overrun and killed. An equal amount became submerged and lost from sight, not knowing which way to turn as they were beset from two sides.

'Fall back to me,' Rickard ordered with fragile calm over the frenetic din. 'To me! Withdraw to my position.'

The combined voices of Kiyami and a burly Marine sergeant backed him up to good effect.

A large number of the survivors managed to comply, pulling back in close-bunched groups and fighting all the way in strenuous hand-to-hand combat, many Marines punching out in hard-hitting viciousness at troopers too slow to defend themselves.

An Imperial captain rounded the corner of the passage

and recognised Rickard as a leading figure in the ranks of
the resisting Service combatants. He took a badly aimed
potshot. Rickard was well out of the way of danger.
Beside him Kiyami got off a shot and successfully downed
the troublesome officer.

The majority of the troopers began pulling back to
order as their casualty rate grew at an ever-increasing
pace. The further they pressed the aggravated Marines,
the harder the Service's professionals fought back. The
fighting slackened off as the two forces separated.

'Now we know for sure,' Rickard said to his first officer,
keeping his attention ahead. He picked off open targets
whenever they presented themselves. 'They're trying to
take as many of us alive as they can.'

'So they are definitely after the *Emputin?*'

'Looks that way. But we're going to have to find some
better cover if any of us want to make it back alive.'

'We should enter the west passage, a few at a time with
the rest holding this exit.'

'Nice idea. We should start right away.' Rickard
signalled to the Marine sergeant and began relaying his
instructions.

In the bewilderingly sudden affray, Bentowski had
found himself battling alongside Bernerds and Stuart.
Now, feeling battered but happy to be alive he caught his
breath in long, chest-expanding gulps of air. The
threesome sheltered in a protected alcove not far from
Rickard's position. 'Oh boy,' Bentowski gasped. 'In this
place it's a case of one wrong move and you're dogmeat. It
just ain't safe.'

Bernerds gave an acidic growl of agreement. 'I'll go
along with that, mate.'

'I hoped you would.'

More intent on matters outside of the alcove, Stuart
carefully noted the enemy numbers, instantly spotting the
increase. 'They're multiplying again,' she commented.
'Looks like they're getting ready for another attack.'

'Oh for chrissake,' complained Bentowski. 'Why don't
they give it a break.'

'They can't do that,' Stuart grinned. 'It'd spoil my fun.'

'You've got a bloody strange idea of fun,' Bernerds told

her.

'You're a one to talk!' she countered. She looked back to the Imperial lines. 'Christ, here they come again!' The solid ranks of troopers charged once more.

'Defend yourselves!' someone shouted.

Shouting colourfully descriptive, but rhetorical, insults at the troopers, Bentowski jumped out of hiding and fired into the thickest part of them in frenzied abandon. Then it was hand-to-hand combat again, rifle barrels being used to block blows from swords, or the chopping butts of other rifles.

'Get back to the west passage!' Rickard commanded above the noise. He could see his people being slowly beaten under the massive onslaught, little by little. The fighting was bloodthirsty. The Marines were struggling ever harder to hold the enemy off and their casualty rate was escalating. They seemed determined to hold the courtyard, even to the death. 'Pull back,' he yelled at them. 'Retreat.'

Service crew split into small, bunched up groups, aiding each other in the hazardous physical conflict. It was an almost impossible task. They were being overwhelmed. Some made it back to the passage. Others did not.

Bentowski fought his way methodically through, all trace of impudent humour gone from his face. Suddenly he was knocked sideways by a blow from the gigantic fist of a trooper. Shaking his head to clear it, Bentowski calmly noted that the offending trooper was constructed like a brick wall. Then he shot him in the stomach, watching with satisfied pleasure as the giant body collapsed to the floor. 'Take that, goon-face,' he spat.

Rickard, Kiyami and Beck, together with many wounded, stayed in a large gathering around the entrance to the passage, helping to safety as many as they could. Rickard watched the progress of his retreating crew with concern. Some of them were taking too many risks.

Stuart remained doggedly stuck beside the ubiquitous Bernerds. She tried tirelessly to make sure he did not fall into trouble he would be unable to get away from. The muscular middie cleared himself piece by piece of his many targets, continually darting to the aid of some failing rating or Marine. He repeatedly put his own life at risk in his dangerous rescues. Stuart fought to keep up with him, never leaving his side until they were separated by a fast retreating band of Marines. As she fought her way clear she could only watch in horror at what happened. She was too far distant to act successfully. She saw Bernerds as he was cornered and smashed half-stupid by the swinging butt of a trooper's rifle. He floundered helplessly, in a totally dazed state.

Hard-fighting in a struggle of his own, Bentowski witnessed the happening of it and quickly dealt with his opponent, diving blindly to the middie's rescue with a lunatic scream.

'Bonzaii!'

'Bentowski!' Rickard screamed but it was too late. The helmsman blew one trooper apart and knocked the senses from another as he smashed his way through. He failed to realise that he was being surrounded until the encirclement was complete. His arms lowered as he faced the stern troopers, daring them to rush him, goading them into action. They recognised the mad glint in his eye for what it was and knew he'd never let them take him willingly. As Bentowski gave a crazed yell and jumped for the attack, two of the troopers shot him with pistols, both of them finding their targets with deadly accuracy. Noticeably weak pulse flashes arced out and caught Bentowski in the chest. He crumpled.

Bernerds' semi-conscious form was hauled off towards the main courtyard.

'Bloody idiot!' Rickard shot angrily at the once again advancing Imperials, dropping two troopers in their tracks. 'Damn it! Why did he have to try that?'

Stuart had not moved from where she stood in the dark shelter of the archway. She had been caught unawares by the sudden finality of events and had looked on, totally unable to help. She cursed quietly to herself in a sibilant tone, determined to make amends to Bernerds. 'I'll be back,' she swore. 'I'll come back and get him if I have to bloody well do it on my own.' There was no way in the world she was going to let anything stop her. She would not be deterred. No way. The determination was clear on her face as she rejoined the captain and his group.

In fitful stops and starts of movement the larger part of the Service forces, numbering about half their original complement, entered the west passage and made for the grid. A small body of Marines, along with Rickard, Kiyami and Stuart, remained to defend its openings to the east and north. Beck also stayed on, a little way back from the front line, while he tended to the newly wounded.

The Imperial advance ceased, and the incessant gunfire abated, as the troopers strengthened their position, sitting in stern mastery over the courtyard. They now held almost two thirds of the residency and were once more massing in overwhelmingly strong numbers, ready to renew the onslaught.

Kiyami could see that the Service people had no chance of survival. If the Imperials charged there would be a slaughter. They were all tired. The fight was leaving them, especially after their heavy losses in the interior courtyard. Perhaps it was their *karma* to die here. Maybe the ghosts of her ancestors had had their fun for the day and would no longer interfere. Curse all ghosts, she thought. They only make more trouble for us.

The double suns finally broke through the thick clouds and cast a wide shaft of light into the courtyard, illustrating to a greater degree the death and destruction over which wafted an amorphous blanket of smoke. It momentarily dazzled Rickard and he swore as he stumbled and grabbed for support, trying desperately to retain his balance.

'Captain,' Kiyami put out a steadying hand. 'Are you okay?'

'This bloody one point three gravity is becoming a nuisance,' he uttered darkly. His fury at the loss of two of his best officers remained unabated. Howarth and Bentowski had both played important roles in the defence and to lose them angered him intensely.

'It is tiring us all. All we can do is to endure it.'

'Not for much longer, I hope.'

There was a timely pause in the firing. The troopers'

attention seeming to be drawn elsewhere. The faint whistle of nearing retro-jets could be heard to the south. 'It's the launches,' Beck shouted joyously. 'They've arrived.'

Heaving a combined sigh of relief the Service people listened in from their covered-over location as, with a swirl of wind and sand, the first of the rescue vessels touched down on the grid. 'Why is it they are not firing at the launch?' Kiyami puzzled.

Rickard shook his head uncomprehendingly. 'It's strange. You'd think they would try to stop us getting out.'

'Never look a gift horse...etcetera,' Beck said from behind.

'Damn right. I want all remaining non-combat personnel to make their way down to the grid now,' he ordered, looking directly at Beck. 'And that includes you, Phil. No arguments this time.'

'Absolutely none proffered, Captain,' Beck affirmed. 'Those people are more determined than we originally thought they would be. They don't seem to mind their casualty figures while I see you suffer for every one of ours. I'll take the rest of the injured with me. See you back upstairs.'

'I hope so.'

With the farewell he was gone, struggling off with the wounded, the few acompanying ratings aiding him. Only a bunch of thirty or so Marines and a few security crew remained.

Rickard's eyes followed the departing figures down the passage. He felt a surge of relief as the doctor and company ascended the stone stairway at the passage's end. Now all who were left were combat trained. Maybe the damned casualty rate would decrease. He somehow doubted it. Firing broke out from the direction of the courtyard and he glimpsed a line of troopers shooting up at the landing grid, spraying it with indiscriminate fire.

Helpless to intervene Rickard swore again in frustration. 'I wish they would make up their minds. Who are they shooting at, us or the launch?' He slammed his fist into the stone pillar. He was careful not to use his damaged hand.

Jumping down the steps from the south-west corner of the residency, and running swiftly along the darkened passage, the breathless rating instantly captured Rickard's attention.

'Captain,' he gasped. 'The cutter's arrived. It's here. Just waiting out of firing range for the last launch to leave.'

'About time too.' New determination lit in Rickard's eyes at the news. the end of what had seemed an unending nightmare was in sight. 'Okay. All remaining crew and most of you Marines go for the grid.'

Kiyami merged with the shadows, intent on remaining inconspicuous. As far as she was concerned, her duty lay in remaining with her commanding officer. Whether he wanted her to remain in the battle zone was immaterial. She wanted to stay. She could take care of herself. It was about time she revealed quite how well to Rickard.

Rickard did not notice Kiyami's silent withdrawal. His mind was fully occupied trying to organise the retreat. 'I'm going to want a few volunteers to stay behind,' he said. 'We're going to fight a final holding action until the cutter's ready for lift-off.'

In a quick exchange of commands the Marine sergeant sorted out his men, picking those to stay from the less exhausted of them. The others were hustled off, their arguments for staying falling on deaf ears. The few security crew reluctantly joined them in heading down the pasageway for the grid, leaving only fifteen in the remaining number, most of them Marines who had borne the brunt of the fighting. Fifteen to hold out for a few minutes against the multitude of troopers until the cutter was ready to depart. It was a singularly unenviable task and the chances were that many of them would not make it through the length of the passage.

Among the number, bravely ignoring Rickard's order, was Stuart, rifle in hand and ready for use.

'Hope we can all get to the cutter in time. I'd hate to get left behind.' Rickard squinted at the smoke-smeared sky. 'Where is the bloody thing, anyway? That coxswain's certainly taking his time.'

'I think he's coming in now, sir,' the rating said from beside him.

'Well, get going, then.'

'Yessir.' The relieved rating hurried after the last of the main group.

Rickard noticed his first officer as she emerged from the shadows. 'Kiyami. What are you still doing here?'

'I will be aiding you in the delaying tactics,' she stated, asserting herself in a tone that did not brook argument.

Rickard shrugged at the candidness, as glad now as earlier for her support. 'Can't say I'm not glad to have you along.' Aside from the encouragement won by her support he felt disheartened and tired, worn down by the successive failures in his first mission as ship's captain. Well, maybe it would not all be failure. He was determined to check out Iad Kitan and his rebel group, especially after it had been proved very conclusively that he had been telling the truth. Kiyami's support of him gave him some extra strength.

With a flurry of movement the Imperial forces, previously closing step by step, suddenly withdrew with great speed, deserting the hard-won inner courtyard.

Two of the Marines abandoned their cover rather irresponsibly to see what was going on. A burst of unexpectedly direct gunfire cut into one of them and the other scrambled for cover, shock making him gasp for breath.

'Stay back. Don't give them anything to shoot at,' Rickard warned. Retreating their enemy may be, but stupid they were not. Kiyami edged up beside him.

'What is going on?'

'Sudden change of heart?' Stuart offered optomistically from the back.

'I doubt it, Stuart.' Rickard glanced at her and it dawned on him that she was there against his orders. He frowned, knowing it was too late to do anything about her. 'I doubt it very much. Let's get a closer look now they've abandoned the courtyard.'

He emerged from behind the protection of the wall and stared at the lifeless scene before him. Bodies were piled high amid discarded weapons. Not a trooper remained.

Leaving their own dead behind they had pulled out completely. He approached the centre of the courtyard and peeped cautiously around the corner of the central passage and through the broken gates.

Before he had a chance to see anything through the dense mist-like smoke there was a sudden high pitched whistling that started loudly and increased steadily in intensity.

'What is it?' Rickard asked of his crew.

'I do not know,' Kiyami answered for the rest of them.

The Marine sergeant arrived behind him and instantly recognised the sound for what it was. He shouted a hasty warning. 'Scarper! Take cover quickly!'

As one they dived for the flagstone floor barely in time. Rickard cringed as the eastside armoury, not completely emptied of explosives, was spectacularly blown up. Its fragile stone structure was completely smashed to bits. Debris was scattered everywhere, pounding the flagstones. Mercifully none of it was very large. The Service crew were covered in rolling clouds of dust that drifted over them like a thick, corrosive fog.

Rickard coughed dust. Around him his crew were choking and spluttering in the same fashion, spitting the profuse brick dust from their mouths. Once he had cleared most of the muck from his own face and roughly brushed down his uniform to rid himself of the worst of it, Rickard exclaimed in anger, 'They're not giving up! They're firing bloody cannon at us!'

'A fucking great mess they made, too,' Stuart swore with a descriptivity that belied her petite prettiness, delivering the words with unsubtle emphasis. 'This is some serious hassle,' she said, deliberately imitating Bentowski for effect. Then she wished she hadn't. The loss of the likeable helmsman still rang in her mind. She liked his cheeky style, his friendly ease with people, officers and crew alike. She was going to give the Imperials hell. Bentowski didn't deserve to be cornered and gunned down like that. There was going to be trouble. She'd see to that.

'I think we'd better get out of here,' Rickard suggested.

Kiyami nodded. 'It would be the wisest course,' she

said.

'You lead the way, Kiyami.'

As the others moved off behind the first officer Rickard peered through the dust haze and the noticably wider gap beside the now half-blocked passage to the outer courtyard. He saw troopers milling around at the foot of the wide steps. Beyond them was the lone cussion cannon, squat and black. Troopers began scattering on orders shouted from an unseen source. Rickard fired a single shot at them through the dust cloud to ward them off and they hit the ground, covering their heads with their hands.

'That's a bloody strange way to react,' Rickard puzzled. 'I only fired one shot.'

To explain the situation more fully to him the cannon whistled piercingly and he dived for cover, his feet losing their grip on the dust-coated flagstones so that he fell heavily. The breath was knocked from his body and all he could hear was the shrill scream of the cannon as the sound filled his head. It sounded like a screeching bird of prey diving for the kill. It was loud. Ever so loud.

The armoury was completely pulverised by the ensuing explosion. A new cloud of combined smoke and dust wafted down to obscure the enemy lines from sight. As the rumbling reverberations faded Kiyami hurried back into the courtyard. She was agitated by Rickard's abrupt disappearance. She couldn't lose him now. Not after he'd brought them this far. Anxious dread gripped her when she found she could not see him anywhere.

'Captain,' she called. Where was he? 'Captain! Christopher!'

A figure made shockingly pale grey by multiple layers of thickly enshrouding brick dust rose painfully from the floor, surrounded by piles of heaped stone and mortar. Rickard gave a deep, drawn out cough, inhaling deeply afterwards to fill his empty lungs and feeling decidedly blurry-headed. Kiyami almost laughed in relief. *Bakairu!* That was a near thing.

'That was too bloody close,' Rickard growled through a mouthful of dust. 'It's getting too damned dangerous around here.' This time he did not bother to wipe off the

227

grime and dirt. He was just too thickly covered by it to make the attempt worthwhile. His hair was grey with brick dust. His whole body was grey with it. He saw Kiyami through a haze of grey. Her features normally so soft, so perfect, displayed extreme worry. Worry that was quickly hidden away when she got closer.

'Are you harmed, Captain?' she asked, once more the unflusterable first officer. The Marines began drifting back to see what all the fuss was about. Kiyami put out a hand to help Rickard up.

'Feel great,' he said. 'Just great.' He stood with difficulty, a hand clutching at his stiff back. He hobbled a few steps before straightening fully, finally convinced that he *was* unharmed.

'You don't look it,' Stuart said. Rickard glared at her through dirt-ringed eyebrows. '...Sir,' she added.

'Are you trying to take over in the funny comments department, Midshipman?'

A third shot from the cannon hit without warning. Not even greeting them with the now accustomed whistle, the destructively powerful charge hit and demolished Rickard's office in a spray of smashed brick, sending most of it, and a good deal of the surrounding balcony plummeting down to shower and crush a Marine who had been standing where Rickard had lain moments before. The brickwork that survived the explosion shattered when it hit the ground, like glass thrown from a great height. A thick chunk of broken masonry caught Rickard a glancing blow on the shoulder as it rebounded heavily, knocking him back to the ground with a gasp.

'Jesus.' Stuart stared unbelievingly at the mess as a new dust cloud settled.

'The cutter's on the grid,' a Marine called, peering out over the armoury ruins.

Avoiding looking at the crushed and bloodied body of the unlucky Marine, Kiyami helped Rickard to his feet. Traces of blood were gathering at the shoulder wound and his face was pale and drawn, although how much of that paleness was from the dust and how much from actual shock she could not discern.

Rickard felt dazed. Confused. His head was clearing,

228

but not fast enough. He bravely ignored his throbbing shoulder and joined the Marine at the open section, looking with him out onto the residency. At this angle the cutter could be clearly seen, its bulky frame sticking worryingly over the small grid's edges. 'It's touched down. Let's go.'

'We can't all go up there at once, sir,' the Marine sergeant said. 'It's too open.'

Rickard put a hand to his head, feeling pain in every joint. All he wanted to do was rest.

Without further pause the Imperial forces charged, rising from their prostrate positions like a giant wave rising from what had been a relatively calm sea.

Rickard heard. He looked up. He hesitated.

'Go. Move out! We will cover you,' Kiyami shouted, revealing a rarely seen strength to her character. She openly admired the way in which Rickard had handled the situation so far. But at the moment he was out of it - stunned into inactivity by the closeness of the cannonfire.

The party split, the Marine sergeant leading off the majority of his men. Seven defenders stubbornly remained with Rickard, including Stuart and Kiyami. The seven trailed at a slower speed after their fast disappearing colleagues. They headed around the corner and dived into the west passage, the swiftly advancing troopers closing behind.

They passed what remained of the narrow connecting alleyway. From the high mound of rubble that now protruded into the passage Rickard glimpsed a hand poking out, almost as if it were searching for something just out of reach. It was a human hand. The crewman - probably a member of Howarth's demolition team - must have been buried when the explosives were triggered. It was most likely a confused and desperate attempt as they had come under direct attack. The Marine might well have made what he thought to be a useful sacrifice. He had certainly not been mistaken.

Rickard felt better. A fresh rush of adrenalin had reawakened his senses. He took command moving back to rearguard the others.

The last of the Service defenders ran past the ruins and

on past the deserted quarters, the doors left wide open, furnishings abandoned in the rush to escape. Rickard happened to glance back as they reached the midway point in the passage and saw the enemy numbers filling the bright courtyard end, standing clear in the light and preparing to open fire.

'Take cover!' he cried, ducking into an open doorway. The others followed suit as the firing started. One Marine was not quite fast enough. The first hail of solid projectiles caught him in a spraying line across the chest.

Rickard risked a fast look out of his doorway to see how the rest of his people were doing, a hand going to rub his badly bruised shoulder. The blood on it was drying rapidly, staining his already filthy uniform.

He saw that Stuart was in the middle of the group along with the remaining three Marines. Kiyami was at the far end, nearest the stairs to the grid. She indicated that she was okay, delivering him a cursory wave. Only one further casualty, then. The unfortunate Marine.

By pure chance Rickard happened to glance upwards. With a cold chill of fear he spotted a lone trooper on the barely visible roof of one of the quarters, in the direction of the grid. He was clambering his way through the narrow gap between the low roof and the thick stone walkway. Fearful of being caught in a crossfire, Rickard tried to aim a shot at the trooper, but firing from the other end of the passage disturbed his concentration and he missed badly.

Just at the wrong moment Kiyami - who had missed Rickard's actions and was unaware of the danger - came out of cover to return a few shots. The adventurous trooper sprang off the roof and landed softly behind her. Before she had time to even realise he was there he had her. A wide arm was locked around her neck and a pistol was aimed unwaveringly at her head, the stubby barrel twisting her hair, as the trooper made clear his intent.

With jarring force Kiyami slammed an elbow into the large trooper's stomach. He did not even flinch, blinking only in surprise at the unexpected strength of the blow. Realising that her best shot had not proved effective she nonetheless tried again, smashing her arm backwards

230

with all the force she could muster. It was to no avail. The trooper's stomach had to be as solid as the metallic hull of the *Emputin.*

The firing from the far end of the passageway ceased immediately the trooper made his unscheduled appearance.

Rickard poked his head out a little further, just to check if it really was safe, before he stepped completely into view. 'I will kill her if you do not surrender,' the trooper growled fiercely at him.

Stuart stepped out and glanced at Rickard in uncertainty. The tension in the air was electrifying.

Rickard concentrated his narrow gaze upon the trooper, unheeding his threat. He had had enough for one day. He was thoroughly vexed, utterly annoyed and fed up at being pushed around, battered, bruised and generally being mistreated by his formerly 'friendly' hosts. Their pathetically messy attempt to capture his ship had ended in failure for them. Most of his people were safely away and he was damned if he was going to let this one moron stop the rest of them doing likewise.

'You slimy, good-for-nothing, untrustworthy turd-ridden bastard,' he uttered vituperatively, defiance written all over his grime-encrusted face. He resolutely levelled his pistol, putting extreme emphasis on the motion for the sake of effect. If ever he needed perfect markmanship, it was now. He prayed he would not miss. There would be no second chance.

'Stop!' the trooper ordered in a flustered manner. This was not happening the way he'd planned.

'Not a chance.'

The trooper was tensing himself to pull the trigger when Rickard made his own shot. Kiyami gave a reflexive yell as the hammering of his pistol jerked back his arm. The target was clear. The shot did not miss. Blood welled at a neat hole in the trooper's penetrated skull, and trickled down his face, and over his glazing eyes. The trooper dropped.

Unharmed but shaken by the daring of Rickard's shot, it quickly dawned on Kiyami that she was standing out in the open. She, and everyone else, rushed to cover

231

simultaneously with the resumation of hostile gunfire.

Himself surprised at his accuracy, Rickard attempted to calm himself and sounded the retreat, trying to steady his shaking hands. 'Make for the stairs,' he called out in a voice firmer than he felt. 'Use the quarters as cover.'

Willing himself to make the effort he enacted the first move by boldly darting out of the shelter of the doorway and sprinting for the next, keeping low as the Marines fired over his head to cover him.

'Go!' he shouted as he reached safety and took up a firing position. He started shooting as, one by one, Stuart and the Marines made their way back a couple of rooms. Then the process was repeated for Kiyami and then himself. They continued this procedure each time, ducking and weaving as they made their dashes, energetically negating scatterings of loose brick and heaps of rubbish. All the while they pulled back amid the enemy's fire. One of the Marines caught his foot on a large block of masonry, not seeing the strewn pile of rubble in the shaded gloominess of the passage. As he began to rise a stray shot hit him in the neck, killing him instantly.

Rickard kept the rest of them going with merciless force, trying not to notice the fresh casualty. 'Move! Come on, don't stop.'

Stuart stopped to check on the downed Marine.

'Leave him, there's nothing you can do for him. Move! Stuart, shift yourself.'

A stray shot blasted the wall next to her.

She moved.

There were only five of them now and they were all tired beyond belief. The extra gravity weighed them down ceaselessly. Their weary spirits refused to give up the fight. They were as determined to win now as they had been at the start. They ducked from doorway to doorway. The chase seemed to be endless. How many more rooms could there be?

All five met up in the last doorway. One of the Marines occasionally returned the fire, but not for the sake of hitting anything; they'd all had too much killing, too much blood-letting for that. It was only to keep the troopers at bay.

'Now,' Rickard decided. 'We are going up those stairs.'

'We'll be wide open,' protested Stuart.

'I know. That's why we're going one at a time and with full covering fire from the rest of us.'

'What about the last person?' Kiyami enquired with raised eyebrows.

'That'll be me so it won't matter.' He stifled any further protests by shoving Stuart forward. 'You first, Midshipman.'

Choking down her rebelliousness, Stuart waited for a lull in the firing before running the short distance to the stairs, taking them two at a time. The others provided more than adequate cover but still wild bursts of fire ricocheted along the passage, knocking out wedges of masonry centimetres from her head as she ducked and yelled in surprise. She made it to the top unharmed.

There were four remaining survivors.

Rickard turned his head toward Kiyami. 'You next,' he said.

'But-'.

'Go on!' he shouted.

She made off, rapidly disappearing from sight.

And then there were three.

The troopers were closing in, using the same tactics as the Service crew, darting from doorway to successive doorway. Rickard made one of the Marines go next. The youngster jumped out and ran. Instantly and with a large dose of bad luck he was hit, the shot catching him in the leg. He fell to the floor, a hand whipping reflexively for the wound. The pain was vividly clear on his extremely youthful face.

'Oh *damn it!*' Hating to act rashly but deeming it necessary under the circumstances, Rickard gritted his teeth and dashed to the fallen Marine, while the remaining man held off the advancing troopers. His tired muscles were starting to feel like rubber but he grabbed the Marine by the arm and yanked him forcefully up the stairs, getting his hair singed in the process by a shot that came a little too close for comfort. 'Come on, soldier,' Rickard yelled at him. Together they clambered up to the grid.

Seeing that they had safely made it, the last Marine in the west passage gave a dementedly wild, nerve-boldening scream and, pumping gunfire back all the way, virtually leaped the entire height of the stairway and raced for the grid. He rejoined the others on the exposed landing pad as he clambered under the raised nose of the cutter, getting around to the hatch side.

From the grid Rickard glared down over the residency at the extent of the damage. Something went cold inside him as he gazed upon the sight. So much destruction. So many deaths. Smoke and bodies were everywhere. There was little relief to be taken from the fact that most of them were Rukan. Bodies were bodies in anyone's manual. Large slivers of broken wood from the wrecked main gates littered the open courtyard. A pile of crumbled and destroyed masonry was spread out where the main structures had once stood at the northern end. A pillar of jet black smoke was pouring from the gaping ruins of the officers' mess.

The grid gave a sudden lurch to one side, almost throwing him off. Suppressing the urge to panic he caught his balance and peered over the outer edge. He was horrified to see a team of troopers in the green shubbery below, methodically cutting through the supporting metal pillars with heat torches. He delivered a shot, scattering them.

'Into the cutter,' he snapped. 'We don't have long. If we don't get a move on we'll be making a close inspection of the Emperor's gardens.'

They jumped into the cutter and sealed the hatch. Inside, space was at a premium. The cutter, although larger than a launch, was fully taken up with wounded and the last of the regular crew. Beck had waited for this, the last evacuation ship. He was right at the back, tending to some of his many patients. He looked up and stared in undisguised astonishment at the sight of the dusty, bloodied Rickard.

Oblivious, Rickard jumped for the empty co-pilot's chair, striving to keep a level head as a picture of the fully laden cutter crashing to the ground filled his mind. 'Lift off!' he told the coxswain. 'Evacuate at max speed. I want the fastest altitude climb you've ever made.'

The cutter lifted away as the first troopers reached the top of the stairs from the passageway. Some of them fired bursts after it but to no avail.

As he coughed and gasped for breath Rickard noted his uniform was filthy. It was also torn and covered in thick, clinging dust. He felt thoroughly and utterly exhausted. His shoulder was a mass of aching, throbbing pain. A thin mask of dried and clotted blood added to the dis-orientating confusion he was suddenly re-experiencing. His adrenalin-heightened senses were slowly becoming oblivious to all outside stimulus as he revelled in the simple fact that he had survived a very traumatic experience. It was a battle Rhos would have enjoyed immensely. So much for adventure.

Through the dimness of his outer perception he felt a hand rest on his undamaged shoulder. 'I must thank you for saving my life,' Kiyami said in his ear. She had decided that he deserved some thanks for bringing them safely through the battle, when he was clearly just as scared and confused as the rest of them.

He did not have the energy to do more than rest his own hand upon hers in a gesture of comfort at her words. He was glad she had said them.

Stuart sat alone, wishing she could have done something to help Bernerds, rather than allowing him to be dragged off a prisoner, and Bentowski to be needlessly killed. She had liked Bentowski. His irrepressible comic-book humour made his charm almost unresistable. To stand by and watch his death without acting was, in her mind, unforgivable and she had to make amends.

She cursed, hating the Rukans for what they had done. 'I'll make sure we come back for Bernerds,' she swore lowly. 'I'll make sure if I have to hijack the ship myself. No-one's gonna stop me.'

She promised herself she would do it if she had to. But she hoped going to such extremes would not be necessary.

11

The *Emputin* was at red alert status.

Everything was prepared for trouble. The defensive shields were actuated, the gunnery posts were charged and ready for action, the engines were on emergency standby, merely awaiting to be programmed with co-ordinates and speed before they gunned the ship into roaring motion.

Bulloch was pacing the length of hanger bay control. The fingers of one hand tapped a brisk tattoo on the palm of the other in unconcealed nervous agitation. He had been impatiently awaiting news, some contact, any contact. Just a message from the surface so he knew what was happening. But there had been nothing bar the calls of incoming launches, and what they had to say about the battle zone was not good. By all accounts it was one hell of a mess down there. Corpses lying all over the place. The pilots had been unable to tell whose bodies. Service or native, so there was absolutely no indication as to the fortunes of Bulloch's crewmates. With any luck he should not have long to wait now. It had been endless minutes since the cutter disappeared through the unusually thick blanket of grey cloud, and it should already be on its way back, hopefully with the last of the evacuees on board. It was a tense time on the ship. Too damned tense.

His work was made no easier by the fact that one of his chief technicians had inexplicably vanished. True, the young man, Crewman Oaks, was renowned for his work-shy attitude, but he was still one of the best technicians in bay control, and it did not explain why he should take an unscheduled break under a red alert status. That would cause him plenty of trouble when he

236

finally decided to turn up.

As Bulloch completed another thought-enmeshed length of control the radio receiver crackled into life. He was at the console before any of his technicians could move a muscle. He flicked a switch and heard the cutter's approach signature, recognising it straight away.

'Hello, this is Bay Chief Bulloch to cutter. Are you reading my signal?' he said into the voice pickup.

There was a slight pause on the other end as the cutter's comm was operated. 'Rickard here. We read you fine.' His voice was thick with swallowed dust.

'Captain, you were out of touch for so long. What happened?'

'It's a long story. Too long a story to go into right now. The main thing is that most of us made it out alive. We have suffered a few...casualties. The last of us are here now, in the cutter.'

Bulloch breathed free once more. His fears had magnified the loss numbers out of all proportion. The wavery voice of Beck came on speaker. He disguised well the weariness he felt in every muscle. 'Rem, it's Phil here.'

'Glad you made it safe and sound, Phil.'

'So am I, believe me. Listen to me. We have a great many injured people here, some of them are in a pretty awful condition and will require urgent attention as soon as we dock. I'll need every single available crash team standing by to take over right away.'

'Will do. They will be here waiting for you.'

'Thanks. See you soon.'

'Any minute now.' As soon as the connection was cut Bulloch was paging Medical, arranging for Beck's crash teams to be on site when the cutter came in. That done he busied himself with the docking procedures. The cutter was guided in through the open outer doors and on to the grid. Once cycling was completed the inner doors were unsealed and the waiting crash teams scampered to the cutter's descending hatchway.

Brushing past them. Stuart wasted no time in hanging around. 'Get out the way,' she snapped belligerently. 'God, I need a smoke.' With that she strode off at a brisk pace, leaving her fellow escapees behind.

Bulloch hurried over to greet the emerging Rickard, his face gawping when he saw the condition the captain was in. 'It must have been touch and go down there,' he said for lack of anything better.

Pale, almost gaunt in appearance, because of the dry mask and of dirt and grime that clung to his normally healthy features, and dropping dust as he moved, Rickard nodded his head slowly and with effort. 'It was. It was easier than I'd feared, though. There weren't too many of us left waiting so the butchery was minimal.'

'How do you feel, Captain?'

'Tired. Very, very tired.'

For all the response he was getting Bulloch felt he'd do better to drop the subject, especially considering the way Rickard looked at present. Instead, Bulloch watched as the survivors who still possessed some mobility trudged wearily out of the cutter, making their way around the crash teams and their hover trolleys as the more seriously wounded were offloaded and whisked away. Beck ran to and fro, supervising the transfer meticulously. Stunned and battered shock victims draped in silver heat-retaining wrap-arounds were caringly guided off, their helpers comforting them as best they could.

Taking the controls of a trolley, Beck did not stop to pass pleasantries. 'Sorry I can't stop,' he said to Bulloch as he started off. 'I've found myself with a lot of work to do. Ginny tells me it's chock-a-block upstairs.' With that he sped off and vanished around the corner.

Kiyami walked straight past Bulloch, barely managing to give him a nod of recognition as she fought to stay upright. Her exhaustion was clear to see, even though she struggled to disguise it. Without a word she exited the bay.

Rickard sympathetically watched her go. There was a new glimmer of understanding in his dust-encircled eyes. He was getting to know his commander quite well by now, her faults, what few of them there were, and her good points. She was a strong-willed woman, despite her outwardly pliant facade. She cared, about the crew and about him. That was what made her so good. He now fully realised why she was reputed to be one of the best first officers in the fleet. He knew he was extremely lucky to have her with him. It was a shame that it had taken something like recent events to prove that fact to him.

He was tired. They all were. Once on the cutter, out of immediate danger, all their energy had left them. They had relaxed, content in the simple knowledge that they had made it. They were alive. He was sure he felt it more strongly. All he wanted to do was rest, somewhere nice and quiet. He was hard put to remind himself that there was work still to be done. They had yet to get out of this system. Doubtlessly, there would be a blockade of sorts to prevent them trying. It would be some time yet before he could rest.

The milling activity abated, slowly dying out as the bay emptied. The final crash team whizzed out of the doors, making for Medical at breakneck speed. The last of the Marines followed at a more relaxed pace. A peaceful silence fell, one suddenly so strong that it could be heard.

One face Bulloch had not seen go past stood out boldly in his mind, as was understandable. 'Where's Lieutenant Bentowski? I...I haven't seen him get off.'

'Bentowski didn't make it.' Rickard said it without visible emotion.

'And Thom Howarth?'

'He was another casualty.'

The flat emotionlessness with which the words were delivered made Bulloch uncomfortable. 'Oh,' was all he could think of saying. The conflict must have been as bad as he had previously imagined after all.

'I have to get to the bridge. We're not out of the fire yet.' Rickard walked off leaving Bulloch alone in the deserted bay.

'Back to work, I suppose,' he said to himself and made for the corridor. It's quite empty out here, he thought with pleasure. Now that all those crates have been shifted off. What was left? Yes, there were still those food boxes to be seen to. He supposed Science should be notified. Best to wait until the ship was out of danger. He was about to enter bay control when something crossed his mind. Crewman Oaks was still unaccounted for. And if he imagined for one minute that he was going to avoid any more of the workload, he was badly mistaken. 'I think it's about time I discovered the whereabouts of our friend Oaks,' he mused.

The crewman had been caught out before, skiving in the storage room just off the main corridor. Perhaps that was where he was hiding this time, trying to dodge the hard work the rest of them had had to endure. Bulloch fully intended to give the young man what for when he finally caught up with him. He would be given the most laborious, dullest tasks Bulloch could think of. That would certainly teach him a much needed lesson or two.

As he neared the storage room he heard a scraping sound. He paused, ears pricked for repetition. 'No, must have been my imagination,' he muttered. To prove him wrong, the noise was repeated, this time very definitively. It clearly came from the storage room. It was Oaks. Had to be. Probably caused as he made himself comfortable. Not this time, though. This time he had been caught out.

Padding forward Bulloch approached the room, noticing that its door had been left open. A darkness from inside merged with the bright lights of the corridor. He frowned at the darkness. There should have been a light on. Perhaps Oaks had heard his arrival? Perhaps Oaks wasn't even in there. The noise could have been made by malfunctioning venting. But then what had happened to the lights?

Puzzling at the anomaly, he tapped the door with the toe of his boot and edged it further open. In front of him in a constricted semi-circle the darkness was pushed back only with effort. It seemed reluctant to give in to the light, unwilling, perhaps, to reveal the mysterious originator of the sounds Bulloch had heard.

He stepped into the pitch black room and felt the tension grip him tightly. The air was musky, almost stiflingly so, and a faint, almost familiar odour reached his heightened senses. He reached blindly with his hand for the manual light control, feeling for it without turning his attention away from the room itself, and was started to find it hanging by its wires from the battered fixing on the wall.

'Uh, oh.' The thought entered his mind. This could be

240

trouble.

Screwing up his courage he walked into the blackness. It absorbed him instantly in an almost greedy fashion. A faint and now shockingly miniscule puddle of light at the door did absolutely nothing to illuminate the dark. Exploring ahead with hands outstretched Bulloch felt his way around the stacked food crates, his back stiff and erect, just waiting to absorb the blow when he finally did bump into....something. What? There was nothing here.

He circled the room, relieved to finally find his way back to the door and the warming light. Stopping just short of the doorway he glanced around and listened intently. He could hear nothing. The room was deadly silent, unnaturally so, now that the clicking of the incapacitated heat lamps did not disturb the quietness.

The sounds must have been in his imagination. True, he had been overworking himself of late in order to complete his part of the evacuation. Maybe that was it. Too much attention to duty? Overwork? Oh, come off it! he thought reprovingly. He had heard a noise. Definitely a noise, not his imagination. Admittedly it could have come from badly operating piping or even heating ducts. Yes, that was it. Oaks was clearly elsewhere.

'Yes,' he said, trying to persuade himself that all was well, 'I imagined it.'

With a shrug he turned towards the door and took a step forward.

He froze when his foot caught on something lying in his path. A mound, a shape which the faint light did not reveal. He tapped the shape with his foot, squirming when he felt the boot dig into a softness. Backing up a pace he widely skirted the strange object on the floor and made for the door. Opening it all the way, he brought himself a minor increase in the amount he could see.

He could see the shape.

Not believing his own eyes he approached it once more, bending over to make a closer inspection. His stomach churned as recognition came to him. It was a body, a human corpse.

It was the dead body of Crewman Oaks.

The body was huddled in a foetal curl with one hand

241

stretched back, as if to fend off his attacker.

Bulloch's hand touched the dead man's neck in a vague effort to discover a pulse, even though the body was stone cold and snowy pale. Instead, his hand was enveloped by a thick, almost dry sticky liquid and he sharply drew it back, looking with dawning horror at the clotted redness in which it was amply covered. Blood also soaked the back of the crewman's skull where the deep, steeply sloping angle of the knife-wound was plainly evident, lacing upwards into the soft frailness of the brain cavity.

Unable to fully comprehend quite what had happened, Bulloch straightened and backed away, his wide, staring eyes still captured by the sight of the profusive, congealed mass of *red* that stuck tenaciously to his hand. His mouth gaped loosely as if his mind had lost control over its actions.

Unthinking, Bulloch backed away from one terror directly into another, this one far more real and malevolent. He came to a sharp halt as he hit the obstacle. The hairs on the back of his uncovered neck prickled at the touch of fetid breath. He made as if to turn but was prevented by the sudden motion of a powerful, roundly muscled arm sliding with startling rapidity around his neck. The tough-looking sleeve that encased the offending arm had in it a jagged rent that stretched from elbow to wrist.

The sleeve was also matted with drying blood.

The arm jerked roughly and Bulloch found his voice very speedily.

He yelled loudly, panic edging his senses, but a giant hand clamped over his mouth. He thrashed and twisted desperately in an attempt to break free but it was to no avail. The arm around his neck tightened its hold and pulled back mercilessly, slowly choking the life from him. He smashed backwards with his elbow and his kicking feet thrashed against legs that were planted to the deck like pillars.

There was no effect. The arm remained. He tried to see the hidden face of his attacker but his head was kept completely motionless, unable to move a fraction. All his fast flicking eyes could see, the single tenuous object to which they ceaselessly kept returning, was that one, ultimately powerful, ultimately deadly arm. The sight of it filled his vision even as that most precious sense began to fade and dim. He was dying and there was nothing he could do to prevent that. Not against this attacker.

He tried to cry out again, to scream against the tortured agony that erupted in his throat, but all that emerged was a strangulated gasp, a dying gurgle, as life slipped away from his meagre grasp. Darkness, all pervading, all enshrouding, crept inwards, covering his mind, filling his awareness. It was drowning him unstoppably. It was a darkness more pervading, much more complete than the inconspicuously faint shadows of the room. It became more dominant even than the arm itself which was now merely a faint blur on a distant, ever-retreating horizon. A deep tunnel loomed in front of him, enlargening constantly. It was a pit. A maw that wished to consume him and he could feel himself toppling over its rim, unable to hold his balance as the encompassing pressure on his neck increased. He tumbled helplessly into it. The smoothness of its walls offered him no grips, no handholds as he plunged down its infinite expanse. The pit was bottomless yet he could see its end. There was a light, a brighter light than ever he had known, that awaited him and he knew that this was the terminal finality of death.

The air left his lungs for one last time in a tight, slowly fading rattle. His body was dropped uncaringly to the cold metal of the deck. The lone trooper grinned humourlessly. All was going well. He was about to become a very useful commodity in the machinations of his Emperor, and his rewards would be sweet and plentiful, of that he was certain.

Chief Engineer Robert Stringer, in one of his rare trips out of his personal domain, strode down the short corridor in large, space-eating strides, humming softly to himself. He was on his way back to Engineering after paying a short but necessary visit to the bridge. The secondary control and monitoring console there had needed readjusting. Extra power banks had to be locked in for engine use and the bridge was the place where the job was carried out, never mind that he had told the designers of the ship time and time again that the console was better suited to Engineering. But some people never listened. Thankfully. All the hustle and bustle of the evacuation had died down. The noise of the constantly used intercom speakers had finally ceased with the conclusion of the evacuation. All the surviving crew were aboard and it was time to leave. There would probably be a blockade of sorts that they would have to run to effect a full escape but in a ship with engines as beautifully powerful as those on the *Emputin* it would be no problem.

Instead of taking the easier route of catching a lift all the way from bridge to Engineering, Stringer had had to stop off at Spares to pick up one or two items of need. These safely pocketed he was heading back to the nearest elevator. He reached a set of doors and as he entered their sensory range they hissed open.

He stopped short at the sight before him.

To his utter astonishment a tightly packed squad of troopers thundered past, slowing to a halt and turning back even as he stared in open-mouthed bewilderment at them.

The bewildered hesitation lasted for a single second. In a sudden spurt of motion the troopers made a dash for him. Stringer leapt back and pounded at the emergency lock feature of the door's control panel, moving *very* fast. The thin metal barrier slid shut, barring the troopers' path. They began smashing at the door with angry might.

He thumbed the intercom button, his usual air of cool collectedness returning as he recovered from the shock of seeing enemy natives running loose on the ship. His page was calmly answered. 'Bridge. Lieutenant Watts here.'

'This is Stringer. I'm three levels down, in corridor nineteen. There are troopers in the passage beyond this one. Imperial troopers.'

There was an exclamation in the background and immediately Rickard was at the speaker. 'How many troopers?'

'About fifteen or so. I would imagine.'

'Okay. I'll be right down.' He continued speaking to Watts, his voice carrying over the still-open channel. 'Get a full security and Marine detail in there right now. Sound internal alert and warn all crew to secure their positions. Kiyami, take the conn.'

A second voice sounded from the other side of the bridge. Stringer could not make out who it was. 'I'm coming along. Sorry, Captain, but you can't refuse-'

Watts cut the connection.

Silence fell in the corridor. Even the muffled thumps on the door had ceased. The troopers had obviously realised that now the element of surprise was lost they had no time to waste. Stringer leaned back against the wall and listened apprehensively as the sounds of gunfire started up in the distance, closely accompanied by the screaming wail of sirens as the alert was sounded.

Rickard ran towards the increasing noise of weapons' fire with more energy than he'd had a few minutes ago, courtesy of Beck and a dose of his 'uppers'. They had been necesary or he'd never have taken them. Without their support he had been liable to collapse any minute through sheer exhaustion. Now he was fine, fighting fit for an hour or two. Long enough to make an escape, or to mess it up.

Karen tagged along beside him, matching his pace. Much as he'd wanted her to stay on the bridge she had been doubly insistent on coming along. She was openly concerned for his safety, especially after he had gone through so much on the planet. She was so pleased to have him back, after being forced against her will to leave him in the residency, that there was no way she would let him out of her sight so soon. Call her overprotective but that was the way she was feeling right now.

She wondered what it had been like, how bad the carnage of which he had described so little had been. Easy was something it had not been. Lieutenant Bentowski had not returned, nor had Thom Howarth. Both she presumed were missing or dead, although there was some talk of prisoners being taken. Later would be the time to prise information out of Rickard. Now he was too tense and weary. At least she had managed to get him to wipe most of the dirt from his face. Now he looked marginally healthier than he had done. It was probably the mothering instinct in her.

'Who let them on board? That's what I want to know,' Rickard said.

'Perhaps Mister Bulloch will know.'

'He'd better. I want some answers; like what a squad of Imperial troopers are doing, prowling the corridors of my ship.' He fingered the thick wad of bandage, covered by his grimy uniform, that clung to his cut and bruised shoulder.

The pair trotted briskly on. Rickard increased his pace at the sound of more intense firing ahead and Karen began falling behind. They both failed to see a large, muscular shape that skulked down a shaded sub-corridor to the left. As they passed the shadowy turn-off the dark shape jumped out and grabbed Karen by the scruff of the neck, yanking her back fiercely, at the same time kicking her ankle sharply with a large, heavy boot. She gave a startled gasp as she was pulled off her feet. Her head jerked forward and her long, free flowing hair was flipped over her head. It covered her face before she shook it aside, spitting a strand from her mouth.

Rickard spun at the flurry of motion, immediately wary of the danger which greeted his eyes. 'Remain very still,' the heavily muscled trooper who held Karen snapped shortly. He raised his free arm. The pistol held in the firm grip of his hand was aimed at Rickard. He tightened his grip around Karen's throat, making the position comfortable to him but distinctly uncomfortable for her. She squirmed and wriggled, trying without result to break free. Her ankle was starting to throb with pain where she had been kicked. She contemplated the situation wondering how best to escape. Then she noticed the rent in the trooper's sleeve - and the dried, congealed mass of blood that surrounded and had seeped into the tear. Then she was suddenly still.

The corridor's luminescent strip lighting reflected off the cold metal of the pistol's jet black barrel. Constant exchanges of rapid gunfire echoed in Rickard's ears as time seemed to stretch endlesly, turning seconds into long minutes.

Rickard sorely wished he could use the same move that had saved Kiyami, startling the aggressive trooper into insecurity. He was tempted to try but this time he did not have his own weapon in his hand. The damned thing was safely and uselessly stashed away in his pistol pouch. He would never reach it in time. The trooper would gun down either him or Karen instantly. His own life he might be prepared to risk but not Karen's. Not by any chance would he dare take that sort of risk. He wondered where Bentowski's legendary US Cavalry had got to when he needed them. Then he wished Bentowski himself was here. Maybe he could wisecrack the trooper into surrender.

'You'd better let her go,' he demanded, squaring up to his opponent.

'Quiet!' the lone trooper snapped.

'Let her go.'

'She will guide me to the docking bay.'

'She doesn't know the way, she's only a civilian,' he procrastinated.

'Then she will have to learn very fast.'

'Honestly,' Karen added, her courage increasing as she realised she was needed alive. 'I don't know the way. I'd only get you lost.'

The trooper revealed the shortness of his patience. 'Be quiet!' he demanded. He slammed the barrel into the side of her head, causing her to cry out sharply.

'You damn-' Rickard started forward.

'Stop!' The pistol pointed directly at Karen. 'Which way is the elevator shaft?'

'Do you honestly think I'm going to tell you?'

'You will,' he replied with malice in his voice.

'No chance.'

The gun barrel dug cruelly into Karen's skin. Rickard winced as her face contorted in pain. 'Stop!' he cried. 'Stop it.' His firmness collapsed. He didn't know how to help her.

'Now tell me.'

'Karen...?' Rickard was drowning in indecision.

Karen managed to give him a smile, wavery though it was. Her head was beginning to hurt where the barrel had drawn blood. 'I'll be okay, Chris. Try not to worry.' She blinked rapidly, the pain in her leg increasing. She looked at Rickard, sensing his confusion. Their eyes met and exchanged a depth of emotion hard to obtain in normal circumstances.

'Where is the elevator?' the trooper repeated.

'I don't like to do this, Karen,' Rickard said.

'I've a feeling you have no choice.'

The trooper was growing steadily more impatient. 'You will tell me what I need to know.'

'Or what?' Rickard made a last attempt to face him down.

Using the pistol he slowly twirled Karen's hair, wiping it over the growing thread of blood. It trickled in a thin line down her scalp and over her ear, dripping onto her bare neck.

'All right, all right, damn you,' he relented angrily. 'It's behind you, back that way. There's a lift around the corner.'

Karen gave a relieved sigh as the barrel was withdrawn slightly. The trooper gave a singularly evil grin of pure delight at his own cunning and began pacing backwards, dragging Karen close to him all the way.

A Marine, rifle at the ready, rounded the corner and stopped at the sight of trouble. The trooper's unprotected back was facing him, presenting him with a clear target. He had no time to make the shot, however. The trooper had heard his rather noisy arrival and turned at the sound, making his intent plain as he threatened his hostage. He used her as a screen to block any potential shots from the Marine.

The Marine shouted a warning to Rickard. 'Mind yourself, sir. I'll take him out.'

'No! Don't fire!'

'What?' The Marine paused in uncertainty and the trooper took his chance. The Marine was given no opportunity to dodge as the trooper fired at him, and he went down, the charred hole at the centre of his chest giving rise to a faint spiral of smoke.

Karen blanched at the sight of the smouldering corpse. For a split second Rickard's anger got the better of him and he made a rush forward. The trooper whirled back just in time to stop him and he checked his run with visible effort. The pistol returned its alignment to Karen. The trooper was a loner and he was dangerous.

'Why don't you let her go? Leave her alone, she can't harm you.'

'I need some protection on a ship full of your scum,' the trooper growled, making a move towards the lifts. Karen staggered along as the trooper's hold on her tightened reflexively. Her ankle was now a vivid red. It hurt too much to put her full weight on it so she was forced to limp awkwardly.

There was absolutely nothing Rickard could do but watch as the trooper and Karen reached the end of the corridor. He did not move as Karen was hauled into the lift and the pair were eclipsed by the closing of the elevator doors. Then he moved. He ran for an intercom, slamming down the transmit button.

'Rickard here. There's a native trooper in liftshaft 9 and he has a hostage. Advise extreme caution in approaching him. He will harm the hostage at the first sign of trouble.'

He abandoned the intercom and sprinted off towards the ongoing battle with the groundeating pace of a hundred metres runner.

Rickard took in the scene in an instant as he arrived at a wide intersection between the bay and its surrounding corridors, leading off like wheel spokes. The Imperial forces held the bay and its adjoining corridor and were using scattered packing crates as cover. Marines encircled the area in tight formation, ensuring the troopers could

249

not advance. They sheltered behind the corners of offshooting corridors, continuously ducking round to return the fire. A once tidy stack of empty lubricant containers, heaped against one wall, provided extra cover. The walls were blackened and pockmarked from the gunfire.

The first impressions Rickard received were of mayhem and pandemonium, complete disorganisation. The intersection seemed gripped in utter confusion. Chaos reigned as pistol and rifle shots echoed and ricocheted wildly. The troopers were steadily being driven back by the superior numbers of the Marines. The firing was profusive but the Marines were hampered by the fact that they had to be careful not to injure the few hostages the troopers had taken.

Rickard made for the stack of containers, ducking as he avoided the rapid gunfire. He reached the comparative safety behind the high pile and immediately recognised the midshipman already there, firing well-aimed shots across the open space.

'Stuart. How's it going?'

'Captain.' She made room for him, pausing to fire another shot. 'Not too bad. We're holding them off. They're bottled up. They can't move anywhere. The corridor behind them is a dead end so we've got them trapped. Their only way is the bay.'

'Which is probably the same way they came in.'

'Yeah. They've taken some prisoners. Nothing we could do about that, they already had them when I got here.'

'I imagine the more they capture, the better chance they think they have of persuading me to surrender the ship. You can't get them back?'

'Not without a full scale battle, and this close to the outer hull that isn't very wise.'

'No, I suppose not.' Oh damn, he thought. He quickly ran through his options and considered the situation. The Imperials seemed bent on taking his people alive, and keeping them that way. That was good. It wouldn't be long though before those captured were used to force him into submission, so he didn't have long to find Iad Kitan and mount a rescue of some sort. But, if he was

250

right, and he desperately hoped he was, then the prisoners would be safe for the time being. He made an instant decision, regretfully consigning the hostages to imprisonment with the crew taken earlier. 'Push them into the bay. See if they will leave of their own accord.'

'I'll see what I can do.'

The doors of an elevator terminal just behind the troopers' front line snapped open. From the lift emerged the loner with his own hostage. Karen struggled desperately as she was dragged along. Rickard's heart gave a painful leap as the shot from a Marine came extremely close to hitting her, scoring the deck bare centimetres from her leg.

'Cease firing!' he yelped. 'Hold your fire.'

The troopers paid no heed to the fact that the Marines had stopped shooting and blindly continued their own barrage of gunfire, punctuating the one-sided ceasefire noisily.

Glancing behind him at the new arrivals, the Imperial troop-commander's eyes widened as he recognised a writhing Karen. The loner swiped at her with the palm of his hand and she became withdrawn and silent. The fight had been knocked out of her and the narrow trickle of blood had dried over the side of her face, marring her pale, normally unblemished skin. She stood still, putting her weight on one foot. The other was placed out in front of her in an attempt to minimise the pain from her ankle. The bruising was already appearing, vividly dark purple in colour.

As that did not matter to the troop-commander, he was free to enjoy the sight of her. He knew from his briefing that she was very important and would be a prime catch for the Emperor. Now was the time to leave. They had achieved as much as they could here and he did not want to lose such a valuable prize. He waved his troops into the bay, ensuring they kept a hold on their prisoners. Then he scurried up to the inner doors to confer with the trooper who had helped him on board in the first place. The dark red human blood around the gash in the trooper's uniform quietly reported the fact that he had been busy that day. He kept a tight grip on Karen.

251

'You've have made an oustanding achievement,' he said once he was out of the firing line, the absence of any firing notwithstanding.

'The Emperor will reward me well for my work.'

'Any rewards will be mine,' the troop-commander told him. 'I am the chief officer here.'

Karen's captor was silent but his mind was extremely active. There was no way he was about to relinquish his own glory to someone else.

'Did you accomplish your secondary task?'

'I did. It has been actuated and will carry out the need perfectly. I still argue that it does not carry enough power.'

'It is all we require. We want the ship intact. Go to the shuttle.'

The loner had absolutely no intention of allowing his superior to receive the applause for his prime capture. He was not stupid. Far from it, he had already realised how important the woman was to the Emperor as a means of bargaining.

The troop-commander started off, intending to enter the bay. Before he came into sight of the remainder of his troop, the loner whipped out his pistol with dramatic abruptness and shot him full in the back. Karen screamed at the close and unexpected nature of the action as the troop-commander slumped to the deck.

'Quiet!' the loner hissed in Karen's ear. She subsided, no longer attempting to struggle. She had witnessed the full maliciousness of her captor's pernicious nature and did not intend to push her luck. She was hauled into the bay. The waiting troopers glanced over the loner's shoulder, searching for their officer in command.

'He is dead,' they were coldly informed. 'Enter the shuttle. We are leaving.'

From his place of concealment Rickard had seen the happening of it but at the time, fearing for Karen's life as he did, he could do nothing to help her. As the last trooper disappeared into the bay he darted forward, pistol drawn. He hoped he might be allowed to exercise his markmanship once again but as he rounded the entrance a badly aimed shot from the bay smashed into the wall, causing him to duck reflexively. The loner's shot left a darkened scorch mark on the wall.

Dodging a second shot Rickard dived for cover. He rolled for the door's edge but in his haste miscalculated and smashed into it, damaged shoulder foremost. The wound was jarred badly, sending pain lancing through the whole arm. By the time he had recovered Karen had been bustled into the Empire-designed shuttle. The hatch was quickly sealed after her.

'Sneaky little bugger,' Rickard cursed at the disappearing trooper. 'He evens kills his own. I'd love to get my hands on him.' Although, he mused, it was doubtful whether his bare hands would do much damage, considering the trooper's overbuilt stature.

'They're powering up for lift-off,' someone shouted from control.

'Damn,' Rickard scrambled to his feet. 'If they try and shoot their way out of the bay we'll be breathing vacuum.' He darted into control, startling the few technicians who had managed to get there after the end of the fighting.

'They're lifting off,' he was told.

'Open the outer doors and seal these ones. Let them go. Quickly!'

The technicians began operating the controls with practised ease, sending the mechanisms into operation. 'Where's Lieutenant-Commander Bulloch?' Rickard demanded, finally noticing the man's absence.

'Don't know, sir,' A technician answered without looking up from his work. 'No-one has seen him since before the troopers turned up.'

'How did they get aboard?'

'Someone let them in. The tech on duty in here was found dead.'

'Then they must have smuggled one of their own people aboard.' It was probably that bastard he'd run into, he thought, remembering once again Karen's evil captor. And he had Karen. The idea of it made Rickard sick. He sorely wished there was something he could do.

Stuart entered control, joining him at the console as the Imperial shuttle could be seen departing the bay, heading off speedily toward the planet.

253

'Now we both have to come back,' she said to him.

Rickard glanced down at her. Her tiny fists were tightly clenched. 'Why?'

'Me for Bernerds, and you've got Miss Trestrail to look after.'

She had a point, Rickard admitted freely. He'd known almost from the first that she was worth watching out for. He had been right. And this time, so was she. They really did have to come back.

'Get some rest, Stuart. You've earned it.'

'Don't I know it.'

To remind him they were not yet safe, the intercom blared out with startling sharpness. 'Bridge to Captain. Emergency alert.'

'What? Another one?' he said in exasperation. 'This is getting ridiculous.' He headed for the bridge at a run.

☆ ☆ ☆

The *Emputin's* nerve centre was at full alert status. The lights were dimmed for battle conditions. Extra crew were dotted at the auxiliary consoles. The complete range of instruments along the bridge walls had been activated. Fire control teams waited out of the way, at the ready in case of need. In a well-controlled bedlam constant readings were being fed to Kiyami who was at the conn.

'What's the problem?' Rickard asked as the door closed behind him.

Kiyami rose from the conn and a steadying hand flashed to the chair's armrest as she wobbled uncertainly. The action did not escape Rickard. She looked completely done-in, he thought. There were dark rings around her normally clear blue eyes.

Kiyami continued as if nothing was wrong. She coolly reported the situation. 'I am afraid the Emperor has learned from his mistakes. He knows that three of his ships are no match for us so he has deployed a total of six and they are presently forming a barrier in our flight path and are begining to close in.'

'Great. Why didn't they invite the rest of their fleet and we could've had a party.'

'Captain?'

'Nothing.' He sat in the command chair.

Kiyami made another observation for him. 'Our exit out of the Belt is blocked. We cannot escape in that direction.'

Rickard was only just catching his breath after the mad flight from bay control. He inhaled deeply, filling his lungs. 'I don't want to go to the Belt, yet.'

'Captain?' Kiyami repeated.

'We're not leaving. There is unfinished business to be dealt with. I've ordered a course to be set for Tibor. I want to see what the rebel group has to offer. We - I owe the Emperor for this and I intend to repay him in full.'

'Imperial flagship is demanding our immediate surrender, Captain,' Watts broke in. 'They say that if we do not comply their superior numbers will defeat us by force.'

'No reply, Lieutenant. Mister Boyd, is a course to Tibor laid in and set?'

'Course is set and ready.'

'We'll have to make a detour, though. Have you programmed an evasion course around the enemy ships?'

'Yes, sir. It's all in there,' he gestured to the nav console.

'Mister Bentow-' Rickard cut himself off. He had become so used to the helmsman's presence that it would take time to become used to his absence. He would soon miss the man's incessant wisecracking. 'Uh, Lieutenant....' he quickly caught the attention of the replacement helmsman. As she turned he caught his breath. Before him sat an exquisitely proportioned, beautifully shaped woman. A veritable Venus, such was her perfection. Her straight, thick blonde hair hung over her shoulders and reached down the length of her back.

'Yes, sir,' she uttered with a faint but noticeable drawl.

Another North American, Rickard thought almost blithely. What are they trying to do, corner the market in helmsmen? 'You are...?'

'Oh. I'm sorry sir. Ehm...Lieutenant Arakelian, sir.' She smiled nervously, revealing even, pearly white teeth.

255

Watts interrupted. 'We are receiving our final warning to surrender, sir.'

'Right, Lieutenant Arakelian, get us out of here, please.'

'Aye-firmative, sir.'

Gleaming, ever-so tidy hair flicked out as she spun back to her controls. She slid and locked the proper instruments, her lightly tanned hands blurring with the speedy motion. An escalating subspeed was entered into the memory giving the ship forward motion. *Emputin* moved ahead, directly toward the blockade.

The Imperial warships open up in a widening blast of fire that moved like a chain reaction, each ship adding its own meagre power to the strengthened whole. *Emputin* bucked under the combined impact of so much fire-power. The shields strained to hold as the enemy ships moved around, closing in a well-formed semi-circle.

'Watts,' Rickard said, gripping the arms of his chair tightly. 'See if you can contact Alpheratz. Inform them of our difficulties. Weapons,' he did not have the time to become acquainted with Howarth's replacement, 'open fire on the flag ship. Concentrate needle beamers on the bridge.'

'Aye, Captain,' the stranger at the weapons desk answered.

A scathing volley of fire was hurriedly returned, causing the flagship considerable damage in the process. It limped out of the firing line, wreckage and debris spewing from the gaping wound in its hull. As if to counter the loss, the intensity of fire from the remaining ships increased recognisably. The shields strained under the mounting pressure.

Watt's managed to speak to Rickard over the rising level of background noise. The whine of straining circuitry was becoming almost deafening. 'I'm sorry,' she said. 'I can't raise anyone. The jamming hasn't stopped. All communication out of the Belt is impossible.'

'Damn. We've got to leave and it's now or never. We're not so strong that we can fight six of them for very long.'

The deep rumbling tremor that vibrated through the framework backed up his words. The main view screen

256

showed the semi-circle of warships drawing an ever-smaller net of entrapment around the ship, closing like a pack of wild dogs ganging up on a well-defended animal.

'Hyperspeed ready, sir,' Arakelian reported in a nervously hushed tone.

Before Rickard could give the word showers of sparks erupted spectacularly from the flight controls. Arakelian reacted straight away, more from fright than instinct, slinging her arms over her face in protection. A fire control man leaped down from the raised platform at the bridge's rear and quickly doused the growing flames, spraying the damaged console with white, sticky foam. The deck shook as another distant explosion rocked it.

'Helm's out, sir!' Arakelian informed Rickard loudly as she recovered herself. She hoped he did not think she was to blame.

'Dammit. Go to auxiliary control! Get the artificers in here right away. I want the damage fixed now.'

Arakelian reached for a communicator and locked into auxiliary, managed from deep in the bowels of the ship. 'Come in, Auxiliary Control. Please take over flight management. Read my settings and activate.'

Watts sharply cut through the confusion of the intraship channels. 'Maintenance, this is a grade one repair emergency. Helm control has been lost to the bridge. Effect immediate repairs.'

'It seems they are moving in for the kill,' Kiyami directed Rickard's attention to the screen. She was too physically exhausted to be daunted by the sight.

Rickard looked up and saw. The warships were almost touching hulls, so close together were they moving. Even as he watched the centre ship launched a stream of torpedoes that could not fail to hit at such close range.

'Hang on!' The torpedoes hit and *Emputin* rocked wildly under the barely sustained impact. The lights glimmered momentarily before regaining full power. The force of the impact and its jarring aftermath made Rickard's damaged shoulder throb as the pain started up once again.

'Shields are weakening,' came a report from Weapons

257

control.

'Helm,' Rickard snapped urgently.

'I'm trying, sir,' the beleaguered Arakelian glanced up, pale blue eyes flickering in uncertainty.

'Return fire,' Rickard ordered to weapons. Then with a faint edge of desperation to Arakelian, 'Helm?'

'We should be in motion now.' She fervently wished she was right.

Her foam-washed console emitted a spate of dull bleeps and the floor gave a lurch as the ship was put once more under control. It shuddered as the normally smooth acceleration ground and rattled under the pressure.

'Subspeed is back on line,' she sighed.

'Go,' Rickard spread his hands in supplication.

'Initiate,' Arakelian called into the comm.

Unresponsively sluggish at first, *Emputin* shot forward at a higher subspeed as the warships began to close in for the final kill. They ceased firing in stupefaction as *Emputin* headed straight for them on what seemed a suicide course, only dipping sharply at the final second to sail underneath their bellies and cruise away in a well-timed move. Arakelian was doing a fine job, despite the damaged controls.

The fact that they had lost their target dawned belatedly on the warships and they were extremely tardy in turning on their axis and giving chase to the rapidly vanishing Service cruiser. Moving sluggishly, they almost brushed hulls as they manoeuvered around, unskilled piloting not aiding their pursuit.

Out of danger, *Emputin* accelerated into hyperspeed in an almost leisurely fashion. Its crew seeming to mock the warships with their time-taking attitude. The ship soared away from the hostile capital of the Rukan Empire and what Rickard considered to be its infestation of backstabbing diplomats.

Peace and tranquility. It had never felt so good to Rickard.

'I *never* want to go through that again.' He rubbed the tiredness from his eyes as he sank back into the chair. He did not dwell on the fact that they still had to return. All he wanted for the moment was a long rest. And he was not the only one. 'Kiyami, I think it's about time you went off duty, don't you?'

'My duty period has ended, yes.' She took the hint and departed with great relief. Only sheer willpower kept her on her feet.

Arakelian released her crushing grip on the comm unit. Visibly tremulous hands were white with the unaccustomed emotional exertion. The comm unit dropped to the deck with a clang and she jumped, catching herself as Rickard looked over.

'How bad's the damage, Lieutenant?' he asked kindly.

'Um...I don't think it's too bad, sir. Should be able to get it fixed up. I could set up a jury-rig as long as things stay peaceful outside.'

'Don't worry. I think we're safe for a while. See what you can do.' he delivered her a smile of encouragement that did much to dispel her timidity. It also hid his own concern of Karen's fate. A concern that was very real.

He hoped his worried face did not show how real.

12

The suns were at their zenith. They burned down from an almost deserted cobalt blue sky with suffocating intensity. Lonely tufts of fluffy white cloud meandered high across the trackless sky, wandering leisurely from one haze-distorted horizon to the other. The moistureless earth rippled with heat. The coldness of the early morning had disappeared with unnatural speed. The day had become very warm, very humid.

Layers of pale yellow sand, ever-present over the less busy streets of the capital city, were still, untroubled by the previously gusty winds like a deadly calm sea after a violent storm. The winds had died almost concurrently with the conclusion of the residency battle, settling the city into a measureless blur of non-motion. A state of almost complete soundlessness existed throughout the city, creating its own sense of unreality. It was as if normal, real life had ceased and an imaginary duplicate with only vague similarities had replaced it. The city was as quiet as the grave.

Howarth was becoming annoyed at just how silent the place was. He could not think for how long he had been crouched in the deep alcove, but his legs were aching like hell. Every joint was stiff and cramped. He must have been jammed into the hole for a couple of hours, judging by the positions of the suns. The recess was in the back wall of one of the city's many mud-brick combination dwellings. Steel supports had been thrown in at the corners, apparently for simple good measure. Many of the local buildings were like this, so Howarth had discovered. It was as if they had been modernised with more advanced materials only a piece at a time and at great intervals. As if modern technology was a late arriving guest at a party already well under way. It certainly did nothing for local beauty. And this was where he'd chosen to hide out.

Not thinking of where he could go after breaking away from his captors, Howarth had simply centred his thoughts on survival. He had headed for the maze of closely clustered buildings that formed a seemingly impenetrable jungle of passageways and narrow alleys around the palace. It had appeared the most sensible means of evasion. With a little skill and a lot of luck, it had been an easy task to dodge and lose the single trooper on his trail. The remainder of the native army had more urgent things on their minds than chasing after a solitary escapee, one who could do little harm on his own without even a pistol. Just a flick-knife and that was it. They were probably correct in their assumption but Howarth did not intend to sit around and find out for sure. It was time he got moving.

Battlegrimed and unshaven, he eased himself forwards. Checking first to make sure the alley outside his niche was deserted, he crawled out of hiding, stretching with relief at being able to unbend his cramped limbs. He heard elbow and knee joints click as he tried to get the blood circulating in them. Two hours. It must have been at least that. It was a long time to be compressed into such a tiny, cramped hole, especially in heat as consuming as this. It was about time he did something positive instead of cowering away.

He peered in the direction of the residency. There was not much to see over the obscuring buildings bar a thinning black mantle of smoke, a coiled air column that refused to dissipate. The battle must have ended by now, Howarth thought. He supposed everyone had escaped. Hopefully. If the evacuation had continued the way it had started then it was a good bet they had. Rickard was doing a good job. He'd made out better than Howarth would have thought. The captain had revealed a strong sense of leadership under hard conditions. It strangely belied the man's usual air of pessimistic downtroddenness. Usually he appeared pretty insecure. Maybe that was simply a false image he fed others to put them off the right track, although why he would want to do that Howarth could not imagine. Rickard was complicated. Too complicated for him to hold an introspective discussion on the man, at least, not at this time and in this place. Look to your own problems first, he thought. But please don't go walking into any troopers, huh?

He took a few tentative steps towards the end of the alley, heading for the wider street at its end. 'It's about time I started thinking about what I'm going to do,' he decided aloud. He glanced up and down the alley and saw nothing but more buildings of a similar nature to the one behind him. 'I'm stuck on this planet-sized oven. What *do* I do now?' he wondered. He thought of counting his options, but he realised that he didn't have any. Lady Luck had not granted him a good hand. In fact he could even picture the Lady herself, looking down upon him and smiling with unpleasant intent.

'Well,' Howarth muttered, risking a peek around the corner of the street, 'she'd better not try anything now. I don't need any more bad luck.' He'd already had one run-in with a couple of inimical citizens, soon after he'd imagined he was safe from pursuit. That had been too close for comfort. Come on, he thought. Get moving. Enough time wasted already.

But where was he supposed to go? So far he'd concentrated primarily on staying alive, dodging troopers and citizens alike. So much so that he'd not thought of what to do, where to go. What he needed was time to settle and think. Unfortunately, all that filled his mind was the thought of how his colleagues were coping against the oppressive odds that faced them. He certainly hadn't planned ahead.

Now it was high time he did so. What he needed was a plan of action. Anything was better than running through the endless twists and turns of the countless mass of city dwellings, stumbling from one fight to another. That was all that would happen if he did not decide where he was headed. Eventually he was bound to run into someone and then he'd be in trouble. After all, he wasn't a superman, despite wishes to the contrary. Instead he felt he should and could do something to help out any other Service crew still on the planet. There were prisoners, he knew. Crew had been captured alive in the battle. He'd seen the Imperials going to great pains to take them. He, himself had been taken virtually unharmed by a sneak attack. All right, so he'd been caught off guard, intent on laying the charges, but that was no excuse. He'd been taken pretty easily. So there had to be others.

The best place to head for was undoubtedly the Imperial Palace. That was the most likely holding place for captured Service crew. All he had to do was work out how to get in. And out. What were the escape options once he'd managed to free any captives? He thought he understood Rickard well enough after recent experience to know he would not abandon his crew. He would try to get them back, there were not many commanders who wouldn't, but how long would it take him to return? Was the ship in the hands of the Empire? Was Rickard even alive? God, he hoped so, otherwise he really was stuck here. But if he could be ready and waiting with all the freed prisoners when Rickard turned up it would save a lot of time and effort. Still, he thought, one problem at a time. The first was to discover just where the prisoners actually were. And he knew exactly what to do about it.

Howarth abandoned the alley, quickly checking that the intersecting street was empty. He made off down one shadow-darkened side of it, keeping low, until he came to a wide intersection. The confined street met a broader one. He halted, confused, wondering which way to go. He wanted the Imperial Palace. But where the hell was it?

The lone trooper trudged along, his stocky pistol snug in its holster. He was bored. He had been hunting for the single interloper for what seemed like a measureless age. The Service officer had somehow escaped capture during the battle and had made off into the city. There had been a sighting not far away but that had turned up nothing.

The imbeciles who had spotted him had even allowed him to escape unhindered! What morons! Wherever that alien was now, he was nowhere near this part of the city, and that was a fact. If he had any sense at all he would have headed for the valleys to the north. There, the lofty crags and outcroppings of rock deflected the worst of the midday heat, creating a sheltered haven for the local animal life - and for many of the local criminal elements.

He remembered a colleague of his who had once chased a thief into the valleys. He had only caught up with his quarry when the thief had met with a waiting accomplice. The pursuing trooper then had the added bonus of a double bounty when he brought the bodies back. That was why, whenever they were hunting, the troopers always thought first of the valleys. He wished that his troop-commander had the sense to think of that, instead of forcing him to patrol this low-life slum area, infested as it was with the sort of scum he would not bother to spit at. He wished someone would hurry up and rid the world of the escapee so he could at last come off duty. A double tour was not the most enjoyable of tasks.

Howarth was greatly relieved when the trooper walked right past him without even glancing down the gloomy sidestreet. A pistol and crowd-control baton. The Imperial had no other weapons. This was his chance to reap a little information without putting himself in any danger. Brandishing his flick-blade, he crept up behind the unwary trooper, his footfalls noiseless on the thin layer of sand. This would be easy. He did not intend to allow the trooper the chance of resisting.

With a sudden spurt of motion he bounded forward and flung an arm around the trooper's throat, gripping it tightly. The other hand in which the blade was securely gripped rose to eye level.

The trooper instantly ceased to struggle when he saw ten centimetres of shining steel pointing directly at his face. He had no intention of playing the hero, even though he longed to gouge flesh from the face of his mysterious assailant in long, tearing fistfuls. He submissively allowed himself to be dragged bodily backwards into the shelter of the side street. His captor hauled him around the corner and into the shallow recess provided by a doorway, slamming him up against it so they were face to face.

'Okay, sunshine. Where's the Emperor's palace from here?' Howarth demonstrated that he was wasting no time on polite smalltalk. The trooper was silent. He glared at Howarth, murder in his eyes. 'Where is it?'

'Release me now,' the trooper demanded. He kept his voice emotionless.

'Great,' Howarth said to himself. 'I always get the friendly ones.' He moved the knife closer to the trooper's unprotected face, wanting to instill fear into his captive. Sunlight glared off the bare metal, reflecting onto the trooper's face. 'Just answer the question.'

'No.'

'This is your last chance, lizard-head. This isn't exactly a meaningful dialogue we're having here and I want some answers.'

'Are you trying to threaten me?'

'*Noo!* I just came here for some fun in the sun! Of course I'm bloody well threatening you!'

The trooper went quiet for a second before coming to a decision and resignedly pointing the way. The fact had quickly dawned upon him that he had been captured by the very alien he was supposed to be hunting. It was not a comfortable idea. 'Follow the main street until it comes to a central road,' he said. 'The way from there will be clear, even to you.'

'Watch it with the backchat. Is the palace where the prisoners are being held?'

'What prison-'

Howarth jerked the trooper's head back, pushing the blade very close to his face. 'Don't mess me around. Answer the question. Is that where the prisoners are being held?'

The trooper gave a short nod. 'It is.'

'Thank you. That's all I needed to know.'

The trooper cynically wondered what his superiors would say and do when he reported that he had found the human and let him go again. He reluctantly came to the conclusion that he would have to make an attempt at capture. It was not a pleasing thought but there was one factor in its favour. The one major argument that persuaded him even to think of attacking Howarth was the realisation that his troop-commander would probably shoot him out of hand if he did not.

'You will now lay down the knife and surrender to me,' he ordered firmly.

Howarth's eyebrows lifted in amusement. 'That's got to be the funniest thing I've heard all day.'

'It would be better for you if you did. At least you will remain alive.'

'Look, after what your lot did to us today I doubt if any of us wil ever trust anything you say again. We don't take easily to war but you're certainly asking for one.' Now that he had discovered what he wanted to know, his captive had become an unwanted nuisance, an acquisition he no longer required. He wondered analytically how to dispose of the acquisition.

'The attack was not my idea,' the trooper mournfully whinged. It was possible that by feigning cowardice he could catch the Service officer offguard. 'I merely follow my orders.'

'I've heard that before. Too many times for it to sound believable.'

'But it is true.'

'You know something? We're not so different after all, the Grouping and your Empire. Both carry their fair share of heroes and cowards. I think it's quite clear which category you fall in. Now shut up. I'm trying to think.' What the hell was he going to do with the trooper? Kill him out of hand, in cold blood? Murder was not his style. It was one thing to fight in open warfare, quite another to kill with forethought.

While Howarth was puzzling over what to do, the trooper decided his chance had come. With courage born of fear he grabbed Howarth's knife arm and jerked forwards, spinning to twist the arm and force the Serviceman to twist his own body or suffer a broken limb.

The trooper whipped out his pistol, intending to end the situation immediately. Howarth reacted straight away. With blinding speed he blocked the pistol with his free

266

hand, forcing it away from his body. At the same time he swung out his foot, hooking it behind the trooper's legs and pulled back sharply. The trooper's legs were whipped out from under him, sending him crashing to the ground, still clutching Howarth but dropping the pistol. Thus thwarted, he tensed himself to make a grab for the weapon. Howarth caught him by the collar of his uniform and punched him heavily in the face. Bone crunched and shattered beneath his fist. The trooper's wide nose became a bloody mess.

Quickly, before the trooper could recover, Howarth retrieved the fallen pistol and lobbed it further down the sidestreet. Then he stood back and waited, unruffled by the affray. The trooper was breathing heavily, wiping away the blood with one hand, while pulling himself up by the doorway with the other. His vision clearing he glared at his enemy, standing only a few feet away from him, holding a knife. He'd managed to see what had become of his own weapon and he wondered what the Service officer was planning. He was larger and more muscularly thickset than he had appeared at first, and he was scowling darkly, waiting for his opponent to make the first move. Well, the trooper thought, angry now that his shock had abated, he should not be disappointed. Keeping his eyes locked on Howarth, he reached down to the side of his belt. Unclipping a leather restrainer, he withdrew his baton and brandished it menacingly. He smiled, sure that a three-feet long baton could not be bested by such a short-bladed knife.

Howarth saw the trooper's anticipating smirk, undoubtedly he was sure that he could not be beaten. It was an attitude Howarth hated. This guy was a hard case and he liked to show it. In one powerfully oversized fist he gripped the metal-tipped baton, wanting to fight. The wooden pole was blunt at one end, slightly spiked at the other, and did not carry much weight, but Howarth knew it still made a dangerous weapon. And that smile continued to bug him. It was an expression that Howarth had seen on the face of many of the troopers in the residency battle. He disliked it fervently, and with good reason. He now relished the chance of a return bout. The opportunity for some revenge had been plainly presented to him. Who said it was a dish best served cold? He was going to enjoy this more than he thought possible.

The trooper brandished his baton in both hands, raising it menacingly. He wiped blood from his face with a dusty sleeve. Howarth steadied himself, waiting for the attack. It was one against one. Equal odds. It made a likeable change. He almost smiled himself as the trooper moved in.

The baton was swung high, aiming for Howarth's head, but he managed to duck. The metal tip gouged a deep groove in the soft material of the wall behind him, spraying him with a dislodged crust of mud and brick fragments. The trooper swung again and Howarth sidestepped neatly. The baton struck deeper into the wall, this time catching between more solid brick surfacing. Before the trooper could withdraw, Howarth grabbed hold of the baton and kicked out, delivering his opponent a vicious blow to the genitals. The trooper gasped and released his weapon involuntarily, staggering back in numbing pain. Howarth yanked the baton free.

The surprised trooper quickly regained himself, reassessing the situation carefully. He had underestimated his enemy. Even though he was well-built for one of his kind, he should not have been able to react with such speed and agility. It was a well-known fact that the homeworld of the Service crew had a lighter gravity than the capital world. That meant they should also be correspondingly weaker. And from what he'd seen of most of them he surmised this to be correct. Nothing so weak and spindly in appearance was entitled to be quite so effective at hand-to-hand combat. He would have to be very careful if he was going to win this. Very careful.

Howarth was understandably pleased with himself. He saw how surprised the trooper was. It was not for nothing that he'd forced his body to familiarise itself with heavier gravities. 'Now who's got the upper hand, mate?' he said and this time he did smile. As if to mock the trooper further, Howarth threw the baton to the ground, aiming it at the trooper's feet. 'Have another go,' he offered.

The trooper was unamused. He picked up the baton,

making sure his grip was tight. He steeled himself for a second attack. This time he would not miss. Howarth's smile changed from one of pleasure to one of calculated anticipation. He intended to make at least a token payment in return for all that had happened.

The baton lashed out and Howarth was quick to parry using the flat of the blade. His stubby knife came into contact with the metal-encased end of the baton and he delighted in the reverberating clang of metal on metal that resulted. The trooper tried again but the thrust was once more blocked. Howarth jabbed forward sharply, poking his opponent almost playfully in the chest. He made a small tear in the trooper's uniform, creasing the flesh beneath. This enraged the reptiloid even further and his deeply boned skull crest pushed forward to emphasise his angered reaction. He lunged at Howarth with an unexpected roar of rage. His sudden show of temper managed to catch the security chief by surprise. It was the last reaction he'd expected. He stumbled backwards, taken off guard. His balance was lost and he staggered, tumbling ungainly to the side of the narrow street. The blade tumbled from his grasp and the native was on him instantly, not allowing him the chance to recover. Holding the baton like a pole, the trooper produced it bare centimetres from his throat, moving it inexorably closer. The tip touched and cut into the flesh and a pinpoint of dark red blood appeared. Howarth struggled desperately, biceps bulging as he fought to hold back the hand controlling it.

In the midst of fighting for his life an unwanted flash of thought raced across his mind; suddenly this was not so much fun. He was in trouble.

While holding off the maliciously smirking trooper with both hands, Howarth snapped his head up and frantically searched with his eyes for the lost blade. With a sinking heart he saw that it was well out of reach. There was no hope of getting to it. His single chance lay with wresting the baton from his attacker. He grabbed it by its near end and concentrated his whole effort into removing the sharply tipped weapon from his throat. Tensing his muscles he pitted his prodigious strength against his

269

opponent's. At first the baton remained dangerously stationary. Howarth's arms shook with the effort, his hands trembled. He exerted more excessive force, desperate not to be outdone after all he'd endured. At last, a centimetre at a time, the weapon was edged slowly but surely away by Howarth's only marginally superior strength. Sweating streams with the effort he forced the trooper's arm outwards, towards the alley wall. Locked in deadly silent struggle Howarth smashed the trooper's bare fist against the mud-encrusted wall trying to force him to loosen his hold. He repeated the action, and again, until the fist was cut and seeping blood. His opponent doggedly refused to release his weapon.

'Drop it. Will you drop it?' Howarth hissed. 'Bloody well let...go!' He put all his energy into one last attempt, swinging the baton-wielding arm out and back against the crumbling wall in a super-human effort. One gasp of pain and the trooper released it, letting it fall to the dirt surface with a solid thump.

Howarth jerked up his knee, roughly shoving the unbalanced native to one side. He jumped to his feet, scrabbling for the knife. He grasped it thankfully and rose, intending to act in a way commensurate to the trooper's actions. He was confident now of victory.

Before he could even straighten fully, the unflagging trooper leapt wildly onto his back, slinging a securing arm around his neck. The arm drew tighter still as the hold was strengthened. The struggling Howarth was struck on the rear of the neck with a tightly clenched fist and the effort was repeated, sending wave after punishing wave of numbing pain soaring up his spinal cord.

In a blind fury and with his head spinning Howarth gave an enraged yell and gripped his assailant's legs in a firm, unyielding hold, still clutching the knife. Simultaneously, he bent sharply forward and levered the trooper up, propelling him over his head so that he lurched and lost his grip, sliding forwards unstoppably. His skull came sharply into contact with the solid unmalleability of the wall with a gruesomely muted *thud*!

He tumbled to the floor. Howarth staggered back, quickly catching his breath and rubbing the sore nape of his vividly bruised neck.

Fearing the scuffle had been overheard he glanced up and down the length of the street but his worry was unfounded. The street remained obstinately devoid of life. He'd never seen the city so empty. Shrugging off the strangeness of it Howarth impassively regarded his dormant opponent, lying as he was, helpless, sprawled in a heap at the base of the wall. He appeared unconscious. Dark red blood was gathering in droplets on the sand beside him from the large jagged cut on his forehead. His skull crest was lowered, flopping limply to give him an oddly displaced look of placidity.

Howarth lowered the blade. 'Stupid sail-head,' he muttered venomously, eyeing the limp skull crest. He sighed in relief that it was over.

'At least you don't bleed green,' he observed in a style that broadly bespoke of Bentowski's influence. He blinked dust out of his eyes, still watching the prostrate trooper carefully, wary of any movement. God, if Bentowski could only see him now.

Perhaps he might find something to help him get inside the palace. It was a faint hope but worth trying. He was that desperate. he leaned over the unmoving body and began checking the pouches in his uniform. In the blink of an eye, what a moment before had been a motionlesss body had become a dramatic blur of activity. The native came to life, lunging for Howarth's throat and grabbing him in a throttling clasping of giant hands. Howarth flailed, momentarily panicking. His attacker's strength was incredible, much greater than it had been, urged on by the desire to alleviate the shame of his defeat. They both fell to the ground, the native not losing his hold.

Once Howarth had recovered from the initial shock he was even more shocked to discover there was nothing he could do to escape from the powerful hold. He curled his fingers into a fist, sinking it into where he hoped the xenomorph's stomach was. There was absolutely no visible effect. Indomitably strong muscles prevented the blow from causing any harm. A greater force was exerted on the crushing grip around Howarth's throat, the two of them thrashing about on the ground.

271

Howarth was becoming increasingly desperate. He fully realised his plight. He had to force his way out of this soon, or not at all. Then sudden remembrance of the knife came to his disorientated mind. He had unwittingly dropped it but it had to be nearby. His breathing was becoming irregular. He had to hurry. Craning his head as much as he was able he saw the blade. It was lying scant centimetres from his grasp, knocked away in the desperate struggle.

He tried to reach it. He had to reach it. Searching with the periphery of his vision, he clawed his way along, stretching out to the limit of his ability. His groping fingers missed the blade, falling short. He dug his hand into the sand, physically dragging himself and his adversary in the direction of the blade. Glancing out of the corner of his eye the bloodied trooper saw Howarth's intention. He resisted frantically, spurred on by sheer willpower. He could not release his hold on Howarth for fear of losing his advantage. Despite his best efforts he failed to stop the relentless movement towards the knife. He tried to dig his feet into the soft dirt, throwing his whole body into the effort. To his immense concern he found that it made no difference. He was too late, anyway. Howarth reached out for the blade, pulling his opponent onto him as he finally grasped the weapon. Suddenly panic-stricken, the trooper smashed his boot down on Howarth's wrist. He had to prevent the blade from coming up. With his other hand he tore at the Service officer's throat, fingers like steel talons raking the skin.

Howarth struck out wildly, uncaringly. His fist caught the trooper's broken nose, causing blood to flow afresh from the wound. He jerked back with his legs and the two entangled figures rolled in the sandy earth, tumbling one over the other until they hit the narrow street's opposite wall. Howarth came out on top but the iron-strong hold on his crushed throat lessened only marginally. The native was still relentlessly intent on ridding him of his life, something he was equally keen on retaining. The knife arm was free now, and he intended to use it.

Jamming his free hand under his adversary's jutting

chin Howarth exerted greater force and pushed back his head. He levered it up with his palm until the trooper's own neck was presented to him, as equally unprotected as his own. Then he brought up the blade, raising it high, pausing and holding it there. Despite his tortured breath coming in wheezing gasps, he made the moment last, so the trooper could see what was coming. When he did his eyes widened in terror. His grip slackened, allowing Howarth to gulp air. One hand flew to Howarth's to prevent the blade falling. It was no good. The blade was lowered relentlessly, closing on him with a black finality. There was no way for him to stop the blow from being delivered. His mind calmly registered the fact that he had lost his battle. The Service man had beaten him. Knowing he was defeated he re-tightened his iron-strong grip on Howarth's throat, wanting to cause his opponent maximum injury. But however much he wanted to, he could not do it. It was no more than an exercise in futility. Howarth's eyes were beginning to lose focus as a sudden wave of dizziness hit him but he did not need to see clearly to hit what was a very easy target.

He thrust the knife down, stabbing into the soft flesh around the trooper's collarbone with a sound sickeningly akin to that of meat being skewered. Blood spurted out in a pressurised jet, flowing freely from the wound. The trooper cried out in a single wail, his face contorted in a rictus of agony. A fountain of blood splattered over Howarth as he yanked free the knife with a sharp tug and slashed again, cutting, ending the fight as he ended his enemy's life. His enemy's arms fell away as the breath left his battered body.

Feeling extremely blurry-headed Howarth dropped back languidly.

It took him some time to regain enough energy to be able to move his exhausted body. When he finally did, his bone-weary muscles were like lead weights as he rolled the corpse off him. It took a great effort to heave it aside but he somehow managed it, then propped himself against the wall. He gasped air fitfully, filling his oxygen-starved lungs. He felt drained. The pain in his throat was intense. A severe, throbbing nullity that seemed to persist endlessly. There was a blackness that was only beginning to fade from the fringes of his consciousness, like a dark shroud that had engulfed the light and was only beginning to give way with great reluctance.

Howarth glanced at his hands. They shook uncontrollably. His head span, making him feel confused and disorientated. He coughed fitfully, each spasm causing him to flinch at the constricting ache he felt in his battered throat. His breathing finally began to steady, coming in hoarse but regular intakes. His entire body suddenly plunged into a short fit of uncontrollable shivering, his teeth chattering despite the humidity. The delayed physical and mental shock, unburdened by thoughts and ideals of combat-hardened strength and mental rationality, ended sharply with a drawn-out shudder that brought him to full awareness. His eyes opened and he took in the corpse lying prostrate before him.

He swore. If he had failed to reach the knife...if...if he *had* failed, then it would have been him lying there, smothered in thick sand and his own drying blood. 'That was too close for comfort.' His voice grated the words. 'How come these guys always go for the bloody neck?'

He wished now that he had not allowed the trooper the chance to fight back. That had very nearly become a costly mistake. He'd been damned fortunate to come out on top. Once the desire for revenge had left him the fight had become distasteful to him. Taking life was not something in which he revelled but it had been necessary. His life or the trooper's. Wiping the sweat from his face with a dirty sleeve, he cast an eye over the surrounding buildings. There was no disturbance. No shouting of evil-minded citizens. No running of heavily armed troopers through the narrow streets.

All was quiet. He tentatively fingered the bright red line around his neck, brushing away the small gathering of his own blood from the tiny wound there. He rested his aching head in his hands, careless of the blood and dirt encrusting them. He sat like that for a few minutes, resting, gathering his strength. What he wouldn't give for a bath and good meal, he thought wistfully. Or even standard Service rations.

Feeling decidedly stronger, he rose to his feet. He did not bother to brush down his uniform. The clinging sand stuck in yellow blotches to the thick blood-spots, patches of darkening red that covered his upper body. It didn't matter, anyway. It wasn't as if he were still on duty.

Crouching over the stiff corpse, he pulled his bloodied knife from the hideous neck wound it had created, gripping its featureless bone handle tightly. He wiped the knife clean on the trooper's trouser leg and tucked it into the snug security of his belt, patting it almost affectionately. It was not much but it had saved his life.

The blood had ceased to flow from the wide open tear below the trooper's broad neck. A deposited caking brown stain was left to mark it. Lifting his body a little, Howarth caught a whiff of the foul odour that emerged from the dusty uniform. He wrinkled his nose in disgust. Ignoring the stink he rapidly went through the pockets, hoping to find something. A pass key. Anything that would help him. He groaned in frustration, finding nothing more than a few coins. He cursed and gave up, allowing the corpse to fall back limply. Now all he could do was conceal the body.

Gripping him by the shoulders of his uniform, he began dragging the dead trooper further into the darkness of the shadowed sidestreet. Glancing along the row of buildings, he quickly found a wide, full-length niche into which to jam the limp, flopping body, pushing it as far back as he could manage. The niche was covered in sand and it flowed around the body, swirling over the stained uniform. That done, he straightened up. He was tired and hot, sweltering in the day's humidity. The brilliantly shining suns boiled the very air with their oppressive heat.

'Christ it's hot out here,' he gasped. He shook sweat from his face.

There was no reason to hang around, he thought. Then he remembered the trooper's pistol. He would gain nothing more from his dead opponent, except that. It was a good job he'd remembered. He'd not get far without it.

275

He trotted up the darkened street to where it lay and eagerly scooped it up, dusting off the clinging grains of sand from its sleek barrel. He was glad of its comforting bulk, its rounded butt resting nicely in his palm.

It would come in very handy, he thought. He'd be certain to find a suitable use to which to put it. He slotted it into his holster, finding he had to force it somewhat because of its bulk. It was not exactly standard issue but what did he care? He was pleased to have something more than a flick-knife for defence.

He set off along the still-deserted street. The wind blew up once more, shifting sand in whirling eddies over the corpse he left behind. The entire disturbance had brought not one investigative enquiry. Not a soul had bothered to spare a moment to glance out of their homes. No-one wanted to know. It was a strange day and strange things had happened, so what was one more strange disturbance? Nobody wanted to be outside, in the streets. Not on a day like this. The unlucky trooper's stiffening body would not be discovered for some considerable time, sand-swept and cold, like a beached sea creature left as a play-thing for the elements.

Howarth arrived at an intersection. The confined street met a broader one. He halted, struggling to remember the directions he had forced from the trooper. Which way did he say? Howarth wondered, annoyed that he'd allowed himself to forget so easily. Making a decision, he set off, taking the right hand turning. This had better be the right way, or he was going to get nowhere fast.

He walked warily down the wider street, heading in what he hoped was the direction of the Emperor's palace. The street was short, ending only moments later in a sharp turn which hid whatever lay beyond. Howarth ventured cautiously around the bend, fully expecting to be presented with another section of the maze. Instead what he saw surprised and delighted him. The way ahead opened out into a wide, expansive area of cleared space dominated by one single, very familiar construction.

He had come face to face with the Imperial Palace.

Its protective dome, presently only semi-transparent, shone brilliantly under the bright light from above. The

276

sunlight was marginally masked by a dissipating black cloud of smoke drifting lazily from the abandoned residency.

'I've been that close to the lousy thing all this time.' Howarth cast his eyes heavenward even though there was no-one to witness the gesture. He had been travelling almost parallel to the palace all along. In fact, his course would have eventually taken him away from it. He was lucky to have happened across the trooper.

Standing in a group outside the main gates he could see a cluster of palace guards. There seemed to be more of them than before, with a good many regular troopers making up the numbers, and they were not paying much attention to duty. They seemed to be entwined in some vividly gesticulative discussion. Doubtlessly it concerned the events of the morning, and one of them appeared to be recounting his own experiences to his audience. They, on their part, seemed eager to disagree with the story teller, and they were disagreeing vehemently.

Howarth looked further on, at the large, ornate doors of the palace's front entrance, which were wide open. If only he could get past the guards, he thought. That would make this a whole lot easier. But he knew there was no possibility of his entering the palace via that route. He would never make it over the open square without being seen. It presented no cover, and he wasn't feeling suicidal enough to try his luck, which wasn't at its best.

No, the best course of action he could follow was to watch and wait. The main entrance was not the only one he knew of. It was about time he showed a bit of patience and merely satisfied himself with conducting a little surveillance.

Howarth examined the nearest building. It was a single storey brick-built affair. Strong metal struts were built into the corners to support the weak walls. On the near side were no windows, just a smooth, featureless surface, not very easy to climb. He walked around to the building's rear.

The wall there was just as smooth and featureless. Again, there were no windows, only a row of tiny ventilation slots along the top. Standing by the base of the wall there was a rounded, mould-covered barrel. Howarth took a closer look, peering in to inspect the contents. No doubt it was a water barrel. It was a shame that the damn thing was empty. He needed a drink more than anything in the dry heat of the day. Even that gunge served at the street corner tavern would do right now. That aside, the barrel would serve another purpose.

Climbing onto the barrel, Howarth realised that there might be someone inside the building. The last thing he wanted to do was disturb them; he wasn't doing so well that he needed to become involved in another fight. He was extremely careful to avoid the tiny ventilation slots dug into the wall. From the top of the barrel he could reach the roof's edge. He pulled himself up on the low, extremely primitive stone balustrade that ringed it, his boots producing an eerie, echoing quality from the empty barrel as he lifted himself off it. A moment later he had climbed to safety up onto the flat roof. Breathing a sigh of relief that he had not been heard, he crawled on his stomach to the opposite edge of the roof where he gained a clear view of the palace.

It was a perfect position for a temporary observation post. From here he could watch the comings and goings of the palace occupants, and discover how active they were before he thought of entering the building himself.

Now all he had to do was to wait a while for something to happen. Hopefully this wasn't going to be too long a wait. He wasn't *that* patient. He tried to make himself comfortable on the roof, settling down under the fiery luminescence of a cloudless blue sky. The flat roof exuded heat to a merciless extent. The scarlet line around his throat began to ache dully and his fingers toyed with the dried bloodspots under his chin. That hard-faced trooper had caused him more trouble than he'd expected. He certainly wasn't going to do that again in a hurry.

His aches and pains were quickly forgotten when he recognised the whine of an approaching floater. He peeped over the balustrade as the heavily-laden floater rounded the far corner of the square. It ponderously hovered up to the palace's gates where it came to a bumpy halt. It was a type similar to the one that had awaited

278

Howarth outside the residency, box-like and completely covered.

As soon as it halted the suddenly alert palace guards moved forward to form a ring around the stationary vehicle. The driver leaned out of his seat and snapped a command to one of the troopers. The nearest of them reached for the sealed doors and unlocked them, stepping instantly back and raising his weapon. His companions did likewise, unslinging their own weapons and pointing them threateningly. The first of the prisoners jumped down.

The lead trooper delivered him a menacing poke in the ribs with his rifle. Others climbed down out of the battered floater to stand beside him in a growing group. Two of them carried between them an immobile, incapacitated form on a very basic light metal stretcher.

An Imperial officer emerged from the palace interior, pistol raised. He gestured to the offloaded prisoners, waiting impatiently for them to move. One by one they trailed in his direction as he led the way into the palace. His unwilling entourage were hastened along by the gun-wielding troopers.

Howarth recognised the prisoners immediately. They were *Emputin* crewmembers - captives. They were the very prisoners he had nobly intended to rescue.

'At least they're still alive,' he breathed softly. It was the first break he'd had all day.

Staring hard, he strained to make out their identities. It was a faint, meagre hope at that range but still he tried. In the few short seconds he had before they disappeared he quickly checked through them. Only the unconscious figure on the stretcher rang any bells of familiarity in his mind. It was strange. He couldn't be certain but the build and stature were vaguely recognisable, half covered as the figure was. Then the stretcher and its load were gone, taken into the palace through exquisitely carved portals in the protective dome.

The rest reluctantly followed, the last of the bunch vanishing into the darkened interior, closely shepherded by the troopers. The figure at the rear was a woman, and limping badly. Someone dressed not in the one-piece regulation duochrome uniform of the Service but in civilian garb. Howarth frowned, puzzled. There was only one person she could be. He easily recognised her shapely figure from when he'd ogled her on *Emputin's* bridge, at the start of the mission. It was the official observer - Karen Trestrail.

What the hell was she doing here? 'I'd swear she got away on one of the launches,' Howarth muttered. 'In fact, I know she did. So what's she come back to this pit for?' The question better have an answer because one way or another, he decided positively, he was going to find a way into the palace. He glanced at his watch. It was 45.50 now. He'd give it a couple of hours.

That would be easy, he thought. Comparatively easy. Then there was the hard part, the bit that he was dreading most. How was he supposed to get back out again, especially with half the population of the Emperor's prison in tow?

Well, one way or another he'd soon find out.

13

Sickbay on *Emputin* was littered with the blood-smeared forms of wounded and dying crew. A heavy atmosphere of sluggish despondancy had settled over the inmates of the ship's hospital like a pollutant-filled fog that was dispersing any coherent visibility.

Nurses worked at double speed as they darted from bed to bed, having to tend to far too many patients. Most of the injured were survivors of the residency battle. Their high number had been added to by the even more recent confrontation on the ship itself. Now sickbay was overcrowded and overworked. Life-sign readouts on compact electronic diagnosis panels clipped to each bed flickered away, relaying the condition of their connectees. Some wavered erratically, plunging suddenly and labouring to rise once more as life support equipment helped stave off death's embrace.

There were a great many not so severely wounded crew sitting propped against walls or at the ends of beds. A few drifted in and out of consciousness. Others moaned lowly in constant unrelieved pain. Many were covered with external lacerations or sported a variety of ills; broken bones; internal injuries; skull fractures and burn marks where some had been fortunate enough to survive direct hits by weapons fire.

Virginia Hicks stood over one prostrate patient, dabbing with a once-sterile gauze pad at a deep cut. The wound, more of a gash than a cut, bled persistantly down the crewman's soot-streaked face. Hicks kept herself aloof, remaining outwardly oblivious to the surrounding groans and cries for aid that pressed in on her sanity. She concentrated on one patient at a time and ignored the rest

281

to the point of dereliction, only acknowledging the most urgent requests. It was the only way to work under such circumstances. The conditions were tough even for her, well practised as she was at her job.

She held a fresh pad to the crewman's wound and made him hold it there before she moved to the next bed. The new case was a projectile wound and fever was beginning to set in. Hicks provided a much needed hypo of phenacetin to reduce the fever. The spray hypodermic was applied sending its contents into a vividly bruised forearm. Tiny droplets of blood remained in a patterned circle on the flesh as Hicks finished. She looked up to see a pair of orderlies enter sickbay wheeling a disposal trolley between them.

The overworked orderlies discovered their newest customer on the bed nearest the door. The stiffening body was covered by a single sheet. The bed's diagnostic panel was dark and silent. Careful to help a badly limping crewwoman out of their path, they then grasped the corpse and lifted it, hauling it irreverently onto a trolley, dumping it like an over-heavy bag of rubbish. They had made the same old trip time after time, far too many times in the last couple of hours for it to be a novelty worthy of holding their wandering attention. Their eyes looked at the surroundings without seeing them. Their minds protected themselves with a kind of vacant withdrawal, as if what was happening was not directly related to real life, to the normality they usually enjoyed. They simply went through the motions with practised monotony. They did not look too closely for fear that the horror would finally dawn on them, bringing with it a pernicious reality of its own.

The numbed orderlies abandoned sickbay with their cargo, steering the laden trolley out through the doors. Rickard stood aside to let them pass. His eyes were dark and heavy, a change of uniform had not refreshed him. He entered the hospital wing to witness for himself the gruesome mess the medical centre was descriptively reported to now hold. He stopped short at what greeted his eyes. What - when he had last seen it - had been a tidy, peaceful, well-ordered ward had become...what? A

282

mortuary? An abattoir? He was momentarily stunned by the sight of so many suffered inflictions crammed into such a small space. It was a stomach-churning vision.

Beck sensed rather than saw Rickard's unmoving form standing statuesque in the reception area. He glanced up, peering bleary-eyed over a blood splattered patient. His face was drawn and pale, his thinning hair ruffled and unkempt, but he still retained his natural vibrancy refusing to let the moroseness that affected virtually everyone else settle on him. He had too much work to do.

Rickard's wandering gaze met Beck's and the latter called out over the low background of noise. 'Come in, come in. Just carrying out a litle elementary repair work over here. Like to keep in practice.'

Rickard wordlessly crossed the space and stood on the opposite side of the bed. He stared laconically at the comatose crewwoman being treated.

Beck finished sealing a jagged wound on the woman's thigh. He pocketed his pen-sized hand laser as he pulled forward the folded covers, tucking them in hurriedly but neatly. He caught Rickard's silent appraisal of him as he straightened up from the bed. He hoped the bloodshed had not affected the young captain overtly.

'Making the rounds?' he asked.

'Something like that.' Rickard remained expressionless.

'How's the damage upstairs?'

'Better than it was.'

'It sounded bad, according to the reports.'

'They were exaggerated.'

'From what I heard it was a miniature device planted so that it was in a position to fuse the helm's junction controls.'

'You heard right,' Rickard said shortly, not bothering to comment on the precision of his description.

'I also heard we lost Karen.'

'We didn't *lose* her. She was taken prisoner...hostage... whatever damn thing you want to call it.'

Beck saw the pain in his face, heard it in his voice. Karen's capture had hit him harder than anything else. The final hammer blow to drive home the nail. 'Sorry, I didn't mean to say it like that.'

His words of regret were shrugged away.

Unsure exactly how to deal with Rickard's disconsolate mood, Beck decided to fall back on tried and trusted ground. 'That was some fight we got ourselves into down there,' he stated. 'I knew from the start the Emperor was not to be trusted but who would have thought they'd want to start another war? They are certainly going the right way about it. That attack was downright sneaky. They hit us below the belt. They hit us above the belt. Damn, they even hit us *with* the belt!'

'That's a hell of a way to put it!'

Hicks stared over, concern written plainly on her face.

Beck acknowledged the warning, realising Rickard's tense outcry had carried. He could see that the man was tired. The pep-pills were wearing off. His shoulder probably continued to hurt and he doubtlessly blamed himself for Karen's capture. He cared for her - that much was starkly evident. He cared for her a lot.

'Christopher. Look, I really am sorry. My morbid sense of humour got the better of me for a second. It's the way I work. It's my way of coping with all this.' He waved an arm at his conglomeration of abject inmates.

Rickard rubbed a hand over his face, attempting to keep himself awake. 'No. It's my fault. Ignore me. I'm just...fed up with my damned awful responsibilities. No-one said command would be easy but I wasn't expecting it to be this hard. This whole...situation is something I simply have to learn to deal with in my own way, at my own speed.'

He received an encouraging pat on the shoulder as Beck moved past him to the next bed. 'Look at it this way; it can only get easier.'

'Yes, but when?'

The surgeon could not answer. He continued his work by making a rapid, precise check of the patient, moving over him with practised ease.

'Listen, I'm sorry about Bulloch - you heard?'

'Yes, I heard. Death by strangulation. I had to make out the certificate myself. Now I'll never get to collect my winnings,' Beck said forlornly, but without looking up. 'He was an old friend. A lot of fights and a lot of bets. And

284

I'll miss him.'

'I'm sorry.'

'I know.'

The results of the micro-detailed brain scan caused Beck to shake his head in unwanted resignation.

'The door is open, the lights are on, but nobody is home. Permanent cerebral damage by the look of the poor fellow. So,' he raised his eyes, 'where are we off to now? Not homeward bound, I'll bet?'

'I can't. Not yet. There are too many things to do. We have people alive on that planet back there to rescue. One way or another I mean to do that. I also want to see what the rebels can offer. They might be able to help us out. I have to try.'

'I understand. I even agree. I only hope it can be as easy as you seem to think.'

'Don't misunderstand me. I'm under no illusions about that. I know for a fact it'll be as hard as hell to make a successful rescue. But we can't back out and leave them, especially not after all that's happened. Anyway, I refuse to leave Karen behind.'

'I wish you all the luck in the world. You'll have your crew's complete backing. Virtually every man and woman on *Emputin* is clamouring for some sort of retaliatory attack. At least, all those who managed to avoid the battle.'

'Revenge doesn't interest me. My first duty is to get our people out and run for safety. At least we have the advantage in speed-'

A buzzer shrieked.

'Oh no.'

The undulating wail was an immediate attention-stealer. It was a low but painfully insistent noise that sounded distinctly ominous. It issued from a nearby bed's diagnostic computer. Beck whirled, taking in the situation in an instant. Immediately the panel's ECG reading began to drop rapidly.

'Cardiac arrest!'

Hicks was already moving.

She tore open a wall-drawer and scooped out the coronary stimulator. She dived for the bed, attempting to avoid the many stunned onlookers.

Rickard watched from a distance, stunned into silence

as another of his crew died before his eyes.

Beck caught up with Hicks in an instant, jumping over sprawled crew in an untypical display of athletic ability. He pulled a well-used crash tray near to the bed and began emergency revival procedures. A nurse hurried to aid him.

'Blood pressure unobtainable,' she read out.

'Try external cardiac massage. No, don't worry, I'll do it. Feed him with intravenous glucose.'

'Arterial blood gasses drawn,' the nurse called out.

Beck was trying desperately to ease some positive response from a failed heart. He ripped open a dust-smeared uniform, baring the man's chest. First striking down hard on the chest, he then pushed with a steady pulsing rhythm, counting under his breath as he did so. The panel's ECG readout flickered spasmodically back to life before falling once more to the zero mark.

Hicks thrust a plastic breather tube into the patient's mouth, careful to hold back his tongue. She felt the loosening of a tooth as the tube went in. Fast attached to that was a respiratory bag which the nurse used to force air into oxygen-starved lungs. All the while Beck's attempts at resuscitation were proving fruitless.

'It's no good,' Beck decided. 'Prepare the electrical stimulator.'

While Hicks was busy with that task, Beck grabbed for a large syringe from the crash-tray. Readying it, he thrust it directly into the patient's heart. He hoped he could shock a response from it.

By now Hicks had readied the stimulator. She crushed the container tube into an oddly crumpled shape in her haste to spread the pale, gooey paste onto the stimulator's contact surface. Beck snatched the stimulator from her as soon as she finished. He raced to position it over the patient's chest.

'Clear!' he warned before he released the strong electrical current to course penetratingly through unresponsive heart muscles, hoping against hope to gain a movement, a bare whisper of life. The body jerked, arching off the bed for countless seconds before collapsing back. He repeated the action. And again.

There was no response. A last, desperate attempt. One more try before accepting defeat.

It was no use. The oscilloscope pattern remained flat. Hicks read out what Beck already knew. 'Circulatory functioning is collapsing. ECG display is fading. He's dead.'

Beck sighed. 'What time is it?'

'46.32,' Hicks told him.

'Fix that as time of death.'

The ship's surgeon stood back. He wondered with uncharacteristic moroseness if any of this was worth the trouble. He hated to lose a patient as much as Rickard hated to see his crew butchered in senseless warfare. It was a hard job. But, of course, in the end his natural optimistic resilience won through the clouding gloom of another battle lost. Inside, he knew that every medical battle was worthwhile if it brought with it the chance of saving more lives. All right, maybe he couldn't win them all. He was not omnipotent. But if he only won half of them it was still a bonus, that many more people allowed by the grace of technology the chance to live a little longer. That was what made the whole thing bearable. For every life he failed to save - and that was not many these days - many more would continue.

It was the only way to look at it. It was a shame he'd been unable to help poor Rem Bulloch in the same way.

Beck emerged from the deliberations of his inner mind and glanced over at Rickard. The captain was still unmoving. 'Hell, Christopher. You look worse than I feel,' he spurted.

Snapping out of his dazed stupor Rickard became aware that Beck was addressing him. 'Thanks,' he drily commented.

'Don't mention it, Captain. I think you need some rest urgently. What are you doing right now? Not anything of major importance, like saving the universe from marauding, many-eyed invaders?'

Rickard made an effort to pull himself together. He assumed the calm, outwardly authoritative facade required of him as captain. 'Nothing. I'm doing nothing. There's nothing I can do until we reach Tibor.'

'Which is how long away?'

'Two...three hours Earthtime.'

'Then that is two or three hours' worth of rest you can grab. No excuses. This is on doctor's orders so even you can't argue. Those uppers I prescribed to you are not noted for their long term reliability.'

'I guess you're right, Doc.'

'I'm always right, and don't you forget it. And most especially this time. Do you need a knockout?'

'No thanks. I'll sleep fine. I'm certainly tired enough.'

'It's all the exercise you've been getting. I'll see you later and looking a lot better, yes?'

'Fine, Doc. It's your party.'

☆ ☆ ☆

The shadowed darkness effectively hid Howarth from view. He was crouched against the high, plain wall of a high-sided building that lay opposite the palace's perimeter.

From his viewpoint he could barely make out the gardens that backed onto the palace further along. Only the light green leaves of the taller trees peeped over the boundary wall. Beyond that lay the residency, its southern walkway edging the splendidly verdant foliage that fought to gain a hold on its crumbling brickwork. There was no more smoke, no dark clouds of burning rubble. The fires had long since been put out.

Howarth had stayed on his rooftop hideout for close to two hours, watching out for any more arriving prisoners, but there had been none. Everything had remained quiet and unnaturally peaceful. Giving up his vigil he had made his way through the local streets to reach his present position around one side of the palace. He now faced onto a road that ran parallel to the residency's west passage. There he had remained for the last five minutes, assuring himself that all really was quiet before he ventured nearer.

Finally feeling there was no need to detain himself any

288

longer he rose from his darkened corner, peering out to make sure the way was clear before darting off, sprinting for the palace gardens' outer wall. He made the wall effortlessly, finding it easy to jump and catch hold of its top and quickly pull himself up and over. He landed evenly. The soft, velvetly grass covered the sound of his arrival.

He studied the gardens carefully for any signs of activity. The whole area was empty. As completely deserted and noiseless as when Bernerds and Stuart had first entered it earlier that very day. Nothing moved. Not a leaf stirred. Nor was there the usual rustling of trees and bushes. It was as if some mysterious ethereal being had removed all sound, banished every decibel of volume from the place. There was total and utter soundlessness. The quietness was so intense, so deafening, that it actually hurt.

'Will someone please say something?' Howarth muttered to himself, if only to relieve his pained ears. He did not expect a reply and he was not disappointed. 'This is giving me the flippin' willies.'

He made his way surreptitiously through the meticulously tended greenery near the wall, a tiny island of shaped and crafted bushes and plants amid a sea of wildness, a minor ocean of overgrown tendrils and reaching branches. It seemed strange that, with the opulent wealth of the palace itself, the Emperor did not bother to look after his own backyard.

Arriving at the exterior courtyard wall he soon found the remains of the wooden door. It was still in its rather dilapidated condition, its smashed remains laying over the grass. There was a dried puddle of blood caking one patch. It had stained the grass blades a deep red as it had spread. 'Must have been a fight here,' Howarth remarked, staring at the marked earth.

After giving it a cursory inspection Howarth entered the courtyard. He stepped gingerly over that part of the battered gate that stubbornly refused to release its hold on rusted hinges, instead creating a barely surmountable obstacle. The courtyard beyond was empty. The everflowing fountain was still. Its waters were calm and undisturbed. There were no guards at the small doorway set firmly into the palace's outer protection dome, thankfully, Howarth thought. He trotted straight over to it, not wanting to be seen lurking in the open space, and tried the door. To his great surprise and relief it was unlocked. It swung easily open to reveal a short connecting passage from the doorway to the palace building itself.

'This is too easy. My luck's changing at last,' he decided but it was possible that he was walking into a trap. He could have been spotted a dozen times from the palace windows while he was in the gardens. It was a nasty thought. A flowing runnel of sweat trickled down his face, dripping onto the stained cloak to create a growing, damp patch.

The passage was dark and confined, the light from the windows ahead made very little headway through the halflight that existed between palace and dome. Howarth tried the inner door. It too was unlocked and in opening it he allowed light from the palace's interior to fall on him in a blinding beam. Blinking fiercely he ventured forth into the hall beyond the passage, finding it to be a replica in miniature of the front entrance hallway. The same distanced arches spanned the walls and ceiling, virtually identical tapestries adorned the spaces between them. Their elaborately intricate designs wove patterns of splendour to warm the heart of the most disinterested of art lovers, made with delicacy in the extreme that shone under the artificial lighting from above.

Howarth surveyed it coldly, no longer moved by this selfish display of wealth. He wondered instead which way he should go.

There was a sound, a scrape of feet on steps. Howarth dived for cover, choosing the concealing bulk offered by the base of a nearby arch. He snuggled in between the arch and a stout wooden door, watching around the base for the originator of the sound. His heart pounded loudly even as he struggled to remain calm. It was not an easy task when he was enacting the part of the fly who had just voluntarily entered the spider's parlour.

Without warning the door behind him opened. With a

start Howarth swung around as a rotund, fat-faced serving-woman stepped into the hallway carrying an empty silver tray. She stopped short, suddenly seeing the strange, rather repulsive features of an alien - one who had managed to find a way into the Emperor's House without the guards knowing.

Howarth was quick to recover, his trained instincts reacting faster and more efficiently than the serving-woman's. He saw she was about to cry out so he slammed a strong hand over her mouth, failing to catch the tray as she released it. It bounced up from the bare floor, hitting with a reverberating *clang* which echoed noisily off the walls.

'Shit.' Howarth said flatly. The woman began to struggle in his grasp so he tightened it marginally. 'Pack it in. I am not going to hurt you.'

She took no notice. 'Keep still. Will you please...keep... *still!'* The woman fought back even harder, giving off muffled groans. Howarth drew his acquisitioned pistol, pointing it at her meaningfully. 'Now give it a rest.'

This time she did understand and she ceased to resist, sagging defeatedly. 'That's better. Now, when I take my hand away you are not going to call for help, are you.' It was not a question.

She shook her head. Unwisely trusting her at her word Howarth withdrew his hand and she screamed, her voice shrill and piercing. Howarth slapped his hand back over her mouth, cutting the scream off in mid flow. 'Will you for Christ's sake shut up? I'm warning you,' he growled in exasperation, waving the pistol threatingly in her face for good measure.

Again the serving-woman was agreeable but this time Howarth was ready in case she tried to call out, blatantly sceptical of her easy agreement. He pulled away, his hand remaining near her coarse-featured face for many seconds afterwards. At last, finally satisfied that she had heeded his warning, he let the tired arm drop, relaxing thankfully.

'What do you want?' The plump serving-woman's voice was wavery and high-pitched. Her hands were trembling perceptively. She was clearly petrified of him.

'You're going to lead me to the palace dungeons, or holding cells, or whatever you call them. Then I'll just tie you up nice and comfy for guards to find after I've gone. I promise you won't be harmed.' Killing trained troopers was one thing but he could not bring himself to harm this palpably innocent female, not unless she forced him to. After all, there must be *some* good Rukans. They could not all be ruthless, coldblooded murderers.

'Why do you want to go to the prisons?' The woman peered myopically at him.

'Because your masters have some friends of mine in them and I want to get them out so we can have a party,' he said sarcastically.

His wit was wasted on the servant. 'The prisons are down there,' she pointed through the door. 'If I told you the way could you let me go now?'

'No! I mean...I'd prefer it if you would show me the way. It'll be a whole lot easier. Especially for me,' he muttered as an afterthought.

The woman pondered on that for a long moment before nodding slowly, as if her mind were minutes behind current events. She led the way through the door and down the cramped, musty spiral staircase beyond, Howarth trailing close behind.

That was great, he mulled. He now had a snail-brained, thicker-than-two-very-short-planks guide to lead him into trouble that he could easily have found on his own. True, she seemed harmless enough. This rescue mission was turning out far simpler than he could have wished for. He squinted, unused to the steadily darkening route.

The dank, damp staircase led down to a dimly lit, flagstone paved corridor that seemed worlds apart from the grandiose magnificence of the floors above. Down here, in the twilight recesses of the servants' habitat all was uncovered, undecorated stone. Floor, walls and ceiling were all made of the same jet black coloured stone, creating a gloomy atmosphere, a dark and dismal stagnancy. The claustrophobic environment exuded an air of stifling oppressiveness, a scenario of abject slavery. The icy-chilled coldness made Howarth long for healthier, cozier conditions.

Searching his way through the near darkness, he trailed after the serving-woman as she forged confidently ahead. She took the twisting, turning maze of corridors in her stride, never faltering or hesitating for an instant as she unerringly led her companion to the prisons. They encountered not a single soul on their endless journey. Howarth's booted feet sounded loud in the emptiness, the noise amplifying itself as it resounded back and forth along the bare, featureless walls. In a series of turns and changes of direction that made his excursion through the maze of dwellings outside seem like a fun-park outing, Howarth completely lost his sense of direction. The faint light provided by flickering, sparking torches spaced at long intervals did not help him in the least. If it were not for his guide he would be lost completely. And that worried him.

After what felt like an age the woman stopped and pointed to a brief flight of steps that ended at another of those ever present wooden doors.

'That is the prison. If your friends are in the palace they will be on the other side of that door.'

Howarth said nothing, merely pushing the woman ahead of him. They descended the stairs. Howarth automatically raised his pistol, indominantly expecting trouble of some form. His unyielding, stubbornly persistent spirit never failed to amaze him when it was faced with difficulty and danger. It surprised him enormously that he could be so optimistic and light hearted under such disconcerting odds.

Feeling pretty pleased with himself at having come so far, he gestured to the woman to call the guard. She spent a moment struggling to understand what it was he wanted before the proverbial penny dropped. 'Ah!' she grinned foolishly. 'Tyr-Hiite-Kand! Open the door for me.'

Howarth felt exceptionally pleased that he'd correctly predicted the presence of a guard inside the room.

There came a drawn-out, disgustingly eloquent belch from the opposite side of the door before the comforting rattle of keys could be discerned in the lock. The door was yanked open and a bleary-eyed trooper glared out, standing atop a second mini-stairway that led into the prison proper. He had no time at all to react to Howarth's unexpected presence as the security chief aimed and fired over the serving-woman's head.

The trooper's corpse, badly disfigured by the short range of the blast, slumped and fell back, rolling unspectacularly down the steps to settle at the bottom, arms and legs spread-eagled. Howarth winced at the rumbling explosion of sound as it thundered down bare, stone-walled corridors. Quickly he pushed the servant into the room and kicked door shut. Only then did he examine his suroundings.

The prison was a slum. Muck and filth lay everywhere as if it had been accumulating over long centuries. The flagstone floor was sparsely covered with foul-smelling, roughly scattered straw that stank of excrement. A powerfully strong and decidedly rotten aroma drifted over the place like a thick country mist over a village pond. Jagged metal bars ran from floor to ceiling in organised rows all around the wide but narrow room, effectively forming a jungle of prison bars through which the hopeless occupants could only stare longingly at freedom. An open barrel stood beside the steps brimming over with dirty, tepid water. Bits of loose straw floated on its surface. A tattered cloak hung from a nail in the wall. The prison gave off an air of abandoned, moth-eaten decrepitude. It was as if the Emperor actually encouraged the needless suffering of his captives.

Howarth mentally corrected himself. The Emperor probably *did* encourage needless suffering.

Voices began to make themselves heard from one end of the prison. Questioning, frustrated, *human* voices. Howarth grinned, a jocular twinkle lighting his eyes. He gave the servant a slight shove in the right directon. Plucking the old cloak from the wall he tossed it over the body of the trooper. As he approached the cells which held *Emputin's* captured someone spotted his uniform.

'It's one of ours.'

'He's from *Emputin*!'

'Bloody hell, it's Commander Howarth!'

'All right, all right. Calm down you lot,' Howarth said over the excited babble of voices. The serving-woman wandered bemusedly to the end of the prison, keeping well out of the way of things.

Howarth glanced over the prisoners, recognising most only from sight. The few he knew by name were grouped together by the stretchered form he had observed before.

'Hello, sir,' Midshipman Bernerds greeted him from the rear of the group. He was fully recovered and for once was genuinely glad to see Howarth.

Howarth gave him a nod, turning his attention to the civilian who promptly hobbled up to the cell bars. 'Miss Trestrail,' he smiled winningly. 'What are you doing here?'

'It's a long story, one you would not believe,' she said tiredly. She looked worn out by her ordeal. This was one residence she would doubtlessly not mind leaving, the sooner the better. 'I'm just glad you've turned up. This place leaves little to be desired.'

'The almighty conquering hero has come to rescue us, I see,' a croaked greeting that Howarth instantly recognised issued from the stretcher as the figure upon it threw back the single blanket. 'Oh my God! What a mess you look!'

'Bentowski. I thought they'd get you. Without me to hold up your trousers for you I guessed you'd soon be tripping over and landing flat on your face.'

'Yeah. And it's the greatest seeing you, too,' a wide-eyed Bentowski, freshly recovered from unconscious slumber, groaned appreciatively. 'How about getting us outta here?'

'No sooner said than done.'

'Great. 'Cos knowing your luck, pal, the Rukes'll crash in just when you're least expecting it.'

As he completed the sentence the prison door exploded open and a tightly packed squad of troopers poured in, bounding effortlessly down the short steps to fill that end of the prison. Each and every trooper was tensely alert for trouble; a disconcertingly large number of pistols and rifles aimed directly at Howarth.

'See what I mean,' Bentowski added.

'I thought it was too easy to be true,' Howarth shrugged helplessly.

'Oh, sod it,' Bernerds said as he settled against the cell wall, fully expecting what life dealt him.

Bentowski valiantly gave up the ghost, muttering a casual profanity before collapsing back on his stretcher.

While Howarth stared at the troopers, and they returned the stare, waiting for him to act, the rotund serving-woman, the snail-brained, thicker-than-two-very-short-planks harmless old female, picked up a handy, well-rounded fist-sized chunk of stone from the corner and crept up behind the would-be rescuer. She cleanly, and with incredible swiftness, cracked him over the rear of the skull with it.

Karen Trestrail watched in open dismay as Howarth gave a stunned grimace, consciousness leaving him as he blacked out, before toppling over to hit the ground with an impact resounding like the crashing of a felled oak.

☆ ☆ ☆

Tibor: The planet radiated an iridescent whitish-grey aura of light. Brightness effused from it while the sun's full rays beamed down. It was a glaring orb of sublime magnificence that was as cold as the ball of heat called the capital of the empire was hot. A thin, extremely tenuous blue-tinted atmosphere enshrouded the ice- and snow-blanketed surface of the bitterly chilled planet in a protective shield. The very weak consistency of its major gases served to heighten the already spectacular glow from the barren wastelands and high peaked mountains far below.

The frigidity of the world-sized snowball was caused by the vast distance, a void of nothingness, between it and its primary, a medium sized star of incredibly average magnitude. The mother star emitted a far away haze of heat that almost totally failed to warm the satellite lying at the fringes of its reach. The single sun had about effect in heating the planet as a live match on an iceberg.

All at once the planet and its parent were not alone. A ship exited hyperdrive in the wink of eye to slow rapidly as it neared the ice world. Turning to match the planet's rotational spin, the newly arrived space vessel settled comfortably into a geostationary orbit. It glided relatively low over a particularly large plain of ice and rock that stretched from what would on earth be the temperate climates up to the polar region.

The blue-grey hull of the ship shone dazzlingly against its paler backdrop. Rigidly spaced lettering along its sides stood out boldly. The dark colouring of the letters and figures revealed themselves clearly under the planet's reflected light. The SNS *Emputin* had arrived.

In *Emputin's* nerve centre all was in calm control. The panic and bustle of before had settled noticeably once the immediate danger had passed. The damaged helm controls had been liberally patched with hastily welded patches of metal, hiding the resourcefully reconstructed maze of circuitry. An intricate web of wires, connections and electronic chips had been repaired and concealed beneath the obscuring cover plates which the artificers had hurriedly knocked together.

There existed a sense of lugubrious mourning among the bridge crew. Their usually indomitable spirits had been subjected to such a hard time recently that they were bound to flag eventually. An air of held-back, almost reserved, exasperation at the hopelessness of their plight had diffused through them all as if by osmosis until it had affected almost every one of them, causing them to tiredly droop with the listlessness they were feeling.

Rickard had not failed to observe the mood of his demoralised crew and he knew that some action had to be taken to prevent them from giving up entirely. He had to make a gesture of defiance against the stupid militaristic atitudes of the Imperial monarchy. Coming here was the only idea that came to mind for the moment.

He was not the only one concerned with the crew's health of mind. Kiyami also held her own concerns, mainly about Rickard himself. As far as she could see he was worrying too much. Far too much. She did not want him going over the edge - especially if they could not get the prisoners out, if they could not get Karen Trestrail out. She was concerned for him, perhaps more than duty called for.

From his seemingly immovable position at the nav console, Boyd gave a standard post-orbital report. 'We are resting in quadrant three, sector twenty-five, sub-sector seventeen. Now orbiting the planet Tibor, co-ordinates as supplied.'

'Lieutenant?' Rickard gestured to Arakelian.

'Oh. All systems are secured from hyperdrive,' she stammered. 'We are keeping station at...um...sixteen thousand above the surface contact location.'

The faint hint of a smile creased Rickard's mouth as he tried to keep a straight face. It wasn't her fault, he chided himself. She'll soon get used to it. 'Very good, Mister Arakelian.'

She hesitantly returned to her controls, unsure if she had messed up in some way.

'Kiyami, what's this one like?' he motioned to the display of Tibor on the viewers.

Kiyami crossed her arms and leaned back in her chair very much at ease. 'I do not imagine you will be overly happy with this one. It is virtually a complete ice planet. Almost eighty per cent of it, in fact.'

'I hope you're not serious.' He saw her face. 'You are serious.'

'Unfortunately, perfectly so. Average temperature is twenty-five degrees below zero, although some places are warmer. Our rebel friend's surface co-ordinates lead us to a garden spot. The temperature reaches what can be called local tropical proportions - of around a mere ten below. I think it will make a welcome change from the dust and heat of the last few days.'

'I glad you are pleased about it. These people certainly believe in extremes of temperature. First an oven, now a fridge. Lieutenant Watts, get the hanger deck to prepare a launch. And they'd also better have a couple of Warm Coats waiting,' he added. 'Now, its time to see if Iad Kitan is as good as his word.'

'I do not see any grounds for doubt,' Kiyami put in. 'Why should he lie? He correctly predicted the Imperial attack.'

'Yes, but that doesn't mean a thing. There are any

number of ways that this could turn into another trap.' He should not have said that but she sounded so sure of herself on the subject. Maybe she needed to believe in the rebels but he did not. He would reserve his judgement until he knew more about Kitan and his group. 'We'll find out for sure when contact is established. Watts?'

'I'll try and raise them, sir.' Although she doubted there would be any reply she turned to her instruments and began sending out a hailing signal, her aesthetically thin figure shifting to her instruments. 'Iad Kitan of the FIO Group. This is SNS *Emputin* calling Iad Kitan on the planet Tibor. Do you read?' She waited before repeating the message. There was no reply.

Rickard threw Kiyami a cynical glance. It was something of a who-was-so-sure-he'd-be-there type of glance.

Kiyami thought she'd rather not answer, instead uncrossing her arms in a mildly disquietened attitude. They had all been pinning their hopes on Iad Kitan and his group, her especially. Perhaps more so than she would care to admit. But the evidence so far said that the group were the good guys of this battle. She wished the ship's comm would hurry up and vindicate her trust in the rebel, justify the evidence by the results.

'Try again, Lieutenant,' Rickard advised Watts. He remained speculative as to the possible results.

Watts repeated herself into the microphone. The reciever crackled unremorsefully as she twiddled with the pickup controls. Harsh, voluminous sounds of intensely atmospheric disturbance issued across the bridge. Everyone winced as a particularly piercing whine roared out. Watts hastily scaled down the noise. Out of the hissing mash of background noise there came the faintest traces of a voice. Watts locked into it straight away, bringing it to the foreground. It rose from the weakest whisper to almost complete, if mushy, normality. The deluge of interference did not abate but was merely forced to assume secondary place.

'I have him,' Watts declared to her audience. 'The signal is pretty weak but I'm boosting it from this end. It'll hold out for long enough, Captain.'

Kiyami smiled relievedly to herself. Rickard was thankful that he had been right in coming here. He'd made one good move, anyway. He leaned over the micro-styled comm attachment on his command chair. 'Iad Kitan, this is Captain Rickard. Can you hear me?'

'...Barely,' came the reply shouted over the background of static. 'There is a storm building in this area so you will have to hurry. The storms on our not over friendly Tibor can be unnaturally ruthless.'

'I can imagine.'

'Nevertheless, hello again, Captain,' his voice welcomed warmly. 'I am pleased to see you took my advice.'

'We took it, all right. I only wish it had come a little sooner.'

'You were attacked?'

'This morning, directly after you left, and by a considerable number of troops.'

'I did try to warn you that it would happen.'

'Yes you did, and I'm grateful for that. If we hadn't already started pulling out the losses would have been far greater.'

'Many were killed?' Iad Kitan sounded concerned.

'Enough. More than enough. Also, quite a few were taken captive, which is why I am here. I need your help to get them back.'

'You need have no worries on that count. We will aid you. With our direction you can attack the Emperor in a way never before attempted.'

'Which way would that be?'

'It would be best if we did not comunicate over an open channel. Carrier waves are vulnerable and there could be an Imperial ship close enough to pick us up. We can talk as soon as you land.'

'Give me the co-ordinates of your base and I'l be right down.'

'I am sorry to say that I cannot direct you to the group's main base. I was marginally outvoted by my colleagues when I suggested that you land there. Most of the others of the group do not as yet place their complete trust in you or your people and your motives. Please, do not be offended, it is just their way. We are all rather suspicious people in these unsteady times. For myself, I am totally confident in you. You are here, what more proof do I need that you have discovered the insalubrious nature of the Empire and its leaders. My companions will soon change their minds about you.'

That did not sound so good to Rickard. 'So what's going to happen if we can't get to your base?' he enquired, mildly suspicious.

'I have a snow sled awaiting you. There is a secondary meeting place I can take you to. Some of the other group members will meet us there. You will, I am afraid, have to limit the numbers of your party to three; the sled cannot hold more than that. Come down at my present co-ordinates, Captain. I will be waiting for you. Until then...'

The crackling and spitting faded to silence. 'Do you still trust him?' Kiyami asked searchingly.

'I suppose so. We don't have much of a choice right now, do we?'

She shook her head in agreement. 'Who will you take along?'

Rickard wondered who he *could* take with him. Much as she wanted to go, he could not take Kiyami. He would not risk both the ship's senior officers down there at once. The first choice was easy; Beck was a perfect candidate. He carried the calm, self-assured air about him that Rickard would need in the forthcoming meeting. That was, assuming he was not still busy in sickbay. His second companion had to be someone he wouldn't have to worry about, someone who could take care of herself with total self-assuredness. Someone like Midshipman Kirsten Stuart. She certainly had strong motivation for getting the prisoners back. By all accounts she and Midshipman Bernerds had been close. She was also fully combat trained. Yes, she would do. That was pretty good thinking, he complimented himself, with, he noted as an afterthought, only a hint of smugness.

'Lieutenant Watts, please have Chief Surgeon Beck and Senior Midshipman Stuart meet me at the hanger deck fully kitted out. Stuart is to have complete armour and armaments with her.'

'Yes, sir,' Watts acknowledged.

Kiyami looked at him disappointedly. Rickard met her dejected gaze and understood how she must feel. 'I'm sorry Kiyami, but I can't risk it. You're more important to me up here. I might need some tough backup.'

'It is nothing Captain. The mission is more important.'

Like hell it was, Rickard thought bitterly. Kiyami had ably proven her abilities to him back in the residency and here he was throwing that proof back in her face. He regretted the decision but it was necessary. He would have to make it up to her at a later date. After all, she did deserve better treatment than this. 'If you will take the conn, please, Kiyami?' he asked her, apology written on his face.

She reluctantly rose and replaced him in the centre seat, saying nothing.

Rickard could not spare time to console her. He motioned to Arakelian. 'Lieutenant, after I send the all-clear, see what can be done about the damage to the controls. I don't want to have to rely on a jury-rig that could fail at any moment.'

Arakelian was quick to nod her luxuriant blonde head in accordance, unconsciously crossing her shapely legs in a manner that would have most men drooling uncontrollably. What the hell was he thinking of at a time like this? Another time and another place, maybe, he admitted, but right now he was otherwise occupied, thank you.

Keeping that in mind he left the bridge.

14

505.99.47-03

The musty prison quarters were shrouded in virtually all-concealing darkness. The only light came from from a single blazing torch, set into the wall opposite the one cell occupied. The other torches had, left untended, burnt themselves out. Their dying flames had slowly waned, flickering and fading as the combustible embers of wood and tar had been exhausted. Slowly spreading gloom ate away at a little more of the already negligible light. The ever-increasing blackness had spread, amoeba-like, across the stuffy confines of the prison. Its grip was steadily strengthening, constantly changing shape, growing until it held all but one lone corner in its power.

The unenviable ambience of the prison still reeked strongly. A pervading concoction of foul, sensorially abusive smells refused to disperse, seeming unwilling to be dispelled from the abysmal surroundings. Its leaving would have been like a breath of fresh air to the inmates in more ways than one and would have done much to relieve their unhappy disposition.

Inside the crowded cell at the far end of the prison, lit by a single torch, the captured crewmembers were snatching what sleep they could. Bentowski lay on his stretcher, snoring gently in peaceful somnolence. He had recovered rapidly from the stun-shot received in the residency battle, and the air had soon been filled once more with his voluminous repertoire of backchat and wisecracks.

Bernerds slept fitfully. He lay near the rear wall of the cell next to Howarth. He tossed and turned restlessly as if locked in some inescapable nightmare that refused to release its nefarious grip on his mind. Sweat was gathering profusely on his forehead, grouping in large blobs and clusters before dripping off his face to stream wetly to the floor.

'He's having a bad night of it,' Howarth commented, himself wide awake after recovering from unconsciousness. He was sitting up against the rear wall beside an equally unsleepy Karen. Looking away from the midshipman he yawned in a manner that was more of a reflex action than a sign of tiredness. His eyes flicked around the cell for the hundredth time, searching for weaknesses in its construction that he knew did not exist, not that he would be able to see anything of them if they did, not in this light. The steadily diminishing torch flames barely illuminated the place, casting broadly perceptible shadows, and doing nothing to drive away the oppressive darkness.

Karen leant forward to cast a quick glance at Bernerds. She stared intently past Howarth at the middie before settling back. 'I feel sorry for him,' she admitted. 'And myself. The sooner we get out of here the better.' She felt a strong wave of boredom wash over her and she tried to suppress it. Prison did not exactly figure in her top ten list of the most fun places to be.

'Why feel sorry for him?' Howarth pointed at Bernerds.

'Look at this pig-sty,' Karen gesticulated demonstrably. 'It's not exactly the latest in five star accommodation, is it? There are over twenty of us in here, all crammed uncomfortably in one squashed hole. It's no wonder he's having nightmares.' She tucked her legs loosely against her body to give a sleeping Marine in front of her more breathing space, pulling her dirtied skirt down in all modesty over her knees. As she did so she felt a twinge from her vividly bruised ankle. She began to rub it soothingly.

'Why is he so special? Look at me, I'm not having nightmares.'

'You're not even asleep so you can keep quiet. I've watched him since I came on board the ship. He's very much the loner, always sticks to just one friend.'

'Yeah, I know her.'

'Yes, but there's more to him than that. I wish I knew

304

what it was.'

'Why?' Howard repeated, intrigued.

'He seems so ...... aggressive at times. Perhaps it's something that happened to him. Maybe it's something to do with his past.'

'No, it's not that. It's just that he's an arrogant little bugger.'

'How can you say that?'

'Easily. What are you? An amateur psycho-analyst?'

'No. Of course not. I was simply wondering, that's all. What's your story? Why did you join up?'

The question caught him by surprise. He should have expected it because somehow he'd known she would get onto this. She was that sort of woman. Direct. Always getting down to the basics, digging into people's personas. He didn't want to tell this story again. He still wasn't sure why he'd told Mori. How could he avoid the subject? With her it would not be easy. 'I don't think you really want to know,' he demurred awkwardly.

'Yes I do.'

'It's a long story and on the whole it's pretty boring. It's certainly not worth the telling.'

'Please,' she insisted softly. 'I'm interested.'

'I don't think so.'

'Thom,' she said quietly, expressing calm sincerity. 'I am interested.'

He'd been wrong. It wasn't that it was not easy. Impossible would have been more accurate. 'Oh... Okay,' he decided, giving in. 'You asked for it.'

His expression became thoughfully demure. The chain of long since happened events slowly returned to his mind. He started with an even voice, looking dead ahead. He was uncomfortable with this. Embarrassed to be revealing his life, his past, in such intimate detail. It felt as though it was the hardest thing he had done in a long while.

'It was some time past, must be nearly fifteen years ago. I was barely seventeen, still wet behind the ears. The war was continuing, day after day, week after week, always in some far away place, nothing to worry about. We heard about it regularly on the newscasts, everything from single pirate raids to full scale planetary attacks, but none of it seemed real. It couldn't affect us. It was only the war, something that had been going on all our lives. We didn't pay it much attention. You know how it was?'

Karen nodded in full agreement, 'I know. Go on,' she prompted.

Howarth shivered. the memory flooded back to him. 'I used to knock around with a friend called Brandon. He was a good friend, one of the best. We'd stuck together for most of our lives, right through school and Post-Ed. We used to mess around a lot, especially where we weren't supposed to, and there was a factory near our housing complex. It was a sort of combined production and storage facility. I don't know what it was they made there, never did find out exactly what it was they stored. Navy ships' parts, I think. Anyway, Brandon and me used to play around in there some nights. We'd found a sort of 'back door', a corrugated iron plate which could be slid aside to give us just enough space to crawl through, so, every now and then, we would sneak in and take a quick look around, inspect all the nooks and crannies to see what was new, what we could make a quick profit on in the local markets. The security patrols were no trouble for us. Brandon had found an easy way around them and we could dodge them and the field beams with ease.

'On one particular night we found that someone had been there before us because the plate had been disturbed and we could see a dim light from inside. At first we guessed the security patrols had found us out but then we saw them walking about outside as if nothing were wrong. I was all for calling it a night and forgetting the whole thing - I was a hell of a lot more timid then - but Brandon, big, brave Brandon, wouldn't hear of it. He wanted to investigate, to look into the mystery. I tried to stop him but it didn't work. He went in and I stayed outside in the cold, not even daring to sneak a look through the hole to see what happened next.

'It was probably a good job I didn't look because the next thing I heard was a yell - more of a scream - from Brandon, followed by the sound of a pistol shot that froze me solid. Seconds later the place exploded, knocking me halfway across the grounds and temporarily blinding me. By the time I'd recovered enough to think straight the police had arrived, trailed very closely by armed soldiers. It turned out to be a Larr sneak-bomb that had destroyed the interior of the building. Luckily for me the shell of the factory had been tough enough to stay intact. The police reckoned that the saboteur, a Larr mercenary, had been in the process of fixing and priming his bomb when Brandon had disturbed him.

'I saw Brandon once more after that. I walked into the smashed remains of the factory's inside while they were scraping his remains off the walls. It brought the whole situation home to me; the war, the fighting, everything. I signed up as a security Marine a week after Brandon's memorial service, much to my parents' dismay. I've never looked back....'

'I'm sorry, Thom,' Karen said consolingly.

'There's no need to be. Like I said, it all happened a long time ago. Just one story amongst many.'

'Well that may be, but I shouldn't have pressed you into talking about it.'

'It's not important. I have people in my own section who have far more lurid and heart-rending tales to tell. That's what the war was about; individuals pulled by circumstance into unification. What happened to Brandon was surprisingly commonplace. Events like that were occurring all the time. It was nothing new.'

Karen did not reply. She was at a loss for words. Her own rather protected and usually 'safe' upbringing had not properly prepared her for life in the front line, where the action was. Howarth was the type of person who might later be called a hero, even though he would be acting out of sheer duty at the time. It came to her that war itself did not make the heroes, it was the people who stayed at home in safety and who did that, perhaps to alleviate their own guilt at staying behind.

Knowing there was not much of worth she could say in response, Karen felt it would be wiser to change the subject, dusting off one of the more prominent troubles on her mind. 'What do you think our chances are of getting out of here?'

Howarth gave a cynical snort, 'Do you want me to be tactful or truthful?'

'That bad?'

'Afraid so. You should have stayed home. Our only hope now is rescue from *Emputin*, or the US Cavalry.'

'Then it's not so hopeless,' Karen brightened. 'Chris.... Captain Rickard is bound to try and get us out.'

'"Try" is the word. And the play-acting doesn't work. You don't have to cover up to me. I've seen how close you and the Captain are.'

'You have?' Karen blushed coyly. 'We thought we were keeping it played down.' Howarth grinned. 'Didn't work, right?'

'Uh-uh. The ship is buzzing with the news. Half the crew know about it already or they did last I heard. Those who don't will soon find out, probably from the Doc.'

'Philip?'

'Yep. If the crew know their commanding officer is happily doing what comes naturally then they imagine they're free to act likewise. You'd be surprised at what can go on, especially on deep range missions. The ship leaves port with a crew full of single people and returns six months later with half of them engaged. It's great to think there's still a spirit of friendly co-operation within the Service.'

'I'm not so sure that Command would see it that way. God, I'll never be able to look Philip Beck in the eye again.'

'Yes you will. He takes a little getting used to but he's fine. Not like the new Captain.'

'Oh yes? Why not like the new Captain?'

'I don't know, exactly. I don't know him well enough to say. But what experience has he got for the job, what training?'

Karen was understandably defensive. 'He's had plenty of training. And I bet he's had more experience than some officers I've known.'

'Is that meant to be a dig at me?'

'It might be.'

'I should hope not.'

'Shut up,' she admonished in a friendly tone. 'Seriously

though, what do you think of him?'

'He's okay. I suppose we just got off on the wrong foot. I took something he said the wrong way - or I may have overreacted a bit, can't remember which - and he got all uppity about it. There hasn't been the time since to straighten things out.'

'But you will.'

'When I get around to it. Maybe.'

'Good. I'm glad you've reached a firm decision.' She fingered the dried bloodstain on the side of her head. She'd got rid of most of it, but clear traces clung to her scalp and hair.

Bentowski stirred with a groan, somnolently raising a hand to rub his sleep-filled eyes. At the same time the door to the prison was flung open with a reverberating crash. Two servants, each loaded down with a deep, rounded plastic container, like oversized mixing bowls, followed a bored-looking trooper down the steps. The trooper waited without enthusiasm where he was while the servants approached the cells, and not without some trepidation.

Karen and Howarth glanced up inquisitively, the latter wincing at the stab of pain he received from the livid bruise on the back of his skull. 'Looks like dinner is served,' he said. His stomach began to react, churning over at the thought of food. He had eaten nothing all day.

'I wonder what is on the menu,' Karen said, licking her lips in anticipation. It had been a long time between meals. 'I bet it's not Cassoulet Toulousain or Raspberry Crême Brûlée.'

Howarth frowned dishearteningly. 'Somehow I don't imagine them giving us anything that sounds that good.' He leant over Karen to tap Bentowski lightly on the head with his foot. 'Wakey, wakey. It's feeding time.'

Easing open his eyes, Bentowski smacked his lips, trying to rid himself of the resinous taste in his mouth. 'Thanks a bundle,' he croaked. 'Just what I need right now; an alarm call that gives me brain damage with a boot. What subtlety.'

'Don't worry about it,' Howarth rejoined. 'There's not much up there for me to damage anyway.'

309

The servant lowered their eagerly awaited deliveries to the floor. Then one of them slid open a small cat-flap type hatch in the cell bars. Nervously agitated, they pushed the bowls through the minute gap, hurridly withdrawing their hands and sealing the flap lest the ferocious captives make a grab for them. They silently departed, waiting patiently at the door while the trooper refuelled a couple of the dead torches. He stuffed a tight bundle of gauze like material into each of the holders and lit them from the sole live torch. That done, he was soon gone, ushering the servants before him and slamming the door shut afterwards. The newly reborn torch flames flickered unsteadily.

Now that they could actually see what it was that inhabited the bowls nobody moved.

They could all clearly see what the loathsome, offensive contents of the bowls were; a pale green, lumpy, slimy mush that oozed and bubbled where it sat. It looks the most inedible, dangerously unwholesome muck they had ever suffered the misfortune to see. Its rank odour struggled powerfully to match that of the prison itself. It appeared as if it would succeed effortlessly.

Karen stared dumbfounded at the uninviting nutrition.

Howarth had eaten nothing that day and it looked as if nothing would change.

Rising with a sudden jerk, Bernerds was instantly awake. 'What happened?' he queried vaguely, wiping his dampened brow and not looking very sanguine about his chances of a positive reply.

Bentowski stretched widely before getting up to massage his numbed legs. 'I think,' he said, directing his attention to the food, 'that they really are trying to kill us.'

Karen nodded, 'I think I agree. Philip's comestibles have gone distinctly downhill since we arrived in our new luxury accommodation,' she observed sarcastically.

The rest of the imprisoned crew were beginning to wake, or were woken, depending on the disposition of their neighbours, and a low babble of stagnant conversation began to arise among them as they each complained to another of their various ills and dislikes. All of them were trying to unsuccessfully to grab space enough in which to stretch out in the badly squashed conditions.

'All right, all right,' Howarth delivered them a sour frown made worse by the wavering glow from the torch light. 'Keep the noise down over there.'

'Have a heart, chief. We've had a hard time of it,' Bentowski put in.

'Haven't we all?'

'I have no idea. I was out of it for most of the time, completely blasted.'

'That reminds me, what happened to you in the battle?'

Bentowski shrugged, appearing suitably sheepish. 'I got carried away. Tried to jump too many Rukes. Never, *never* again will I allow myself to go bananas like that. It's too dangerous to the delicate state of my health.'

'Idiot,' Howarth told him with all sincerity. 'Trust you to try something stupid. It was only bad luck that got me caught.'

'Yeah. An' my grandmother grew wings and flew off into the sunset.'

'Funny. You must be running dry on material. Phil Beck used that one some time ago.'

'Imitation is the best form of flattery.'

'Yeah. Well it was only bad luck that I got caught. She crept up behind me and got me when I was otherwise occupied. Bad luck, nothing more.'

'Oh, of course. Couldn't be anything else.'

'Still, it's not the first time on this trip, is it? We've been plagued by bad luck ever since we got here.'

'Tell me about it.'

'Ever heard of Murphey's Law?' Howarth asked.

Bentowski looked puzzled but Karen knew what he was talking about. 'It means that anything which can go wrong, will go wrong.'

'That's nice. So what?' Bentowski said.

'There's a second one, Murpheys other law, which is not so popular,' Howarth continued. 'It states that if anything is going wrong, then it will get worse. Don't you think that's appropriate for us? I've never known a mission to have so many bad calls, especially when we're doing everything right.'

311

'Yeah. I see your point. I also see why it's not so popular.'

'We're dead anyway,' a sullen Bernerds spoke up.

'Bull,' Bentowski rejected his words out of hand.

'How can you say that? They only wanted us alive so they could kill us off nice and slow.' Bernerds turned away in an attitude of defeat. Depression was settling heavily upon him. He wished he had never set eyes on this godforsaken dirtball of a planet. Life was hard enough before with one and all continually on his back, without having all this extra hassle. 'They can't let us go,' he said. 'We'd have the fleet on them inside a day and they know it.'

'Maybe not,' Howarth said ominously.

'What?' Bentowksi's eyebrows did a little dance of sheer amazement across his forehead before settling back.

Karen stared at Howarth in surprise before enlightenment was granted and she understood how the problem would seem from her father's point of view. 'I see what you mean. Command may be afraid of another war. We might not get any help at all.'

'That's right.'

Ever the indefatigable wag, Bentowski had to put his oar in. 'Maybe the Rukes just like our company.'

Karen and Howarth chorused unintentionally. 'Shut up!'

'Sorry, I'm sure.' He noticed that the food merely bubbled nonchalantly away to itself, probably used to being ignored.

Humour aside however, the thought of no rescue at all sobered them. The idea brought with it a cold hand of fear that caressed each and every one of the worried prisoners.

Feeble light gleamed dully from the torches. They seemed to be fighting a losing battle against the readvancing darkness.

They entered the caverns. Wind-swept flurries of snow followed the whitened figures a short way in as they approached a bend in the tunnel. Rounding it, they came into one of the small secondary encampments of the FIO Empire-opposed group.

All three were draped in heavy Warm Coats with thick pads of fluffed artificial fur hemming the slung-back hoods. Rickard and Beck fitted snugly into their coats, Stuart had on combat armour under hers which made it stick out oddly in places. Her heavy rifle was slung over her shoulder. All three had on dark-lensed anti-glare goggles that fitted tightly over their eyes, protecting them from the blinding whiteness of the snowy tundra.

Their solitary guide abandoned them to rejoin his comrades. Lifting their goggles from their faces they stood where they were.

Large flakes of ice clung to the base of the rocky walls inside the cavern, twinkling softly under the pale light of spot-lamps. The secondary encampment was very basic and very sparsely heated. The visitors decided upon keeping on their heavily insulated coats as Rickard exhaled sharply, watching the faint vapour vanish into frosty air.

Rickard took in the cavern and its contents; thick rush matting covered much of the floor space, stacks of grain and water filled one corner. Beyond that was a parked snow sled. It was decidedly basic, comprising of a thin cylinder for the main body with twin ski attachments on either side surmounted by four unprotected seats that were placed one behind the other. It looked a very unsophisticated but extremely useful piece of transport that was probably very necessary in this environment. The machine was a sister to the one that had carried them from the rendezvous site.

Rickard peered further on and recognised the leader of the FI0 group, Iad Kitan. Kitan looked around at the same time and caught sight of them. With a whirl of elation he took his leave of the people he was talking with and hurried from the far end of the cavern to greet his guests. He was still dressed in his all-covering protective cloak, its overlapping flaps jumping up and down as he bounded along. That he was pleased to see them was evident - it was plainly written all over his kindly face.

'Welcome, welcome,' he gushed, bright-faced. He grasped Rickard's arm and squeezed it in an emotive gesture of his friendship. 'I am so pleased you have come. You do not realise how much this moment means to me. Finally, after all these years of hard struggle we have an ally. A strong ally.'

'We had to come,' Rickard said.

'I couldn't help but notice the inclement weather you're having outside.' Beck chuckled, shaking snow from his coat.

'The storms are usually appallingly ferocious at this time of year. It is caused by the planet's unusual rotational spin, so I am told.'

'I think it's getting worse. Our launch landed with all the grace of an eagle wearing lead shoes.'

'Then we must commence at once. We have a little to discuss first but I am sure you will wish to know more of my proposed operation against the Emperor.'

'I think so,' Rickard agreed before Stuart broke in.

'Do we have to do it standing up?'

'No, no. Please, sit. The rush matting is quite comfortable, I assure you,' Kitan said. 'Over here, where it is warmer.'

He led them over to sit beside the supplies. He crouched down beside them, waving someone to join him from the crowd of watching rebel members. A surly, bad-tempered looking young person elbowed his way through the gathering and squatted on the matting. He had about him a purposeful air, the air of a person who intended to get something done and would allow no distractions.

'This is my close companion and second-in-command, Tor Chen. He will be with us on the expedition to rescue your captured crew members. He is a good fighter.'

'A good fighter is not what we need right now,' said Rickard. 'A well thought strategy would be more use. For instance, how are we supposed to get back into the capital's system when it is very likely to be tightly blockaded?'

314

'You need not fear on that count, Captain,' Kitan smiled. 'A small diversionary tactic in the next system will draw them away for the necessary amount of time.'

'What sort of diversionary tactic?'

'The Empire has a minor base on the moon of one planet. It is badly protected and will come under attack shortly before we arrive at our target. That is what some of these people behind me are to do.' He gestured to the waiting crowd.

Rickard's eyes examined them. All he could see were young native faces, openly eager and innocent. All carried with them a desire for revenge. 'Is this all your group?' Rickard asked.

'No. This is only one cell. We are spread all over the Empire.

'I hope it's going to work,' Beck said.

'It will,' Kitan promised.

A drawn out howl, the not-so distant wail of a creature of the ice wastes, suddenly sounded, reverberating through the wide cavern and bouncing off its glistening walls. The noise prolonged itself almost unnaturally in the cold wind outside.

The heads of the three visitors snapped up in unison. The rebels ignored the howl. 'What was that?' Beck mouthed what they were all wondering.

'I don't know,' said Rickard. 'And I don't want to find out. Whatever it was it didn't sound at all friendly.'

The disembodied wailing repeated itself. Its rancorous inflection boded ill will to anyone it met. The shrillness of the cry rose to a crescendo before fading to be concealed by the mournful whine of the wind.

'Whatever it is,' Stuart observed, 'it doesn't bother them.'

'No,' Kitan said. 'We are quite used to the sound of Tibor's rather cruel wildlife. You are perfectly safe so long as you do not leave the caverns unescorted. The king of this particular ice plain is very partial to a carnivorous diet.'

'Thanks,' said Beck. 'I'll bear that in mind next time I go for a stroll around the pond.'

'Enough frivolity,' the unfriendly second-in-command

315

snapped. 'We have matters to clear.'

'Like what?' Stuart backchatted.

'Are your people trustworthy? Are they capable of the task ahead? Can we rely on their aid in our cause?'

'Hey-'

'You must answer if you want our aid.'

'I don't see why.'

'Hmph. And you call yourselves intelligent.'

'Excuse me, but I was under the impression that it was you who was helping us, not the other way around,' Rickard protested.

'I am sorry, Captain Rickard,' Kitan said placatingly. 'Tor is unpractised in the fair art of diplomacy. What he may lack in the conversational field he more than makes up for in hard results.'

'That doesn't excuse his lack of manners.'

'No, of course not. I apologise on his behalf,' Kitan bowed his head.

Beck gently restrained him. 'There's no need for that. It was simply a misunderstanding that's all.'

Iad Kitan thanked him with a humbleness the visitors had not seen in him before. Apparently he was deeply ashamed at Tor's outspoken rudeness.

As if to snub Kitan's apology, Tor snapped out more questions. They were delivered with an unsoftened dislike of the strangers. 'Why are you here? What do you really want in the Empire?'

'This was a peaceful mission to establish contacts with your people and ours,' Rickard told him, becoming distinctly annoyed with the vexatious second.

'Then we got involved in the funny games your Emperor plays,' Beck inserted.

'And you,' he poked a finger at Beck. 'What do you do that you are so offhanded on the matter?'

Kitan raised a hand to placate Tor but Beck quickly intervened. 'Pardon me for not promptly deigning to dignify your question with an answer,' he said innocent-faced, 'but, and under the circumstances I thought I would ask so please don't take offence, when do you bring out the thumbscrews?'

'How dare you - ' Tor bristled angrily but Kitan forced

him down.

'Be silent, will you. I invited these people here and I will not tolerate your continual interference. Be silent or leave.' Tor fumed but stayed where he was. 'This is a great task. We have a mission to free the people of the Empire from the tyranny of their subjugator.'

'How'd you know they want to be freed?' said Stuart.

'Of course they want to be freed,' Tor replied indignantly, refusing to stay quiet. 'Our first major strike will be our greatest. We will strike at the very heart of the Emperor's rule - the palace in capital city.'

'Oh, yeah? An' how are we gonna get in? Walk through the walls?' Stuart asked sarcastically, peeved by the second's apparent naivety.

'We already know a way into the palace,' was the smug reply.

'That's convenient.'

Rickard intervened before fresh hostilities broke out. 'Cut it out, Stuart. Stop baiting him.'

'Captain, it's so easy.' She smiled at the look of outrage that appeared on Tor's contorted face.

Beck returned to the more serious questioning. He directed his question to Kitan. 'How will we get into the city?'

'That is where our network comes into operation. Transport will be waiting by the time we reach the capital. We will travel in safe concealment to the residency and from there we shall descend the southern wall and traverse the Emperor's private gardens.'

'I think that bit has already been done,' Beck said, glancing pointedly at Stuart who shrugged nonchalantly.

'I am sorry?' Kitan frowned in confusion.

'It's not important,' Rickard said, 'Please continue.'

'The remainder is easy. Once we have located the holding cells inside the palace we can be picked up in the gardens by your launch craft. The Emperor will not know what has hit him until it is far too late.'

'You've got it all worked out, haven't you?'

'This moment has been long in coming. This small band of fighters has waited years for one moment such as now. We are ready to fight.'

'Yes, you might be. But will anyone else be ready? You can't rely on hordes of the city people rushing out to join your noble cause,' Rickard pragmatically pointed out. 'Despite wishes to the contrary you are only a small group with an equally small support.'

'It is of no consequence,' Tor brushed the matter aside. 'We are ready to leave. We can move immediately.'

'Hold on. We only just arrived,' said Stuart.

'To wait any longer is unnecessary. The Emperor is weak and can be defeated now.'

Rickard shook his head. 'It might not be so easy as you think.'

'My companions have waited long for this attack,' Kitan said. 'They desperately want this time, this chance. They have suffered much at the hands of the Empire and its militaristic oppressors and they fully intend to right some of those wrongs.'

'Only some of them?'

'However, heroic and romantic our cause may seem, we are still realists. We admit that the battle will be long and hard.'

'He has a point, though,' Beck said to Rickard. 'Let's face it. The Emperor and his mob have been under-estimating us all the way. They didn't reckon on the strength of our defence in the residency. Their explosive plant on the ship was too weak and ill-placed to cause any serious damage or long-lasting harm. Their plan to enter troops via the hanger bay also failed dismally. They aren't up to it, no matter how hard or desperately they may try. They are not the all powerful conquerors they would have you think. They are hopelessly weak and feeble compared to some of the races beyond the Belt. I am beginning to think we can beat them, despite help from people like our friend Tor, here.'

Rickard stared at Beck's supportive outburst in open astonishment. This far in Beck had been solidly against engaging in revenge attacks, or attacks of any kind. This came as somewhat of a revelation to an unsuspecting Rickard. The FIO members were also plainly impressed with his monologue, even the argumentative second.

'Good speech, Doc,' Stuart complimented him.

'Hmm...Thanks, yes,' Beck said, and cleared his throat loudly to cover his uncharacteristic embarrassment. It was worth it, he thought, for Bulloch.

'Perhaps you're right,' Rickard smiled grimly. 'I'm starting to welcome the chance to fight back.'

'Are you thinking of revenge?'

'Damned right. It'll give us a chance to kick their backsides for a change.'

'Very eloquent.'

'That's the way I feel.'

'Then I am pleased that we all agree on the matter,' Kitan said, climbing to his feet.' 'Shall we start off?'

'I think we'd better,' Rickard said, cocking an ear to the wailing wind. 'I'd hate to get caught in this weather.'

They readied themselves for an immediate departure. The crowd of young rebels silently broke away to finish their final preparations. All of them were apprehensive. No matter how much they were looking forward to the strike it was still an immensely daunting prospect - to attack the very home of the Emperor himself.

☆ ☆ ☆

The steady sinking of the suns heralded the end of another day. The exceedingly long, eventful day in which so much had occurred was drawing to a close. The suns' weakening light, their gradually softening heat, gently pulled a concluding veil over a long line of extraordinary diurnal events. The lower of the two suns tentatively reached out and touched the distant mountain tops as it levered its way out of the sky. The rocky crags and peaks were enveloped in an effusive glow, a fading halo of orange. Darkness began to obscure the rim of the sky. A wind was blowing, its strength growing noticeably with the night. The overhead sky was alive with hues of darkening red and purple. The vividly, augmented streaks of cloud combined their colours where they touched, merging, mixing them, producing indeterminably vague textures of shading that defied description. It was an unusual sunset for an unusual day.

Shadows deepened. Darkness loomed.

Out of the gloom of the evening sky there appeared a shape, an object which rapidly grew in size as it neared the ground. Eventually, the shape lost its tenuity and took solid form. Like a descending eagle, wings held close to its side, the launch swooped vertically, reaching for the rocky surface of a cliff top, eager to set down amid a cloud of retro vapour and disturbed sand and deliver its living cargo.

Once the noise and disturbance of landing had ceased the launch's hatch hissed open, hinging out and down to hit the ground with a muffled thud. Rickard, cold weather insulation discarded, stepped out. He made a quick survey of his surroundings and noted with satisfaction that his vantage point allowed him to overlook capital city below. The launch had set down on a high plateau, one of many ringing the verdant, compact valley in which the city was situated. It offered an unoccluded view of the rescue party's destination.

The rest of the team followed Rickard out of the launch. Stuart led with a squad of Marines and Tor marched an impatient group of FIO rebels close behind. The rebels stood apart from the Service crew in a tight cluster, anxious to begin their war of resistance against the Empire.

Trailing behind Iad Kitan and an attendant 'tronics and tracking Marine was Kiyami. Once on the ground she joined the others well away from the launch. As the combined group of Marines and rebels stood back, the hatch sealed itself with a faint whine of pumping motors and the launch blasted off, heading directly upwards and vanishing into the lurid colour scheme of the sky.

While the others were busy witnessing the launch's departure Rickard was studying Kiyami.

Her build was smaller than Karen's, and her hair darker. She was very beautiful but seemed extremely delicate. Yet she possessed courage and strength enough to rival Stuart. She was there, with the team, because Rickard did not want to leave her behind yet again. He had done that once too often already. After the

320

performance she had given in the residency she could not be refused the opportunity to take part with the rest of them. She was quite able to take care of herself and this time Rickard wanted her with him. Besides, he had decided, she *was* the best first officer in the fleet.

He walked over to the plateau's edge and stared at the sprawling city. Kiyami broke away from the main group while they prepared their equipment for action and joined him. She was pleased with him. He'd shown the strength she knew he had by including her in the team. She was glad of that. She had known right from the start that he was right for the job. It was a pity things had turned out so difficult for him. She turned her eyes from him and followed the direction of his gaze.

'The place looks dead,' he said.

'Indeed,' Kiyami observed, 'the city does carry a funereal air about it. Perhaps they know we have arrived.'

'Not a chance. They're not that good. Their equipment isn't that precise yet. Another couple of years and maybe, but we're safe for now.'

'I hope so, otherwise this could easily become the most unsuccessful rescue in history.' Rickard smiled at the Beck-like humour, so unusual from her. 'Shall we move off?' she said. 'Before the FIO members try to run the show themselves, with or without Iad Kitan's agreement?'

'Yes. I'll admit Kitan doesn't have very good control over some of them, especially young Tor. He's going to cause us trouble one way or another. I can see it coming.' They returned to the main group. Rickard singled out Iad Kitan for attention. 'Where do we go from here?'

Kitan signalled to his second. 'Lead the way, Tor. A short walk, Captain. Off the plateau by a secluded mountain path to an awaiting transporter. From there into the city and on to the residency. We can go over the south wall into the palace gardens. All is taken care of,' Kitan promised and followed on after his team.

'So I'm beginning to understand,' Rickard muttered. He waved the men and women of his own team forward.

They made their way off the plateau via a rugged, pot-holed mountain path which led in a winding spiral down to the valley. The end of the path was reached

321

amidst the to be expected moans and groans from the Marines that the walk was too long and that they should have landed closer. It was all light-hearted banter amongst professional soldiers who were nerving themselves up for a fight. The moaners amongst the team soon changed their tune when they saw that transport awaited to take them the rest of the way. A battered old van-type floater had been supplied by Iad Kitan's contacts in the city. They gladly filed in and were driven off into the capital of the Empire.

Rickard need not have worried about secrecy in entering the city - it was, or at least, it seemed to be, utterly deserted. Hide curtains fluttered aimlessly under the mild breeze on the outskirts of town. The main streets were bare and quiet. The church was unattended and the market place had been abandoned. It was certainly a very different atmosphere to the one they had experienced on their first guided tour with Kal Nyr. It was now more a scene of empty desolation. If he had not glimpsed the occasional movement from inside open doorways Rickard could well have believed it.

Peering out from his concealed peephole in the back of the floater, Rickard saw when they arrived at the residency. The main gates were still strewn widely over the open main courtyard. The shattered guts of the officers' mess were still lying scattered over the north end. A mound of unmoved rubble still protruded from the remains of the connecting alleyway that Howarth had made such a good job of blocking.

The floater's rear doors were snapped open and the rescue team moved out. 'Come on, come on,' the Marine sergeant urged his troops as he led them into the residency and down to its southern end, taking the steps to the walkway. 'This is no time for sightseeing.'

Nevertheless, while setting up and securing the ropes that were to get them into the gardens, they continued to stare and pass comments on the battleground they had left such a short time before. The palace gardens were unchanged in the noiselessness they had maintained almost since dawn. The breeze that ruffled what sparse shrubbery there was out in the sandy streets of the capital refused to be lured further than the boundary walls. All was still and very, very quiet.

The gardens' side of the south wall was just as pitted and pockmarked as ever. Figures moved at the wall's top. A command was passed along and ropes dropped to cover the wall like hanging vines. The rescue force streamed down, running for concealment as soon as they touched the bare brown earth.

Rickard and Kitan took the lead as the team filtered through the gardens, Kiyami and Tor fell in close behind. Working her way to the front alongside the first line of Marines, Stuart coolly unslung her rifle and positioned it menacingly in her arms. Its overwhelming size made it look far too big for her tiny stature but she coped with it in an expert fashion, sure and confident of her abilities.

Leading the way alongside Rickard, Kitan and the burly Marine sergeant, she circumnavigated the wild, overgrown bushes and shrubs along the way. Remembering the route from before, she required no prompting from Kitan on which directions to take in the gloomy sublight of late evening. She was the first to reach the smashed remnants of the gate to the courtyard, impatiently waiting for the remainder of the team to catch up while they did their utmost to remain unseen from the palace.

Iad Kitan came up behind her just as she was edging around the gateway. He leaned forward trying to peer past her. A single trooper, standing as if planted, by the protection dome entrance was quick to react. He quickly levelled his rifle and got off a shot as Stuart ducked back.

Iad Kitan was not so quick to react. The shot took him full on the thigh and he collapsed in a heap, clutching at the wound.

Stuart wasted no time in consoling him. She ducked back to the open gateway and ruthlessly dealt with the trooper, out in the open as he was.

Beck hurried to examine Iad Kitan's bleeding leg, producing his bag of tricks from thin air. A Marine helped Kitan to get comfortable, propping up his head. The flow of blood was quickly staunched and the wound was cleaned up. While Beck was at work, the rest of the team, who had bolted for cover at the first shot, emerged to gather around Kitan, looking on in morbid fascination.

Rickard pushed his way through the crowd of rebels and Marines, not pleased that the Marines seemed to have forgotten their training to gawp at a minor injury.

'Break up this bunching,' he snapped at them. 'Sergeant, place our men.'

'All right, you lot. This isn't a party. Positions! I want full circle cover, move it,' the veteran Marine sergeant rapped while trying to keep his voice low. He found it hard to do both at once.

Rickard squatted beside Beck. He was concerned that their prime ally was out of action. 'How is he?'

'He'll be great, once we get him out of here.'

'I can continue, Captain,' Kitan croaked weakly.

'No you can't,' said Beck. 'You're not going any further with this leg, I'm afraid.'

'But I have to.'

Rickard tried to placate him. 'I'm sorry, but it's impossible. Look, we'll be okay. You've done well in getting us this far. I think we can find our way from here. And with your people to help out...You can't manage it like that, can you?'

'I...suppose I cannot.'

'This woman,' Rickard indicated the Marine propping Kitan's head, 'will stay with you until we get back. We'll pick you up on our way out. I'm sorry that you couldn't finish this but there must be someone reliable in your group that you can transfer command to?'

'There is Tor.' Kitan motioned his second over before Rickard had a chance to disagree.

Tor bent down to hear him. 'What is it?' he asked sharply.

'I am entrusting you with the leadership of our people for this mission. You must aid the Service and Captain Rickard but you must also follow the Captain's directives. Do as he asks and try to control your emotions. Do you understand me?'

'I understand you perfectly. But you need not worry. I will find us the glory we seek against the Emperor.'

'No, Tor, that is not the way you were taught.' Kitan

tried weakly to grab hold of Tor's collar but the stronger rebel pulled away, straightening.

'Never worry. We cannot fail.' He marched away, triumph in his very stride.

'You can't trust him,' Rickard said plainly.

'I have to, Captain. He is all there is.'

'Not on something this important, surely?'

'My apologies...but I cannot do anything more...'

Kitan slumped back into the Marine's arms. His complexion had turned pallid and he appeared to be in some pain from the wound.

'You said it wasn't too bad,' Rickard protested to Beck.

'It's not,' Beck firmly assured him. 'He's in some shock, nothing more than that. It's what I expect from a pulse wound.'

'Well, we can't wait around. We have to get a move on.'

'Okay,' the Marine sergeant took his cue and got the team mobile. 'Shift your arses. Let's get on the move.'

'I'm sorry to have to leave you behind,' Rickard said to Kitan as the rebel leader opened his eyes.

'I will still be here when you return. I promise.'

'You'll be okay,' said Beck. 'Don't go away now.'

As they started off Rickard located the 'tronics Marine. 'From now on I want continuous tracking. Scan one hundred and eighty degrees ahead of us. I want to know what's coming before it gets here.'

'Yes, sir.' The Marine unlimbered and actuated his portable motion tracker, slowly swinging it before him in a wide arc.

Thus reassured, the rescue team made their way unmolested into the palace. Tor led the way, not hesitating the slightest as he followed Howarth's trail down the winding spiral of stone steps and into the subfloor tunnels and pasageways below the ground level. With the 'tronics Marine beside him they encountered no-one, either avoiding what few patrols there were by taking side passages or waiting in silence until they had passed. Utilising the FIO Group's knowledge of the underground maze the prison was found with ease. They clustered around the top of the steps leading to the door. There was no guard.

Inside the prison all was quiet and calm. More of the torches had been lit and now flamed with rekindled resilience. The captured crew were lounging listlessly in their small cell saying very little. The conversation had faded and died as time passed and even Bentowski had become subdued and silent. There was nothing to do but wait. Wait until something happened or someone came for them.

Then the main door of the prison was hurled open and a tightly grouped bundle of Marines charged in, the others close on their heels.

At the first sound the imprisoned crewmembers instantly bounded to their feet. They desperately tried to see what was occurring, some pessimistically wondering if their end had finally come.

One of the first in after the Marines was Rickard. He sniffed the thick air once. It was enough. The prison air was enriched with vile odours which assailed his sense of smell without mercy. Attempting to ignore it he strode the length of the prison to where the prisoners were apprehensively awaiting their fate. At the sight of him and the party of armed Marines behind him they cheered. Their jubilant relief was self-evident.

'He dun do'd it,' Bentowski spurted, eagerly trying to shake Rickard by the hand through the cell bars. 'He came back for us.'

'What did I tell you?' Howarth said as if he knew all along that it was the truth.

'Oh, Cap,' grinned Bentowski. 'You're the greatest. You know that? The greatest.'

Rickard was slightly taken aback by the helmsman's gushing welcome but he valiantly rose to the occasion. 'Like him or hate him, you certainly can't ignore him,' he admitted in good humour to Howarth. He was pleased to see the helmsman. Actually *pleased* to see him!

'Don't I wish we could ignore him,' Howarth joked. 'I've been stuck in here with him for hours so you can imagine how I feel.'

Kiyami joined Rickard, Stuart trailing along with her. At the sight of the middie, Bernerds jumped to the bars in a flash to greet her.

Kiyami watched with interest. Never before had she seen Bernerds reveal so much emotion. He and Stuart had to be closer than anyone had suspected, closer, perhaps, than they themselves suspected. She witnessed a similar expression on Rickard's face when Karen Trestrail appeared at the cell bars. Their eyes met and shared their own experiences in a kind of intimate telepathy. The intensity of the reunion between them had moved beyond mere speech. Kiyami glanced back to the middies and was surprised to see that they were at imminent risk of descending into the same starry-eyed state. She was about to intervene when Beck sprang up behind her and executed the task for her.

'Now we're here, how do we get back out?' he asked, breaking the mood between the two couples.

'Through the front door?' Bentowski offered brightly.

'Over my dead body.'

'The Rukes are working on it.' Bentowski was back on form.

'Stop wasting time,' snapped Tor from further down the prison. 'We must move. Free your people and hurry.'

Bentowski grimaced, curling his top lip. 'Hey, who's the geek-brain? He's a real bundle of laughs. What charming company you keep, Doc. Really makes me feel wanted.'

'The only ones who want you are the troopers out there,' Howarth quickly retorted.

'Captain,' Bentowski pleaded through the bars. 'Please get me outta this cage before I lose my cool and attack him.'

'Sergeant,' Rickard prompted, standing back from the cell door.

'Yes, sir,' the sergeant replied and hustled forward a Marine armed with a specialist, low-intensity cutter. 'Move back now,' the sergeant waved to the prisoners as the Marine went to work on cutting around the heavy metal lock. With a subdued flash of sparks the lock fell away in seconds, not even a spiral of smoke remaining to commemorate its departure. The Marine stood and pulled open the door.

'At last, we're out,' Howarth breathed as he left the cell. The freed prisoners went with Kiyami and Beck to join

327

their rescuers in the main section of the prison, excitedly exchanging their stories while they were rearmed. Stuart and Bernerds also drifted toward the crowd. They had broken out of their haze and were conversing animatedly, Stuart mercilessly berating Bernerds for his lack of sense in the residency battle. They were far removed from the immediate worries of life and seemed simply pleased to have found one another.

Karen waited until last before leaving the cell. Rickard met her at the door, his arms sliding around her waist when she held him to her. 'How's your ankle?' he asked.

'Not bad. I'm still limping, unfortunately.'

'You'll make it.'

'I hope so. Never again do I want to go through that,' she said.

'You won't have to,' Rickard promised. 'Not long from now we'll be at the Belt and into safe space. Then I can submit my report on this place and arrange to get some decent leave.'

'Good. I missed you.'

'I missed you, too.' It gladdened him to know it was true. The thought crossed his mind that their exchange might sound rather mushy to any onlookers but he was pleased that he could actually say it, instead of hiding his feeling away as he had always done before. 'All we have to do is get out into the street. The launches will pick us up from there.'

'Let's not wait around.' She puckered her lips in expectation and he took the hint, easing down into the kiss. They remained like that for an eternal second before drawing away, their eyes once more saying to each other what words could not. Thus fortified they rejoined the others, he helping her along.

The first thing they noticed was that Tor was arguing again, this time with Bentowski.

'We have to use this chance to defeat the Emperor,' Kitan's second was saying. 'Why wait for years when we can do it now?'

'Hey! Not me. This guy wants out!' Bentowski turned on him. 'We've already had our asses shot off, enough for this life-time at least. What are you? A glutton for punishment or just plain masochistic?'

Howarth spoke up, but not to Tor. 'Don't start using long words, Bentowski. You'll only get confused.'

'Thanks for your immovable support, Thom.'

'Okay, Bentowski. Keep your wig on.'

Rocklike, Tor was not to be shaken. 'This is our task. Our true task. I do not expect you to understand but we can win. The Emperor must be destroyed here and now and we are the ones to do that. We can win.'

Rickard had strong doubts but he did not voice them. Instead he sounded the retreat. 'No way, Tor. This is a straight in-and-out rescue. You're not ready to confront the Emperor yet. Iad Kitan knows that, why won't you accept it?'

'I will never accept that we cannot defeat lowlife scum such as he surely must be!'

'This is not the time for a damned debate on the issue. We are leaving. Now. Whether you like it or not.'

'We are not under your orders, Captain.'

'No, but you are under Iad Kitan's and his orders were clear on the subject. We leave-'

The disagreement was saved from developing into a full scale argument by the intervention of the 'tronics Marine who was worriedly examining the small screen of his tracker.

He finally decided that he did not like what it said to him. 'We've got company! Captain, I have a large signal here. Troopers, lot's of them. Heading this way.'

15

'We've got to get out of here fast,' Rickard said. He knew he could not stress how fast he desired to leave the murky passages of the palace's sub-level floors.

'We're going to be fighting our way out,' Howarth warned.

'It's either that or stay here and wait for them to come and get us.'

'Well said,' Beck piped. 'Why don't we leave now?'

'And give the Emperor something to remember us by along the way,' Howarth finished.

Bentowski was typically more direct. 'Yeah! Let's kick some ass!'

'No,' Tor suddenly snapped. Everyone stared at him in astonishment. 'To leave is the last thing we should do,' he continued. 'This is our chance to fight back. Here and now. Why leave when we have been presented with such an opportunity?'

'Excuse me once more for butting in,' said Beck, 'but don't we have half the Empire's armed forces waiting for us out there? In my mind it is not a very wise decision to fight that many troopers through choice.'

'Damn right,' Bentowski backed him up. 'We ain't come all this way to get blasted for you guys.'

Tor spluttered with indignation. 'How could you *imbeciles* possibly-'

'Listen, pal. Anyone as narrow-minded a mor-'

'Lieutenant,' Rickard hurriedly intervened. 'Shut up. Tor, you are acting madly here. You're supposed to be following Iad Kitan. His orders were to come out alive, not throw your lives away in a senseless slaughter. Are you going to disobey him?'

330

'This is not disobedience. This is a war, and I will fight it.'
'You're just speaking in clichés. Why won't you listen?
It's suicide to attack those troopers.'
'We will see. If you are so spineless as to be afraid you
may wait here for our return. The people of the group will
follow me even if you will not.' The FIO rebels behind him
muttered their half-hearted support. 'Follow me,' Tor
shouted to them in overzealous eagerness as he made to
leave. 'Today we destroy the Empire!'
The Marine sergeant boldly blocked the doorway with his
large frame. 'Shall I stop him, sir?'
'No,' Rickard decided. 'Leave him. He's made his
choice. Let him go.'
Tor rushed from the prison, the majority of his followers
dutifully following after him. Only a few rebels and the full
force of Service crewmembers remained behind.
'He's a bloody nutcase!' said Howarth.
'Yeah,' Bentowski wisely nodded. 'A total fruitloop.'
'They've turned off, away from the exit,' Stuart said from
the door. A shockingly loud burst of trooper fire
accompanied their disappearance. 'And now they've blown
whatever cover we had down here.'
'I knew Kitan shouldn't have trusted him. The
hot-headed idiot. All he's achieved by his impulsiveness is
to alert the Emperor to the rest of us. We're going to have a
hell of a job getting back out of this rabbit warren.' Rickard
was feeling a ridiculous compulsion to yawn and he barely
managed to stifle it. He had to be more tired than he'd
guessed. 'This is going to set the Group back a few years - if
it doesn't destroy it completely.'
'We can still put Tor's stupidity to good use,' Kiyami told
him. 'His attacking the troopers will cover our own retreat.
I think we should use that advantage.'
'Good idea. Let's get out before the shooting starts.' He
ran to the door and eased himself around the frame,
carefully eyeing the corridor outside for any signs of enemy
troopers. There were none. No sign either of the FIO
rebels. 'It's clear.' He glanced back. 'Mister Howarth,
would you please detail a couple of Marines to escort Miss
Trestrail, seeing as she's injured. I don't want to
accidentally leave her behind.'

'No, of course not.' Howarth winked at Karen, amused that Rickard was maintaining his pretence even under these conditions.

Following Rickard they poured out of the prison, heading for the exit. Beck, Kiyami and the injured Karen - supported by her Marine escort - stayed up front with Rickard while Howarth kept rear-guard with the helmsman and the middies. Rickard was not so inexperienced that he did not think to have the route mapped on the way in, and they followed that electronically recorded map back, the 'tronics Marine providing the information on his tracker. In a tightly-packed group they made their way at the double along the cold, damp corridors. At every twist and turn they checked the way ahead, ensuring it lay empty of all life. Trigger fingers at the ready they ploughed through the underground tunnels below the palace.

As they dashed past an access corridor a prowling squad of troopers spotted them and gave instant chase. Shots were soon forthcoming in the direction of the fleeing Service crew.

'Mind your backs,' Howarth warned the Marines ahead of him. 'There's company on our tail.'

Rickard heard and increased the pace to a full run. 'Don't waste time with them. Just move!' he shouted back.

'Oh God,' Beck puffed. 'I don't think I can manage this sort of pace for very long.'

'Nonsense, Phil,' Karen chided him while she hobbled along, aided by the two Marines. 'Look at me. If I can do it with this ankle then so can you. You'll be running long after I've given up.'

'I wouldn't place any cash on it. I wasn't built for this kind of exercise.'

'Then we will have to get you in training when we are home,' Kiyami said from behind, herself keeping the pace effortlessly.

Rifle shots suddenly sounded from the way they had come.

'Blast!' Beck gasped through clenched teeth. 'Now the horrible little buggers are becoming a nuisance.'

Rickard was feeling unusually bouyant and high-spirited. Things were going right at last. He put it down to the ease with which the operation had so far run. They might even get out of this with only one or two casualties. 'Keep up, Doc. This is where it gets interesting.'

'You mean, will we make it out of here without the troopers catching up with us or are we running straight into another trap?'

'Precisely.'

The retreat had begun in earnest.

The troopers continued to fire as they pursued their prey and chunks of stone were smashed from the walls left right and centre as the troopers fought to aim a straight shot in the narrow passageways. One such shot came close to hitting Howarth and, while running, he twisted his body to return it.

Bentowski was finding it a little warm at the back for his liking and tried to move up, all the while protecting himself in his own off-centred manner, simultaneously cursing at the troopers and goading them on.

'Why is it we're always running from these creeps?' Stuart cried to Bernerds as Bentowski came scuttling past.

'Don't ask. Just run,' Bernerds replied breathlessly.

She did run, but that did not prevent her talking. 'Where's Kal Nyr?' she asked. 'I've got a goodbye present for him.'

'Dunno, I ain't seen him. Been too busy.'

'Well I hope someone gets him. I'd hate him to miss out.'

They raced along the passages at breakneck speed, the insubstantial lighting failing to slow them down. Marines stopped only occasionally to return the sporadic fire. Bernerds took up the rear-guard position, only too willing to cover his colleagues' backs with a blanket of pulse fire. Masonry exploded from the walls, ceiling and floor as he let loose, uncaring of what he hit. He simply concentrated on creating an impassable wall of debris and flame. He became so engrossed in his task that he started to fall behind the main group.

As they passed another intersection Stuart glanced behind her and saw they were leaving him. She held back to call a timely reminder to him. 'Hey, Pete! Keep up!'

He turned and delivered her a genial wave, telling her he was fine. Before he could move to rejoin her a second squad of troopers flowed out of the intersecting passage, cutting him off. They immediately turned on the Marines who formed the bulk of the Service numbers and opened fire. Bernerds remained unseen.

The Marines, along with Stuart, ducked together and returned the fire. The corridor suddenly became a battleground.

Bernerds was stuck for options. There was only one way he could go. He saw straight away that he would do himself no good by remaining where he was so he ducked into the shelter of the side passage, more to avoid the gunfire of the Marines than to escape the troopers. The corridor became consumed by the building conflagration of fire and heat, lit by the flash-bursts from so many rifle snouts.

Stuart searched desperately for any sign of Bernerds over the heads of those troopers still standing. The smoke from several small fires suddenly cleared in a brief swirl of wind and there he was. All she caught of him was a mini-second glimpse through the enemy ranks.

Their eyes met and locked for one brief moment. A frantic heartbeat later he was gone, safely esconced up the side passage. Stuart stared helplessly after him until Bentowski caught her arm and dragged her away.

'Come on,' he cried in her ear. 'Let's hack it out of here!'

'I can't. We've left Pete behind!'

'Stuart, we are leaving. There's nothing you can do for Bernerds so move your ass!'

'Bentowski, you obnoxious bastard! Get off me,' she protested.

'If you want to insult me go ahead. I don't give a damn. I saw where Bernerds went. Right now he's got more chance of making it outta here than you have if you try to fight through those Rukes. So you're comin' this way.' He yanked her to her feet.

She reluctantly allowed herself to be led off, feeling more than a twinge of regret at having to abandon Bernerds.

The troopers, suddenly reinforced by the late arrival of the first squad, closely pursued them, pushing on relentlessly. The battle moved on, dragging through the ill-lit maze towards the exit.

A pair of young Marines were holding the very rear of the

departing rescue force, successfully holding back the threatening troopers under heavy pressure, protecting the back of their colleagues - until the most forward of the troopers stepped boldly out to fire one precisely targetted blast of searing heat. One of the brave Marines went down, folding and slumping against the wall.

Bentowski jumped once more into the fray with vigour, pumping fire into flaying bodies. He made a particular point of shooting down the troublesome trooper in the front line, commenting loudly to himself, 'Zapped!' The flash from the muzzle of his rifle illuminated a great many corpses as he sprayed shots down the corridor, homicidally killing everything in range.

He looked ahead and saw with relief they had arrived at the stone staircase that lead upwards, to freedom. *'Yahaay!'* he hollered victoriously. 'We're outta here! We're gonna make it!'

A trooper decided he looked too victorious and fired at him, missing his bobbing form by millimetres. He ducked appreciatively, returning the shot in kind. 'Take that, sucker!' he bawled. The heavy pulsefire impact jerked the trooper back, spinning his corpse carelessly aside.

Rickard was at the head of the team, this time having no thoughts of acting the hero. He was concentrating firmly on getting his crew away from the danger zone, back to the protectiveness of his ship. That thought came very close to being his last as the wall violently exploded a hairsbreadth away from his head. In dodging the explosion of brick and stone Rickard damaged his already hurting shoulder, wrenching it when he hit the ground.

'Chris!' Karen cried, and Kiyami rushed to aid him. 'Captain, are you hurt?'

'I'm all right. I'm fine,' he insisted, scrambling to his feet and rubbing his hurting shoulder.

'You don't look it.' Karen told him plainly.

'I'm okay,' he reassured her. 'Keep moving. We're almost out.'

He led the way, breathless and aching, up the stairs into the over-decorated grandeur of the palace chambers which were mercifully empty of troopers. He glanced back to ensure Karen was still safe with her personal bodyguards before making for the door to the gardens.

Officers and Marines alike exploded into the night-darkened gardens in a controlled panic. Virtually every one of them was on the lookout for more troopers heading their way. Only one or two were otherwise occupied; like the many Marines who were firing back to cover themselves; like Karen who had her hands full staying mobile with her damaged ankle; like Beck, red-faced and flushed from the sudden exertion of trying to drag a hurt rebel along with him, one of the very few who had remained behind.

Iad Kitan and the lone Marine with him were waiting when the others burst out of the palace. The Marine quickly scooped Kitan up as Rickard and Kiyami reached her, bringing the wounded rebel leader to his feet. 'Everything okay out here?' Rickard asked the Marine, making her out clearly in the haze of light coming from over the garden wall.

'Dead quiet, sir. Not a whisper until the launches touched down over the wall.' She pointed to the boundary wall of the palace gardens. 'Then some gunfire started up for a while. Now it's quiet again.'

'The launches are there now?' asked Kiyami.

Kitan, looking more recovered, smiled. 'They are. Thanks to perfect timing this rescue mission will pass without problem. A great blow has been struck today.'

'Not quite,' Rickard said.

'What? What do you mean?' He glanced around and failed to see more than a couple of his rebels amongst the many Marines. 'Where is Tor, and the others?'

'Tor did not want to stay with us,' Kiyami told him gently. 'He imagined he could win your cause and finish the Emperor for good.'

'They were all killed?'

'I think so. A lot of firing accompanied their disappearance.' The darkness could not hide his sense of loss. Kitan's face fell dejectedly. 'But you said yourself that it wasn't your only cell of resistance,' Rickard told him.

Kitan nodded his head. 'No, it was not the only one, but it was one of the best. We have many others and our aim

336

can still be achieved but it will not be today, not now. And all because I trusted Tor...'

And it was a pretty stupid thing to do, Rickard thought. Anyone could see Tor wasn't up to the job. But, he reminded himself, this was not the time to mention it.

'Captain,' Howarth caught Rickard's attention. 'The troopers are massing inside the palace. We have to move.'

'Damn. Yes.' Rickard snapped a hurried order to the Marine sergeant. 'Blast the wall, Sergeant. That's our escape route.'

The sergeant needed no further bidding. He collared two Marines armed with grenade launchers and aimed them in the direction of the boundary wall. Once space had been created around them they fired their launchers simultaneously. With ear-shattering loudness a sizeable chunk of the wall was reduced to a scattered pile of smashed brickwork. A halo of dust and smoke surounded it, clearing with annoying slowness to reveal what remained - an unobstructed escape route to the street where three of *Emputin's* launches sat awaiting them, whisps of vapour still rising from their cooling landing jets. Warm rectangles of light shone from their open hatches, where figures moved within. Remote-controlled beams on the top of the hulls revealed the way to safety in a passage of white light.

A coxswain could be seen at the hatch of the nearest launch, waving them on. He shouted a warning that Rickard heard clearly. 'You'd better hurry, sir. We have trouble out here. There's a squad of troopers down the far end of the street and they're waiting for you to come out.'

Rickard turned to Howarth. 'We are going to need some protection. We'll never get everyone safely across without it.'

'Then some of the Marines will have to go first.'

'Okay. See to it.'

Howarth nodded and snapped a command to the Marine sergeant who then chose the men for the job. The rest of the team moved towards the exit, readying themselves to run the gauntlet of enemy fire. Only Bentowski remained, with Stuart and a few others, to

337

hold off the troopers from the palace.

The Marines went out first, placing themselves to give covering fire for the others. A bunch of them ran out into the open street, rolling to the ground at spaced intervals in a line facing the city guards. They began firing at the troopers immediately, forming a protective shield.

'It's safe,' Rickard decided. He glanced quickly at Karen, making sure she was safe. Seeing that her Marine escorts were close by her, he turned back to face the way ahead. 'Run for the launches,' he said.

He led the way with Beck, helping the medic with his patient. They, closely tailed by the other non-combatants, scampered past the prostrate Marines for the shelter of the launches. Rickard almost pushed Beck into the first one as a burst of enemy fire fried the air over their heads. Gunflashes illuminated the line of troopers at the far end of the street. Remaining in the open, Rickard aided first Kiyami and then Howarth as they raced for cover.

'Where's Karen?' Rickard demanded as Howarth knelt inside the launch's hatch. He pulled Stuart up by the hand as she and Bentowski leaped in.

'She's still in the gardens,' Howarth shouted over the noise of pulse fire.

'What's she waiting for?'

'I don't know, but you needn't worry. She's safe enough. The two Marines you detailed are still with her.'

'Well she had better get a move on. I want her over here.'

'The same as Stuart here would like to see our friend Bernerds again,' Bentowski said, kneeling beside Howarth. He was adrenalin-pumped and wide-eyed from the fight.

'Why?' Howarth asked.

'The twithead got lost.'

'Lost?' He stared at Stuart for confirmation.

Bentowski nodded. "Fraid so. Took a wrong turn when we met up with the second buncha goons back there. He'd better catch up soon or he'll get dumped.'

Howarth could see Stuart was worried about the missing Bernerds. 'He's probably in one of the other shuttles.'

'I didn't see him come out of the palace,' said Stuart.

'Don't worry,' Bentowski glanced up at her. 'He'll make it. It's not as if the Rukes can shoot him. He's so thick he's bullet-proof.'

The acidic curse she growled at him did not hide the worry on her pixie face.

The last few stragglers bolted for the cover of the launches, including Karen and her Marine escort. They flanked her one on either side and were deliberately keeping their pace matched to hers, slowed as she was to a fast limp.

With no-one left to stop them, the troopers who had been kept at bay in the corridors of the palace suddenly burst out into the gardens. At their head was an officer Rickard was sure he recognised from the fight on *Emputin*. He resembled the loner who had murdered his own commander but the uniform was different, higher ranked. An Imperial guardsman's uniform.

Rickard had no more time in which to think of the matter. The Imperial guardsman and his troopers reached the rounded gap in the wall. They were clearly illuminated by the launches' beams. It all happened very slowly and very clearly. It was as if he was a spectator at an event completely separated from the normal flow of reality. He was looking on from a great distance.

He was standing years away.

He was helpless to intervene.

-He saw as the Imperial guardsman drew his troopers to a halt when the most forward of them fired a single, well-targetted shot that struck one of the fleeing Marines dead-centre on his unprotected leg, causing him to stumble as he fought to keep his balance. And the Imperial guardsman raised his pistol, narrowing one eye as he peered through the gun sights, so that he could ever-so gently pull back the trigger to fire and hit one of the escapees full in the back.

-He saw as the Marine was caught by the

blast of one of the trooper's rifles and staggered when he reached for the wound but managed to keep on his feet. And Karen turned to cast a brief glance back over her shoulder so that, upon seeing ranked troopers chasing them no longer, her features relaxed a tautened mask of fear, for she thought they were free, but then the guardsman's shot hit her full in the back to send her tumbling to the ground with a stunning impact.

Rickard froze.

He could see that Karen was not moving.

The nightmare-calm quality of it left an unwipeable imprint on his memory but still there was a recognisable delay in his actions as the real-time understanding of it hit him. When it did it sent him cold with shock.

'No,' he uttered in realisation. Then louder. 'Oh *God!*' He darted to where Karen's motionless form lay and skidded to the ground beside her.

Dark-dispersing bursts of fire from the end of the street sounded. The enemy shots falling all around went completely unnoticed.

Beck glanced out of the launch and what he saw made his stomach flip over. 'Ohmigosh! Howarth, quickly, get out here.' He leapt from the hatch. Oh, why her? he asked himself mournfully. She wasn't a threat to anyone. Didn't even carry a weapon.

'Bentowski, Stuart,' Howarth ordered, trying to keep his voice steady at the sight that greeted his eyes. 'Covering fire!'

Rickard was becoming frantic and he had to consciously force himself to calm down as he checked for a sign that she was alive. One flicker of movement, anything, but all he could see was the growing, spreading bloodstain on her back. It was useless. She couldn't possibly have survived. He couldn't think straight. All he could see was Karen lying there in the dirt. Surrounded by red. There was too much blood. Far too much blood.

She had to be dead.

The uninjured member of Karen's Marine escort moved to aid him. 'Help me lift her, sir. We can get her into the launch,' he said. Rickard did not answer. 'Sir. Grab her arm and we'll move her. Captain.'

But Rickard remained unresponsive. Gunfire continued to fly overhead. He took no notice of it. 'All right, Marine,' Howarth said reassuringly as he and Beck reached them. 'How is she, Doc?'

Beck crouched over her, fast-moving hands a blur of motion as he desperately searched for a pulse. He found one, wavery and tremulous though it was. 'She's alive,' he breathed.

Rickard almost laughed out loud with relief. A new drive moved him. All at once he had the motivation to stir himself. All at once he could cope again. He felt a solid determination to carry this through to the end. Damn the bloody Emperor, he cursed. I'll see him in hell before I give up. He straight away resumed command. 'Let's get her out of here,' he ordered, rising with strengthened resolve.

'Lift her gently,' Beck cautioned. 'Don't put any strain on her back.'

Howarth took Karen's arm and together the four of them eased her unconscious form into the launch. Bentowski and Stuart making way for them as they passed.

Once they were in, the last of the Marines strung out across the street broke for cover. As they reached the launches, Stuart began pulling back, nudging Bentowski before her. 'Hey!' he cried indignantly. 'Quit shovin.'

'Shut your face,' she told him. She had still not completely forgiven him for dragging her away from Bernerds. 'We aren't out of this yet so get your backside in motion.'

'Whatever you say, little lady,' Bentowski smiled and allowed himself to be bustled into the launch.

Stuart was the last in. She glanced over at the still unmoving guardsman by the wall. He was staring with pleasure at the spot where Karen Trestrail had fallen. Murdering sod, Stuart thought angrily. She didn't see why he should get away with that. Not without some

341

retribution. She let off a shot, hitting the brickwork beside him, causing him to duck. Then the hatch started to close and her view was cut off. Cutting her off from her target...and from Bernerds. He had not made it to the launches. She knew that to be a certainty. He was lost for good. He'd never make it out now. 'Goodbye, Pete,' she said softly. She knew she would not see him again. Kirsten Stuart grieved for him.

Hatches hissed closed and the launches lifted off from the street, creating downdraughts as they rose, whipping up tormented swirls of sand and dust. They were fast in disappearing from sight, showing scant respect for gravity, treating it only as if it were subject matter in a book to be ripped up and discarded.

The launches sped for the safety and protection of their mother ship, fleeing the bloody battleground and the lives it had claimed.

☆ ☆ ☆

Unaware of events outside the palace, Bernerds found he had to shrug his shoulders in resignation. He was lost, he conceded sheepishly to himself. The twisting, turning maze of passageways had finally got the better of him.

Since being separated from the others he had done nothing but wander from one empty corridor to another, finding all of them equally deserted. He had eventually managed to struggle out of the gloomy sub-levels but that had only brought him into a totally unfamiliar section of the palace. Now he hadn't a clue where he was. Lost, that's what he was. Totally bloody lost. He wondered if Stuart was faring any better. She probably was. She always did have a knack of coming out on top of a situation while he usually seemed to end up in life's intensive care department.

'There has to be some way out of this bloody rabbit warren,' he cursed, and punched the wall in frustration.

Starting forward once more, he remained careful to keep a steady watch of the ground ahead, even though

342

just about all the palace guards seemed to be occupied in the sub-levels with their escaping prisoners. Arriving at a wide corner he peered around, at last spotting something familiar. Guarded by two annoyingly alert troopers were the twin, heavily ornamented doors of the throne room.

His earlier antipathy vanished in a flash. He smiled grimly and readied himself to attack, checking that his rifle was properly actuated. Action at last! Without further deliberation he jumped out and fired a dead-hit shot at the first trooper who crumpled without making a sound. As his companion became a blur of action Bernerds dropped and rolled to the far wall, holding the rifle steady to fire again. The second trooper collapsed, halted in the motion of drawing his own weapon. The ante-chamber drifted back to its originally quietened state as the deafening echo of gunfire faded away.

Without pausing to admire his handiwork Bernerds rose and ran for the throne room doors, crashing through them awkwardly and bruising the length of his arm in the process. Managing to cut through the pain, he righted himself and brought his rifle to bear on the startled occupants of the chamber who were all huddled defensively around their Emperor.

All activity in the throne room ceased. All eyes fell on Bernerds.

'Freeze!' Bernerds shouted with as much menace as he could muster while he covered the group, hoping they would not decide to charge him en masse. One trooper by the far wall tried his luck, imagining he was fast enough to draw and shoot. Bernerds brought him down with a single shot, scarcely breaking his attention away from the Emperor and his entourage.

This was certainly a change for the better, he briefly thought. How much he had changed in such a short time. How long ago was it he had made his first kill? A day? Not much longer, anyway. Now here he was gunning down bad guys all over the place, acting like a one-man army. Why did it have to come now? Why did he have to cut himself a piece of the action now, when all he wanted was to be with Kirsten, back on the ship?

'Now, you're all gonna do exactly what I tell you. I want

you all to ease out your weapons and throw them over here,' he gestured to the side of the chamber. He had not moved from his position in front of the half-open doors. He wanted to feel a lot safer before he ventured any further inside what was a potentially lethal trap. The Imperial officials and troopers in the protective barrier around the Emperor sullenly complied with his command. Malignant animosity was evident in their every move but he knew they dared not act against him, so greatly did they fear for the Emperor's life. A small arsenal of pistols, rifles and personal firearms quickly built up in a scattered heap against the wall. The last trooper to throw his weapon away did so with angry force, sending it smashing into the wall so that it crashed noisily down on top of the others.

At last Bernerds felt able to relax. Straightening up he edged around the tightly knit group towards the dais where the Emperor sat, silently fuming at the incompetence of his own guards to stop one single intruder. Bernerds kept a wary eye on the group in front of him, not doubting that at least one of them had kept a weapon of some sorts. But he still noticed the dimmed lighting in the chamber; the ominous shadows at its distant edges where blackness overtook the comforting, but greatly darkened illuminants that hung, spider-like on single threads from the distant ceiling far above his head. He prayed that there was no-one lurking within the shadows. He could not hope to cover the Emperor's bunch of lackeys and keep watch over every unlit nook or cranny for unknown assailants at the same time.

Reaching the dais, he jumped up and placed himself to one side of the Emperor's high-backed throne. He turned his rifle to aim its sleek barrel at the Emperor's crested head, nonchantly leaning over him to tickle his ear with the rifle's tip.

'One wrong move, mate,' he said, imitating Bentowski's acidic growl to perfection, 'and you're dogmeat.' Saying it in that fashion was a mistake, he realised. It made him wish the helmsman were here to help him out. He needed all the help he could get and for once he didn't mind admitting it.

'You're going to be my passport out of this place.' He raised his voice to include the cluster of uncertain officials below him. 'None of you will give me any trouble if you want your Emperor to keep breathing. None of you, do you hear?'

He decided to take the ensuing silence as a positive answer. A familiar tall, broad-shouldered figure pushed his way out of the group, halting at the foot of the dais. A smug, deriding smile played at the corners of his mouth. Bernerds recognised him instantly. 'Well, well. If it isn't our friend Kal Nyr, the biggest scumbag in the galaxy.'

'How apropos,' Kay Nyr's voice was ice cold.

'What?'

'The barbarous savage delivers himself to his tomb, his deathplace.'

'Shut it,' Bernerds warned. He was not sure what the aide was playing at but it was bound to be beneficial to all but himself.

'How far do you imagine you will get? How far before you are captured and exterminated like the animal you really are?'

'I said be quiet.'

'And I should imagine that we all heard you, exceedingly loud as you are.'

Bernerds was beginning to feel flustered and, for some reason, panicky. Why? he wondered. He was supposed to be in control of the situation. 'I should have killed you when I had the chance,' he said.

'But you did not possess the courage.'

'Listen, if we're talking about courage-'

'I do not imagine for one moment-'

Bernerds shouted him down. 'If we're talking about courage, you and your squirming little friend here,' he playfully squeezed the Emperor's neck, 'aren't running very high in the stakes! You're a bunch of two-faced hypocrites! You go and invite us down here by pretending to be so very sorry about attacking us earlier, and then try and wipe us out and take over the ship in the sneakiest way you could. Well, that little effort just about wins the gold bloody medal in gutlessness!'

'It is not us who are gutless. It is you, a prime example

345

of what the Empire and its people must be protected against.' Utterly pathetic.' Kal Nyr continued his denunciating tirade, almost ignoring Bernerds. It was as if he was trying to goad the middie into action, addressing himself almost exclusively to his audience.

That was his mistake. In a flash of inspiration Bernerds suddenly saw that the aide was attempting to provoke him into releasing the Emperor and moving into a position where the troopers could safely deal with him.

'Soon the palace guards will have dealt with every single one of your pathetic little band of rescuers,' Kal Nyr rambled on, 'as well as those disgustingly traitorous rebels your people have associated themselves with. Soon they will all be dead, then there will be only you. And how long can you last on your own?'

Now that he knew what was going on, Bernerds acted more confidently. 'It won't work,' he said with a grin. Kal Nyr was caught off guard by his suddenly relaxed attitude. 'It's not going to work. Not this time. And I'm not going to warn you again. Shut your mouth.'

Despite catching the aide off balance, he might as well have whistled in the wind for all the effect it had. 'Aah! Tut, tut, my friend. There is absolutely no need to lose your self-control. That will accomplish nothing at all.' Kal Nyr had soon recovered his composure and was almost laughing aloud at him.

Bernerds finally lost what little patience he had remaining. Although he exuded an external visage of calmness, inside he burned with uncontrollable rage as he thought how these people had treated their 'guests'. Who the hell did they think they were? They couldn't get away with treating people like this, like dirt. He certainly didn't have to take this! Emotion clouded reason in his mind for an instant and he swung his rifle around. The shot blew a wide hole into Kal Nyr's unprotected stomach and carried through to strike the trooper behind, knocking him clear off his feet.

The surprise on the aide's face at the complete unexpectedness of it was clearly evident as he slowly toppled to be caught by his colleagues and lowered to the cold floor. His body twitched spasmodically for a few

346

seconds before it lapsed into final stillness.

The rest of the Emperor's servants stared at Bernerds in a state of stunned immobility. While he still held the upper hand Bernerds quickly whipped the rifle butt back to their master's head, pressing it hard into his flesh. He was surprised at himself. he hadn't thought himself capable of it. But he had to stay clear-headed. He couldn't afford to relax now.

'Anyone else want some of that?' A frustrated trooper took a pace in his direction, clearly intending to jump him. 'Yeah?' Bernerds screamed at him. 'Come on, then. Come on! 'Cos I'm just about ready for you slime bags!' The trooper's superior put out a restraining hand, holding him back and Bernerds was greatly relieved to see that there were no other takers.

He failed to catch the slight movement from the balcony overlooking the chamber.

The Imperial guardsman peered inquisitively at the scene below, awaiting his chance. This would be too easy, he thought gleefully. He was pleased he had taken the trouble to enter via the little-used balcony doorway rather than announcing his presence by using the main doors. One never knew what one might overhear from the many high-ranking staff who frequented the chamber, and for an ambitious and only recently promoted trooper it was a godsend. He had only just returned from the palace gardens where he had been busy chasing off the invading Service force, unfortunately not being able to retake the freed prisoners. That was the only mark against him at the moment. For his successful role in the otherwise failed takeover bid of the Service ship he had received his promotion and had been transferred to the Emperor's personal guard. It was a highly prestigious position in the army and he was still feeling intensely proud of himself.

He had cautiously sneaked onto the shaded balcony only moments before the Serviceman's abrupt entry and had been unable to be of any assistance in saving Kal Nyr - not that Kal Nyr deserved saving as far as he was concerned. With the snobbish and self-opinioned aide out of the way he might be able to find a foothold in the officer classes. The possibility was not to be sniffed at.

All the time that the Service midshipman had been in the chamber the guardsman had been preparing an attack. He had speedily, but quietly, ripped off a length of braided ornamental trimming from one of the numerous tapestries without alerting the Serviceman - who was obviously running on a knife-edge of calculated sadism and total paranoia. After an age of painfully slow work, in the process making a ruinous mess of a priceless heirloom, he cut through the last stitch and curled the freed braiding under his arm. He tied one end of the rope-like braid to a nearby support column, making sure the knot was secured. Then he eased himself out over the balcony rail, pulling tightly on the makeshift rope and began lowering himself centimetre by centimetre.

As he started down he thought of the prestige he would gain from single-handedly rescuing the Emperor from the clutches of his would-be captor. There was more to life than just duty, more than blindly following orders, he knew that now. He had already achieved some notoriety for his accomplishments, most notably in his capture of the civilian member of the Service crew. Perhaps he would be acclaimed once more for shooting her. She would not be celebrating a successful escape. He had developed a taste of power, a desire to be one of the rulers rather than one of the ruled. Success and reward brought more pleasure to him than the sheer drudgery of duty. And it was more enjoyable.

From his position in front of the Emperor's dais, one of the high ranking military officials of the Emperor's personal advisory staff calmly watched as the lone guardsman made his descent. He glanced quickly to the Serviceman and was glad to see that he had no inkling of what was occurring behind him. Deciding to help out the guardsman and play for time, the officer stepped out of the group, instantly gaining Bernerds' attention.

'What do you want?' the middie questioned.

'I am Bian-Tojo-'

'I don't want your bloody pedigree,' Bernerds ruthlessly interposed. 'I said what do you want.'

'That is the question I should be asking you.'

'Just back off and let me get out, I'm leaving.'

'I merely request that no harm should come to our Emperor. Safe conduct cannot be otherwise assured.'

'Don't threaten me.'

'I would not dream of doing so.'

The middie began edging away from the throne, dragging the silent Emperor alongside. The rifle did not waver from the Emperor's head.

'You will not reach the exit,' the officer told him.

Bernerds considered his position and wearily realised that the odds were stacked heavily against him. High against him. In fact it was very unlikely that he would make it out of this alive. Added to that his arm was starting to hurt like mad. So, he mused, this was what it was like to play the doomed hero. It was not all it was cracked up to be. Now he was stuck with the role he found he did not want it. Rather, he would happily swap places with some other unwary idiot.

He just hoped Stuart had made it out. That way at least half of their team would survive. He certainly didn't reckon his chances.

The lone guardsman stepped off the braid and crept stealthily towards him.

And the officer watched - and acted. As Bernerds was negotiating the step down from the dais the officer rushed him. To the open astonishment of his fellow officers he darted at the middie, whipping out a pistol from his tunic.

Bernerds shot him down. Too late he realised there was someone else behind him. The guardsman appeared as if from nowhere to yank back his rifle, directing it away from the Emperor as it fired, barely missing its intended target. A granite-hard fist hit him full in the face, the high-ribbed glove encasing it tearing at his skin. The fist hit him again and he staggered back, blood streaming from his nose. Momentarily stunned, Bernerds let go of the Emperor who scuttled eagerly away.

Bernerds managed to recover enough to block the next punch and he swung out with the butt of his rifle. The move gave him vital seconds as the surprised guardsman caught the blow straight on. He hurriedly reversed the rifle and fired at point blank range. The total force of the blast ripped open the loner's throat and hurled his corpse to the floor.

'About time you got your's,' Bernerds hissed vengefully.

He turned and saw a maddened gang of troopers bearing down on him. They were oblivious to the backdrop of smouldering cloth as a tapestry smoked where his stray rifle shot had caught it.

In that instant he knew he was dead.

The anger and frustration of having come so close to escaping only to be thwarted at the last minute suddenly got the better of him and he released himself to the whole force of the suicidal rage that had been steadily building inside him. With a blood-curdling scream he leapt into the bunched mass of troopers, firing wildly at them. One went down, his head a gaping pit. A second followed. But ultimately there were too many of them. He could not shoot them all.

The rifle was ripped from his grasp as he was weighed down by the sheer numbers. Countless punches and kicks rained down on him, pummelling at him. The pain increased, growing and spreading until it merged into a numb emptiness in which he felt nothing. He discovered he could not see any more. Something was obscuring his vision. Something warm, thick, running with slow liquidity over his eyes. It had to be blood. He guessed that it was his own but he could not be sure.

In the far distance, at least a million miles away, he could hear the angered tones of the Emperor snapping orders, barking them with the virulence of a frenzied dog. 'Send all available vessels after them,' the voice growled. 'I want that ship!'

It became a meaningless jumble as his LTU was smashed. With a placidity of mind that somehow amused him he wondered what the Emperor was getting so overheated about.

Surely nothing could be that important? Not now....?

There was no-one outside the throne room to pay witness to Bernerds' dying breaths as the troopers methodically beat the life from him. The antechamber was deserted but for the rapidly stiffening corpses of the two guards that were sprawled over the floor.

Bernerds died without any of his crewmates knowing he had died.

'Beck, how is she?' Rickard demanded as the crash team whizzed across the bay deck to meet them at the launch's open hatch, directing a stretcher before them through the cluster of disembarking Marines. Beck made sure that Karen's still unconscious form was loaded with care onto the hover trolley before turning back to answer him. 'She's not good,' he said firmly. 'I have to be honest about it. I can't tell the extent of the damage until I get her down to sickbay.'

'You'll let me know if...?'

'Yes. I'll let you know.' Beck led the crash team off at a run, whisking Karen away while Rickard watched with concern.

Kiyami placed her hands gently on Rickard's shoulders, easing him towards the exit. 'You have work to do, Christopher,' she told him. 'Do it, while the Doctor does his.'

'Huh? Yes, of course,' he said. He attempted to compartmentalise his worry, putting it to one side for the moment. It was not easy. 'We'd better get to the bridge.'

'Precisely.' She guided him off.

Bentowski and Howarth followed while a bemused Iad Kitan stared in awe at the size of the bay. Stuart, on impulse, decided to trail Bentowski to the bridge, knowing that she was unlikely to be noticed there under the circumstances. If they were about to be wiped out she at least wanted to see what was coming on the bridge's main viewer screens.

Both bridge doors snapped open to allow the returning crew entry. They hurriedly took their positions; Howarth replaced the stranger at the weapons console, Bentowski took over from a relieved Arakelian. She subsequently positioned herself to one side at an auxiliary panel. Helm was not fully up to par as yet, so she thought it better to stay nearby. Kiyami went to the science section and straight away began scanning the immediate area. Stuart slipped in behind them, going unobserved by all except Bentowski, who delivered her a wink of encouragement.

'Nice to see you again,' Boyd said genially to Bentowski. 'I thought we'd lost you.'

The helmsman turned his attention to the navigator. 'Nope. That was just wishful thinking on your part.'

'Yeah, wasn't it just.'

'Aww, now don't be like that. Underneath it all I know you like me.'

Rickard stood by the conn, a hand going to rest against the miniature console there. He was far too agitated to sit. 'There are Imperial warships closing on us,' Kiyami soon reported.

'Hang on,' Rickard said to the bridge crew in general. 'We're not out of this yet.'

The first blast impacted against unprotected hull, rocking the ship and throwing Rickard back against the railing. It took him a moment to recover before he scrambled to his chair and fastened the seat restraint. Blast the agitation, he thought.

'Shields up,' he ordered. 'How many of them this time?'

'Seven,' said Kiyami.

'Bloody hell,' Stuart swore under her breath but Rickard still heard her.

'Ever had the feeling that you're somewhere you shouldn't be?' Bentowski asked as he glared at the screens.

Rickard stared meaningfully at Stuart and saw that she had taken the hint. But he refrained from asking her to leave the bridge. She knew who was boss. 'Set a course for the Belt,' he said to Boyd. 'They won't catch us this time.'

'It's already set, sir. Just give the word.'

'Go, and prepare for immediate hyperdrive.'

No directional positioning required, *Emputin* simply glided straight off, at last under way for home. She slowly accelerated, steadily gaining speed for the jump into hyperdrive. The Imperial warships began to fall behind. They did not allow the fact to stop them firing in profusive bursts.

'How about returning some of that fire?' Rickard suggested.

'We can't do that,' Howarth said, shaking his head.

'What?'

'We can't fire the ship's weapons when we're about to jump, no Eagle-class ship can. It's a design error.'

'But we've done it before.'

'No we haven't. We've never actually been preparing for hyperdrive while under battle conditions. We couldn't do it.'

'Kiyami?'

'I am afraid he is quite correct, Captain.'

'That was uncool,' Bentowski put in. 'That was major uncool.'

'Another bloody cock-up! It's no wonder we've got nowhere.'

Another direct hit from the enemy warships crashed into *Emputin's* shields. The ship shuddered noticeably under the impact.

'Okay. Forget the weapons. Just get us out of here.'

'Prepare for jump. Going to hyperdrive now.'

Bentowski slid the controls and the ship coasted off at a plus-light velocity. They were in hyperdrive - on their way home. The capital planet of the Rukan Empire and its binary suns dropped into the mishmash pattern of stars behind the ship. The stars ahead coalesced on the main screen, with a constant flow-by as the nearer ones were passed.

The Imperial warships were quick to give chase. They soon moved up into hyperdrive speeds to pursue *Emputin*.

Kiyami calmly noted the fact. 'The Emperor is reluctant to give us up. The warships have followed our course and are pacing us...barely.'

'Go to speed ten,' Rickard said with a smile of

anticipation.

His anticipation was not to be disappointed. As *Emputin* increased her speed the warships gradually began to drop back, no longer able to keep up the pace. *Emputin* sailed on unhindered and free. The Belt soon came into sight on the screens.

Arakelian was staring at her panel in puzzled bemusement. Something was wrong. Very wrong. Readings were beginning to fluctuate unnaturally. 'Sir,' she murmured lowly. 'Captain, I think helm is about to-'

Helm went. It failed, and rather unspectacularly - no noise, no flames. It just went dead, Bentowski's console blanked out. The ship dropped from hyperdrive.

'What happened?' Rickard demanded.

'The jury-rig couldn't take the pace. Main control's gone,' Bentowski said, sliding from his chair to inspect Arakelian's unit. It was equally dead. 'We're stuck.'

'Main control's non-functioning shouldn't affect the drive. Why did we stop?'

'A fail-safe system,' Kiyami instructed him. 'If the main control centre is out then everything kicks out after it.'

'And the warships are on our ass again,' Bentowski added.

'Oh, well that's just great.'

Shots were instantly forthcoming, once more rocking the ship.

In sickbay Beck was working furiously to save Karen's life. With the aid of the medical equipment he had managed to revive her but she was still critical, and worsening by the second. It did not help when the deck began to shake and shudder every other minute, coming very close to causing him to slip on more than one occasion.

'What the hell fire is going on up there?' he cursed as he glanced up from the operating table. 'How am I supposed to work like this?'

Under him, despite mild sedation, Karen writhed and

354

moaned almost in simultaneous accord with each lurch of the deck.

We're almost at the Belt,' Rickard pointed at the screen. 'Can't Auxiliary Control do the rest from downstairs?'

'Not through an asteroid field, they can't. The ship won't jump now until we've passed it.'

'Then get them to supply maximum subspeed,' he grasped for the arm of his chair as the deck shook under him. 'We can at least try and make a run for it.'

'Oh Lord,' Bentowski muttered as he stretched for a communicator circuit. 'I bet those Rukes can't believe their luck. Auxiliary, we need you. Give us max on sub, pronto. Heading...' He glanced questioningly at Boyd.

'Two-nine-three by two-eight-two,' Boyd said.

'You got that?' Bentowski said into the communicator. He was greatly relieved when they gave the affirmative. Rickard was even more relieved when the ship resumed forward motion. Blasts from the closing warships had reached new heights and the deck was rarely still now. 'Can you repair the damage?' he asked.

'No way. Not in time to make any difference. It's this or nothing,' he gestured at the screen and the auxuliary control that now moved the ship.

'They are gaining on us.'

'We just have to keep running. We might make the Belt.'

'Yeah. And we might not.'

'Kathrynn, see if you can contact Alpheratz yet. Maybe they will be able to help us.'

Watts turned quickly to check on it but she soon found it was no use. All she got was interfering static.

'Sorry, Captain. We are still being blocked. I can't raise a whisper on any channel.'

'Keep trying or we really are in trouble.'

'Torpedoes astern!'

'Rear viewer.'

They were in trouble. A wide stream of glowing torpedoes flowed towards them from the warships. There was little chance of avoiding them all.

'Evasive!'

'Move it, you suckers!' Bentowski bellowed into the communicator.

Under Bentowski's expert management, auxiliary helm control threw the ship into a wildly desperate course of manoeuvres, *Emputin* slewed erratically left to right to dodge the rapidly oncoming missiles. It was enough - almost. Two of the widely spaced wave hit home with harsh impact, noticeably weakening the shields. A broad flurry of needle shots followed to pound ceaselessly at the Service vessel. Briefly the shield power fluctuated under the intense strain. In a fountain of sparking, vaporising metal, a jagged scar was burnt into *Emputin's* hull. A confined but destructive explosion resulted.

'We just lost power on four main banks, ' Howarth said in amazement. 'Christ, how the hell did that happen?'

'It means your ol' pal Murphey's up to his tricks again,' said Bentowski.

Rickard had to think through the confused conglomeration of blaring computer warnings and screaming circuitry. The situation was getting desperate.

'Still no reply on distress calls,' Watts called out. 'Trying on all channels.'

And it was worsening by the second. 'Send a local distress call. We just have to hope one of our ships is in the area.'

'I'll give it a try, sir,' she replied, frankly not expecting any reward on that tack.

'We're coming under fire again,' said Howarth.

'It's no good. We can't run any more. We are going to have to stop and fight.'

Bentowski found he had to laugh. 'This is gonna be one short battle.'

'Fire aft torpedoes,' Rickard immediately decided, intending to return a little of the same treatment.

Kiyami spun to face him. 'Aft tubes out of action. The last hit cost us that.'

'Then fire needle shots at them. Howarth, concentrate

on the leader.'

'Right.' Bolts of visible light reached out to smash at the Imperial command ship that cruised at the peak of the enemy's oval formation. Its shielding stubbornly held against the first strike.

Howarth shook his head in resignation. He tried again but with no better results. 'That's the best I can do. Energy readings are too far down the scale to give me a decent shot.'

'Try again,' Rickard said firmly.

'We don't have the energy for it.'

'Try anyway. It's all we have.'

'Yeah, whatever you say.'

More needle-thin laser shots lanced out at the command ship, hitting it hard, this time not relenting until the ship's screens broke and the hull was hit. A bright yellow puffball of exploding gases and machinery blossomed out from its side. It veered off sharply, ceasing to fire. A cheer went up from *Emputin's* bridge crew. It was a victory of sorts, although by no means anywhere near enough. 'That's the lot. We can't take any more of them,' Howarth flatly revealed.

'Then we're history,' the helmsman told them. 'Look at the screen.'

They all looked. *Emputin* was steadily closing on the Belt but would not reach it, that much was patently clear to everyone on the bridge. The Imperial warships were on them, encircling them, as was currently being revealed by the two secondary viewers. They were being entrapped in an ever-tightening circle of warships. They could not possibly hope to survive the combined onslaught of so much fire power.

The deck rolled and pitched as the ship was once more hit. This time it did not stop. More explosions jarred them, some sounding ominously close to the bridge. All three viewers showed the warships engulfing them in a tunnel of blazing death. On the port side a warship closed threateningly on *Emputin,* spraying the Service vessel with a devastating volley of broadsides that rattled it to its very frame.

Watts snapped a hand to her ear in an attempt to hear

internal signals more clearly over the deafening whine of failing consoles and a dying ship. What she had heard was not good. 'Section twelve reports massive depressurization along sixty per cent of its length. Corridor three on the hanger deck is holed and sealed. There's a complete power blackout on all of deck nine!'

'We're not going to make it,' Rickard said, stating the obvious. His hands were sweating profusely, his nerves were tension-wracked.

All eyes were locked on the viewers, as if by sheer willpower alone they could escape. But the intensity of the attack increased even more. *Emputin* trembled to its very core, losing energy at an alarming rate. The drain of power was excessive. The banks were rapidly being exhausted, reserves included. 'Kiyami, can't we return the fire?' Rickard pleaded with undisguised desperation.

The science officer shook her head. 'It is not possible. All power is being channelled through the shields. If we divert even enough for a needle shot the drain will kill us before we can kill them.'

Rickard flicked his eyes to the viewers. The circle around the ship had tightened to its narrowest possible limits. 'I don't think it's going to matter very soon.' An overhead circuit overloaded and a rain of sparks showered down from the ceiling, filling one corner of the bridge with a puddle of flickering shards of light.

Stuart swore to herself, followed by Kiyami, this time in Japanese. *'Bakairu!'*

Rickard looked at her in surprise. It quickly turned to horror when he heard what she had to say. 'There are more of them. I read four more ships, approaching fast from the Belt!'

'We're dead!' Stuart blurted.

'Hey, that's great,' Bentowski mused. 'At this rate I'll never get to collect my pension.'

'Bugger your pension.'

'That aside,' Rickard said drily, 'we are also trapped. They've got us in a very well-executed pincer movement.'

'How can you talk about their flippin' movements at a time like this,' Stuart gaped.

Watts made a timely interruption with some more bad

news. 'Engineering reports it can no longer provide shield power.'

'And my circuits are dead,' Howarth added.

And then it came thick and fast.

'Backup power is down ninety-five percent. All mainlines' power is failing.'

'Shields are collapsing, Captain.'

'New ships are closing and firing.'

'We don't have a bloody chance!'

This is it, Rickard told himself.

Kiyami suddenly raised a hand. 'No wait-'

And the lights failed.

The bridge was plunged into a darkness broken only by the pale glimmer of numerous console lights... And there was silence.

'If this is someone's smart idea of an afterlife, it's not funny,' Bentowski's disembodied voice cut through the blackness. 'Who shut off the lights?'

'I'm still here,' Stuart uttered in astonishment. 'We're still alive!'

'Kick in the backups,' Rickard ordered.

The emergency lighting rose to be straight away replaced by the returning mains power. The bridge appeared deceptively normal. There was little to reveal that moments before they had come within a hairsbreadth of certain death.

With a crackle of static the viewers flickered back to life and immediately caught everyone's attention. The Imperial warships were clear to see as they retreated at maximum velocity, speeding for home. The larger bulks of three Eagle-class Service cruisers glided slowly into the picture, sending the warships packing with a fusilade of needle shots.

'What the hell...?' Howarth gasped.

'They're ours,' Watts muttered dazedly. 'They're our ships.'

'Yahaay!' Bentowski cheered shrilly. 'Send us a postcard, guys,' he shouted at the fleeing warships.

Rickard almost joined the helmsman in cheering. It seemed as if his US Cavalry had finally arrived to save the day. He stole a glance at Kiyami and saw that she was beaming radiantly, unashamedly revealing her emotions for once. She caught his gaze and returned it with a wide smile, one wholly heartfelt. He returned the sentiment and his eyes switched back to the viewers. The cavalry were letting the Imperial ships go, waiting until they had accelerated from subspeed to vanish into the zone.

Out of the corner of his eye Rickard glimpsed Howarth turning towards him, grinning widely. 'I didn't get to tell you before, but you're okay, Captain. Definitely okay. One of Bentowski's good guys.'

'Thanks,' Rickard replied, a little taken aback. He was grateful for the gesture. He too had felt their disagreement should not have happened. They had merely lacked the opportunity to right the situation between them. At last things were looking up.

On screen the flotilla command ship closed to hover near *Emputin.* So close, in fact, that Rickard could pick out the vivid lettering along its hull. It confidently advertised itself as being Eagle-class vessel SNS *Caliburnus,* and it was in a remarkably improved condition compared to the last time Rickard had seen it, smashed and half-dead after colliding with a suicidal mercenary ship.

It was a much welcomed sight for eyes that thought never to see a friendly face again.

'Commodore Bartlet of the *Caliburnus* for you, Captain,' Watts announced.

'Put him on screen, please.' Rickard made himself comfortable in the centre seat, his hands moving surreptitiously to wipe clear droplets of sweat from them. The picture on main viewer faded and metamorphosed itself into the rounded features of the commodore, his moustache, a thick bundle of hair cascading over his top lip, twitching magnanimously.

'Captain Rickard,' his bass voice rumbled. 'I'm extremely glad to see that I made it to your rescue just in the nick of time, eh?'

'Believe me, Commodore, you're not the only one,' Rickard said, not taking to the man's slightly over-bearing attitude but glad for his presence nonetheless.

'It's a good job we happened to spot you. I don't know

how much longer we were going to be here for. Between you and myself,' he said with the bridge crews of both ships listening in, 'I think Command were about to pull the plug on you and order us home.'

'I had wondered what an Eagle-class flotilla was doing all the way out here in the first place.'

'I was posted here in temporary command of this ship by Admiral Trestrail just in case you should bite off more than you could chew. Good job too, eh? Call it a precautionary move on his behalf. It was meant in the best intent.'

'Yes, I'll bet.'

'And it saved your bacon.'

'Well, I'm duly grateful.'

'There's just one other thing before I pop off. I've a message to relay to whoever is in command of the zone. It was dictated by Admiral Trestrail to be broadcast if you failed to return and reads to the effect that the asteroid belt marks the territorial edge of the zone's inhabitants - so they can stay here, no venturing into our territory, not until we can handle them safely at any rate. Command is going to set up observation posts on the larger asteriods to keep an eye on them and there will be regular patrols along this way from the word go so there will be no more trouble in this sector, I can tell you.'

'It sounds like the sort of thing the Admiral would come up with.'

'Quite, and it sounds rather bold to me but that's Command for you. So, if you do know whom I should contact,' he said as if expecting a mailing address.

'Just post it to "The Emperor", Bentowski piped. 'It'll get there.'

Managing to stifle a smile, Rickard said, 'I think a wide band broadcast will do, Commodore. They'll pick it up, don't you worry.'

'Oh good. Is there anything else you need before I sign off? You can make it back under your own power, can't you?'

Rickard glanced quickly at Kiyami who nodded firmly. 'Yes, thank you, Commodore. We'll be all right.'

'That's excellent. Goodbye, Captain.' The viewer

361

blanked out to be replaced by the standard magnification starfield picture.

'Pompous asshole,' Bentowski said, voicing everyone's opinion.

'Pompous or not,' Rickard said, 'He did save our bacon, didn't he?'

'Good point,' the helmsman agreed. 'An' it damn well needed saving, that's for sure.'

'Okay,' Rickard breathed deeply, glad for the chance to take it easy, even if the ship was a flying cripple. 'If you would take us home, Mister Boyd?'

'Be pleased to,' Boyd said, and pushed the buttons. The ship glided unsteadily forward, making for the uppermost portion of the asteriod belt.

'Captain,' Watts said. 'Doctor Beck requests your attention in sickbay. He says it's urgent.'

Rickard's very nerves froze at the words. His face bleached pale white. He and Kiyami exchanged glances and he felt his heart go cold. 'Take over,' Kiyami heard him say and she experienced a sharp twinge of sympathy towards him. She hoped he would not be receiving bad news. He wasted no time in jumping up and vanishing through the door...

☆ ☆ ☆

...To enter sickbay in the same manner he'd departed the bridge - at a run. Dashing through still-opening main doors and into the second, smaller bay section, he ignored the recumbent patients he passed. He did not even stop to wonder how they could still be sleeping after all the commotion from outside. His thoughts were centred entirely on one person and he stopped short as he caught sight of her. The main lights were off. Three small illuminators were placed around the bed where they cast soft-edged shadows around the room, creating a tiny pool of light in the midst of a sea of darkness.

She was there, with Hicks and Beck, in an otherwise deserted section, lying on a very standard bed in a very standard sterile ward with a single thin sheet draped over her body...and she was hurt. Badly hurt. Rickard glanced at Beck with the question plain on his face and his heart sank as the surgeon approached him with a sad, melancholy look in his eyes. Even from there Rickard could tell it was hopeless.

His fears were cruelly vindicated when the surgeon spoke. 'She came out of emergency surgery a few minutes ago. I patched her up as best I could but...' he faltered, hesitating to deliver the final, irrevocable verdict, '...but there's nothing more we can do for her. The internal damage is far too great, even for all this,' he waved a hand at the complicated array of life-supporting equipment situated closely around the bed. 'I'm so sorry. You have my deepest sympathies, Christopher.'

He felt numb, stupefied into inaction. The shock must have been too great for him, he thought in confusion. This wasn't really happening. He was imagining it, all of it. Of course she wasn't really dying. Was she? 'She's not, Beck. She's not,' he said softly, as if by saying the words he could make himself believe them.

'Christopher,' Beck took his arms and turned him gently away. 'Karen is dying, I've done all I could to help her and it wasn't enough so I've reduced the pain for her. She'll feel nothing. When she goes it'll be like falling into a deep sleep for her. Believe me, it's the best possible way.'

'No.'

'Christopher, you have to accept it.'

'No!'

'Chris-'

Rickard tore himself free and all but ran to the bed, falling to kneel beside it. He stared at her for a moment, not wanting to believe. A hand went to move a damp strand of hair from her face. She was so pale, so pallid. So near death. He wanted to cry, such was the extent of her pallor, but the tears were denied him. She was like a fragile doll, seeming so weak and lifeless.

Standing over the other side of the bed, Hicks glanced to Beck for guidance. He motioned her to him. She moved a little way back from the bed to join him in the gloom beyond the bed's illuminants. 'Karen,' Rickard said. 'Karen, it's me.' After a long moment her eyes opened. They opened with a heaviness that was unbelievable to her. She was so exhausted. Sleep now would be a great comfort to her but there was something she had to do first. And there was Chris, sounding so distant, so worried.

'...Chris.' She tried to smile but her leaden muscles couldn't seem to make the effort. Instead it came out as a tightened grimace.

'Look at you,' he said. Her forehead was beaded with multiple sweat droplets and he scooped up a tissue from the bedside tray, carelessly scattering neat arrays of surgical and anaesthesiological equipment in the process. A scalpel was knocked to the floor with a clatter but the noise barely registered in Rickard's brain. Hicks started forward, intending to move the tray, but Beck held out a hand to hold her back, motioning silence.

Rickard used the tissue to wipe the sweat away, murmuring with concern to her. 'You're all hot.'

'Hot. Very hot. I hear you've been busy,' she croaked through moistureless lips.

'Don't worry about me, that's not important now. We've made it. We're going home.'

'Home?'

'Back to Earth. Back home.'

'I don't think so, Chris. I don't think I'm going to get there. Not this time.'

'Of course you're going to get there. Don't say that.'

'If you say so, I suppose you...must be right.' Her eyes slid closed and were a long while re-opening. 'It's been a long time since we had the chance for a quiet evening together, hasn't it?' she finally said.

'It has been a while, yes.'

'I was remembering how it was, that night.' She seemed pleased with the memory. 'We should do it again.'

'Oh, Karen, I wish we could.'

'I don't see why not.' She frowned, her eyes suddenly focussing sharply. 'I can't feel any pain.'

'And I'm glad for that,' he said, glancing back at Beck. 'Very glad. How do you feel?'

'Sleepy. It's been a long day. I'm glad you came back for

364

us, Chris. Some of the others didn't think you would.'

'I wouldn't have left you there. That place was a pit.'

'My hero,' Karen said, her voice weak. Rickard went silent, unable to think of anything more to say to her, knowing it was all pointless. 'What are you thinking?' she asked.

'I was thinking just how beautiful you are,' he said, a faint smile of regret played at his lips.

'Yuk,' she whispered hoarsely. 'That's mushy.'

'Yes, it is. But I don't care.' The sudden reminder of what she had been like before...*this*...came to him, hitting him with the force of a runaway pile-driver. He blinked furiously, trying to clear his reddening eyes. He was unable to stop his vision from blurring over. 'I don't care,' he reiterated mournfully.

'Yes you do. You should show your feelings more often. You're too enclosed in yourself.'

As if he cared about that now. 'I'll try harder in future,' he said simply.

'Good. I'll make sure you do. Don't give up on the Service. It needs you. Oh, if only...' She coughed and a thin trickle of fluid dribbled over the corner of her mouth and ran down her chin. Rickard was quick to wipe it away.

'What was it?'

'I won't be here. I can't help you any more.'

'Yes you can.'

'I feel so tired. So tired.'

'We can go back to that restaurant, in Paris.'

'...Chris.'

'I'm due for some leave. We can make the reservation as soon as we get home.'

'No.' With stark clarity, through a thick mist of dreamy haziness, Karen saw the reality of it. She could see it where Rickard desperately refused to. 'I'm dying, Chris-'

'Of course you're not.'

'Yes...I'm dying. Do you think I can't tell? I only have...' she winced at a sudden muscle spasm that shot through her despite the drugs, forcing her to fight for breath, her chest heaving, '...have to look at Phil to see that.'

Beck hurriedly tried to hide the truth of what she said from his face. The attempt was in vain.

'I don't want to die, Chris.'

'You won't.' He touched her cheek, so much wanting it to be true.

'It hurts to talk, but...'

'You won't die, Karen. You can't,' he was almost pleading now, coping with such a dreadful feeling of inadequacy. 'You can't die. I need you.'

'I feel so tired, though. I just want to sleep.' As she struggled for air sweat was streaking her face. She was soaking in it, the thin sheet over her clinging and damp with it. Rickard watched in utter helplessness as her life slowly slipped away from her.

'Don't sleep yet, please,' he begged.

'Chris, I can't stay awake. I *want* to sleep.'

'No! Please, no.'

'You worry too much. Don't worry, it's not good for you. I've told you that before.'

'I know you have. It was good advice then, but not now. Now things are different.'

'How are they different?'

'Because this time it's you.'

'Me?'

'You were hurt, Karen. You were wounded when we escaped from the palace.'

'Hurt? Oh, yes.' She was barely audible. 'Yes, I remember. I was running...and I was hit.'

'Yes.'

'It hurt, and I...I fell. But that was a long time ago. A long time. I've been resting since then, and I'm still tired. Still sleepy. I have to rest a little longer. It doesn't hurt anymore,' she said, smiling wanly in astonishment. Her voice was so weak now. 'I don't need to be afraid of it. It won't hurt, I know.'

'Karen, don't...'

'Hold me, Chris. Hold me tightly.'

She closed her ever-so heavy eyelids with enormous relief. The tiredness was all-consuming now. All she wanted was to go to sleep. Just to rest for a while, a long while. Because she was so tired. Her face relaxed with sudden tranquility.

'Karen...'

And Beck was there, standing over her, searching for a pulse. It was there, faint, almost imperceptible. Then it stopped.

Rickard stared at him with tremulous anxiety. There was no hope in Beck's eyes. He knew with stark clarity that it was over, finished, but it was an impossible reality in which to believe. Utterly unbelievable.

He turned his eyes back to Karen but she was sleeping. She had to be sleeping, she had said she was tired. But why then was she no longer breathing?

He stared at her for long minutes before the answer finally came to him. Then the tears came, and he wept.

EPILOGUE

505.99.51-56

She seemed so peaceful now. The soft light gave the illusion that she was merely sleeping. It was an illusion he so dearly wanted to be true.

Rickard stood in the open doorway and looked back at her for one last time before he finally abandoned the mortuary. The features of her face were relaxed and without pain, at rest forever. The plastic screening over the stasis container protected her body from the ship's atmosphere and would continue to protect her until they reached Earth, where she would be buried in the Trestrail family mausoleum. Home, he had told her. They were going home. But not for him. No longer could he call his mother world home. This was his world now, *Emputin*. The ship and all its inhabitants. This was all he had to cling to. He said a silent goodbye to Karen and sealed the door.

He trudged wordlessly to his quarters, not bothering to return the salutes he received from crewmembers in passing. He reached his private rooms and entered. He ignored the dimness of the single phosphorescent bar that was the only actuated lighting there. Instead, he made straight for a compact drinks cabinet in the corner and drew out a half-empty bottle of Scotch. A generous amount of the warm brown liquid was poured into an unwashed glass. It was the ideal remedy for drowning his grief. Rickard tried hard to convince himself that it was true. Just as he flopped down on the edge of his rumpled, unmade bed, the door buzzed piercingly for his attention.

'Go away,' he said to the door.

'It's me, Beck.'

'I'm busy.'

'I think we should talk.'

'I am busy.' The door slid aside and Beck walked in. 'I said I'm busy,' Rickard flatly repeated.

'I heard you. And I can see what you were busy at.'

'What I do in my private quarters and in my free time is my own business.'

'Not when you're in charge of two hundred other lives, it's not.'

'Just leave me alone.'

'So you can start drinking your depression away? It doesn't work like that, Chris. You'll only make it worse on yourself.'

'Why the hell shouldn't I be able to get drunk once in a while? I should have thought that it was the captain's prerogative on occasions like this. A celebration for all the joyous escapees on the day of their release!'

Beck sat down beside him on the bed. 'Look, I know it's hard for you. I know how close the two of you were, everyone does-'

'And you think that makes it any easier on me? Whenever I leave my room just knowing that behind all those blank faces they're saying "Poor Captain. What bad luck. Don't you just feel sorry for him?"'

'Believe me, Chris, you greatly underestimate your crew, and you're doing them an injustice by viewing them in this light. They only want to help you. You've got to break out of this depression.'

Rickard glared at him before taking a deep swig from the glass, almost emptying it. The burning heat in his throat pained him, but it was a satisfying pain. One stimulating sensation in an ocean of nothingness. 'Every time I try to reassemble the rush of events in my mind it does no good. All I can see, all I can recall, is a jumbled blur of shooting and running, fighting to stay alive. But Karen lost the fight. She didn't make it and I did, and that's what's breaking me up.'

'That you're here and she's not? You can't think like that. She wouldn't have wanted you to, for a start. Can you just imagine how she would feel if she saw you destroying yourself like this? Can you?'

Rickard nodded glumly. 'It's not too hard.'

369

Beck studied his features carefully. It had been a full ten hours since Karen's death in sickbay, and in that time Rickard had left his cabin only twice, both times to visit the mortuary. No-one had seen him come near the bridge and his command seat even though Watts had announced their impending entry into Sol System only moments ago. He looked pale and gaunt and had clearly not taken much rest. 'You've been working under too much pressure for too long. I've seen this before. You went straight from Intelligence services to commanding a full crew, without a break. You are a physical and emotional wreck, Christopher Rickard, kept up only by sheer stamina. You are going to need a few solid months of rest and recuperation now that this is all over.'

Rickard, silent in his grief, stared at the empty glass in his hand, turning it ever so slightly so that it caught the light. He found that if he twisted it to certain angles he could visualise shapes moving deep within it. Dark flecks of animation in a crystaline world. One particular shape reappeared time and time again to haunt him. He stared harder and it was there once more. 'She often wore high heels,' he murmured out of the blue, and for a brief moment in his mind he was far away, a long time ago. 'They used to make quite a noise when she walked.'

'Chris,' Beck tried to intervene on his thoughts.

Rickard subsided, returning to silence as he drifted over his memories. A particular one came to mind and he re-examined it aloud.

> ". . . Out, out, brief candle!
> Life's but a walking shadow, a poor player
> That struts and frets his hour upon the stage
> And then is heard no more;. . ."

'What was that?'

'Something,' he said absently. 'Nothing. It's from a play that Karen knew, a very old play. She quoted from it all the time.'

'Was it important to the two of you?'

'She'd studied that play. She seemed to like it a great deal. I looked up the quote in the main library last night.

It seems very apt. In some ways it could almost have been written with her in mind. They certainly had the same temperament, that's for sure. Except of course that the original character was a murderer's accomplice. Karen certainly wouldn't...'

'It's all right, I understand.'

'How can you understand! I can't get it out of my head!' he snapped. Then softer, 'I was thinking it all over. God knows I've had the time to. Normally we can step back from death, withdraw our feelings. Normally we can ignore it, like you would ignore a screen programme you didn't like, or a neighbour you didn't get along with. But not this time. The hurt is far too strong this time. This is personal, far more personal than anything that's ever happened to me before. This time it was Karen.' ...Lying cold and unmoving in the ship's morgue. Dammit! Why couldn't he clear his mind of that picture? 'I know this job is dangerous, hell, that's why we signed up, isn't it? For the danger and adventure. But not for it to end like this. Not this way. I feel so bloody... *frustrated!* There's not a damn *thing* I can do about it!' He startled Beck by hurling his unemptied glass at the wall where it shattered explosively, littering that side of the room with its fragments. He rose to his feet, staring at the dripping whisky stain on the wall. 'I can't feel anything but numbness.'

'Chris,' Beck said softly, worried for Rickard's state of mind. 'You have to take a hold of the situation. Control your emotions. You have to. You certainly can't carry on like this, tearing yourself apart.'

'I can't do it, Phil. You're right. I can't carry on like this. Why me? I keep asking myself. Why did this all happen to me? One last shot of bad luck in a mission full of it, that's all it took. One last push.'

'Come on, now. Stop that right this minute. It does absolutely no good to anyone, least of all yourself. She's gone and you did all that you could, and it's about time you realised the fact. Isn't it?'

Rickard turned away, not wanting to face what he knew was the truth. Beck jumped up and spun him around. 'Dammit, Christopher! You are going to hear me out even

371

if I have to sedate you and have you secured to make you listen. There was nothing you could do. Not a thing. She was a casualty of war, just as much a casualty as Rem Bulloch. They weren't the only two people to lose their lives in this conflict. You did your best to help the whole crew but there had to be one or two losses along the way. You know it and I know it, so stop killing yourself over the fact. It's not doing you any good. No good at all. There was nothing you could do! Believe that!'

'I...' he shook his head. 'I *can't*, Phil...'

'No! Shape up, Captain. This is your last chance. The ship still needs you even if you think you've given up. The crew need you. They know what you've lost, what Karen meant to you, we all do. They will help you, support you. Surely you've learnt that much about them by now. But you have to help them in return. You have a job to do. I don't care how corny this all sounds. Eventually you will put all this behind you. Life must continue, as they say, so shape up and stop feeling so damned bloody sorry for yourself! Right?' He held Rickard firmly by the shoulders, forcing him to make his decision on the spot.

'Right,' Rickard eventually mumbled. He sighed and squared his shoulders, bringing up his head to return Beck's hard stare. 'Right,' he repeated more strongly.

'That's my boy,' Beck grinned warmly, and delivered him a reassuring pat on the back. 'Back to work, eh?'

'I don't know if I should. I appreciate your help in pulling me out of an alcoholic daze but to go on as captain of the *Emputin* seems pointless after all this. I'm thinking I should pack it all in.'

'Don't. That's my advice.'

'It means nothing to me now.'

'Rubbish. Utter twaddle. I hope I'm a good enough judge of people to realise that. You've plenty more to look forward to. I must say, you've settled in pretty well since you first arrived. You were a bit green around the gills to start with but you're coming along nicely now. Don't spoil it by resigning your post. Together, myself and the crew have just about kicked you into shape - think how it would upset the crew if you left them after everything we've been through together. It's not a good idea. Do me a favour, Chris. Don't even think about resigning in the next year. Let this all drift into your past and then think about it, when you mind is clearer, okay?'

Rickard looked away, locked in thought. His troubled mind refused to make the choice easy for him as the pages of his memory carried him through the last twenty-four hours in seconds; the anger experienced in that time, the pain, the heartache. Things had changed. His life had changed irrevocably, but it still remained *his* life. He was the only one who could choose. His choice, his decision, the second in the space of a few minutes.

He decided. 'Okay,' he said as he looked back. 'I stay.'

'That's the spirit,' Beck congratulated him. 'Never say...'

'Die? You can use the word.'

'Of course. I simply imagined...'

'Doesn't matter, Doc. You can't hide away from it forever so you might as well say it. We all die sooner or later. You can't escape it, doesn't matter how hard you try.'

'I thought morbidity was my line.'

'Sorry. It's going to take me some time to recover from all this. I'll be all right eventually. For me it's business as usual. Definitely business as usual.'

'I have to congratulate you on being good at your job. I know it's been said before but it's true. Not many could cope with the sort of pressure you've been under, and you know what I mean, Admiral Trestrail included.'

'Bugger Trestrail.'

'That's the spirit. You know, at least he won't be able to trouble you. You've saved much more than you lost. Trestrail can't harm you over Karen, mighty as he thinks he is. A demonic twinkle lit Beck's eye and a grin came to his lips. 'All he'll be able to do is throw a fit like an asthmatic goldfish swimming in a tank full of sulphuric acid.'

Despite himself, Rickard found he had to raise a laugh, however half-hearted it might be. 'I think I'd better get up to the bridge, don't you?'

'I couldn't have put it better myself,' Beck said. He was relieved that at last Rickard seemed to have escaped the worst of his turmoil, and his guilt, however misplaced it might be. He was out of it. 'I think you'd better get cleaned up before you go marching off. You have ten hours' worth of stubble and half a bottle of whisky to rid yourself of. I can provide you with something to neutralise the whisky, but the stubble's all yours.'

Rickard entered the bridge with Beck and waited as the doors hissed closed behind them both. All eyes were on him and the air had suddenly become tense, expectant. They were all there; Kiyami, Howarth, Boyd, Watts, Bentowski, and even Arakelian. And they were all concerned for him, he could see that clearly now. He wondered how he could ever have missed it.

Kiyami watched the captain carefully, surprised at how well he seemed to be coping, now that the doctor had talked to him. She had wanted to go down there herself, to shake him out of his self-induced depression, but she had discovered she could not carry it through. Although in the short time she had known him she had grown to be greatly fond of his non-assuming character, she was still attempting to keep herself marginally aloof from her feelings and from other people's, and the idea of pulling someone, even Rickard, out of the depths of despair was something she just could not cope with, not yet. But with luck, and *karma,* he would pull through. She hoped he would. He had only to break through the atmosphere on the bridge. Perhaps she should help in doing that.

What did break the mood, before Rickard could utter a word, and before Kiyami could move, was Kirsten Stuart's unexpected entry through the other set of bridge doors. Without looking around her she made straight for Bentowski, plonking herself precariously on the edge of his console. The eyes of everyone of the bridge switched from Rickard to her.

'Hi, Bentowski. We're home at last! Ain't it great?' she said bouncily.

'Knock your eye out,' he agreed, amused that she hadn't noticed the captain.

'Is that yes or no?'

'That's a positive aye-firmative, little lady,' he drawled. He promptly received a playful punch on the arm from Arakelain. 'Oww! What's that for?' he spluttered.

'For making fun of the way I talk.'

'Serve you right,' Stuart chuckled. Then she saw Rickard and stopped. 'I shouldn't be here,' she mumbled, and started to leave.

Rickard raised a conciliatory hand to halt her, pleased that someone had lightened the atmosphere. He had been unaware up to now of Bentowski's friendship with the middie. 'It's all right, Stuart. I think you've earned the right to be up here for a while.'

She stared at him in surprise before gladly accepting the reprieve. She settled back against the helm panel. He wasn't so bad, for an officer. A wish that Peter Bernerds were still with her caressed the back of her mind. He would have liked the captain, too. She was sure of it. It was a shame he'd never had the chance.

The rest of the bridge crew relaxed with Rickard's words, thankful that things were at last back to normal. They returned to their duties. Rickard was out of the spotlight for a while.

'Magnanimity is much loved among leaders,' Beck whispered to Rickard as the latter took the empty conn.

'I wish I'd been more magnanimous when everyone was warning me not to enter the zone in the first place. What was it you said? "Open the lion's den and in walks Daniel"?'

'I could also have said don't look a gift lion in the mouth - it'll bite your head off. You did what you thought was right. And being the man in the centre seat we followed you in that, no matter what our arguments were. You're the man in charge, duly elected by the powers that be to take this command. And there art a great number of years left in thee,' he said theatrically, 'so don't waste them.'

Rickard put on a brave face. 'You're full o' blather,' he returned, and not without a hint of wistfulness. But that had to stop. He had said his final goodbyes at the door of the mortuary. 'Earthward bound at last. We've lost a few good people on what turned out to be a highly risky scouting job for Command, Rem Bulloch amongst them, although I can't really say I got to know him that well.'

'I think you would have liked him,' Beck assured him.

'Then there's Stuart over there. She was pretty close to Midshipman Bernerds.'

'She mourned for him in her own way. I think she has also become rather attached to our friend Bentowski. I was speaking to him and you know what he's like. "She needed some comforting and, big softy that I am, I decided to fill the vacancy," he said to me, quite genuinely as well.'

'They would make a strange couple,' Rickard noted, trying to imagine two people with their temperaments as a couple. It would be an interesting relationship. He was pleased that they had found their own kind of peace. 'I feel comfortable here,' he decided, gazing around the bridge. 'At last I feel comfortable here.'

'You do belong, Captain,' Kiyami reassured him as she approached the conn. 'We all think that, even Thom Howarth.'

'I found that out a few hours back.'

'Then believe that it was well meant, because it is true.'

'Thank you, Kiyami. Did I ever tell you? I think you're the best first officer in the fleet.'

'Oh, compliments now,' said Beck.

'I do not mind. *Domo arigato, Taicho-san,*' Kiyami said. Although he would not know it, she had paid him a compliment by speaking in Japanese rather than in English. The people of her country had become a greatly conservative race, and they did not pass on the essence of being *Nihon-go* readily. Perhaps he would know what she had said. In time.

Rickard frowned in amusement. 'I think I'm going to have to take some lessons Kiyami,' he said to her, and perhaps not so jokingly? he wondered. Kiyami smiled, gratified at his confirmation of her thoughts.

'It'll certainly keep you out of harm's way,' Beck said to him with a broad grin.

And it was clear that he needed some distraction to occupy himself, he realised. However little Admiral Trestrail could punish him for his daughter's death, life in the Service would be hard going for a while. The admiral would doubtlessly press for a full enquiry and court martial once he got back to Earth. He would never be the same free person again, never live the same happy-go-lucky lifestyle he'd known before. From now on it was duty first and foremost, all the way. Ship's captain first and last. It sounded like a life sentence. But even that did not totally exclude some enjoyment, he realised with a wry smile.

His expectations of the future were certainly brighter than they had been before.

'Well, would it keep you out of harm's way or not?' Beck asked.

'I don't know about that,' Rickard said, his expression becoming thoughtful. 'I don't know. We'll have to see.'